May I Leave Stars

WRITER'S CUT

CATHERINE C. HEYWOOD

MARAIS media

Copyright © 2020 by Catherine C. Heywood
Published by Marais Media, LLC
All rights reserved.

Epigraph by Victor Hugo, from *Ninety-Three*, copyright © 1874 by Harper and Brothers, is in the public domain in France.

"Je te veux," composed by Erik Satie to a text by Henry Pacory, is in the public domain in France.

"Au clair de la lune," composer and lyricist unknown, is in the public domain in France.

ISBN: 978-1-951699-00-0

Cover Design and Interior Formatting
Qamber Designs and Media
Cover Images
Salome Hoogendijk
Zhenikeyev
Christian Mueller
Author Image
Jenny Loew Photography
Illustrations
Timea Gazdag at Qamber Kids
Editors
Cheri Johnson
Devon Burke at Joy Editing

For Jeff—the X axis to my sine wave

GLOSSARY

OF FRENCH TERMS AND PROPER NOUNS

atelier – private workshop or studio for a professional artist; can also be an artist's residence

blanchisserie – a professional laundry

blanchisseuse – a professional laundress

bohemian – one who practices an unconventional lifestyle such as free love or voluntary frugality; associated with artists, writers, and musicians

brasserie – an informal restaurant often open late into the night and offering a large selection of drinks.

courtesan – originally a courtier; clever, talented, charming; a woman who is a paid mistress to powerful men; the top of the demimonde

croque-mitaine – bogeyman

demimondaine – a woman who belongs to the demimonde

demimonde – "half world," hedonism financed through a steady income of cash and gifts from wealthy lovers; used to refer to the official world of prostitutes and courtesans in France

goguette – a place for drinking, singing, and socializing; it tended to attract literate men from the artisan class who were associated with revolutionary politics

le Fauborg – refers to the French high nobility; after the Revolution, the great or "old families;" an idiomatic expression for "old money"

grande horizontale – another name for courtesan

le gratin – "the upper crust" of society, includes both le Fauborg and Tout-Paris

grisette – a working-class woman who combines one occupation, typically in the garment trades, with part-time prostitution; the entry-level of the demimonde

hôtel particulier – a grand, free-standing townhouse, typically with an entrance court and a back garden; a common gift for a woman moving into the demimonde

lorette – the "respectable prostitute" or mid-level of the demimonde; named after the Church of Notre Dame de Lorette, where many of these ladies took to making their assignations

Père Fouettard – "Father Whipper," he accompanies Father Christmas on his rounds, dispensing lumps of coal and spankings to naughty children

réveillon – a night-long feast celebrating the birth of Christ; typically commences after returning from midnight mass

Rive Gauche – the "Left Bank" or the southern bank of the River Seine

Tout-Paris – refers to the most influential of Parisian high-society, setting trends, tastes, past times and holidays; generally, but not always, "new money"

vernissage – "varnishing," before the formal opening, a private viewing of an art exhibition during which artists would apply the coat of varnish

PARIS
1889

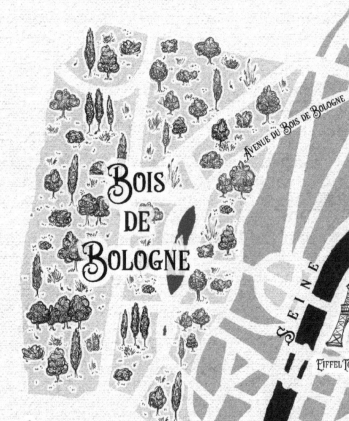

BOIS
DE
BOLOGNE

AVENUE DU BOIS DE BOLOGNE

SEINE

EIFFEL TOWER

← CHÂTEAU DE SAINT-CLOUD

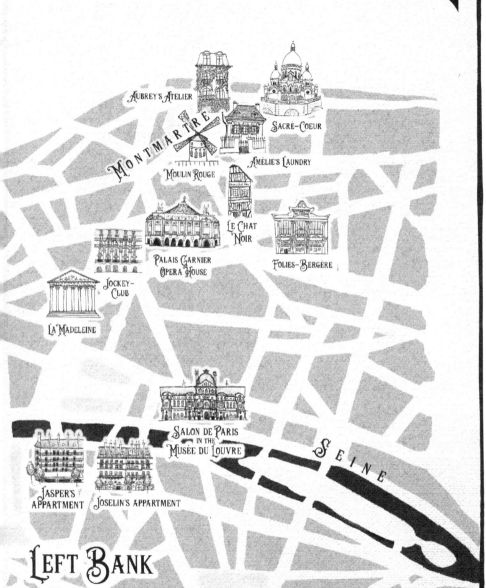

AUBREY'S ATELIER

SACRÉ-COEUR

MONTMARTRE

MOULIN ROUGE

AMÉLIE'S LAUNDRY

LE CHAT NOIR

PALAIS GARNIER OPERA HOUSE

FOLIES-BERGÈRE

JOCKEY-CLUB

LA MADELEINE

SALON DE PARIS
IN THE
MUSÉE DU LOUVRE

SEINE

JASPER'S APPARTMENT

JOSELIN'S APPARTMENT

LEFT BANK

Whatever causes night in our souls may leave stars.
—Victor Hugo, *Ninety-Three*

PART ONE

GIRL IN BATH

I

*F*ew people employed a needle and thread as badly as Amélie Audet. And yet she sat amidst piles of stained linens, fingers thimbled, turning needle and thread to repair holes. On this darning day, she'd returned from her early-morning deliveries, back already aching from the thirty-pound basket she bore, only to sink her sore fingers into rank laundry, separating those that needed repair before washing. She hated the little laundry at No. 13 rue Ravignan. But so did everyone else, so she suffered it to hide.

Beside her, Léonie fell into coughing. Amélie glanced at the other women who flicked inscrutable glances back. When Léo coughed again, three short barks, small and swallowed up but still persistently there, Amélie cringed, fear burning in her chest.

"No better today?" she whispered as she drew a needle through a limp and smelly sock.

"A little." Léo poked herself, dropping her needle and thread.

Again Amélie dared a look at the other washerwomen. They worked alongside them. And spied for the laundry mistress, too.

"Can't you wear a thimble today?" She handed her one.

Her friend gave one small shake of her head.

Léo, once so deft with her flying fingers, now struggled as they swelled and grew sore. Too often she complained of exhaustion and a scattered mind. A cough would seize her chest, her whole body, and she'd be racked with it. Days at a time she seemed to improved. Amélie lived on those, hoping and praying one would lead to the next and the next. But inevitably the bad days returned.

Amélie glanced again at Léo and worried her lip. Working from five in the morning until eleven at night but for Sunday and with the madame hawkishly monitoring their every move, there remained little hope of Léo being seen by a doctor. Unless her condition should miraculously improve, the best they could wish for was to conceal it.

Amélie took a sip of Bénédictine and peered out the window. Paris sloped below her to the south, its soaring spires and streaming smokestacks, pinched gray sheet roofs and rust-orange chimney pots crammed into crooked rows. The tight city looked as tipsy as she felt.

At five, Amélie went next door to their boarding room. Fixing her long mane of midnight-brown hair into a fashionable pompadour, she scrubbed her skin until it stung, then changed into a fresh skirt and shirt. The city scorned washerwomen as disease-riddled slatterns. Amélie seethed just thinking about that. Before resorting to this position, she'd always prided herself on her cleanliness and fastidious care with her clothes. Yet now she could hardly blame them. The grime of ash and animal-fat smell of lye seemed to cling to her always. Dabbing on some eau de cologne, she breathed in the fresh citrus scent as she studied her reflection in the mirror.

A month before, she'd pleaded for a shorter shift for one day a week, and Madame Pelletier had nearly sacked her for it. The laundry did brisk business on six days and only sighed like steam on the seventh. She should be grateful for the job, for the room and board, still she'd had to take the risk. Finally, she pinched her cheeks and sighed.

No sooner had she stepped onto the street than biting fingers snaked around her arm.

"I won't have a consumptive girl working in my blanchisserie," the short and bosomy Madame Pelletier hissed into Amélie's ear. "Bad enough they force us to the damn outskirts for fear of disease. Do I give them a girl who proves them right?

"I can't tolerate Mademoiselle Thomas and her hacking for much longer." She pierced Amélie's chocolate-brown eyes with a black gaze. "And if I should see even one drop of blood, you're both gone. Do you hear me? Out of a position and out of your room."

Amélie shook on the short walk to the café, the laundry madame's threat racing through her mind along with everything she might've said had she not been so stunned and tongue-tied. Had she not been such a coward. Madame Pelletier cooed like a mother hen over her "girls" in one moment, then reigned like a bitch of the first water in the next. They all knew she'd just as soon cut them as hold them. She issued no idle threats and had cast out a girl who'd gotten pregnant only two months earlier.

Amélie couldn't bear to think of Madame Pelletier putting them out. They wouldn't sleep on the streets, of course. Wouldn't starve. And it wasn't that she didn't miss her old life. Sometimes. But she could never go back to that. She simply wouldn't. They would have to find a way to make Léo well and, in the meantime, see to hiding her condition.

She slowed as she came to the picture window of Café Mignon and dared a glance inside. *He came.* Her heart galloped in her chest, and her mouth went dry. There he sat, his nose in *Le Temps*, his hand caressing a glass of red wine, so sublimely at ease with his power. A stack of papers rested on the table beside him, résumés, perhaps, for her competition.

Amélie had a secret. A talent and a longing that burned unabating inside. She breathed life into it, and it breathed life right back. It remained her one chance—her one *honorable* chance—to escape this wretched life. If only she could summon the courage to take it.

Here and now, after Léo's coughing and Madame Pelletier's threat, if there were any clearer sign, she couldn't imagine it. Then she knew, and it whispered in her heart as clear as a bell:

There is no peace in hiding. I can't bear it anymore.

Shifting the odious madame and her threats to the back of her mind, Amélie pasted a smile on her face and breezed into the café.

"You're late," the café's owner, Monsieur Étienne, said, slapping her bottom as she collected her tray.

She grit her teeth, nearly swallowing her tongue along with all the sharp things she wanted to say.

"I am not," she said, ducking away from his stinking breath. He loved the café's onion soup and indulged in it far too much. Didn't he know it was coming out of his pores?

Rude and handsy with his staff, but for his upper-class patrons, Étienne held a wide smile and his arms out. He loved them nearly as much as he loved himself and managed to maintain a cordial formality, even if somewhat fawning at times. That was why they came to Café Mignon, a Tout-Paris enclave in the midst of bohemian Montmartre. And that was why Amélie had begun working there—for one very important member of le gratin.

Furtively, Amélie studied Monsieur Degrailly as he stroked a neatly groomed auburn beard. He and Monsieur Zidler owned the dance hall soon to reopen on boulevard de Clichy. They promised it would be bigger, better, and more beautiful than all the rest. That it would transform the district—the whole city!—with its thrilling entertainments and electric lights, leaving lesser dance halls in its shadow.

For weeks after first hearing of it, Amélie had floated on clouds of conjecture. *Am I good enough? Can I secure an audition? Whom* do I know? How do I approach them? Can I dazzle them, or will I humiliate myself? These thoughts ran like a river through her mind, at times making her feel ten feet tall, confident with her talent, and at others making her want to shrink with insecurity.

One thing she knew for certain—there'd be no answer for any of it unless she tried.

Two days a week for the last four weeks, Amélie had waited tables at Café Mignon. Eight shifts, but he'd only come on three. Three chances she had. Three chances she didn't take. Just as Étienne required, she kept her head down and her smiles small, drifted in and floated away as if invisible. All the while, fear and insecurity had dogged her as she served Monsieur Degrailly's food and replenished his drinks.

Now today, even with her determination bolstered and that clear-as-a-bell voice urging her on, she couldn't seem to devise a suitable plan. Every clever thing she imagined saying suddenly seemed pitiable. No doubt he was approached by hopeful starlets everywhere he went. He probably had a merciful dismissal at the ready. She had to find an unusual way to engage him. Something memorable.

Amélie jerked at a vicious pinch to her bottom to see Étienne had sidled up to her with a serpentine grin. "Are you sleeping, mademoiselle?" He nodded to Monsieur Degrailly. "His wine's nearly empty."

The man had taken perhaps two temperate sips, his glass nowhere near empty.

First Madame Pelletier and now this. Why do people always assume they can take advantage? One day. One day I will have them all at my feet, and they will see.

Amélie obliged her slavish boss with a simpering smile, then turned to Monsieur Degrailly. Rehearsing every introduction she'd imagined, her heart beating so loudly she could hear it pulsing in her ears, she strode to his table.

Distracted by her musings, when a customer stood behind her, he bumped into her. The glass that held Monsieur Degrailly's cabernet tumbled off her tray, sending the wine splashing on him and shattering on the floor.

Amélie gaped in stunned horror. From across the café, Étienne made a sound like a cross between a quack and a gasp and bounded to the table.

"What did I tell you about those stilts for legs? The wine falls harder for your height. You're dismissed! Get!" He turned to Monsieur Degrailly. "She's an idiot girl. I never should've hired her."

Monsieur Degrailly stood, shaking his hands of the wine as Amélie desperately apologized and blotted his papers. She hoped they were résumés for other performers, now ruined.

"If you hired an idiot, monsieur, what does that make you?"

Étienne had a face like a potato, and it went blank as he was struck dumb. Amélie couldn't help but laugh.

"Don't laugh, you insolent girl." He pinched his face in disgust. "It makes you sound half-mad, and we both know that's only half right." Turning to the gentleman, he dabbed frantically at the red stain that bloomed on the man's milk-white vest. "I assure you the cost of wash or repair will come out of the girl's wages."

Monsieur Degrailly chortled. "I can't ask that. And in any event, there is hardly a wage amount this poor girl can earn that could begin to cover it."

"Then I'll have her under heel for a year. *More!*"

"A fine arrangement that is, given you just dismissed me."

"I'm sure I could think of something." Étienne didn't even try to hide the lascivious look on his face. Despite his devoted wife, he'd propositioned her at least half a dozen times.

"Monsieur, I do hope you're not suggesting what I think you're suggesting," Monsieur Degrailly said.

"She's no maiden, monsieur, I assure you, but a common slut who hangs around every atelier in Montmartre, ready to drop her dress for every man-of-the-brush who gives her a smile and a franc."

Amélie froze. Impossibly, it seemed Étienne knew. Then her gaze fell on Monsieur Degrailly. His wide eyes looked on her as if he'd never heard the words *slut* or *atelier*. Looked on her as if he were seeing her for the first time, and perhaps he truly was. He surveyed her from head to toe, his eyes alight and the corners of his mouth turning up. Once again, she felt herself back in the Salon de Paris. Felt Aubrey's eyes on her, pleading for understanding. Felt the eyes of fashionable Paris on her, fascinated and ravenous for more.

After that scandalous season, when everywhere she'd gone she'd felt bared, felt eyes on her, stripping her, never did she think she could feel more naked. But she did now. Mortally embarrassed and feeling the heat of a blush flood into her cheeks, she turned on a heel and left.

Amélie had taken perhaps thirty steps down the narrow cobble street when she heard him.

"Mademoiselle."

A part of her wanted to run from him, yet an equal part wanted to run *to* him. It made no sense. Imperceptibly, she slowed but didn't stop. If she could've kept that cabernet from falling on his pristine shirt, she would not have.

"Mademoiselle, please stop. If I must, I'll chase you down this street. And we both know it'll be you who looks the ridiculous one."

She stopped. Because she knew he spoke the truth. Tout-Paris couldn't look ridiculous when compared to the bohemians of Montmartre if it tried. Cagily, she turned when he approached.

His chest rose and fell against his stained shirt, and his close-cropped auburn hair was slightly mussed over his florid face. But against his searching sage eyes and aristocratic features, against his magnificent height—she had yet to meet a man who towered over her own height of five-eight by some half foot—and clothing, an impeccably cut midnight-blue suitcoat over dove-gray trousers, she did look ridiculous, and he looked, well, magnificent.

In all the rumors of his charisma, in all her scrutiny of him these past weeks, never had she realized just how handsome he was. Yet now, with his arresting gaze fixed on her, she didn't know how she could have missed it. As they regarded each other, something warm and alive cut a path between them Amélie had only ever felt once before.

When his eyes continued to travel all over her, she folded her arms across her chest and narrowed her brows.

"I'm sorry to be so rude," he said.

"Yes, you are."

He smirked. "I don't believe I've had the pleasure. My name is Jasper Degrailly." He extended a hand.

Reluctantly she took it, for his bold appraisal had been the height of rudeness, and had he been any other man, she might have slapped him.

"And you are?" he pressed.

"Amélie Audet."

At length he appraised her from head to toe and not without a hint of awe. Finally, he said, "This may sound peculiar. By chance, do you know Monsieur Talac? The painter?"

On the outside she stood plain-faced while inside she screamed. To anyone on the street, she would appear appropriately dressed. Yet inside, she felt naked. Would she never be able to run far enough from Aubrey Talac? Hurt and spiteful—a worse pairing she couldn't imagine—he'd set out to ruin her life. And succeeded. Now the devastation of that relationship poured over her like an acid rain. What possible hope could she have with Monsieur Degrailly now?

"If you'll excuse me, monsieur."

Shattered, she turned and walked away.

"What are you doing home?" Léo asked when Amélie returned.

"I was dismissed," she said, still dazed by her dashed hopes.

She poured a full glass of Bénédictine and drank it down in one swallow, then refilled her glass and took up her sewing.

"Dismissed? Did you turn Étienne down one too many times?"

"I wish. I would go back and cut him where he stood if he reached for my bottom again."

"So, what happened?"

"I spilled wine all over Monsieur Degrailly."

Léo chortled, then swallowed and tried to cough politely.

"I don't suppose he offered you an audition after that?"

Amélie shook her head. "It's difficult enough to even get a chance to be seen by him and Zidler. Now he'll take one look at me and cross me off the list before I even have a chance to open my mouth."

She wouldn't tell her about his mention of Aubrey. Léo would only politely entreat on his behalf, and she couldn't bear that. Not today. She would have to find another way. Because, come what may, she would get that audition.

2

*F*ive nights later, Jasper sat in Le Chat Noir. Drumming his fingers, his gaze skated over the stained-glass windows, iron lanterns with cat motifs, and the motley collection of arms and armor in Rodolphe Salis's cabaret. Five long days he'd bided his time after mining every bit of information he could find about the alluring mademoiselle from the café. Never could he have imagined she was a performer. And at one of his regular haunts.

"Why am I here?" his sister asked. Marie-Thérèse sat rigidly beside him, adjusting her perfectly kept ensemble.

"I couldn't bring Daphne tonight, you understand."

"Would she object to accompanying you as you search for her replacement?"

"She would, I think."

"Liberal in her appetites, but only to a certain degree?"

"Quite." He smiled tightly. "And I'm not searching for her replacement. This girl is merely a… curiosity."

"A curiosity." Marie-Thérèse slid skeptical eyes to him.

Salis, a shorter man with slick hair and a pointy beard, stepped on stage, and the room grew dim while the stage warmed.

"What is Montmartre?" he began. "Nothing. What should it be? Ev-ry-thing," he declared, booming with greater emphasis on each syllable.

Salis had dedicated himself to agitating for anarchy through the divine subtlety of poetry and song. He wanted Montmartre to secede from France and made certain everyone knew it.

"Degrailly, is that you, my friend?" Salis asked.

Jasper nodded.

"Where is Madame Degrailly tonight? Does this poor girl beside you not know you're married?"

"I can only guess that my *ex*-wife, Madame *Travers*, is tucked tidily at home, knitting her rosary beads. And, believe me, this poor girl beside me knows it very well." The drunken crowd laughed uproariously.

Salis focused more feigned ire on some other patrons, at which the crowd whooped and laughed. It was his regular bit, and you wouldn't attend if you were the sort to be easily pricked.

Finally, Salis introduced a poet who recited a lengthy collection of poems. Then he returned to the stage.

"And now, for your pleasure, Belle Étoile."

Amélie Audet stepped onto the stage, and Jasper leaned forward, peering intently to see her better. If she was, in fact, the woman in the stunning painting—and how could she not be?—it hadn't done her justice. Captured in silky oils in ripe pinks and peaches, she was soft and used, wanton and sly. Now she stood poised and impenetrable. Lovely. Straight as a blade and tall. Never had he seen a woman so tall. The sleeveless gold brocade dress she wore hugged her trim curves and was striking against her peaches-and-cream skin and dark-chocolate hair and eyes. And there was something else, something in her gaze he couldn't fathom exactly but wanted to. Desperately.

Yet her beauty fell to nothing when compared to the voice that broke into the room when she began to sing. She started small and grew smaller still, but her voice was so strong and sure he was certain she could take down a wild boar with the needle of it. This was a sign of any singer with true talent. It was rich and crystal clear, only the pure cream of her voice. And it poured over him, over everyone in the room, as they sat spellbound.

This was no mere waitress who played at singing but a true and rare talent. Now he saw her physical presence went far beyond any searching look in that devastating painting. And her musicality was like nothing he'd heard before. She didn't merely hit her notes—she remade them.

Then her eyes slid to his and warmed as the corners of her mouth curled into a soft smile. When the song came to a close, he sat forward as if he could draw more from her even as she pulled back. His hands came together without any thought. He wanted more. And he would have it.

"She's good," his sister declared.

"Yes."

When Amélie finished her set, Jasper went in search of Salis.

"Why didn't you tell me about her? Why have I not seen her before?" Jasper came often in search of talent but never on a Sunday night.

"I don't know," Salis replied. "She's delightful, isn't she?"

Jasper arched an incredulous brow. "More than delightful." Then he knocked on the dressing room door. "Belle Étoile. Are you decent?"

"Just a moment, monsieur."

The door opened, and Amélie stood in her gold dress with something calculating in her eyes. To the other girl in the room, Jasper nodded toward the door, and she scurried out. He sat on the sofa and motioned for Amélie to join him. After a long pause, she did. There was nothing appropriate in sitting so close with no chaperone. Still, they settled beside each other as if their closeness should be a perfectly natural thing. He dearly hoped it would be. And soon.

"You're a talent, mademoiselle. It is *mademoiselle*, is it not?" He knew very well.

"It is. I thank you, monsieur."

"Belle Étoile. Are you a star amongst the sky of performers in this district?"

"I think so," she replied without hesitation.

There was his dilemma, for he thought so, too. The businessman in him would see her on stage when his greatest experiment, the Moulin Rouge—which had to succeed—opened later in the year. But the man in him would see her in his bed, where no other man could get to her.

"Tell me, how did you come to be Monsieur Talac's figure model?"

"I don't know what you're talking about, monsieur," she uttered.

She'd paused. Paused and seemed to choke on her denial.

"Yes, you do. It's you," he said breathlessly. "You're *Fille dans le bain*. The figure model who vanished."

After a pointed pause, she said, "Are you in love with me, monsieur?"

She'd tried to sound confident, yet her eyes looking everywhere but on him and the color flooding into her cheeks belied it.

"Any man who's ever looked upon that painting is," he said, "and if he says otherwise, he's lying. But I think you already know that, don't you?"

"Perhaps you might secure the services of Monsieur Talac. After all, it was his keen eye and deft hands that rendered me."

"Talac did indeed capture something in your eye. But it was that something, that… passion, that is entirely you."

"Hunger, Monsieur Degrailly. A desire to eat when the day is done. And to perform. That's what you saw. If you think otherwise…"

Propriety be damned, he slid closer to her, his mouth mere inches from hers, the lower lip lush and shiny in the center, just begging to be kissed. "I know otherwise. You're hungry, mademoiselle, for all that you say. And something more, I think."

Abruptly, she stood and walked to the door. If his reputation preceded him, he had to take care.

"What are you doing now your set is done?"

"It's late." Her hand fell on the doorknob.

"Not so." He walked to her. "Have a drink with me. You'll meet my sister. She's a good, honest sort." Though he hadn't known it consciously, this was why he'd had the forethought to bring the painfully prim and proper Marie-Thérèse.

Amélie smiled tightly and shook her head.

"Come on." Jasper took her gloved hand in his, and the warmth of it there seemed so right that he looked at it, then she did, too.

Hours later, Marie-Thérèse called out the door of their carriage. "You must come, mademoiselle! Tell her she must come, Jas."

Amélie had joined them for one drink that became three as they watched the remaining performers close out the night. And though he knew she was a young woman of humble means, she gamely carried her end of the conversation—music and art and literature, even politics and, most surprising of all, horse racing.

Marie-Thérèse had been gape-mouthed as the singer countered her prediction that Bull Dog would break his maiden on the short course at Boulogne next Sunday. "He's a firm middle-distance colt," Amélie had said, predicting that instead it was Kildare who loved the sprint and the soft conditions expected after the rain forecast for later in the week. Rarely did people surprise him, but this woman seemed to be one revelation after another.

Now this. After insisting they drop her at her doorstep, she'd directed his driver to this modest house a block away from her address. Jasper knew exactly where she lived and was beginning to think he wanted to know everything about her.

They stood at the random doorstep, his sister no doubt watching.

"I thank you for the escort home, monsieur."

"I would feel better had we dropped you at your actual address, mademoiselle."

Her eyes darted around as she fiddled with her skirt.

"It isn't far," she admitted.

"I know."

She seemed to vibrate with a magnetic energy that drew him to her. He struggled to remember the last time a woman had so moved him. His hands, his mouth, his whole body he wanted to place on her.

"May I see you again?"

"You're kind, monsieur."

"I'm not kind. And I promise you'd be doing me a great favor."

The flickering gaslight warmed the blush on her cheeks. From the drinks or perhaps something else. He took a small step closer, breathing in her faint orange-blossom scent.

"I'm flattered, monsieur. But I haven't much time to indulge in that sort of thing."

He considered her deft answer even as he wondered when last he'd been turned down.

"What does that mean?"

"If you know where I live, then you know where I work. I'm not complaining, mind you. I'm happy to have a position and a place to live. But the life of a blanchisseuse is not an easy one, monsieur. The hours are long. The Sabbath is my only free day, and I spend part of it rehearsing for Le Chat."

"But you must come with us to Boulogne next Sunday. To see your Kildare take the thousand-meter."

"He'll get on just fine without me."

"Shall I? How shall I get on without you?"

An indulgent smile caressed the corners of her mouth. "I think you get on just fine. And even if I could, I haven't anything to wear. I wouldn't embarrass you."

"Is that all? A circumstance easily remedied. I'd be happy to buy you anything you'd like."

"You misunderstand. You needn't give me gifts."

He couldn't help himself when he nuzzled his nose, his beard, his mouth, so near her face their lips nearly brushed. He heard her suck in a breath and felt her chest press into his. But she didn't pull away.

"You wouldn't want to disappoint my sister now, would you?"

"No, but—"

"Good." He slid his hand into the warmth of hers and drew it to his lips for a kiss. "I'll call on you."

3

The next morning, Amélie steadily cranked the mangle, feeling how close Monsieur Degrailly had been, reliving every look and word they shared, the subtle seduction of his warm hand sliding into hers and that polite kiss that felt anything but. How she wished he'd kissed her.

"What time did you get in last night?"

Léonie stood mere feet from her, folding and feeding water-soaked clean linens through the mangle. But Amélie, so lost in her distraction, scarcely noticed her.

"Late."

Léo pulled the wrung linen from the mangle and handed it to Claire, a diminutive, sloe-eyed girl, who stood on a step stool to hang it from the drying rack that soared into the beamed ceiling. The drying white linen hung in ethereal rows as the gentle breeze from the open window moved through them. They appeared like dove's wings fluttering and not the hardest labor of their hands.

"Mm-hm. Why so late? If Salis kept you for another set, I hope he paid you for it."

Léo had sometimes played piano at Le Chat Noir and loved to talk performing.

"What aren't you telling me?" Léo prodded.

"Monsieur Degrailly came to see me."

"He did? To hear you sing? Why didn't you tell me? And did he love you? Of course he did. Did you get an audition? Tell me you got an audition. What am I saying? Of course you did." She squeezed Amélie's arms fiercely. Thankfully this seemed to be one of her good days. She had some vigor and some good color on her cheeks. "Oh, what shall I wear for opening night with all those fine gentlemen from the Rive Gauche?"

"I didn't get an audition."

"You didn't? He didn't like you? Was it the wine you spilled? You promised him you weren't that ungainly, right? You do have long legs, but you're never awkward. He should be lucky to have your legs for his high-kick lines. What did he say? Did you talk to him? Tell me everything."

"I will if only you'd stop talking. He called me 'a talent' and asked about my stage name, if I thought I was a star."

"What did you say?"

"I said yes. Or I think so. Something like that."

"There's no thinking. You are. And everyone in this city will know it soon. So, he came to Le Chat to see you. Called you 'a talent.' Wait." She paused in contemplation. "Where were you when he called you a talent?"

"In my dressing room."

"With Penny."

"Penny left," Amélie said after a pause.

Léo chewed her lips. "You were in your dressing room. Alone. With Monsieur Degrailly."

"Yes. But nothing happened."

Léo shook her head as if Amélie were a complete innocent.

"Don't shake your head at me. I know what I'm doing."

"Do you?"

"Not every man is like Aubrey."

"No. Monsieur D is worse. He moves Tout-Paris with a word and a wink. And money. He has so much money I can't even begin to imagine."

"All those years Aubrey wanted Monsieur Degrailly's interest and you encouraged it. A word from him or his patronage and Aubrey would've been made. Now *I* have his interest, and suddenly you disapprove?"

"This is different. *You* are different."

"Nothing happened. I promise you."

"So, what did happen? You were late because of him, so tell me."

"He wanted me to have a drink with him. And his sister."

"His sister." Léo rolled her eyes. "You mean his mistress."

"No. It wasn't Madame Kohl. Her name was Marie-Thérèse, and she had the very same distinctive auburn hair as he."

"Mm-hm."

"Don't 'mm-hm' me. She did," Amélie insisted.

"You had a drink with him and his sister."

"A few."

"How many is 'a few'?"

"Three."

"Wine or absinthe?"

"You know me. I can't think clearly with the green fairy. Wine, purely wine."

"Good, because you have to keep a level head with him. And never, never let yourself be alone with him. Never again."

"I don't think we need to worry about my reputation. Aubrey did more than enough to ruin that. I might as well be in the demimonde for all the good he did me."

"But you're not. And you needn't be. Right? You convinced me there was another way. That you have talent enough without it. You didn't need Aubrey, and you definitely don't need Monsieur D. He's dangerous."

"You don't really believe those rumors, do you?"

"You don't? After all, they weren't born from a few careless whispers, but a divorce complaint so detailed in its decadence it would make the devil himself blush."

"I don't know if I believe it. He doesn't seem the sort."

Amélie couldn't explain how safe she'd felt with him. When they were alone, sitting improperly close, when he nuzzled her, she'd felt not a sliver of fear. But something else. Something, despite what she'd told him, she wanted.

"What does 'the sort' seem like?" Léo asked. "He's violent, or he'd still be respectably married, and we both know it."

That was the word around town, the true teeth in the bite of those rumors. For it must have been truly something to warrant one of the first divorces in France in nearly a century.

"Still, I don't think he's as menacing or powerful as you think."

"Girls." Madame Pelletier strode in with two full carafes of white wine. Routinely she furnished wine and Bénédictine with feigned beneficence when they all knew it dulled the bite of labor.

"I have the best news." She filled a glass for each of the women and raised hers. "Inexplicably, an investor from le Faubourg has taken an interest in this blanchisserie. Can you believe it? Some effort, he said, to better the working conditions. To shorten your hours and raise your pay. If you begin your workday at five in the morning, you are to *end* your workday at five in the afternoon. *The. Afternoon.* Can you believe such a thing? I cannot. He doesn't seem to have any head for business, but I don't care. His frivolity is our gain. His investment, well, it's made us." She clinked their glasses so hard the wine splashed on their hands.

Léo leveled Amélie with a cynical look as they took a sip.

At six that evening, Monsieur Degrailly's carriage pulled up.

"Did you invite him here?" Léo folded her arms across her chest as she watched him alight.

"No."

"I don't believe you. Your ambition will get you hurt and worse than your heart. You can't work if you're hurt."

"We don't even know what he wants. He could be here for Madame Pelletier."

Léo rolled her eyes. "No one comes here for that bitch."

"Keep your voice down."

Madame Pelletier trilled outside their door as she knocked. "Mademoiselle Audet, you have a visitor," she sang.

Amélie opened the door to the madame's bug-eyed delight.

"Ah, Monsieur Degrailly," Madame Pelletier drew out his name as if puzzling over the pronunciation, though everyone in France knew the name and he was almost certainly her mysterious new investor, "is here to see you, my dearest girl."

Amélie wanted to gag herself with the woman's own preening claim. The only things about her dear to the laundry mistress were her strong back and calloused hands. She pulled a shawl around her and went to go downstairs when Madame Pelletier stopped her.

"You might want to freshen up some, dear. He's quite fine, that gentleman."

"We've met, madame. He's more than aware of my circumstance."

Madame Pelletier's eyes narrowed. "You've met, have you? What does he want with you? I run a respectable business here. This is no brothel. Need I remind you what happened to Michelle? She got herself pregnant."

Amélie leaned in toward the woman. "I don't know if it works that way, madame. I know you're Catholic, and she was hardly the Virgin Mother, you would agree."

Madame Pelletier pursed her lips. "You've got a mouth on you."

Amélie found Monsieur Degrailly in a charcoal suit with a matching top hat tucked under an arm. He stood and gave her a radiant smile that made her feel warm and loose, as if it thawed frozen skin.

After introducing him to a dubious Léo and exchanging

pleasantries, he said, "A little bird told me you might be free this evening."

"Did it? What a nosy little thing."

"Would you be so kind as to take a walk with me?"

"A walk?"

"Perhaps even share a meal. If you're feeling hungry."

Amélie peeked out the window. "Have you got Marie-Thérèse tucked in your carriage?"

Monsieur Degrailly made a show of looking out at it. "Not today."

"Hm."

"Yes. Hm."

Amélie changed as Léo hovered. The ridiculously outdated day dress could only look inadequate beside Monsieur Degrailly's haute couture. But it was the only proper dress she had. The gold she wore to sing belonged to Salis's own collection.

"Where are you going?" Léo asked.

"For a walk."

"With his sister?"

"No."

"Still, that sounds nice. If you don't mind, I think I'll join you."

"I do mind."

"You're going to speak with him about an audition."

"I suppose. Yes."

"You. Suppose. What are you doing? You insisted you weren't like other performers, women who only use the stage to get into a wealthy man's bed. This is exactly what you're doing."

"I'm not climbing into his bed." Amélie refashioned her hair into a tidier bun. "We're going for a walk—"

"A walk—"

"Perhaps a bite to eat."

"What does he want with you?"

"Maybe he likes my singing."

"If he liked your singing, he would've offered you an audition. It's your body he wants. He'll cut you loose when he tires of you. Do you think to supplant Madame Kohl? She's rumored to be as daring in the bedroom as she is elegant in the salons. He'll never leave her. He's using you."

"For what?" Amélie stood at the door, her anger rising. She knew everything Léo said was true. "If he's so enchanted by Madame Kohl."

Léo shrugged.

"Thank you for your confidence in me."

"I just don't want to see you get hurt."

4

*M*onsieur Degrailly offered his arm, and they ambled slowly through the winding streets. As the sun fell closer to the horizon, striations of blush, taupe, and gray painted the evening sky. The air, which had been pleasant in the ripe afternoon, now held a slight chill, but he was warm, and Amélie found herself leaning into him.

After long minutes that seemed to grow heavy in their quiet, he finally said, "I can't help but wonder what makes the city's most sought-after figure model become a laundress. Of course, no offense intended to your position."

"Of course," she mocked. "Don't you know every girl dreams of floating down the boulevards during the Mid-Lent feasts? Queen for a day."

"I'd forgotten. Were you a queen for the parades, then?"

"Just this year. In my gown and mask, attended by my courtiers."

"I'm sorry I missed that. I keep thinking one of these years they should crown a Queen of Queens. Naturally it would be you, mademoiselle. The Queen of Paris," he said, framing it with his hands in the sky. "I can see it."

"You flatter me, monsieur."

"It isn't flattery when it's true." He paused. "Queen of the Mid-Lent feasts. And why else does one such as you become a laundress?"

"I'm sorry to disappoint you, monsieur—"

"Please. Call me Jasper. I hope I may call you Amélie."

"There's no great mystery. Merely a small truth that becomes embellished for want of more. Monsieur Talac and I were dear to one another and had a falling out. Things were said in the heat of hurt that can never be unsaid." She paused. "And I never aspired to be a figure model."

"Does he know where you are?"

It was rumored the painter, despite looking, didn't know where she was.

"He knows." She looked at him, his sage-green eyes cool amidst the warmth of his face. He met her gaze. "Why do you care so much?"

"I don't know. I find you a curiosity. The painting is all I know."

They sat for dinner tucked into a quiet corner café. And though he studied her, he had the good grace not to comment on her dated dress.

"I wonder what Madame Kohl would say if she should see us here."

He smiled mischievously. "You know about her, do you?"

"I do." She squared her shoulders. "And Madame Travers."

"You've kept abreast of me. I think I'm flattered."

"My friend keeps abreast."

"The tiny ball of disapproval?"

"That's the one. And a man in your position begs attention, whether he wants it or not."

He nodded. "True. As to the other, I have a healthy appetite for beautiful women. And at thirty-three, I'm hardly a young man."

"Quite a healthy appetite, I hear. I'm afraid I can't indulge you in that way, monsieur. If I misled you, I do apologize."

"You didn't mislead me, Amélie. You've been refreshingly plain."

"And still you invest in Madame Pelletier's blanchisserie."

Comically, he looked up and tapped a finger on his chin. "Did I invest in a blanchisserie? I can hardly think why I should do that. But I do have interests in many properties." He paused. "Are we speaking frankly?" He leaned forward, his eyes flitting all over her face, the soft candlelight making his beard appear fiery.

"I think so."

"If you were a grisette, I could approach you on fair terms. At the very least help you to rise, if that was your wish. But that doesn't seem to be your wish, Amélie. So, tell me, what is?"

"Why is it you must give me something?"

He gave her a heated look that held the answer. Her mouth went dry, and she took a sip of her wine, caressing the glass nervously.

"I'm not a grisette, as you seem to know. Nor do I have any desire to be a lorette or a courtesan."

"May I ask why?"

Indignant and embarrassed, Amélie felt as red as his beard and stood, dropping her napkin on the table.

Monsieur Degrailly grabbed her hand. "Sit."

He hadn't even looked at her. Yet his steely grip, not painful but unyielding, and the commanding tenor of his voice, it made her drop too easily back into her chair.

Gently he pulled her chin up and looked her in the eye. Why had her chin been down? She'd never been a coquette who feigned humility in the face of a handsome man.

"Don't be narrow to suit something I suspect doesn't serve you. For a woman in your position, what I'm offering you is quite simply the world."

"But not respect."

"When weighed against all the rest, is that so important a thing?"

Unflinching, she met his gaze. "It is to me."

His face pinched in puzzlement. "You're not a virgin."

"You know I'm not."

"Why, then, this false modesty? Means are made in such ways."

"Ends are made in such ways."

He tipped his head and made a face as if saying *touché*. "I could help you, Amélie. I would very much like to help you if I can."

"That's kind of you. And as I said, I am flattered, but—"

"But nothing. If you resort to working in a laundry, your financial straits can only be dire. You're beautiful, intelligent, amusing, articulate. And more than any of that, talented. The picture of a woman destined to be a great courtesan." He leaned in, his warm breath falling on her ear before saying, "I could make you a woman of independent means."

Though it wasn't the first time she'd been propositioned for the demimonde, the suggestion coming from him, a man her body crackled with intensity to be around, was perhaps the most forthright and vulgar thing she'd ever heard. Even the whisper in her ear had made her wet. Shamefully she wanted more.

"And keep me in an apartment on the rue Leblanc next door to Madame Kohl?"

"Forget about her for a moment."

Amélie chuckled. "You're so arrogant, monsieur."

"And you like it."

"And infuriating," she added.

"Then we're well matched. Because I've never been more intrigued and equally infuriated by a woman as you."

"Well, then I've done my part." She made a mock bow.

After dinner, they walked up the hill. The Basilica of the Sacré-Coeur stood at the summit. Still under construction, its milky-white travertine was encaged by iron latticework. A contradictory thing to see, as paradoxical as the summit upon which it stood.

In the five years she'd been back and as close as she'd been, Amélie hadn't dared to come to this hilltop that had known so much horror.

Was it here? she thought as she dragged her feet. *Or perhaps here?* She would never know and didn't want to know. *Mont des Martyrs, indeed.*

The church, they'd been told, would stand as a penance for the anarchist district. A memorial too, for those who'd lost their lives.

Maria Álvarez Audet had given all she could spare to see it built. Even in her joy-swallowing grief, Amélie's mother had dedicated herself to seeing that bloody place consecrated to the sacred heart of Christ.

Penance and memory and Christ's love. The Catholic Church could say whatever it wanted. But those in the district who still harbored rebellious hearts knew better. The city wanted order and a reunification with its guiding church. What better place, what better way, than to turn this siege-guns peak into an unquestioned place of peace.

Amélie was torn. Their cause had been just. But the means… and the end… She swallowed a hardened lump of tears threatening to crest. This was why she hadn't come until now.

The sun was setting as they stopped at a railing. Paris stretched before them, salmon-tinged under gathering flint-and-periwinkle clouds. Monsieur Degrailly grasped the railing, his fingers brushing hers.

"Are you all right?"

So lost in her painful thoughts, she'd nearly forgotten he was there. "I'm fine, monsieur." She gave him a reassuring smile.

"You're shaking. Are you cold?" He took off his suit coat.

She supposed she was shaking but wouldn't admit to why. "Perhaps."

He wrapped her in his coat, which smelled of his clean scent—a blend of citrus, chamomile, and earthy tobacco. Layered. A rich man's scent.

Brushing the back of a hand down her cheek, Monsieur Degrailly regarded her with those keen eyes that wanted everything.

Several minutes passed in patient silence. Somehow the weight of it made him grow. He crowded into the corners of her sadness and anger, making her light and hot, making her heart pulse in her core.

"I believe I've made myself clear as to what I want," he finally said.

"You have."

"But the mystery remains. What do you want, Amélie? And how can I give it to you?"

At length she considered her want and his, how to separate them and whether or not they could be.

"You could help me with something," she finally uttered.

He turned to rest on the railing, facing her. "Tell me. Please."

"I'd like a chance to audition for you and Monsieur Zidler."

"I see." He paused. "But there's a problem. Our girls will be in the demimonde. At the café, you cut that idea to shreds."

"Surely not all of them."

He nodded, but she couldn't tell if he was assenting or thinking.

"If stars are courtesans and courtesans stars, we want the brightest on our stage. We'll cater to le gratin. If they want a night's entertainment, something more bohemian and decadent, the Moulin Rouge will be the place. Decadent but high class. Spectacular and diverting. And when it's over, the night doesn't have to end. If we can pull it off, it will be radical. But we need our entertainment to be… well, entertaining, you see."

"'Entertaining.' Yes, I see very well." She felt an iciness seep into her body. Straightening her back, she turned from the railing.

"Wait." He took her hand and stroked it. "I'm not sure you do."

"As you said, I'm no virgin, monsieur. I do. Tell me, is it in a girl's contract?"

"Nothing so spelled out as that. But since you're not naïve, how did you come to think you could perform without making yourself available? That is why women take to the stage, Amélie. To secure a wealthy benefactor such as myself. Surely you know that."

She did and had confronted it, at times even tried to talk herself out of her dreams because of it.

"That expectation is changing," she said.

"Perhaps. Still it remains."

"I'm a good actress. A good dancer and a talented singer. You said so yourself. I want to perform. And I don't think I should have to sleep with a man to do it."

"Will you let me think about it?"

She nodded.

He moved to stand behind her. The tickle of his beard and fullness of his lips dragged slowly across her nape. It felt like a tension line to her muscles had been cut, and she sagged into him and exhaled.

"You've put me in a delicate position." He pressed small kisses in a neat row along her nape, then up to the hollow below an ear. "You won't have sex to sing, but I wanted you from the first moment I laid eyes on you. Well before I knew you performed." He pressed his arousal to her bottom, and she sucked in a breath. She could feel her blood trickling steadily to her sex, filling it. Glancing around, she saw the walks that ringed the church seemed to be deserted for now. But anyone could come at any moment.

His fingers laced through hers, stilling her. "Relax." He took her lobe in his mouth and suckled. "What'll they see?"

She swallowed. Her sex felt so tingly and full her mouth was agape to catch her breath. *What'll they see?* They'd see how much she wanted him.

Monsieur Degrailly urged Amélie to turn around, his eyes narrowing on her lips. "May I have one small favor?" He dragged two fingertips over her lips, back and forth, back and forth. Unconsciously, she opened her mouth, and his eyes widened. "Nice." He slid the pads of his fingers to her tongue, and she kissed them. "Oh," he breathed as if in wonder. "You're perfect." Her skin puckered exquisitely as if reaching for more praise.

He tipped her chin, leaned deliberately in, and kissed her. He was no fumbling boy desperately jabbing at her lips, but measured and seductive. His mouth moved over hers rhythmically, his tongue sliding in so that she could almost feel him inside her already.

An arm slid around her waist, and a hand skimmed down her chest, lightly caressing a breast. He pressed his sex to hers through the layers of fabric between them and slowly rubbed, mimicking his tongue as it continued to thrust. Her body felt enflamed as her breathing grew faint.

When he finally pulled back, she couldn't help the moan that escaped. He smiled warmly and cupped her cheek.

"Something for you to think about," he said.

5

*T*he next day, Jasper strolled under the great glass dome of the Salon de Paris for the vernissage when he spotted Amélie. She meandered arm in arm with her friend. But the waiflike blonde was nearly missed beside the beautiful and statuesque woman who grew in his mind by the moment. All he could think of was how eagerly she sank into that chair for him, how willingly she took his fingers in her mouth, that soft, sucking kiss to their tips, the way her breath hitched as he played. Even as he felt his heart rate quicken, he became infinitely aware of Daphne on his arm.

"Jasper, you're holding on too tight. What's got into you?"

"Sorry, darling." He pulled himself away. "I'll get us some champagne. You'd like that, wouldn't you?"

Daphne put a handkerchief to her nose. "Why not? I'm nearly gone from the varnish fumes as it is. A glass of champagne might send me right to the floor. I'll be an easy mark tonight."

Jasper laughed, too loudly he could tell. And still he couldn't stop. This was comical. How could she be here? he thought. Then he knew and turned, searching frantically. He scanned the ladders and the artists applying their final coats. This was an exclusive preview. Only the artists themselves and their honored guests.

He grabbed two glasses of champagne off a tray floating by, then went in search of Talac. Yet when he found Amélie, she stood not with Talac, but another man he didn't recognize. They were laughing, their bodies easy, intimate, and so familiar.

"Mademoiselle Audet."

She turned to him, and her bright smile slipped. "Monsieur Degrailly. Fancy running into you here."

"Yes. My ex-wife has some paintings here."

"Your *ex*-wife," Mademoiselle Thomas taunted with an arched brow.

"Madame Travers," Amélie said. "Of course. A woman painter. It isn't done. Why, it's downright scandalous," she teased archly. "For a woman to have such ambitions so clearly outside her sex."

These two women, thick as thieves with their barbed tongues. He could hear his heart thumping while they exchanged tight smiles.

"Who do we have here?" Jasper indicated the man who stood proudly by a painting.

"Daan Thomas." Daan extended a hand, which Jasper shook. "I'm Léonie's brother." He put an arm around his sister.

"A dear friend," Amélie added.

Of course Jasper wondered just how dear. But he also didn't get the sense Monsieur Thomas had designs on Amélie. So, he relaxed.

"It's a handsome piece, monsieur. Is it your first here?"

"I had one some years back, but it didn't make the same impression I hope this one will."

"I think it will." The painting was a scene of naked bathers by a riverside. He'd employed subtle geometric shapes to provide definition to the figures, an avant-garde technique. "You're quite a talent. Really."

"Monsieur Degrailly does have an eye for talent," Amélie said.

"With only one word from him, you could make your mark."

Her face was a picture of earnestness, but her eyes were flinty. She was taunting him, and it was working. All he could picture was getting her alone and giving her a sound spanking. His trousers strained with the image of it playing in his head.

"That's awfully kind," Jasper managed. "But I wouldn't go so far as to say that."

"Oh, Jasper, here you are." Daphne slipped an arm into his and took a glass. "Have you been offering my champagne to every pretty girl in the Salon?" She chuckled amiably, and he knew it wasn't feigned.

Daphne had been widowed at twenty-six. Her husband had been nearly thirty years her senior and, the rumors held it, had been quite controlling and cruel. She would have danced on his grave had it been the proper thing to do. Because Daphne Kohl was the picture of propriety—*in public.*

Jasper had met her by chance nearly two years earlier on one of his visits to No. 9 rue de Navarin. Chez Christiane was known for its *special appetites.* Daphne, with her white-blonde hair and guileless baby-blue eyes had seemed quite out of place in the den. And upon closer inspection, she was glass-eyed from intoxication. He'd thought—rightly it turned out—someone had taken advantage of her, and he spirited her from the club like a white knight.

Yet Daphne Kohl was an unusual woman. The image of an angel—it did occur to him just how much she physically resembled his ex-wife—yet in bed, her appetites were anything but innocent. They shared this interest and affection, exploring their passions in heated gasps, but it was little more than that. For now, it served them well.

"Is this your piece, monsieur?" Daphne asked.

"Yes, madame," Daan replied.

"The bathers are abstract, and yet it seems to give some weight to the piece. And the dimensions under the canopy of trees seem to be just right." She looked at Jasper. "Wouldn't you say, darling?"

"I would."

"You've captured it, madame," Daan said.

Daphne smiled prettily. She hadn't been educated in art as well as some. Certainly not his ex-wife, Joselin, who claimed it like an unusual pet. But Daphne was unafraid of her ignorance and eager to learn. A happy combination.

"I don't think we've had the pleasure of being introduced." Amélie extended her hand to Daphne.

"No, we haven't."

"I'm sorry," Jasper said. He wasn't sorry. The last thing he wanted was for his current and future to be acquainted. "Mademoiselle Audet, this is Madame Kohl."

While the women exchanged greetings, Jasper was struck by how physically different they were. One tall and dark, even something mysterious in her beauty. The other shorter and blonde, somewhat angelic. Yet both stirred him.

"Amélie."

They all turned.

"Aubrey."

Daphne gasped. "Is it—could it be? Are you Monsieur Talac?" Slack-jawed, she looked at Jasper, then back to Talac.

"You know my work?"

The artist smiled and appeared approachable. Yet there was something overweening in his weasel eyes. He stood tall, nearly as tall as Jasper. His tie and shoulder-length chestnut hair seemed deliberately askew, as if he couldn't be bothered with the simple social grace of grooming and wanted to be certain everyone knew. Jasper decided right then and there he didn't like the man.

"I was hoping you'd be here," Talac said to Amélie. "May we talk? Somewhere private."

"Wait a moment," Daphne said. "You're *Fille dans le bain*. Of course! This is Monsieur Talac and you his mysterious figure model all the art world raved about two years ago. Do you remember, Jasper? Is it not her?"

"Perhaps."

"There's no 'perhaps' about it. The resemblance is uncanny." She slapped him teasingly on an arm, then turned to Talac. "Will you paint her again, monsieur?"

"I'd like to, madame." He took Amélie's arm. "It was a pleasure to meet you. If you'll excuse us."

6

"You came for Daan," Aubrey said after he'd pulled her into a corner.

"Yes, we came for Daan. It's a beautiful piece. And we miss him."

Aubrey ran a hand through his hair. "What about me? Do you miss me? Do you ever think of me?"

He looked at her with pleading in his eyes. Once again she marveled at the idea that this man, so gifted, could be so insecure. He had made her his sun, happy to orbit around her if only she would shine on him.

Eighteen months had passed since she'd last seen him. When she left, she'd been heartbroken, as if he were the one leaving her. She'd missed him terribly, only to discover he was spreading a scurrilous rumor, running his mouth and running her down in equal breath.

She'd hated him for so long. Just imagining lashing him with her tongue made her breathless with anticipation. But the sharpness of that anger had dulled over time. Now, standing before him, she was reminded of his dark beauty, his warm eyes when fixed on her, his open heart. How he'd loved her. And how she'd loved him.

"No. I don't miss you. Honestly, I don't really think about you."

She knew she sounded bitter and didn't care. And she also knew, when she couldn't seem to summon her righteous anger, that she lied. Aubrey had been the great love of her life. So great, in fact, she'd allowed him to swallow her up in it. She'd come to Paris to sing and fallen for a promising young artist.

The sitting that became *Fille dans le bain* was the only time she had ever modeled. New to the wonders of her body and sex, she hadn't given any thought to baring herself to Aubrey.

The fragrant bath steamed, and she gathered her wild sable hair up to secure it.

"Beautiful, my love. Now turn your body slowly and look at me."

So languid and drunk from the orgasms, her eyes were sleepy, and her body soft and pink and used.

"What are you doing? Put that away."

"Can't," he said, scribbling frantically. "I wouldn't be an artist if I didn't at least try to capture the most beautiful thing I've ever seen."

That was true. He'd sketched often. Half-finished scrawls of her littered his studio. But never nude.

She moved to climb into the tub.

"Stop. Whatever you do, don't turn away. Don't move a muscle. Your beauty and this light, it's perfect. You must allow me to capture it. Please."

She sighed. "You're not going to show my face, are you?"

"The face of a goddess? Yes," he said absently. He'd slipped seamlessly into another world, where the light of inspiration meets the beauty of subject and everything else falls away but the rush of that thing so divine it feels handed to you by God. "Look here." He pointed to his square jaw. "Look right here."

"You're not going to show that to anyone, are you?"

"You're so provincial, Amélie. Will your Brazilian maman spray you with holy water?"

"Yes."

He smiled sweetly at her, and she relaxed a bit.

When weeks later it was finally finished, they stood before it.

"It's an incredible painting, Aubrey."

He nodded. "It's the subject."

"No."

"Yes. You have to let me submit it to the jury. It could be my big break."

She exhaled sharply. "You can't be serious. I thought you were painting it for yourself."

"Are you so selfish you would deny me my success?"

"That's not fair. You have great talent. You can paint another of someone else. Of something else."

"It won't be the same. This is a singular work. I've never captured anything like this before. Surely you can see that. There's something there." He pointed to her rendered face, her eyes.

And that was the greatest irony of all. What he had captured was her vulnerability. That hidden quality she wanted to hide more than she wanted anything. More even than performing. Naked in all ways, the painting threatened to expose her.

They fought over it for months, but in the end, he submitted it without her consent. Its reception was all he'd hoped for and more. Everywhere they went, his unsteady arm was wrapped around her waist as if the two of them had somehow created it together.

He had captured something, he said. To art critics and art lovers. He had. *Her.* And he held on so tight she couldn't breathe. She loved him, and she had to leave him.

She couldn't be anywhere near him, or she could so easily fall back. He knew it.

"Are you seeing anyone?" he asked.

She glanced at Monsieur Degrailly, who seemed to be keeping an eye on them out of the corner of his eye.

"No."

As if sensing they were being watched, Aubrey took her arms and pushed them behind one of the towering palms that seemed to sprout among the exhibits.

"I miss you, Amélie. So much. I can't paint without you." There was the truth. She gave him a perturbed look. "I-I can't *live* without you."

"Don't be so dramatic, Aubrey. You seem to be doing quite well for yourself."

"Clothes. A steady following. An income that allows me to paint. But it's nothing compared to you. I want you back."

She shook her head.

"Why are you being so stubborn? You love me. Still. I can see it."

"And do you love me? Or do you just love what we had?"

"Of course I still love you. Of course. There could never be anyone to compare to you. You know that. You're my muse."

"I need to go. Léo will be looking for me."

"Daan misses her. You can't be happy in that wretched blanchisserie. Come back to me. Just come back. Please."

"I need to go." She pulled away.

"Yes. That's what you always say. But I won't give up."

Monsieur Degrailly appeared. "Is there a problem?"

"No," Amélie said. "Thank you, but no."

If she went back to Daan and Léonie, Aubrey would only follow as if he were meant to be there. And if the four of them carried on together for even a few moments, she might be reminded how good they once were. So, she wandered for a while.

Finally, she stopped before a series of three small nudes tucked away from much of the Salon's exhibits. When she saw the scandalous signature—Joselin Travers—she knew why.

"They're unusual," she said to Madame Travers, who stood before them. "But remarkable, I think."

The willowy blonde in a robin's-egg-blue dress had an ethereal beauty about her. Yet she appeared sad as she studied them.

"You think so?" Madame Travers gave her a watery smile.

"A woman's eye can't help but see the female form differently.

They're really something special. Congratulations."

Madame Travers's brow furrowed as she studied Amélie. Then her jaw dropped, and she pulled in a breath as if to speak—

"They are something special, aren't they?" Monsieur Degrailly said as he greeted his ex-wife. The embrace wasn't perfunctory or polite. He held on a beat too long; his lips on her cheek lingered.

"So special they're tucked away over here where no one can see them," Madame Travers said.

"One step at a time, Jos."

"Right. And if it weren't for my ex-husband, they'd be outside on the street somewhere, clamoring to get in."

Monsieur Degrailly shook his head. "Joselin got in on the merits of these paintings. Anyone can see it."

He looked at his ex-wife with something more than admiration. Not simply pride. Love. Amélie was struck. She'd been so intent on the lovely Madame Kohl that it never occurred to her he was still in love with his ex-wife. Here was the woman who held his heart. If he loved her, perhaps Amélie could manage a flirtation with him and it would be nothing more.

"Here you are." Aubrey stalked toward her, exhaling in exasperation. "I thought I'd lost you."

The four of them stood beside each other, their arms wrapped around their partners. As Madame Travers and Aubrey talked about the optical effects of color, the use of saturated shades and broad brushstrokes to evoke an artist's inner turmoil, Amélie and Monsieur Degrailly pasted polite smiles on their faces. They nodded, adding to the conversation here and there, but they were not a party to it. Their gazes, tense and searching as they flitted to each other, were having another conversation entirely.

7

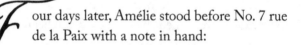our days later, Amélie stood before No. 7 rue de la Paix with a note in hand:

Amélie,
My carriage will arrive for you at noon on
Saturday.
JD

The House of Worth. She couldn't afford even a speck of dust on the floor of the place, let alone a haute-couture gown.

After seeing Aubrey at the Salon, she'd felt certain it would signal an end to Monsieur Degrailly's interest. But when she walked in the door, he was waiting.

"What am I doing here?" she asked after exchanging courtesies.

"You need an evening gown, and we need to get your measurements." He directed her to a room filled with cast figures wearing the most elegant dresses she'd ever seen.

"They're beautiful, but I can't afford these."

"I can afford them."

"Have you suffered a head wound?"

He chuckled. "My mind is perfectly sound."

"Need I remind you we haven't come to any arrangement."

"I know, and I've been giving it a lot of thought." He folded his arms across his chest and leaned against a sofa. "You have this idea of how wonderful your life will be when you get on that stage, but you haven't any idea how wonderful it might be with me. I intend to show you."

She raised her brow.

"This is merely a costume so that you may play your part."

She sighed. "What part is that? I'm almost afraid to ask."

"My mistress, of course."

She shook her head.

"One night. Give me one night, and I'll give you your audition."

"I've told you I won't have sex to sing."

"This isn't that. It seems like it, looks like it, feels like it…"

"But it isn't."

"It isn't. You paired the two together. I didn't."

He was right. He hadn't.

"And before you say her name, Daphne's a good sport. She sees other people. *I* see other people. We see people."

"Your ex-wife? Do you see her as well?"

"Jos has no interest in seeing me."

"But you have an abiding interest in her, I think."

He smiled flatly as he stared at her. Finally, he said, "I'm not looking for love, Amélie."

"Neither am I."

"Then why do you hesitate?"

One week later, when Amélie came down the stairs in a sapphire silk gown with detailed deep-blue-and-black embroidery, Monsieur

Degrailly's eyes widened. His gaze traveled from her pompadour—grudgingly done up by Léo with tiny braids and sapphire ribbons—to her low pumps.

"Will this costume suffice?" she asked.

"You're exquisite." He took her hands and bussed her politely for Madame Pelletier's and Léo's watchful benefit.

"And you've dusted that unfortunate suit off from the back of your wardrobe. No doubt intending to be handsome."

Monsieur Degrailly wore a haute-couture Inverness cape over an elegant matching suit. His bearing was straight with one arm neatly tucked behind his back while the other held his top hat. His auburn beard was a neatly trimmed shadow on his face, and his hair was devoid of the slick of pomade so many men favored and Amélie detested. Instead it appeared he'd run a hand through it, sending his soft waves into a riot. Though his eyes were cool, he knew very well how good he looked, and his smile was smug.

He extended his arm. "Shall we?"

"What time will you bring her back?" Léo asked.

Amélie frowned at her while Monsieur Degrailly appeared to think.

"It could be very late," he pronounced. "I wouldn't wait up. But I promise to return her safe and sound."

"I'll have your word on that," Léo said.

No sooner had they gained the carriage when he kissed her, his fingers pulling down her chin to open her mouth. Her breasts tightened, and her sex seemed to pulse and pant. She'd been attracted to Aubrey, but for this man, she ached.

"Monsieur, please," she said when he broke the kiss.

He looked at her, his face filled with wonder, as if he'd been outside himself and slipped back in, holding all the secrets of the universe. Then he pulled the tie on her cape and peeled it open. He took his time admiring her bodice, the intricate beadwork on the tight curves was its own work of art. Then he pressed a wet kiss at the hollow where her collarbones met.

"Tonight you'll call me Jasper." He retied her cape. "I insist. I think you'd like to do that, but your misplaced pride is holding you back." Once again, he bent over her mouth and kissed her, this time soft yet somehow more sensuous with how he teased and pulled back.

"Really? Tell me more about me."

"I intend to," he replied with such promise she was equal parts excited and worried.

When the carriage pulled up to the creamy Beaux-Arts exterior of the Paris Opera House, Amélie felt the sudden press of terror. With her dreams and ambition and the dogged sense she could achieve whatever she imagined, she'd never really thought herself inferior to any crowd, for neither ignorance nor class were anything to be ashamed of when they were dynamic things. Yet now she felt conspicuously out of place. For the first time, a pretender.

As they climbed the stairs to the entrance, she squared her shoulders and straightened her posture. Still, her fingers bounced nervously.

At the top of the stairs, he paused to look at her, then slid his hand into hers. "Relax," he breathed warmly into her ear. "You're the most beautiful woman here. And if you know it, they will, too."

When they walked into the stories-high grand foyer, she was stunned by the magnificent marble stairs that wound up into balconies, the carvings and gold leaf, and all the grand chandeliers. The dark sculptures holding tiered trays of lights like glowing desserts.

"It really is something to see for the first time," Monsieur Degrailly admitted.

For a moment of unchecked awe, she'd forgotten he was there.

"I don't want you to be intimidated," he continued, "but I think I need to tell you something."

"I'm not easily intimidated," she said, though she just had been.

"While you're studying all this beauty…" He leaned in and whispered, "Everyone is studying you."

She looked around them and saw men and women hiding behind their glasses and fans, flicking furtive glances at them.

"They're looking at you," she said, "wondering what kind of rubbish you picked up."

"You don't believe you're rubbish. Do you?" He waited until she shook her head. "I promise you they're not thinking that. They're thinking, 'Who is that enchanting woman, and how did he get her to stoop for him?'"

"Jasper, you're flattering me."

"Is it working?"

His praise fell down her spine like fingers on a piano. "It is."

He leaned in and pressed a wet kiss near her ear. "I like the sound of my name on your lips."

She looked at him. *Was that the first time I said it?* He nodded as if a party to her thoughts.

After an elegant dinner accompanied by more glances and murmurings from Tout-Paris, Jasper and Amélie were tucked comfortably into a red-velvet private box when the lights went down and the orchestra galloped into the opening bars of *Le Cid*. As soon as Fidès Devriès opened her mouth to sing Chimène, Amélie was lost. She leaned forward as the soprano's voice climbed up and up, dipped and turned, pulling the audience into the tale. That diminutive woman with the large voice held everyone in the theatre enrapt.

Well into act 4, Amélie felt Jasper beside her. She'd been so taken by the performance she nearly forgot he was there. He moved closer and slightly back from her, then put his arm around the back of her chair. Facing the stage, he tipped his head to hers.

"Are you enjoying the opera, Amélie?"

"It's unlike anything I've ever felt."

"Good. Keep watching the stage."

"What are you do—"

"Whatever you do, whatever *I* do, just keep watching the stage."

"Pardon me?"

"Watch. Just keep watching."

Her gaze froze to the stage when she heard Jasper clear his throat and bend over as if he'd dropped something. Then she felt his hand under her dress. She gasped and grabbed it, glancing to the right and left of them.

"What are you doing?"

"Let go."

She squeezed even tighter and looked around again.

"No one can see," he said silkily. "If they look, they will see me smiling politely, my lovely date entranced. Now let go of my hand." Reluctantly she did. "Good girl. Now, keep watching."

Warmth flooded her face and chest, and her breathing grew faint against the tight corset as his questing hand smoothed up her stockinged leg through all the layers of her underclothes and into her knickers. She sucked in a breath and whimpered as his hand met her bare thigh. Again she grabbed his hand when it hovered near her sex.

"Ah-ah. Let. Go. You're enjoying the opera, aren't you?"

"Yes." Although she'd completely lost the thread of it.

"Spread your legs."

"Not here."

Her sex felt so flooded and thick she couldn't let him touch her there. Not now. Right here in the opera house with Émile Zola and his wife in the very next box. *What is he thinking?*

"No one can see." He traced two fingers up and down her thigh, getting closer and closer to the crease at her core. "I promise."

Fixing her watery gaze on the stage, she shook her head even as she opened her legs.

"More."

She licked her lips and spread her legs further.

"More still, Amélie," he said in a lust-laden lilt.

It felt like her whole body was burning up when she spread her legs further, more than enough room for his hand. And when he slid a finger through the down of her sex, deep into her wet core, she swallowed a cry.

"Shh. Ah, sweetling, your cunny is soaked. I think you want this.

I think you like me touching you here." He waggled his finger. "Right here in the middle of act 4. Are you watching?"

She nodded, some sort of ridiculous squeak sound, like a mouse saying yes, coming out of her mouth.

"What's happening?"

"I have no idea."

He *tsk*ed. "What am I going to do with you?"

"I don't know."

"Lucky for you, I have some ideas." He slid two fingers up and down, up and down, and up and down her slit.

She moaned, and her head fell back.

"Ah-ah. Keep watching."

"I don't know what's happening anyway."

"Then pretend. We'll playact. I'll play the role of a gentleman sitting close to his lovely date with a placid hand on her thigh, wishing, hoping, praying he might stroke her naked thigh later if he's very ardent and she's very game. And you'll play the role of my lovely lady, so entranced by her first time at the opera she hasn't any idea she's being fucked by his finger. Can you do that for me?" All the while, he worked up and down the outside of her swollen lips, playing in the crease where it met her legs, gliding just over the top of the button that held her release. Teasing, so mercilessly teasing.

She looked at him, and his lopsided grin was sly and pleased. As much as she wanted to slap it off his face and yank his hand out of her skirt, she wanted what he wanted even more. That realization was so surprising that barely without thought, she opened her legs even more.

He thrust two fingers inside her to the knuckles, and she moaned.

"Shh. Not a sound. Open your eyes. Close your mouth. Concentrate. What's happening?"

"I'm going to come."

"I meant on stage."

"I have no idea."

He chuckled and pumped his fingers in and out, moving his thumb to circle around, then finally press into her bundle of nerves, kneading it. She gasped and jerked.

"Easy. Stay still. Can you come without a sound?"

She shook her head.

"But for now, you will. For me. Won't you?"

She felt like she was going to go up in flames. Fall off her chair. Make an utter ass of herself. And she didn't care. Never had she clung so desperately to the blissful edge and wanted to hold on and let go in equal measure.

"I feel you getting close. Tightening up on my fingers nicely. Any moment. Any second. La petite mort. And you'll do it without a sound. Just for me. Won't you?"

When finally she tipped over the edge, she bit her lip hard, grabbed her chair and his arm, anything to hold her steady and keep her quiet. The tingling rushed through her core and up her spine. She felt her sex clench his fingers over and over and over again.

Finally, she was able to take a breath and turn to him. His satisfied smirk was devastating as he smoothed her dress and tasted her on his fingers.

"Why did you do that to me?"

He leaned in and whispered, "Because I knew you'd like it. Tell me I'm wrong."

Amélie glanced at Monsieur Zola, the famously prudish writer who seemed to reserve his particular ire for wanton laundresses. The man glimpsed her out of the corner of his eye and squirmed.

"You're not wrong," she admitted, though it tasted like a defeat.

When Jasper pulled back, he held her cheek tenderly. "Good."

8

rich dinner, the exhilarating opera, then a stunning orgasm. When they finally climbed back into the carriage, Amélie felt so languorous she could have sunk into the squabs and fallen asleep.

"This has been a night I'll never forget. I thank you, monsieur. So much."

"My pleasure. Believe me. You've ruined me for any other date for the opera. I never imagined how good it could be to bring someone so livened by it."

She rolled her eyes.

"Not that," he continued. "Well, yes that. But I really meant that you were so struck by it all. It only made me want to show you more. I hope the night doesn't have to end yet."

She peered out the window. The carriage was wending away from Montmartre, not to it. "Where are we going?"

"I thought we'd stop at my apartment for a drink.

If you'd like."

Amélie felt all the blood in her body race to her core. There could be no question what he was suggesting, and after his taunting in the opera, she wanted desperately to say yes.

Still, she could feel her mother's condemnation all the way from Rouen. Her mother, though she'd once been so daring as to follow her dashing French captain from the streets of Salvador to France, couldn't seem to conceive of a woman who wanted more for her life than the meager bounds her sex and religion would mete out. Amélie should be focused on being a wife and mother, she'd always said. Sleeping with any man who showed an interest was no way to that. So many times Maria had said it that Amélie could hear the words in her mother's voice even now.

Amélie shouldn't have gone for that walk. Should not have answered Jasper's summons to the House of Worth. Should certainly not have accepted his invitation for tonight. And definitely should say no to this.

After crossing over the Seine, the carriage finally pulled to a stop in front of a cream stone building on the majestic boulevard Saint-Germain.

"Perhaps one drink."

After a tour of Jasper's apartment—it was a Haussmann and very modern, with parquet floors and soaring ceilings, arched doorways and carved fireplaces in every room—she wandered out onto a balcony.

"It's every bit as monstrous as they claimed," she said, staring at the massive illuminated wrought iron tower in the distance.

Jasper slipped his arms around her waist and rested his head on her shoulder. It felt so good and warm and right, as if her body were built to tuck into his.

"It was much worse when they first began building it," he said. "I seriously considered moving. But I'd only just bought the place and I like it."

"I suppose there is something to the electric lights."

"Like the lighthouse from ancient Alexandria." He brought her into the drawing room. "Anyway, I'm used to it now. And it can't be there forever."

They settled on a plush oriental rug with a bottle of cabernet between them, talking about the opera and its attendees. About his family—he was the youngest of four, his older siblings all women. About her mother living in Rouen with Amélie's father's family.

"And your father?" he asked.

"A good man. A wonderful father. He was a captain in the army."

"Was?"

She hated this part. Telling someone new. She didn't like to be pitied.

"He managed to outlast the Prussians but succumbed to radicals in the bloody spring of '71."

Jasper paused as his mind seemed to turn. "At the Battle for Montmartre." Another pause. "The Sacré-Coeur. That's why you were so moved when we were there. I'm so sorry, Amélie."

"Yes, well, it's all right. It was a long time ago."

She sucked in a breezy breath and took a sip of wine. All the while, she could feel his gaze on her but couldn't meet it.

"Not so long ago for a girl of five? Six?"

"Five."

Jasper tipped his head to find her gaze. Reluctantly she met it and found a soft smile of sympathy and reassurance. It was a look that said more than any words could. *I see you. You don't have to pretend. It's all right.*

"Tell me more about your work. Hotels? And entertainment? An entrepreneur. I thought your set looked down upon that."

"Oh, they do. Believe me. They live to look down on people. But I don't have the stomach for genteel poverty like some. Leisure all day and living on the credit of an increasingly worthless name. I can't do that.

"And my father made some bad investments some years back. When it comes right down to it, there wouldn't have been much for me to inherit. The girls didn't care. It wouldn't be left to them."

"They all married well?"

"Two of them. Though they took their fine time of it. My sisters are… a discerning lot." He sighed. "And quite independent."

"You sound plagued by discerning and independent women."

His deliberate gaze fell on her. "It feels that way at times."

"Can you find a more amenable sort?"

"Easily. They're everywhere. But they bore me."

They exchanged an amused look.

"Marie-Thérèse and Marie-Louise are married. With children for my mother to dote upon, thank God. I was a terrible disappointment in that respect. Well, in many respects. Marie-Élise is a nun."

"Is she really? How my mother would love that."

"Her only child? I don't think so. No matter how devout she is."

"You don't know her, monsieur. She's quite taken with Christ."

Jasper chortled. "It seems we're both terrible disappointments to our mothers. Let's drink to that."

After swallowing another sip of wine, Amélie said, "You mentioned an increasingly worthless name. Aren't you descended from the great Comtes de Foix and the House of Foix-Grailly?"

Even as the words came out, she blushed feeling like such a patent climber and wished she could take them back. Léonie fed on these things, not her.

"Yes, indeed. Some say the last male of my line. No small pressure there. But since the Revolution, there is no more House of Foix-Grailly. At some point the *de* became married to the *Grailly*."

"Sometimes we must adapt to survive," she said.

"Exactly."

"And Madame Travers? She didn't mind your work?"

"She didn't have a choice, really. The Travers are the genteel poverty sort. She likes nice things, and I like giving them to her."

Amélie didn't fail to notice the present tense, and Jasper shifted as if realizing it, too.

"Do you think it possible," he said, "to love someone and know that person isn't right for you?"

"It's certainly possible." She didn't think it true in his instance.

They peered at the empty bottle, then he surveyed her. "That looks uncomfortable."

"This old thing?" She indicated her dress. "I'm never taking it off."

"It may be difficult to bathe."

"Do you think so?"

"And the silk may never lay the same. I'm afraid you're going to have to take it off eventually."

"I suppose you have some idea as to when I might do that."

"One or two. Yes."

Suddenly all the excitement of the night seemed to drain out of her and, combined with the smooth, dark red, she yawned.

"If you're sleepy, we might move to a bedroom so you can be more comfortable."

"I was thinking, if I were sleepy, it might be time for me to go home."

"But it's so late." He laced a hand through hers and pulled her toward the bedrooms. "Wouldn't it be so much easier if you just slept here."

She'd known the inevitable outcome when she accepted his invitation for a drink. But as they approached the bedrooms, she couldn't help but remember what Léo had said.

He's dangerous.

A divorce complaint so detailed in its decadence it would make the devil himself blush.

Was she being terribly naïve? Did she simply miss intimacy? Or was there something about this man in particular? He stirred her blood, but he didn't frighten her. Perhaps he should have, but he didn't.

"I suppose it would be easier. And you do have all these spare rooms with their empty beds."

"Exactly." He drew her into the first and bent to light the fire that had been neatly prepared. "They get downright mournful if they're not used."

"And how convenient the fire was ready for you to light in this room."

"I was just thinking the same."

After the fire caught, he switched a bedside lamp on low and turned to her. For what seemed like long moments, he stared at her with dancing eyes over placid features, his head tipping so his gaze could move and scrutinize. She opened her mouth to speak, but he brought a couple fingers to his lips. They lay carelessly on them as if he would tell her to be quiet but couldn't be bothered. His manner unnerved her, and he almost certainly knew it. Had any other man examined her so, she might have called him on his arrogance. But he wasn't any other man. That Jasper made a study of her sent her blood racing, her nerves crackling, and made her breath faint.

"You look uneasy. Is something the matter?" His tone was curious, as if he truly didn't know what he did to her when he certainly did.

"No." Though her voice was tremulous.

"Would you like to be more comfortable?"

"Yes."

"Would you like my help?"

"Please."

He twirled a finger, and she slipped out of her pumps and turned around. She felt the warmth of him behind her and his breath on her nape as he began slowly sliding her long opera glove off her right arm, then the left. Next he moved unerringly to the tie of her bodice.

"How do you do this without help?" he asked.

"The answer to that is very simple. A woman who can afford such a gown as this *has* help."

"Mm-hm. Of course."

His lips ran along her nape, his nose running up and down the back of her neck and around her ears. When the bodice sagged, he drew it up her arms, tickling deliberately over the fine hairs, then pulling it over her head. Next he untied the outer skirt and the small bustle.

"Step out."

The tone of his voice was firm, almost coarse, and she moved immediately to obey him as if she were a child. For some reason, something in his voice or the way he carried himself, she felt an unconscious desire to bend for him in a way she couldn't remember with Aubrey. In a way she couldn't imagine with anyone, save him. It both alarmed and intrigued her.

The lamp burned a low amber, and the fire crackled and popped. All the while, he worked methodically, deliberately, his fingers skimming over her skin, his breath rising and falling so warm on her neck. Taking his time as if he knew that drawing out every single small act was crueler. It was, and for some reason she couldn't fathom, she liked it.

Finally, he untied and dropped her corset.

"Step out."

She did.

"Now turn and face me."

"I thank—"

Again he put a finger to his lips, and abruptly she buttoned up. She stood in a plain, white cotton chemise, knickers, and stockings, and his eyes skimmed over the demure, shapeless form as if she were in the raw. And, honestly, the burning in his eyes as they moved made her feel raw.

Taking a seat next to the fire, he leaned forward, resting his elbows on his knees.

"Continue."

She moved to a stocking.

"Knickers first."

Knickers were easy enough. The chemise nearly came to her knees. After dropping those, she waited. He wanted to lead, and she wanted to follow.

"Chemise."

She dropped her chemise, and his eyes flared wide. Once again, he looked at her at his leisure, his gaze moving up and down and over and back as if memorizing every curve. It was bad enough when she was dressed, but now that she stood naked but for her stockings, his searching perusal made her squirm.

"Relax. Stand up straight but relax."

She took a deep breath, then slowly exhaled.

"You have the shapeliest, longest, and most beautiful legs I've ever seen. Those dark stockings and your dark hair frame such flawless peachy-cream curves. They draw my eye exactly where I want to go." His gaze drew deliberately up her legs to the down of her sex, up her belly, and around her breasts, then up to her eyes. They were filled with a simmering satisfaction. "Can you count?"

"Yes," she replied. She felt indignant about that, but her voice was scratchy, and she'd sounded pathetic just then.

"I'm sorry, Amélie. I should know better than to underestimate you."

"Yes."

"When I say begin"—he stood and approached—"you'll count in your head."

"Fast or slow?"

"I'll leave that to you."

"What am I counting for?"

"You leave that to me. Now you'll undress me. Are you ready?"

She nodded.

"Begin."

One, she slipped his suitcoat off his arms. Two and she turned to the buttons on his waistcoat. Six, she loosened his cravat. Eight and she began on his shirt. By twenty, she was lowering his pants. All the while, his eyes never left her body, naked but for the delicate stockings on her long legs. Finally, she undid the buttons on his shoes and pulled off his socks.

He took her stockings and slid them slowly, seductively, down her legs. "Are you still counting?"

"Yes."

"Good. Keep going." He stood and deliberately pulled each individual pin in her hair until it fell loosely to her waist. "And stop." He cupped her face tenderly. "What number do you have?"

"Thirty-three." It had occurred to her to slow down.

"Thirty-three. We'd better get started." He smothered her question in a kiss and laid her down on the bed.

When he moved to kiss a wet trail down her neck, she asked, "What does thirty-three mean?"

He held a breast and paused with his mouth taunting over the nipple. "You're going to have thirty-three orgasms before I'll consider letting you move on to someone else." Then he flicked her nipple with his tongue and began drawing a wet line around her areola.

"Pardon?" But the word was lost in a moan. "I didn't agree to that. One night, you said." Then he slowly drew his cock along her sex. "Oh, God," she moaned again. With his hard length sliding on her full sex, she began to squirm. "If you can give me thirty-three orgasms tonight…"

He kissed over to her other breast and took it in his mouth, gently lapping and suckling while he squeezed her bottom, pressing his cock into her throbbing nerve, dragging and rubbing, teasing.

She wrapped her legs around him. "Please."

But he only smiled mischievously as he continued his merciless teasing. He kissed the corners of her lips, the tip of her nose, and apples of her cheeks, along her jaw and over to an ear.

"Please."

"Mm-hm," he murmured in her ear even as he shook his head. "Please, what?"

She squeezed her arms and legs around him. "I-I want you."

"Mm, that does sound serious."

"It is. I am."

"Do you want to come for me thirty-three times?"

At that moment, she would have agreed to three *hundred* thirty-three if only he'd put his cock inside her.

"Yes… I… Please," she croaked out. "Please."

"Mm, I love to hear you beg. I knew you'd love to please me. Now say my name." He worked his cock closer and closer to her cunny opening.

"Jasper."

"Now say, 'Please fuck me, Jasper.'"

"Please fuck me, Jasper."

He *tsk*ed. "I'm not convinced." He slid his cock along her slit and pressed into her nerve while she panted and begged.

"Try again."

At length she begged, and mercilessly he remained unsatisfied.

"Now say it and make me believe it. Are you desperate for me?"

"Yes," she whimpered before she said, "*Please* fuck me, Jasper."

And before she'd even finished his name, he thrust in so hard she shot up on the bed. "Oh, God!"

It hurt, and it was so good. For long moments he slammed into her repeatedly without let up until her body felt like it was melting into the bed.

"I'm going to come," she said.

"Not yet."

"Pardon? I'm going to come."

"No, you're not."

She felt him slowing down and gripped him tighter. "No! What are you doing?"

"Relax. You'll come when I say."

"Are you mad? I come when my body says."

Abruptly he pulled out and sat on the side of the bed, his rock-hard cock glistening with her arousal. The man had the audacity to look at his fingernails. Her jaw dropped.

"Are you playing with me?"

"Yes," he said evenly.

She threw the covers back and reached for her clothes when he pulled her onto his lap, his cock resting at her bottom.

"Let me go."

"No, sweet girl, you'll sit right here. Now just relax."

But she was so rigid with anger that she didn't want to obey. His hand skimmed up and down her arm, the other stroking and pinching a breast as he pressed tiny, wet kisses along a shoulder.

"Jasper, I—"

"Shh. Just relax." He slid two fingers inside her sex. Reaching, swirling, pressing into the walls of her cunny until she couldn't help it, her head fell back, and she moaned.

"Please let me come."

"I will. I want you to come. You've been a very good girl for me. I know you like to obey."

"No, I don't. I don't like to obey."

He chuckled. "But for me you will, won't you?"

"Yes." *Yes, yes, yes.* For him she would've done anything just then.

"Yes," he said as if coming to a decision.

He placed her on her hands and knees before the fire and thrust inside her again. He held her hard and fucked her harder. For excruciatingly long minutes, he worked her nerve until she was dangling over the edge, desperate to let go.

"Please, please, please, please, please," she moaned in an urgent chant.

"Come."

When finally she tipped over the edge, it was like nothing she'd ever experienced before. A firework, warm and wet and shattering, pulsed in her core and raced up her spine. She shuddered violently, blissfully. Cried out as she lost her breath, stars blinking in her eyes. Still he continued to fuck her until he pulled out and came on her back.

Tenderly he stroked her hips and torso, then he moved her hair and caressed her nape and upper back.

"Don't move." He left and returned soon after with a wet linen to clean her up. When he finished, he pressed tender kisses up her spine, turned her head, and kissed her lips. "Are you all right?"

She had no words, so she nodded.

"Come to bed, beautiful."

Jasper closed the grate on the fire and slid in beside her. Amélie had one thought as she drifted off to sleep—*thirty-two.* Then one more:

If that's one, I'll never survive him.

9

Jasper sat in his carriage thinking about Amélie. Four days since their first night together—he was determined it would be the first and not the only—and he couldn't get that goddess out of his mind.

Amélie was submissive; he had little doubt. But unlike most women he knew in that scene, she didn't keep her head down as a matter of course. She didn't simper or reach to obey. Even suggesting it made her bristle. That made him smile. She was strong. Perhaps the strongest woman he'd ever known. From the heat of her laundry life and the pressure of her abiding dream, she'd forged herself as hard as a diamond. And like the gem itself, seemed resistant to being tamed. He chuckled at that. He had merely to suggest her obedience, and she curled away from the word as she beautifully submitted. He'd call it whatever she liked if only she'd bend for him again as exquisitely as she had.

His mind retreated to the morning after. The sleepy

gray light of early dawn had crept into the room as he lay beside her, watching her sleep. She lay on her belly, her arms crossed under her pillow. The coolness in the room would almost certainly wake her if he pulled the covers back.

Sliding a soft hand down the tousled mane of her dark hair—it was a crime to tie that beautiful hair up in a bun all the time—he drew the covers off her back. At the luscious curve of her bottom, he stroked up and down as goosebumps lit her skin. Her back rose as her breathing changed. She shifted and moaned. He placed wet kisses on each plump cheek.

God, she's beautiful.

Jasper couldn't imagine a more perfect diversion while he waited for Jos to come to her senses. Perhaps if he played his hand well, he might even coax Amélie into joining him with Daphne. Black and white. Strong and soft. A fierce tigress and a coquettish kitten. There was a picture. And he suffered just envisioning it.

He adjusted himself. On his way to visit his ex-wife, the one woman he loved above all others, and he couldn't get on for moments at a time without panting over Amélie.

Joselin had a small studio set up in her apartment just down the boulevard from his. Jasper was not a man for navel-gazing, but if he took a moment, he might have been able to acknowledge just how fucking pathetic it was, being so close to her still. Yet all he'd wanted when they divorced, all he still wanted, was to be available to her.

It was there Jasper found her. He stayed in the doorway for a moment, watching as she plied her paints. While he loved her with all his heart—his regal queen—here, as she worked, he loved her most of all. In her smattered smock, her butter-blonde hair falling loose from her bun, she tipped her head and worried her lip.

This was as unrestrained as she allowed herself to be. When she reached for her art. And she did. Despite the reputation of women painters, despite how she shaded her own reputation, she needed it. If only she needed him just as much.

"I know you're there."

A tricolor Cavalier King Charles spaniel perked up her head from the sofa she rested on.

"Quit standing around like you await my permission."

"Don't I?"

The spaniel leapt off the sofa and ran for him.

Jasper scooped her up. "Good morning, Bijou. Do you miss your papa?"

The dog smothered him in kisses, and Joselin grimaced. "Why do you let her do that?"

"She misses me." He set the spaniel down and wiped off his face, leaning into his ex-wife. "At least someone here does."

They exchanged polite kisses on the cheeks, then he sat on the sofa as she went back to her canvas—another nude woman.

Joselin was gaining a reputation as a sapphist, and that irked her to some degree because on a list of things that were scandalous to her, that was one. But when she'd consecrated herself to her art, a woman and against all odds, she'd made it clear that though she wasn't allowed in certain artistic societies and certain studios, though she couldn't paint alongside men, she would not be reduced to painting the limited subjects of a woman's sphere—the domestic sphere.

Joselin had nothing against children or the help or fruit, per se. It was only that she was expected to paint them. And in that, she took umbrage. She was the picture of refined elegance, *and* she liked to paint. Two things diametrically opposed. She navigated them with a small chip on her shoulder. That chip manifested itself in the nude female form.

"I hear you attended the opera the other night." With a subtle, churning hand, she manipulated her brush in ochre.

Jasper smiled to himself. This was too perfect. Three years before, Jos had set him out like a punished dog on the back step. But she was a jealous sort, sniffing around when he'd taken up with Daphne. Now this. She feigned indifference as she dabbed at her painting, yet she was anything but.

"Yes. *Le Cid.* It was quite good."

"And Madame Kohl is well?"

"Fit as ever, last I heard."

They stared at each other.

"I worry about you, Jasper."

"Why is that?"

"Because I love you, silly."

"Do you still? I hadn't noticed."

"You know I do. If you would give up your... *peculiar* interests, we could return to our deep friendship."

"Could we?" She'd hinted but never so boldly declared it as this. "What would Monsieur Durand say to that?"

"Martin's gone on holiday again with that bland wife of his. We've been"—she sighed dramatically—"at odds lately."

"I'm sorry to hear that." On the contrary, he felt a triumphant thrill race through him. But it was the polite thing to say. And this was just the kind of seduction Joselin responded to—the genteel kind.

"Are you really?" She gave him a look of scolding and skepticism.

"You know the answer to that better than anyone."

"He doesn't understand me like you do, Jas."

Was there something in her voice that sounded sincere?

"Do we understand each other, Jos?"

He loved when they traded their shortened names. It was their bedroom talk. Like a secret, intimate language only the two of them could speak.

"In a manner of speaking."

"What manner is that?"

She sighed and went back to her painting.

Could it be possible she'd finally gotten beyond her affair with Monsieur Durand? Maybe she'd finally gotten over her bitterness that Jasper had dared to change.

Joselin had insisted on divorcing, on making such a public show of their hostilities. Theirs was one of the first high-profile divorces in France when the practice had been reestablished only five years before.

It wasn't enough they took different lovers as so many of le gratin did. It wasn't enough everyone knew they were splitting. She made certain they knew why. He wasn't merely a deviant in the bedroom—for half their set were—but a brute as well, which was a patent lie. The idea that now they might have an understanding about anything seemed laughable. Still he loved her. Persistently, achingly loved her. If he gave up his *peculiar* interests, might she really take him back?

"And now you've taken up with this figure model."

Feeling victorious, powerful, and spiteful, Jasper sat back and propped an ankle on a knee. "Are you jealous?"

She cleaned her brush. "You know I am."

Do I? Why is she being so plain today? Could it all be because of Monsieur Durand's absence? Perhaps there's more than mere jealousy.

Jasper's heart suddenly felt lighter. Could all his patient waiting be bearing fruit? Might she actually come back to him?

"For more than a year, I've been trying to find her so I may ask her to pose for me. Suddenly there she was at the Salon, standing right beside me."

Her statement so jarred him with its disparate thread, so different from where he'd imagined this conversation going, that for a moment he had to consider it again. He felt like he'd been shot down from the sky.

"You're not jealous of her. You're jealous of me."

She looked at him as if he were an idiot. "Every painter in this city wants her to pose for him. Why not me?"

Jasper chuckled, a mirthless laugh, and shook his head. He heard a ringing in his ears and felt a sick acid in his belly. Rubbing his brow absently, he tried desperately to gather the strands of power he'd held only moments before.

"She's not a figure model, Jos. That's why she's not posing for you or anyone."

"Is she a demimondaine?"

"Stubbornly, no. She'd surely be more manageable if she were a member of that set." Though the idea didn't seem to hold as much weight as it once had. Why should he make her into the most eligible courtesan in all France for other men to vie for her time and affection?

"I dare say there are a few men who would be only too happy to build her her own hôtel particulier," Joselin said. "You, perhaps."

"Perhaps," he acknowledged, guarding his gaze. That was an idea growing in its appeal. But not even for appearances, not even for a woman as lovely as Amélie, could he risk his tenuous investments with another one.

Joselin came and stood before him. "Are you so taken with her?"

He didn't know what to say. On his way here, he could think of nothing but Amélie. Yet Jos had only to hint, and he fell too easily back.

"No. She's a dalliance."

But even as he said it, it felt strangely untrue.

Joselin stepped closer, and Jasper opened his legs. She kissed him as if dusting off her sweetness, and he wrapped his arms around her, deepening it. When finally she pulled back, she stroked his cheek. He looked at her speculatively, wondering where her heart lay and his.

"Do you ever think about us?" she asked. "I do. Sometimes I wish so strongly that we could go back. Maybe even start again."

Slack-jawed, he stared at her, feeling his heart pounding wildly in his chest.

"Do you really?"

"Yes."

Joselin said it so firmly Jasper knew it was a lie.

She returned to her canvas. "Will you see her again?"

"Mademoiselle Audet?"

"Yes."

"I think so."

"Could you give her my name, please, darling? Perhaps say a few words on my behalf?"

His heart had been everywhere in that studio, and now it cratered to his gut. Of course *this* was what she wanted.

"Are you serious?"

"Completely." There was the sincerity he sought.

"I told you—she's not a figure model."

"There's something charming in that. You saw it. She's both sensual and sweet."

Sweet was not the first word he would've used to describe Amélie.

"And perhaps she can be seduced to it. If anyone can do it, you can. Can't you? You're very persuasive."

Her audacity stunned him. He didn't know what to say.

"It could launch me. Don't you want to help me?"

"Jos… I don't know what to say…" He rubbed his neck. "Talac is a great talent. But more than that, I think he loved her when he painted that. There's something to that. It can't be recreated."

"But you'll try, for me, won't you? I'd be so grateful for any entreaty on my behalf." She turned and looked at him with such promise in her eyes. Promise that somehow felt more like a twist to his balls than a tug to his heart. "Very grateful."

More than a week later, Jasper sat in the ultra-fashionable Grand Café, once again thinking about Amélie and that incredible night.

Her hands had been white-knuckled as she gripped the headboard. *Do not let go*, he'd told her. Her back was arched and mouth agape as her breathing grew light and jagged. All the while, he played with her breasts. Licking, teasing, back and forth.

"Jasper, Jasper, Jasper," Amélie pleaded breathily as she squirmed.

He held himself over her, hovering so close, giving her just enough and not nearly enough. She was falling apart, and he loved it.

"Monsieur Degrailly?"

A waitress stood before him, jarring him from his memory. "Your guest is here."

The simple social graces required he stand, yet he was hard as a rock.

"Yes." He cleared his throat. Then shifted. Thought about his grandmother. Tried to imagine her taking a bath. Worse, stepping out of it. Conjured awful smells. Anything.

"Monsieur Degrailly."

Amélie appeared before him in the garnet silk-damask dinner dress he'd sent.

"Amélie." They exchanged courteous kisses and sat. "I'm so glad you came."

"You gave me little choice."

Jasper had asked his driver, after delivering the dress and a note, to wait for her.

Nearly two weeks had passed since their night at the opera, and he'd found he had to see her. Joselin's plea turned over and over again in his mind. If it were anyone other than Amélie, if he'd never met Amélie, there'd be no question what he would do—anything for Jos. Yet somehow he no longer felt that desperate urge to please his ex-wife.

"What am I doing here? I can't be at the Jockey Club. Not with you."

"Who *can* you be here with?" He bristled, indicating the mostly ennobled men who sat in the dining room of the most exclusive club in Paris. That she'd added the last part made his dormant jealousy flare. He'd only ever felt that way about one other person.

"This is a gentleman's club," Amélie hissed.

"Don't be ridiculous. Look, there's a woman, *two* women, right over there." He indicated the women dining past her shoulder.

"Grande horizontales," she said after a quick glance. "And you know it. The more I'm seen with you, the more they'll assume the same of me. Worse, they'll assume I'm a grisette reaching too high."

"Would you forget about all that, please? I just wanted to see you. Wherever I am—whatever I'm doing, it seems—my mind drifts to you."

That was the stubborn truth. When he could see beyond his pathetic grasping for Joselin's favors, he could admit Amélie might be more than a lovely diversion.

"And Madame Kohl?"

"On holiday in Nice."

"How nice."

"Nice? I suppose it's nice."

She rolled her eyes.

"Order something. Please. You're far too thin, darling."

"Don't call me darling."

"What may I call you? Dumpling? Dove? What?"

"You shouldn't call me anything. This affair is scandalous."

He leaned forward. "The best ones always are."

After placing their orders, she said, "I assume I'm here to hear of my audition scheduled with Monsieur Zidler."

"Ah, no. I haven't arranged that yet."

"You promised me."

"And I will. I just haven't gotten to it." He studied the sheer cream ruffles coyly hiding her décolletage. "Spend the week's end with me."

"No."

"Why not?"

"I have to work."

"Has Madame Pelletier not given you your Saturdays off?"

"She already gives us the Sabbath. Why should she give us Saturday as well?"

"Because I've asked her to. If she hasn't, I'll have a problem."

"I sing at Le Chat."

"Not until Sunday night. I'll bring you and stay to watch. Then bring you home. It's settled."

"It isn't settled."

"Why do you resist? We both know you want me." He leaned in and whispered, "You're thinking of taking my cock in your mouth even now."

"I'm not."

"Spend the week's end with me. Where are we at? Thirty? We could shave a good number off."

She shook her head.

"Stop shaking your head at me. You're so stubborn, Amélie. I hate it. And I love it. But I hate it."

She continued to shake her head, licking her lips, chewing on them as if she were swallowing something.

"I can't fall for you."

He tried but couldn't suppress a small smile. "Why?"

"I'd like to think I'm cold and ruthless when it comes to getting what I want. That I'm utterly single-minded. But I'm not. That is, I haven't always been. I let myself get distracted."

"You fell in love with Monsieur Talac."

She nodded. "Too easily I forgot who I was and what I wanted. I'll never do that again. Even for great sex."

He smirked.

"I'm serious."

"As the grave. I can see that. And I admire it, though I may not understand it entirely."

"How can you say that? You have your passions. I have mine."

"Yes. But you're a woman. It's different."

"It isn't different." She exhaled and looked around the dining room. "Have you seen your ex-wife? Do you even know the woman you love?"

His mouth gaped, and he felt a blush of embarrassment at how transparent he was.

"You needn't pretend with me, Jasper. I have eyes to see."

He wanted to deny it because the truth was his visit with Joselin had unsettled him. Perhaps she'd been lonely with Monsieur Durand gone, but she had fallen so easily into manipulating him. She would use him without a second thought for his feelings. He'd never imagined he could love someone so ruthless. Then there was Amélie, who wanted to be and couldn't even if she tried. The contrast between the two—one so cunning and callous, the other so honest and earnest and honorable, more noble than most of the noblemen in this room—was startling in its clarity. He could finally see that what he took for Jos's strength and determination, when compared to Amélie's, might be something else entirely. And he didn't like it.

"You're determined," he said. "I can see that very clearly."

"You won't interfere, no matter how good the sex gets."

"I wouldn't dare. No matter how good the sex gets."

"You won't fall in love with me."

"You're feeling confident today. I like that. What I'm proposing will be a harmless lark. I promise."

"And you'll schedule my audition."

"Consider it done."

IO

nxious and bored, Amélie looked around the room. Night had fallen, and the space grew amber, lit by the fire and a dim lamp. Though the ceiling was tall, perhaps twelve or thirteen feet in height, it wasn't particularly large. But for the elaborate moldings carved around the chandelier, arched doorway, and windows, it seemed a forgotten space. Apt since, sitting naked and alone for some time, she felt forgotten.

I just need to take this, he'd said with his hand over the mouth of the telephone. *Go into your room, take off your clothes, and wait for me. I won't be but a moment.* That was possibly half an hour ago. What a peculiar intrusion, this telephone. A friend could monopolize your time without even bothering to make a visit. It struck her as the height of rudeness. She seriously contemplated getting dressed and leaving.

Why had she agreed to come? Because for eighteen

months, she'd turned off the woman inside and become the tool Madame Pelletier needed her to be. What her hurting heart needed her to be. Yet with Jasper, she'd spent the past two weeks so aware of her body and its needs. She felt like winter ground under a persistent spring sun. Warming and yawning open, growing soft and desperate, remembering she was still alive. She still wanted. And the shameless truth was she liked it that way.

The door opened, and Jasper peered in, a pleased smile lighting his face. "You've done it."

"Yes." She walked away from his perusal.

"I shouldn't be too much longer."

She turned to see the door closing with him on the other side, and her jaw dropped.

Moments later—record time for her, really—she was dressed and striding past him for the door.

"One moment, Charles." Jasper lunged for her arm. "What are you doing?"

"What does it look like I'm doing?"

"Would you like me to answer that?"

She grabbed the doorknob. "I don't really care."

He closed the door and caged her in with his arms.

"You're obviously busy, and I have other things I'd rather do than be ignored in a lush apartment on the Rive Gauche. Now let me go."

"I don't think I will. No." He turned her to look at him. "Now, I'm going to finish this call with Charles Zidler, a call I took because I also wanted to arrange your audition." He raised a pointed brow. "Are you going to go back in that room and wait for me?"

Amélie took a deep breath. She was fuming and knew she had a right. But for some reason she couldn't fathom, it only added to her desire.

"Yes."

"Good."

He brought his hand to her chin and his gaze to her lips as if to kiss her, then skated a finger slowly under her chin back and forth. It was a little nothing gesture. Still, it made her soften.

He appeared in the room only a minute after she'd returned.

"Shall I lock you in this room for the week's end?"

"No." She smiled slyly.

"You're wearing far too much clothing."

"Am I?"

He crouched before her so that she looked down on him, and still he seemed to own the space between them.

"I'm sorry, Amélie."

"You're not sorry, Jasper."

"No. I'm not."

She sighed. He infuriated her with all his taunts and tests. Still, she was drawn to him. The air between them felt like tinder in need of friction.

"Get undressed." He added another log to the fire.

She reached for her bodice laces, then hesitated. Defiant by nature and irritated by the whole of mankind being so assuming, why was it she seemed eager to obey this man without so much as a thought?

He glanced at her, then smiled smugly. "Would you defy every man you meet?"

"If I can, yes."

"Yet you reached for those laces so beautifully. Fall to a chair at my command, come when I call, spread your legs at my urging. Why?"

She felt such shame in that moment. So weak. "I don't know."

"I know." He paused, as he was wont to do. Every word or touch a great anticipation. "It isn't that you're a good girl. You're not. And that makes you grit your teeth"—he waggled a finger at her mouth—"as you're doing right now, because you're the least like a girl of any woman I've ever known. It isn't that you want to obey me." He shook his head. "You *need* to obey me. And, happy coincidence, all that spirit in that obedient heart, I wouldn't have you any other way."

"No."

"No?" He slid a hand along her cheek, threaded it up through her hair, then began pulling pins. "It's all right, Amélie. I know you feel like you need to fight this. You love to obey me, but you hate that you love it. Isn't that right?"

She wanted to deny it, could feel her head shaking, yet she knew he was right. Worse, she knew *he* knew she knew.

He reached around and began untying her bodice. "You love being submissive to me."

"No." She tried to pull back from him, but his hands on the laces held her firm.

"Shh, just relax." He pressed wet kisses down the column of her neck. "It's your inborn character. There isn't anything wrong with that."

"'Inborn character.'" She bristled. "I don't know what you mean. But I'm not docile like most women."

"I know. Perhaps that's what's so intriguing about you."

He removed her bodice, outer skirt, and bustle. All the while, she spoke.

"What is it you think you know? Do you know I'm as strong as any man? More so because if I wield my womanhood, I'm dismissed as a plaything or a dim pet. I won't be dismissed."

"I wouldn't dream of it."

"But if I think like a man, behave like a man, fight like a man, I'm already lost. Because I don't want to *be* a man."

"Mm." He stroked her breasts. "I don't want you to be a man either."

"Don't mock me, Jasper." She tried to pull away, but he held her close.

"I'm not. Only consider this…" He pressed a kiss to her ear, then dragged a trail down a cord of her neck. As he did, he said, "Can you be strong and soft in one person? Can you bend without breaking? I think you can." He paused. "No. I know you can. And what kind of man wants a weak woman on his arm? In his bed? To bear his children? No kind of man at all."

When he stepped back, she was naked but for her stockings. "Take them off."

Amélie bent to do it, then paused. For some reason, at that precise moment, it felt as if she'd reached the edge of all she knew for certain.

She knew she should turn back. If she were sensible, she would. They exchanged a look, all her convictions and independence held in the still water of it.

Then she took off her stockings.

Jasper began removing his clothes. When he stood naked before her, he slid a hand to her sex and pressed a finger inside. "Ahh, this right here is everything." He played with his finger inside her. "You're so perfect for me. Do you know that?"

Everything inside her screamed yes, and still she felt her head shaking in denial. Gently he stilled it, then slid a finger around her hairline, tucking her hair behind her ear. He nuzzled her cheek, her jaw, all the way to her ear, then whispered, "Yes. And I'm perfect for you."

He pressed his hard chest and even harder arousal to her, and she couldn't help it—she moaned. She felt her knees buckling, and he picked her up and brought her to the bed. Sitting beside her, he played with a breast as he looked at her. The fire lit his soft smile and the hard lines of his torso.

"Have you ever been tied up?"

She should have been appalled. Should have been frightened. Should run and not look back. But she wasn't any of those things. Didn't want to do any of those things. Her sex only felt fuller.

"No."

He held up her stockings. "Would you allow me?" When she hesitated, he added, "We'll stop whenever you say. You have my word."

She could feel her heart beating against her chest. But that still, small voice inside that says yes and no with such infinite wisdom chanted *yes, yes, yes.*

"All right."

He straddled her, then wrapped the stockings around her wrists and tied them to the headboard. "Are you all right?"

She nodded.

"I need to hear your voice."

"Yes. I'm all right."

"It's not too tight?"

"It's tight but not too tight."

He held her cheek and grazed a thumb over her lips, and she arched toward his hand. He smiled and pulled away. Then he drew fingertips down her neck and along her collarbones. Skimming too lightly, he circled her nipples and breasts, slid into the thimble of her bellybutton and around her hips, then where her bottom met the bed and down her legs. Back up between them, pausing to kiss sweetly on the insides of her knees.

All the while, she met his teasing, squirmed and gasped and moaned. What was it about him? A hundred tiny things. And this—a touch so small it made her weak with wanting more. When he finally spread her thighs wide and she felt his warm breath on her sex, she nearly cried with relief.

"Please!"

"Please what?"

Now he moved his mouth as featherlight as his hands, pressing the barest of kisses up and down her inner thighs, over her belly, and all around her sex. Then he bit where her leg met her core. The pain was sharp, and she arched and hissed. Yet a moment later, a wave of warmth rushed over it that was inexplicably good.

"Again."

He didn't hesitate, biting again on the other side.

"Jasper, please."

He climbed up her body and combed a hand through her hair. "What do you need, sweetling?" He slid a finger deep into her sex. "This?"

"Yes," she moaned. "More."

"More?" He slid another finger alongside the first and pumped slowly. "How's that?"

"Good. So good. But I need more."

He *tsk*ed. "You're so needy, Amélie." He thrust his fingers so haltingly and slowly that her arousal was catching, *building*, on his control, and he knew it. He loved to torment her. God help her, she loved it, too.

"How about this?" Finally he replaced his fingers with his cock and slid slowly inside her to the hilt.

"Oh, God, yes. Now harder."

"Harder?"

"Please."

He pulled out and slid back in, biting where her neck met her shoulder. She lost her breath at the confusing and delicious complement of the pain to the pleasure.

"More."

"More?"

"Make it hurt."

He cupped her face, and she opened her eyes to look at him. The gaze he returned was filled with wonder. "Make it hurt? You're certain?"

"Yes."

With bruising strength, he gripped her thighs and spread them wide until she felt her muscles burn. Then he began to slam inside her as if he were reaching right to the heart of her. His strokes were punishing and went on and on and on. The pain was deep and pulled the pleasure down with it so that she felt both of them fused into her marrow. Bound and desperate, she let go of her control and fight, her shame and fear, let go of everything. Her release barreled up through her.

"Oh, God, Jasper! Please!"

II

The next day, Amélie emerged from her room in a forest-green velvet walking dress. But for the floor-length skirt, it looked in every way—from the cuffs and buttons on the sleeves to the intricately beaded lapels and waistcoat, and the creamy lace cravat—like a men's Georgian suit. For some reason, the singular ensemble thrilled her to the tips of her toes. And as much as she didn't want to go to the races with Jasper, she wanted to wear the dress more. And damn him, he knew that very well.

"You look beautiful, darling."

"Why must we go?"

He was intent not only on seeing her, but on being seen with her.

"Would you wear such a distinctive promenade dress and not be seen?"

"No. It would be an injustice. I agree. But…"

He took her hands. "But nothing. The sooner you

get used to being seen with me, the sooner you'll get used to seeing me."

"At least with this lace and the heavy cuffs, my bruises are covered." Her neck, wrists, and thighs were bejeweled with his marks.

He winced. "I'm so sorry."

"Would you stop apologizing? I told you I wanted it. We just don't need anyone to know."

He brushed a thumb along the apple of her cheek. "Why does it seem like I'm your dirty little secret?"

She sighed. "When we're out together, it just makes you and this all the more real. And I can't fall for you."

"Too late, I think." He shrugged into his coat and extended an arm. "If you're worried, I promise you, when they look, they'll see the Pingat first, then the lucky lady who's wearing him. Today is not about whom you should be with, but whom you should be wearing. Now come."

The avenue du Bois de Boulogne teemed with le gratin. Framed by chestnut trees and leafy alleys leading to ornamental lawns and gardens, smart carriages conveyed polished people down the grand promenade. Steel-spined riders jogged their horses. Ladies in their susurrating silks gripped candy-colored umbrellas against the bright sun. A man held fast to a cloud of red balloons while holding a single one out to each wide-eyed child that passed. "Sure to delight. Sure to delight," he promised. A flower girl in a dull, blue dress and two thick braids gripped a wire basket bursting with sprays of spring blooms. "For the lovely madame," she called out.

Jasper strolled in a perfectly rehearsed charade. The dip and send of his cane, how he tipped his hat and to whom, the way his eyes slid across the avenue, his tight smiles and subtle nods, when they stopped and how he introduced her. "Have you had the pleasure?" he asked, indicating her, then introducing her as if she belonged with them. This walk was as much a performance as any Amélie had done on any stage.

And it was a thing to behold.

"Do you care about any of them?" she asked when there was a break in the crowd.

"Jas."

Marie-Thérèse strolled toward them, arm in arm with a darkly handsome man. Three lively children trailed behind.

"Some more than most." He indicated his sister. "Mademoiselle Audet, you remember my sister."

Marie-Thérèse gasped, running her hands along the intricate detail on Amélie's cuff. "You devil! How did you manage to secure this Pingat? He's been notoriously stingy this spring. I can't get over him. Of course, it only makes me want his dresses more."

"Don't be so rude, poussin," Jasper said.

"Really, Thérèse," the man said.

"And my brother-in-law, Monsieur Blanqui."

"Please excuse my wife." Monsieur Blanqui took Amélie's hand and decorously bowed and kissed it. "She has an interest in fashion that clouds her sense at times."

"There's no excuse necessary, monsieur. I understand completely."

After introducing her husband as Olivier and their three children as Charles, Félix, and Nor, Marie-Thérèse said, "It's so good to see you again, mademoiselle. Are you here for the races?"

"We are," Amélie said.

"Have you placed your bets?" Jasper asked.

"We have," Marie-Thérèse said. "But I think I'm changing my mind."

Jasper shook hands a final time with Olivier, then they moved on, promising to find them at the track.

"Poor soul, he isn't completely plain," Amélie said.

"Do you find him more alluring than me?"

"If I did?"

"Then I'll collect for it later," he whispered and playfully bit at her ear.

"Do you promise?"

He gave her a lecherous look.

"Do they think we're seeing each other now?"

"I should think so. And the news will be of some interest to my parents."

"Are they so interested in your affairs?"

"Actually, no. Likely they'd rather forget. My mother's still in her drink over the details of the divorce complaint. But there are two items of note about you."

Amélie suspected, and still she asked, "What are those?"

"You're a mademoiselle still and an unknown in the demimonde."

"And you want them to know about me?"

"Strangely, I don't *not* want them to know." His smile was warm and curious, as if he couldn't stop looking at her and couldn't figure out why.

12

Four days later, Jasper sat amidst a glossy lake of wood in the cavernous space that had once been the White Queen Dance Hall. Beyond the columns and archways, beyond the cathedral ceilings soaring with possibility, it stood stripped and sad. Still, four months remained until opening night, and the glittering adornment that spoke to the red-letter decadence they planned would begin arriving any day.

As he waited for Charles, he thought once again of Amélie. She was a revelation. Much more than a perfect companion to him in bed, Jasper found he wanted to spend time with her and thought of her when he wasn't.

Daphne amused him, and the feeling was entirely mutual. Comely and quick-witted, lovely and experimental—and above all, shamelessly submissive—she'd been the perfect diversion after his divorce when Jos had left him on his knees, a begging half man. But he'd never been able to summon more than breezy affection for her. He'd thought himself incapable. No matter their divorce, he loved Joselin and always would.

Until Amélie.

He could tease her all he wanted about falling for him when the truth was he liked her more than he cared to admit.

Just as soon as Daphne returned from Nice, he would end his affair with her. And he would talk with Jos about her peculiar request. Did she really think he should persuade Amélie to pose for her? He supposed she did. After all, she would send for him, and he would come running. He would have to make it clear his abiding love for her now had its limits.

Amélie was another matter. He'd dropped her off on Sunday night with great reluctance. Ravignan felt like a world away from Saint-Germain. Increasingly, he didn't like being that far away from her. Still, they couldn't be further apart than on the matter of her performing at the Moulin Rouge. He'd secured an audition before Charles Zidler, but he'd be damned if he would do anything more.

The electric lights burst on.

"Damn!" Jasper bent and shielded his eyes. "Do you have to turn on all those lights? I'm blinded, man."

Charles had insisted upon electric lights. He flicked them on at every opportunity, as if he were responsible for supernatural light. "Only the best and brightest for 'Le Premier Palais des Femmes,'" he liked to say. Though Jasper had balked at the expense, he knew the bright lights would dazzle and entice.

"How am I to see this girl you'd like me to consider?" Zidler asked.

The director pulled up a chair and slapped Jasper's leg. One hand smoothed over a rounding belly; the other fussed with his receding amber hair and muttonchops.

"How are you to see her now?" Jasper asked.

"I can see fine. Get used to it, man. It's the way of the future."

Zidler was as bright and loud as the electric lights he favored. With his booming voice and unmatched presence, he might have been a ringmaster, and he walked into any room as if the people had been waiting for him.

By anyone's measure, Jasper Degrailly and Charles Zidler were an odd pair, Jasper as understated as Charles was bold. But they'd happened together one night at the Moulin de la Galette, watching the show with the same idea. Rather than be rivals, they'd struck up a partnership. After all, Jasper needed Charles's keen artistic vision and showmanship, and Charles needed Jasper's contacts in le gratin and his money.

Charles scuffed his foot along the floor. "It shines like a river, this finish. So, tell me about her. Did you see her at Galette? Can she dance the cancan?"

"Ah, no. Not at Galette. She's a singer. Primarily."

"'A singer. Primarily.' And you want her to perform here? At a dance hall?"

"She's a dancer, too. An all-around performer. I thought that was what we wanted. Not just dance-line girls, but a show." He was torn between his desire to speak well of her—he felt a growing pride in her—and wanting her to go unnoticed. There was no way he could convince himself to see her performing here night after night with the men, his friends most likely, vying for her favors after the show. "She does have great legs, though."

"You've seen them, have you?" Charles nudged him with a wink.

"Yes."

Charles pulled out his watch. "Well, where is she? I have a schedule to keep." This was certainly an exaggeration. Zidler loved performers and would carve out almost any time to see an intriguing one.

Jasper looked at his watch—five minutes past four. Amélie wouldn't be late for this audition. A worried feeling crept up his neck. He walked slowly back to the doors, peering closely at the high-gloss, chocolate-brown floors. They'd just been finished. The malted-milk smell of the varnish still hung heavily in the air, faintly sweet and addicting. Like the place, he hoped. It was Madame Pelletier. She was reluctant to allow the girls anything. If she hadn't given Amélie this time, he would have strong words for the obstinate woman.

Finally, he heard the clip-clop of horses on the stone street and exhaled. He hated to acknowledge just how much he missed her. Yet when he strode through the garden, he met his driver and not Amélie.

"Where is she, Louis?"

"Gone, monsieur."

"'Gone'? What do you mean 'gone'? And her friend? Mademoiselle Thomas?"

"Gone as well."

"How can that be? She was supposed to be working."

"The madame was not very agreeable to questions. But she did give me this." Louis handed him a note:

> Monsieur Degrailly,
> I cannot give Mademoiselle Audet the afternoon off.
> I fired her three days ago.
> I warned them.
> Mme. Pelletier

Jasper raced to Ravignan. The front door opened before he was out of the carriage. There the madame stood with pleading arms open.

"Monsieur, it's not my fault."

Jasper glared, holding up the note and crowding her with his imposing frame.

"You have a head for numbers," the laundry mistress said, "but I have a nose for linens. If I'm known to employ sickly girls, I'll be closed down."

"Sickly? Is Amélie—"

"Léonie. I told her. I warned her, I tell you."

"So, you fired them. Where did they go?"

"I don't know, monsieur."

"You don't know. You don't know?" he shouted. He went for the stairs, taking them two at a time. He bounded in on scantily clad women working amidst a cloud of steam and lye. They froze.

He stalked from room to room, sifting through beds and

belongings, questioning each woman for their whereabouts. But he could find nothing to indicate where they'd gone. He headed for the door. All the while, Madame Pelletier scuttled beside him defiant, indignant, then begging.

"You let a young woman and her sickly friend walk out these doors without so much as a 'by your leave'? Have you no heart, woman? My God! Who is your confessor? You should make haste to him before you're struck down, because it would be a very short trip for you to Hell."

On the street, he bit to Louis, "No. 8 rue Cortot," before climbing into the carriage and slamming the door.

13

Three days earlier...

"*L*éo."

"I'm up," Léonie said wearily, swallowing a cough.

"You're not up."

"I'm awake." Léo coughed again.

So, it would be one of her bad days. In truth, Léo could have had a bad week's end, for all Amélie knew. She'd spent a glorious couple of days on Saint-Germain with Jasper. When she finally came home late the previous night, Léo had been sound asleep.

Despite everything she'd promised herself, Amélie was falling for Jasper. His wit and beauty, warm arms and a warmer bed, a man who moved her mind as he stirred her blood. The sex was an enlightenment. As he'd promised, he revealed her to herself. To obey him made her body burn. Being bound somehow made her feel free. And the pain made the pleasure flare all the brighter. All this was not to mention the finest clothes and food, a box at the opera, a day at the Boulogne. How nice to pass some hours with no cares but for the lay of rich fabric, the taste of fine food, and the number of orgasms. He'd made it too difficult to resist.

Still, she bristled at the idea she was submissive. Men had always held the presumption women were the weaker sex and, therefore, meek creatures. How convenient that men had divorced themselves from the childbed. No one who was a party to that could claim women the weaker sex.

Certainly some were like that, but she was not. That Jasper thought so and she confirmed it every time she jumped to do his bidding was like a constant assault to her senses. There seemed a string between them that tied his commands to her obedience, and when he pulled it, she got aroused. And the more time they spent together, the more time she wanted to spend together.

Performing at the Moulin Rouge would be a point of contention. She had an audition with Jasper and Charles Zidler on Thursday. Whatever came of it—she still hadn't any idea what she would do about the expectation she be a demimondaine—she would go forward with or without Jasper Degrailly. After all, it was only a lark. That was what he'd promised. That was all a man still in love with his ex-wife could give. Soon enough he would tire of her. In the meantime, Amélie would have to steel herself against him or end it. The choice was simple, really. She would be fine. And she would tell herself this until it was so.

Tying her hair up, she glanced at Léo, now sitting. Hunched and coughing, she appeared worse than ever, so painfully thin and pale.

"Go back to sleep. If I skip breakfast, I can make your deliveries, then hurry back in time to do mine. I shouldn't be too late. I'll get Zara to start the fires." She looked out to the still-dark streets. She hated carrying the heavy baskets, especially in these early dark hours when the streets seemed too quiet, almost poised for something dangerous. But doing the deliveries had made her aware and strong, stronger and more aware than most could credit.

As she slipped on her boots, Amélie looked at Léo. "Did you hear me?"

"Yes."

"Then answer. I'm doing you a favor, but I need your cooperation."

Amélie stood above her friend like a chiding mother. That was when she saw the blood on Léo's hands. Without thinking, she yanked Léo's hand to inspect it closer, then dropped it immediately. Her gaze fell on Léo's pillow and sheets. There were small spatters of blood there, too.

"How long have you been coughing up blood?"

"I don't know. A few weeks?"

"A few weeks?"

A cold chill of fear sluiced over Amélie's body.

"Get up. Now, Léo, get up! Don't touch anything. Don't—just—move, please. Wash your hands right now. I need to get these."

Amélie stripped the blood-spattered linens from the bed. On closer inspection, they weren't that bad. She could easily hide them while they soaked. But even as she went for more water and a bar of soap, she heard the house waking up. At any moment she might hear the indelicate steps of Madame Pelletier.

Feeling like the walls were closing in on them, her mind raced. Amélie stripped her bed and put her linens on Léo's. Then she sank into a chair. Everything would be all right. For now. But she would have to find some time to bring Léo to a doctor. They couldn't very well send for one to come to the washhouse. She had no idea what a doctor cost, but she had some francs saved. They would be fine.

Then she felt her plan replaced by the heavy weight of guilt. Eighteen months before, Amélie had broken the only home Léo had ever known. With few francs to her name and a position open at Madame Pelletier's laundry, Amélie had had to leave. Either that or the dream she'd nourished since she was a girl would wither on the vine.

Before she could remember, Amélie could sing, her little voice always singular, clear, and strong. Singing in the church choir had fed her, but not nearly enough. Soon she began singing at a goguette for smiles and applause, then francs. On stage she felt at home. And as she grew older, it brought more warmth and comfort than the only other home she had. As soon as she'd turned eighteen, she came to Paris with a small amount of money and an impossible dream.

The Montmartre of her girlhood had been a hilltop village of vineyards and cherry tree orchards, windmills and gypsum mines. Yet after twelve years in Rouen, she'd returned to a village transformed. The agrarian butte was now a metropolitan place, brimming with workhouses and ateliers, brasseries and dance halls. Whole streets and entire families had moved. It was a bewildering change. Until she met Léonie Thomas.

In one of Amélie's first auditions, the pianist had smiled encouragingly, dragged her smoothly through a difficult key change, and, when the song was done, pronounced her the best singer she'd ever heard. When she didn't get the part, Léo quietly pulled her aside and told her why.

"He's promised it to Odette. They're sleeping together."

Incensed she'd wasted her time and embarrassed she'd worried over it, Amélie had followed Léo to a brasserie where they proceeded to get good and drunk. That very night, those sisterless souls became friends.

Kernel-small and fierce as a fist, with a cutting wit and a deep fount of knowledge on the city's ways and players, Léo had given Amélie an education, then given her a place to stay. Amélie moved in with Léo and her brother and their friend. On rue Cortot, she found a camaraderie in their dreams and struggles. They cursed and cried and laughed together. Three years she'd been happy there in their peculiar family of friends.

Léo had left all of it—for her.

"Why did you follow me here?" Amélie asked.

"What?"

Léo was moving about, washing her face and fixing up her hair.

"You didn't have to leave Cortot. But two months after I left, here you were, eager to fill the open position. Why?"

Léo sighed. "We've been over this a dozen times, and I'm too tired for it today."

"That's just it." Amélie strolled to her. "You're too tired because you're sick. Desperately sick when you didn't have to be."

Just then, Madame Pelletier poked her round head in.

"You're awake, then, girls." She was turning to go to the next room when her eyes narrowed on Amélie. "What's the matter there?"

"It's nothing, madame," Amélie said. "My monthly course is all."

"Your monthly course? I meant that fine necklace of bruises around your neck."

Amélie's hands flew to her neck. She'd completely forgotten them. Léo looked at her with disapproval.

"These are nothing," Amélie uttered.

"That upstanding nobleman choking you? Because if he is…" The thought trailed off because they all knew she'd do absolutely nothing that would threaten Jasper's financial support.

"He isn't ennobled, and he's certainly not choking me."

"Oh, well. It seems the more money they have, the weirder their bed sport, am I right?"

"Yes, madame."

Finally, she noticed the linens. "Your monthly course, you say?"

Amélie nodded.

Madame Pelletier took an unusual interest in their courses. She thought them all sluts and made sure they knew it.

"Good. That fine gentleman will drop you faster than a hot brick when he finds you pregnant with his bastard. If you can't keep your legs closed—and clearly you can't, spending the last couple nights with him like a sweet tart—I hope you're using your vinegar sponge."

"Religiously, madame," Amélie said.

"Religiously." The laundry mistress snorted, then narrowed her eyes. "That's a laugh."

When she left, Amélie and Léo exchanged a look.

"I'm sorry," Léo said. "I don't mean to get us in trouble."

"It's not your fault. It's my fault. I never should've allowed you to come here."

"Do you think you could've stopped me?"

"I should've tried harder. I should've insisted."

"I missed you. Desperately those two months. I saw you a few hours on Sundays, and it was never enough."

"You had Daan and Aubrey."

"It's not the same."

Léo gasped for air and fell into a fit of coughing.

"This is why," Amélie said. "This. Now you're sick…"

"I never had a sister," Léo continued when she finally caught her breath. "And you looked so sad. So beaten down. You needed me, and I needed you. Remember? I'd lost my position at Friday, and the piano wasn't paying. You know that. Anyway, it's only temporary. Right?"

Only temporary. That was what they always said. But time slipped by and eventually *only temporary* would turn into a crystallized age of regret.

Grimly, Amélie nodded. "There's no sense in worrying about it now. It's going to be fine. We just need to get you to a doctor. Can you work today?"

"Yes, of course."

"Thank God Jasper insisted on shortening our hours. I don't know what we'd do if we had to work until eleven each night without you being seen."

"Yes. He's a fine one, isn't he?" Léo scowled at Amélie's bruises.

"It isn't what it looks like."

"They're not bruises? Did you give them to yourself?"

"They don't hurt. I don't know how to explain it."

"What are you doing, Amélie? We uprooted our whole lives. I left my brother. You left a man who loved you. Now, it seems, you've just replaced one man with another. What's worse, he hurts you."

"It's not like that. It's—I like it. We do some peculiar things in bed. But I want it."

"You. Want. It. He hurts you, and you want it."

"You don't have any right to condemn me when you haven't the faintest idea what you're talking about."

"I don't have any right? I love you. I don't want to see you hurt."

Her voice was raised, and she fell into a coughing fit, blood spattering all over her hand.

Amélie felt immediately contrite as she sat her on her bed. "We'll talk about this later. When you're better."

"You're falling in love with him."

"No."

"No?" Léo indicated the fine dresses hanging near Amélie's bed. "Amélie Audet would not be taken care of by a man. This man, he isn't taking care of you? Where are we going to have to run when Jasper Degrailly's completely taken over your life?"

"He hasn't taken over my life, and he's not going to. He's amusing. I enjoy spending time with him. That's all."

Léo gave her a skeptical look.

"I should be here more," Amélie said. "For you."

"Don't use me like that."

"For me, then. You're right." Amélie only hated what Léo said because her friend was right. Jasper took care of her, and she let him. And what could she have with a man who couldn't love her? A lark? She seemed incapable of that. Maybe it was time to end their affair. Better to feel a small loss now than to endure a greater hurt in the end. "I have an audition. This Thursday. I'll end it with him then."

Finally Léo's eyes widened in delight. "An audition."

Amélie nodded, a smile curling up the corners of her mouth.

After Amélie cleaned the blood out of the linens, she and Léo went on their laundry deliveries. It wouldn't do for Madame Pelletier to be further curious about them. When they returned, they found the madame standing below the drying pillowcase.

"That's a neat trick," she said.

"Madame?"

"Do you often bleed from your cunny onto your pillow?"

Amélie's mind froze.

"During your courses," the madame prompted.

"Uh, no," Amélie said, her throat so dry it seemed to be closing up. Madame Pelletier turned around, narrowing her eyes on Amélie, then flicking to Léo speculatively, then back. "I thought I would wash the whole set, madame. That's all."

"Oh, well, yes. Stands to reason." Madame Pelletier turned back to the pillowcase. "Still, I was perplexed and so curious I just had to take a closer look. What did I find but the faintest specks—really so faint, when they're dry, you mightn't even notice—of blood just here?" She pointed to the pillowcase. "Like spatter"—she looked at Léo with a mix of pity and malice—"from a cough."

No one moved nor made a sound as their gazes flitted from one to another.

"You're quiet this morning," Madame Pelletier said to Léo. "Did you pass a rough night, mademoiselle?"

Amélie felt the heat of tears flooding up from her chest to her throat, stinging her nose and eyes.

"No, madame," Léo said as she tried to swallow a cough.

"You've had that cough for a while, haven't you?"

"No, madame."

"It isn't what you think," Amélie said.

"What do I think?" Madame Pelletier asked. "Hm? What do I think?" The laundry madame scrutinized them with a menacing look. "Could it be that Mademoiselle Thomas is riddled with consumption and putting every girl in this laundry in jeopardy, not to mention all our customers?"

"I'll go," Léo said. "Amélie's done nothing wrong, and she needs this position. I'll go."

But the madame stalked to Amélie with narrowed eyes.

"I warned you, mademoiselle. You can't say I didn't, because I did. Get your things together, too. Both of you. I'll not have this in my house."

"No, madame," Léo said. "Amélie didn't do anything wrong. Please let her stay."

"She did do something wrong. Now get your things and go! I want this room clear of the pair of you in ten minutes, do you hear?"

Amélie had known it was possible. When Léonie's cough wouldn't go away. When her fingers started to swell. And still, faced with the only option they had, the short walk to the atelier they once shared with Aubrey and Daan felt like the longest walk of her life.

A year and a half before, she'd practically sprinted away, chased by the fear that if she paused, if she looked back and saw Aubrey's heartbreak and Daan and Léo's confusion, she'd falter. The first dew of Aubrey's success after *Fille dans le bain* had begun to burn away under the harsh glare of an art world clamoring for more. Could the vision that had infused that work and splashed a new style on the Paris art scene be recreated? Aubrey had made some attempts. Dancers. Picnickers. Some portraiture. But he dabbed punishingly at the canvas, which returned his discontent in kind. For none of them were her.

Foolishly, Amélie imagined if he were delighted with his success, he might cheer hers. Yet even amidst the accolades, Aubrey was still an insecure man.

Why should you continue to audition when I can take care of you now? We're a pair, you and I. With you as my model and my paintings, we could have all that we want.

He couldn't tolerate that anything in her heart existed apart from him. And the more she insisted, the more he persisted.

She had little money and few prospects; still she had to leave. Could she turn away from the comfort of love and security to feel hungry enough to chase the dream she'd had since she was a girl? It was the same decision she'd made when she left Rouen at eighteen. If she stayed, she'd be consigned to a life of domesticity. A good and beautiful life. But Amélie wanted more. She'd always wanted more. When she finally summoned the courage to leave, it was the hardest decision she'd ever had to make. And the most important.

Now as she and Léo stood before the vine-covered stone-and-brick house, she looked up to the open attic windows and could almost hear the tinny plunk of the terrible out-of-tune piano Léo always played. Could taste the cheap wine and feel the warmth of their laughter. Could remember when she first met Aubrey, his gaze fixed on his canvas until he looked absently up at his name being called. The way he blinked so deliberately as he looked at her. The warmth that cut between them.

Amélie felt a terrible sense of dread. When they walked into this house, she would be changed. By love or fear or comfort or an inevitability, she wasn't exactly certain, but she knew she would be. Her feet felt like lead even as Léo went to the door and pulled the knocker.

Daan opened the door, his sandy hair shaggy and his shirt only partially closed. A bright smile broke wide upon his face.

"What are you doing here?" He turned into the house and shouted, "You'll never guess who's here!" He threw the door wide. "Have you come home, then?"

He hugged his sister, then Amélie.

She tensed, and he pulled back to study her. "What's wrong?"

Amélie hated to be the one to break up his happiness. Again.

"Do you mind if we stay here for a few days? Perhaps more? And we need to fetch a doctor to see Léo. Right away, Daan. It's serious."

Daan examined Léo with a deliberate eye. "You do look thin. And those dark circles. Are they not feeding you enough? Are you not allowed to sleep?" He scowled at Amélie, then put his arm around Léo. "Come on. Let's put you to bed and get you some food. Some of my rich sauces—I can cook now. A good night's sleep and you'll be good as new in no time."

Daan and Léo went upstairs as Aubrey appeared, sleep-rumpled, his shirt open to reveal his lean torso. They exchanged wan smiles.

"Amélie." His voice was hoarse.

"Léo's sick. Gravely."

Aubrey looked at the stairs.

"I'm sorry to bring her back to you like this, but we had nowhere else to go."

"Are you staying?" He looked at the dresses from Jasper she had slung over an arm.

"For now, if it isn't too much of an imposition."

His gaze was inscrutable. Then he turned for the stairs, leaving her standing helplessly in the entryway.

The doctor arrived, shooing the three of them from Léo's room.

"How dare you bring her back to me like this?" Daan said. "You had better hope she recovers, or so help me God…"

Aubrey put a hand on Daan's chest. "This isn't Amélie's fault," he said, though the defense was half-hearted.

"The hell it isn't! She ran away from us. From you. And Léo followed. 'My sister,' she said." Daan shook his head bitterly. "Where could they have gone but to a brothel or a blanchisserie? Both ripe with pestilence."

"I'm sorry, Daan," Amélie said. "I can't tell you how sorry I am. She's my sister as much as anyone could be. You know I love her." She paused. "The doctor will fix her. That's what she needs right now—rest under a doctor's care. Thank you for taking her in. I can go, if you'd like."

"Don't be ridiculous." Aubrey threw an arm around her. It felt so good she wanted to lean into him. So, she did. Just a little. "You're not going anywhere. You'll stay right here where you belong, sweetheart."

The kindly white-haired doctor finally emerged with his face crumpled into his snow-white muttonchops.

"Consumption, I'm afraid. And quite advanced. I can keep her comfortable until she passes on, but that's all I can do. I'm sorry."

"'Until she passes'? Pardon me?" Suddenly Amélie felt the hallway and the men grow dim around her. Her limbs felt strangely disconnected from her body, and she felt alarmingly exposed. So, she wrapped her arms around herself and held on tight.

"It can't be," Daan said, the rims of his eyes red and filling with tears.

"I'm sorry, son." The doctor clapped Daan on the shoulder. "Is she your…?"

"Sister. She's my sister."

"Of course," the doctor said. "You had better call your parents, then."

"We have no parents."

The doctor regarded them with pity, then tipped his hat and went down the stairs.

Daan went into Léo's room, and numbly Amélie followed. Léo lay sound asleep and suddenly seemed even thinner and paler than she had before the doctor's fatal prognosis. Consumption. It could hardly be borne. The persistent cough, the swollen fingers and blood spatter—it seemed both inevitable and unreal. She couldn't be dying.

"We'll get a second opinion," Amélie uttered. But it was faithless.

With reverence, Daan took his sister's hand and kissed it. "Just rest." His voice was tremulous. "You'll be better soon."

Days passed, and they sat a steady vigil at her bedside. They moved her up to the attic and threw the windows open wide for the restorative fresh air so prescribed for consumptives. Easels were pushed to the side, canvases in varying stages lined the walls, rolls of canvas leaned against shelves of paints and brushes and palettes. Amélie played the worn piano, and the boys sang badly—and loudly for all their badness. They told stories and laughed, ate and drank as if nothing had changed when it had all changed.

Still, as if the diagnosis, the very name itself, lent the disease some fervor, Léonie seemed to be wasting away. She sweated away the nights and slept away the days, her flesh melting off, her face sunken. Each day the doctor came, administering heavy doses of morphine and purging her blood, anything to try to arrest the blood-drenched coughing, which only seemed to grow worse.

As Wednesday turned to Thursday, in the deadest part of night, Amélie sat in a daze of pure exhaustion when she felt fingers slide into hers. She jerked alert on the sofa and saw Aubrey beside her. Glancing at the bed, she saw Léo asleep and could hear the wet strain of air swimming in her lungs. Daan sat beside her, slumped over, fast asleep.

"Not much time now," Aubrey whispered.

The emotion Amélie had been trying to suppress surged through her, and she broke. Heavy tears fell in rivulets down her cheeks as her body shook.

"She was fine on Monday," she sobbed. "She carried her basket." Even as she said it, Amélie remembered how strained it was. Léo could barely breathe as she shuffled along. But that was before, when hope had colored everything.

Aubrey pulled her into his arms and held her tight. Tucked under his chin and resting against the warmth of the hard furrows of his chest, it felt so warm and right. How had she ever left this man?

"Shh, my love." He petted her hair. "It's going to be all right."

Amélie woke to midmorning sun. She'd slept on the sofa in Aubrey's arms and pulled up even as she felt him tighten his hold.

"Aubrey, let go."

Reluctantly he did, and she crept to Léo's bed, fearful because she could no longer hear the wet rasp of her chest.

"Is she?" Terror shot through her as Daan opened sleepy eyes to look at her, then he looked at Léo and pressed his head to her chest.

"Sleeping," he said, swallowing a sob. "But her breathing is too faint." He looked at Aubrey. "When does the doctor get here?"

Aubrey checked his watch. "Soon. It's nearly eleven."

When the doctor arrived, he confirmed what they all feared. The coughing had all but stopped because her breathing was growing shallow. It was only a matter of time.

14

mélie faintly registered the knock at the door, the gruff voices in the entryway, and the sound of boots on the stairs. Because she was doing the only thing in the world she was meant to be doing at that moment—holding Léonie's hand, stroking it and singing softly, as her sister struggled to take her last breaths.

"Just go to sleep. Fly to Him, my sweet sister. I'll see you soon."

Amélie felt him before she saw him. Would have known his presence in the same room as her. Somehow he felt as strangely familiar as the back of her hand. Jasper stood in the doorway. In an Ulster coat with his hat tucked under the cape, his bearing regal and features even, he seemed like an untouched island in the midst of their buffeting grief. Then she remembered.

"I'm sorry," she mouthed.

His cool sage eyes fell. "Don't be," he mouthed in

return, shaking his head and giving her a tender smile.

They stared at each other for a long moment, then he tipped his head, indicating Léo, and left.

Aubrey resumed his seat next to her. "What's he doing here?"

Amélie looked across the bed at Daan, his expression unreadable, then turned her body an inch away from Aubrey.

"Not now, can't you see?"

Five hours later, under the soft light of her bedside lamp, surrounded by the warmth of the three people who loved her most, Léonie Thomas breathed her last.

But the moment was far too gentle. Barely a ripple when it felt like a rip. Amélie stared in horror at the quiet room around them and the unshaken world beyond their window. How could that fierceness gutter out?

Then she remembered that knock on the door a lifetime ago. The bag-of-bones sound of her mother's body crumpling to the floor. Her flameless face when she'd told young Amélie her father would not be coming home. Ever again. A five-year-old girl, she'd sought refuge in her mother's arms. But the passionate woman Maria Audet had been had died, too. So, Amélie had crawled into her own broken heart. Held her to herself. Dared not rely on or love anyone. Until she met Léonie.

Amélie felt anger and blame coming up and slapped a hand over her mouth, strangling a sob. If she cried, she might never stop.

Aubrey's arm came around her, and she flinched. "No."

"I'm sorry. I just…"

She put distance between herself and the bed. The boys stared at her. In the oppressive quiet, she felt their grief and blame and had to get out of there. She desperately needed some fresh air.

Throwing the front door open, she ran out onto the walk, bent over, and sobbed. For some minutes she held herself as she cried. Her sadness felt like a heavy living thing pressing down on her chest. If only she could cry enough, she might be able to breathe.

She heard footsteps and felt a presence close. "Just leave me alone." But even as she couldn't manage Daan's blame or Aubrey's neediness just then, she realized it wasn't either of them.

"I'm sorry, Amélie." Jasper stood nearby. "I'm so sorry." The tender tone of his voice made cleansing tears crest again. When he opened his arms, she gratefully fell into them and cried.

"It's my fault," she said, clutching his lapels. "It's all my fault."

"Shh, sweetheart." He held on tight. "Of course it isn't."

After a time, she sagged. All the tension of fear and waiting, laughing when she might have been crying, being there for Léo and the boys even while feeling Daan's steadfast blame and Aubrey's neediness, unable to sleep or eat—her body gave out.

Jasper scooped her up and cradled her in his arms. She heard his driver's voice and saw the door of his carriage open.

"No." She sat up as he was about to climb in. "Where are you taking me?"

"Home."

"I can't leave here. I need to stay with her. Please put me down."

A muscle ticked in Jasper's jaw. Only reluctantly, did he.

"When was the last time you slept? Or had a decent meal?" He took her face and examined her. "She's gone, Amélie, and you're wasting away with her for all your holding on. You'll fall ill yourself if you don't take care."

"I will. I will. I just…"

"Just what? You're coming home with me, and I'm going to take care of you whether you want me to or not. When you've had a good night's sleep and something to eat, you can see to laying her to rest."

Amélie looked up to the attic windows. She could hear Léo's chiding voice even now: *This man, he isn't taking care of you?*

"I insist," Jasper said.

She hadn't any fight left and nodded.

Inside the house, she found Aubrey. They hugged and whispered sweet condolences to each other. But when they pulled back, he glowered over her shoulder.

"She'll be back to help you see to Léonie," Jasper said.

"Where are you going?" Aubrey asked.

"She's coming home with me."

"Why? She should stay here. Where she belongs. *This* is her home. It always was, and if I have any say, it will be again."

Jasper and Aubrey crowded each other, their faces hard.

She put a gentle hand on each man's arm. To Aubrey, she said, "I'm just going to sleep. I'll be back first thing in the morning."

"You're choosing him over me?"

"I'm not choosing anyone. I'm not a prize to be won."

When she turned toward the door, Aubrey grabbed her arm.

"We need to talk."

She nodded.

The gentle rocking of the carriage and soothing sound of horse hooves on cobble put Amélie right to sleep. Vaguely, she felt Jasper's arms around her as he brought her into his apartment. He called for Bertie to start her bath and Sophie to prepare a tray. Somewhere inside her, Amélie felt she should protest, that she was capable, but that part of her felt so tired.

Her exhaustion only made her want to cry more. To be so weak and needy felt worse than a scarlet letter because the condemnation felt true. Tears stung in her burning eyes as she sat limply, allowing Jasper to undress her before the steaming and fragrant bath.

Absently, she grabbed the laces of her corset. "I-I can do it."

"I know you can." He pulled the laces from her fingers and held her chin. "But you needn't prove yourself every moment of every minute of every day. Tonight I live to serve you. And the only thing you need do is let go." He nodded, and mechanically she nodded back.

Amélie slid into the hot bath with a sigh, then under the scalding water to lie at the bottom, where there was no sound, no death, no men fighting like boys. Only heavy tendrils of hair, suddenly floating freely all around her. Finally, she surfaced to see Jasper sitting beside the tub.

"Are you going to be my body servant tonight?"

"Yes." He began to roll up his sleeves. "If you'd let me, I would do it every night. Now turn around." He twirled a finger. "We'll start with your hair."

She could hear him working the soap in his hands, building a lather. Then his fingers slid the soap through her hair from roots to tips and returned to begin massaging at her temples. She relaxed back with a moan, her head and hair dangling over the side. Slowly and steadily, he worked, kneading her brow and scalp and all around her ears to her nape, up and down the back of her neck and along her shoulders.

He lifted her head, which she could barely lift herself, and rinsed. Then he smoothed rosemary oil from the tips to the roots and drew a comb slowly across her scalp and through her hair. When he finally secured it to the top of her head, she sighed and fell back.

Amélie heard the rustle of clothes and opened her tired eyes to see Jasper climbing in.

"I pride myself in my attention to detail." He winked. "Only the best for you."

She shifted to make room. It seemed impossible with his tall frame. Yet when Jasper unfolded himself under the rising water, he crooked a finger, and she nestled neatly into him, her back to his front like a spoon.

So languid from raw emotion, lack of sleep, and the heat of the water, she couldn't brace herself against him even if she wanted to. He slid his arms under hers, resting his clasped hands on her belly. She lay her heavy head on a shoulder and closed her eyes.

"I could fall asleep like this."

"Go ahead." He kissed her hair and relaxed back.

Amélie might have fallen asleep. The next thing she knew, a wash linen was drawn over her face, then dipped into the water and squeezed. The gentle trickle felt and sounded so good. Then his sure hand dragged the soapy linen down her neck and chest, around her breasts and belly. Down her arms and legs. Even between fingers and toes.

Finally, the used linen was slapped down, and he rinsed away any remaining soap.

Perhaps she drifted off again. The water was cooling when she felt firm fingers skimming up and down her neck. It wasn't a sexual touch but an imprinting one. A hand caressed her breast and played with the nipple. Gentle tugs and soft strokes. Then the hand at her neck slid down her belly.

"Open your legs."

She moaned.

"Open your legs, Amélie."

"We shouldn't."

"*We* aren't doing anything. I'm merely playing with the body that belongs to me."

"I don't belong to you, Jasper."

"You do. You're just too stubborn to know it. Now open your legs."

When she did, he slipped his hand over her sex and squeezed. He dragged a trail of wet kisses along her shoulder and slid a finger around her button. 'Round and around, then squeezing over it, then a nail grazing it. The telltale tingling grew more acute, and she whimpered and mewled.

"Mm. That's it. I love those broken sounds. Good girl. I'm not going to make you beg. Not tonight. Just release. Whenever you're ready."

He played and played with her bundle of nerves as she squirmed and moaned and her breathing grew faint. Finally, he thrust two fingers deep into her core as he pinched her nerve, and her release broke, pulsing up through her.

"I think you needed that," he said, kissing just below an ear.

She nodded.

After insisting she eat, a vegetable stew and some butter-slathered bread, they crawled into bed together around midnight. She couldn't believe, when she looked at the time, that when the day broke, Léo had been alive, and now she was gone. Amélie's eyes burned when she thought of it, but at the moment she had no tears left.

15

*I*n the dark early-morning hours, a low fire burned its last crimson embers as Jasper sat awake, staring at Amélie. She lay on her side, her silky, rosemary-scented hair in disarray and her mouth ajar as she slept soundly. After the days she'd passed, she was likely to sleep for some time.

When Louis had arrived at the Moulin Rouge without Amélie, Jasper felt something he would've sworn he could no longer feel—the naked vulnerability that could only exist in feeling true tenderness for another person. He'd planned to seduce and play with Amélie. He'd never imagined he'd enjoy her so much. Be so amused by her. So moved by her. But true and deep caring? That he'd thought locked away along with his mangled heart.

Monsieur Talac obviously still had feelings for her. That made Jasper burn with jealousy. If anything revealed the proof of his feelings for Amélie, it was that. If Talac loved her still and if Jasper were a better man, he'd leave her to him. But Jasper had never been mistaken for being the better man.

Her dreams of performing were another matter. Clearly she couldn't fathom the expectations of men. Those who would come from all over the city and beyond to see her perform. Hoping as they watched for a chance, given all the money in their pockets, to see her after the show. There was no way he was going to permit that.

He didn't want to squash her dreams. If she allowed, he'd give her anything she desired. *Except for that.* Whether she was a known member of the demimonde or not, night after night he would still field requests simply because she was on stage. She had to know that. He had no idea how, but he would simply have to make her see reason.

Carefully he threaded his fingers through her gorgeous blanket of dark hair. If he allowed the merest thought of another man seeing her like this, he felt red-hot. She belonged to him; she just didn't know it yet.

His gaze raked over her exquisite form. Though he wanted to do more, he merely closed her mouth and kissed her.

Later that morning, they rode back to Cortot. To Jasper's frustration, Amélie had refused to wear one of the dresses he'd bought her. She'd said she wasn't a prize to be won, but she couldn't be more wrong.

"I'd like you to consider staying with me," he said. She looked ready, eager even, to deny him, and he took her hands. "At least until you can find something else. I don't want you to worry about where you're going to sleep each night—"

"*Whom* I'm going to sleep with, you mean."

"That, too, of course." He smirked. "This time is trying enough." Her face fell, and she appeared ready to cry again. "She was dear to you, Mademoiselle Thomas."

"As dear to me as a sister. I never had a sister. Nor a brother. No one, really, who loved and understood me until I came to Cortot. When I found them, I felt... *found*, if that makes any sense."

"You're grateful."

"It's much more than that, but yes."

"Gratitude isn't love, Amélie."

Something passed between them that made it clear they were no longer talking about Léo.

"Don't insult me, Jasper. I'm not a child."

"I don't mean to insult you. Truly. It's an easy mistake to make—gratitude and love. Believe me, I know."

"How do you know?"

He paused, considering. "I've held onto... things longer than I might because of gratitude. But that kind of obligation is the worst perversion of love. It's weight when it should be wings."

She straightened as if steeling herself, then peered out the window as they pulled into Montmartre.

"I'm sorry about missing the audition. I would never want to appear uncaring or difficult. And I certainly didn't want you to appear foolish for having recommended me. I'm so sorry about that."

"Nonsense. I completely understand. And I sent a note to Charles this morning explaining everything. No doubt he'll understand, too."

She looked at him, the request written all over her face.

"We'll reschedule as soon as you're able."

"Thank you. I won't disappoint you again. I promise."

He squeezed her hand. "I know you won't."

"I appreciate everything you've done for me. Really."

He leaned forward, tipping his head to chase her gaze. "Why does it sound like you're saying goodbye to me?"

She took a deep breath and looked at him squarely. "I'm going to stay with the boys for a while."

"No."

"Jasper."

"No."

She sighed. "I owe them—"

"We just talked about that."

"It's easier for now."

"No."

She gave him a perturbed look.

"I need to go into my office. But I can send Louis to collect you at any time. You needn't stay with them out of some obligation."

"Not out of obligation. To make the arrangements. We'll have a small wake at the house."

"I can help you with that. With anything you need."

"I know you can. And I thank you. But we can manage." She paused. "I need to have some time to speak with them."

"With Talac."

She looked at her hands fiddling on her lap. "We need to talk. Yes."

Is he in love with you? Are you in love with him? Will you go back to him? Given half a chance, he will use you again. To pose for him. Can't you see? I would never use you. I don't need to. I don't want to.

Jasper could hear this frantic pleading in his head. But he sounded just like the pathetic man he'd become with Joselin. So, he said nothing.

If he had to, for now, he could appear the man who respected Amélie's wishes. Who backed away gracefully. Who gave her time and distance. But if she thought he would do any of those things for too long, she didn't know him very well. He'd never forfeited a contest in his life. And he sure as hell wasn't going to start with one he knew he could win.

The carriage stopped, and he turned to her with as much resignation as he could feign.

"We loved her together, the three of us," she said. "We need to say goodbye to her together."

16

*L*éo's body was taken away and arrangements made for a small wake at the atelier. After making those plans, Daan glowered at Amélie, then went to bed.

She sat with Aubrey, who clapped his hands pensively. He looked, as usual, unkempt. But this time, the strain in his eyes told a different story.

"He'll get over it," he said.

"He has every right."

Aubrey looked at her, his face a picture of pain and regret.

"Monsieur Degrailly. Are you—"

"No."

He gave her a look of skepticism and disappointment.

"We've seen each other. There's a fondness there, I think."

"You think?"

"He would like more, but…"

Aubrey chuckled breathily. "Amélie Audet will not be held down by a man. Isn't that right?" He leaned over the table as if to reach for her. "Isn't there a difference between being held down and simply being held?"

"Perhaps. For some."

"There isn't any 'perhaps.'" He paused. "You punished me. And for what? Wanting to take care of you?"

"You fell in love with me knowing who I was and what I wanted. Yet as soon as you receive some accolades and some francs, somehow you conveniently forget."

"I love you. I want to take care of the woman I love. I'll not apologize for that."

"You say I punished you, but you punished me, too."

"I was upset."

"A poor excuse! You told anyone who'd listen that I'd spread my legs as easily as I'd model for a few francs. When you knew, *you knew*, I'd never done that with anyone else."

"I was angry. Very. Angry. All I did was love you, and you walked away." He appeared to be deep in thought. "You once said you'd love me forever. Have you stopped?"

Amélie had said that. She'd loved him so intensely, even when she left him, it was difficult to fathom ever stopping. But that was before the vicious rumors. Before Jasper.

Aubrey blinked his red-rimmed eyes. "Do you still love me? Because I still love you."

"It isn't that simple."

"Yes, it is."

"We loved each other before," she said.

"But you changed."

"*You* were the one who changed, Aubrey."

"Can't we just go back to how we were? I'd do anything."

"Can we talk more about this after Léo's wake?"

Two days later, Amélie stood sandwiched between Daan and Aubrey to receive the condolences of their friends. Jasper, so distinct in his haute-couture suit amongst the avant-garde bohemians, appeared in the line. After extending his sympathies to Daan and Aubrey, he held her cheek. "How are you holding up?"

It was a conspicuous claim, and she felt the furtive glances of the other mourners.

"It was kind of you to come."

"I wanted to see you. To see how you're doing." He glanced at the stalled line behind him. "When you have a moment, I'd like to talk with you. In private. It's important."

She glanced at Aubrey, who wasn't even trying to conceal his agitation.

"When I get a chance."

Jasper took a glass of wine and began talking animatedly with the illustrator Gaston Bussiere. He knew everyone, it seemed. Periodically he'd glance back at her, his expression opaque.

She looked at Aubrey, whose face was tight. How was it that while she was so intent on not being kept by a man, not one, but two of them seemed determined to keep her? They appeared content to dance around every step she took. She had to find her own place. The sooner the better.

When the crowd waned, Amélie wandered out to the back garden just beginning to burst with peach and yellow roses. Many summer days she'd spent in idyll here as Aubrey painted. Like the sun as it fell so unevenly there, casting the garden in perfect light and troublesome shade, it was a contradictory place in her memory.

"Here you are."

She turned to see Jasper strolling toward her. He was too beautiful just then, with his strong frame and arresting smile. She took a step back, and still she felt unsteady.

"I didn't know if you'd gone," she said.

He shook his head as he maneuvered her through ropes of flowering vines cascading down from an arbor.

After courtesies about the wake, he said, "I've spoken with

Charles, who was as understanding as I imagined. We've rescheduled your audition for this Friday. I hope that pleases you."

"Yes. Of course." She felt an immense need to hug him but instead managed a bright smile. "Thank you so much."

Jasper pulled her into his arms and slid a deliberate hand down her back. She sagged into him in relief, as if her body knew it was home. Combined with the heady floral fragrance that surrounded them, she wanted so much to linger there with him in their enchanted bower. He moved her. So easily. And, no matter how she tried to convince herself otherwise, she wanted him to.

"Are you ready to come home with me?" he whispered as he pressed light kisses down a cord of her neck.

"Ah… no." Her breasts instantly grew tight.

"No?" He dragged his mouth along her jaw. "You don't sound certain." There was a sly smile in his creamy tone.

She wedged her arms between them. "I'm certain. I've been distracted. By Léo. And your attention has been very nice indeed. But I can't go home with you."

"So, you'll stay here with Monsieur Talac."

"Only for a few days. Until I can make other arrangements."

"What if I could make you other arrangements?" She shook her head. "Not on Saint-Germain. Nor Leblanc. How about Ravignan?"

"I can't go back there." She pulled back, and he let go.

"I've spoken with Madame Pelletier, and she's agreed to give you your position back."

"Why would she do that?"

"It seems she found her heart somewhere between my financial support statements."

"You bribed her."

"I merely persuaded her to see reason. Is it my fault she finds my money so persuasive?"

"No. Money is very persuasive for those who never have enough."

"So, you'll go back."

Returning to the laundry would solve her immediate problems

and take a great deal of pressure off her relations with Aubrey and Jasper. But how could she accept it knowing Jasper had arranged it? He might as well have set her up on rue Leblanc. Could she take a small hit to her pride for greater distance?

She nodded and uttered, "Thank you."

An hour later, everyone had gone home but for Jasper, who stood by the front door, holding Amélie's belongings.

"How kind of you to secure her position at the blanchisserie," Aubrey gibed with undisguised animosity.

"It was what she wanted. Surely you can see that."

"What I can see is how neatly it works out for you."

Jasper smiled blandly at Aubrey, then looked at her. "I'll just bring your things, then. You come along whenever you're ready."

"Thank you."

Jasper kissed her. It wasn't short or chaste. When Aubrey cleared his throat, they pulled apart. Jasper gave him a long, even look of blatant challenge that Aubrey returned. Finally, they said goodbye. Amélie could barely stand Madame Pelletier, but she looked forward to getting back there with the men here getting on like boys.

Some time later—likely time enough for Jasper to deposit her things and leave—Amélie walked with Aubrey back to the washhouse.

"I saw the bruises," he said.

Absently she put a hand to her neck. They were nearly gone now, but they'd been evident when she arrived.

"He hurts you, and still you let him come around? I could kill him for hurting you."

If she stayed with Jasper, would she have to explain all the time?

She sighed. "It isn't what you think."

"I know all about his escapades at Chez Christiane. Everyone knows. It's not even that you're his whore—it's that you're his punching pillow. Do you need to be hurt to come to release? That's not the girl I loved. I never needed to hurt you for you to find satisfaction."

He hadn't. Whatever he'd been to her in the end, Aubrey was always an adoring lover. Generous and attentive. The perfect gentleman. It was beautiful and sweet. Exactly what she imagined making love should be.

Aubrey stopped and faced her. "Why do you let him do that to you? Is this what you like now? Help me to understand. Because I can't. You've told me time and again you're not one of those weak girls who would give herself over to anything a man desires. I just don't understand it."

Amélie felt torn. Half his questions she had herself. She couldn't reason it out or explain it away. Not to herself and certainly not to anyone else. The closest she could come to understanding was the raw feeling of it. As if with Aubrey, she'd been happily swimming underwater, not even realizing she couldn't breathe. Yet with Jasper, she crested the surface with a great gulp of air. He made her feel alive. Made everything seem electric-bright. Did she feel shame? Yes. For it was so good. And no. For the very same reason. Might she have been content in the murky, cradling water? Never to know? Perhaps. But now, could she ever go back?

"He's never hurt me in any way I don't allow." She stopped to think. "I can't explain it, and I don't need to. Not to anyone, but certainly not to you."

"What does that mean? 'Certainly not to you.' You may have stopped loving me, but I never stopped loving you, Amélie. Never. If you need to be bound and hurt, I'll do it. But I don't think you need those things. I think he's charismatic. He's interesting. He gives you fine clothes and nights at the opera. I know it might be hard to resist. I could give you all that. Without hurting you."

"I won't say it again because I trust I won't have to." She gave him a pointed stare. "He doesn't hurt me for cruelty. It's a sublime agony. And I don't even know if I'll see him again or what I want but for some time to myself."

Aubrey nodded contemplatively. "I'm sorry to tell you this, but he's in love with his ex-wife. Everyone knows. He makes no secret of it."

"I know."

Aubrey's mouth fell open, then he rushed on.

"He's using you. Don't you see? He's using you, and he'll set you aside when he's done without a backward glance."

"I know. Perhaps I'm using him, too. Did you ever think of that?"

He shook his head incredulously. "He'll never love you. Not in the way you deserve. And you deserve to be loved, Amélie. Though you see it as a weakness. I can't understand."

They stared at each other for a long moment. Aubrey was needy, but he also had an endearing way of laying her bare. And his devotion, but for the wounded man he'd been when she left him, had never been in doubt. He did love her. She felt certain he would fashion a new heart to love her differently and well, if only she'd give him a chance.

"Come to Cortot," he said. "Just for a visit. When you're ready."

When Amélie closed the door on the inside of the washhouse, she sank with relief against it. Sunday night. A mere one week before, she'd returned from an incredible week's end with Jasper, bruised and sated and happy. Little had she known when she woke the next morning, she'd be put out of a room and position. That she'd return to the atelier on Cortot. That she'd have to say goodbye forever to her best friend and sister.

Now she came back to the same house carved into the hill, and everything seemed different. With dread, she looked at the stairs. She didn't want to go up to confront an empty room.

"Mademoiselle."

Madame Pelletier poked her head out tentatively. Then she came into the entryway as if on the balls of her feet. The laundry mistress had never moved so peculiarly. She didn't tiptoe into a room but trudged with ham feet as if it were a chore.

"I was terribly, terribly sorry to hear of Mademoiselle Thomas's passing." Her voice was syrupy and her face a picture of doughy sadness. She wrung her hands, shook her head, and *tsk*ed. "The poor girl. Fortune smiled upon her to have a friend in you, and that's certain. I'm so glad you're back." She patted Amélie's hand and went to leave.

"Madame?"

"Yes, dear?" Still her face was furrowed with compassion.

"Are you drunk?"

The madame went rigid, arched a brow, and pursed her lips. "Oh, well, see if I try a drop of kindness for you again, you ungrateful girl. Monsieur Degrailly thinks to tell me to be nice to the girls. If it were up to him, he'd have me tucking you into bed each night with a pot of chocolate and a kiss to the forehead. What does he know? You'd all run to laziness if I gave an inch.

"You've had your week holiday for your friend. That's more than most." She turned to leave, mumbling as she went, "And don't be expecting any more favors. I'm plumb out."

Amélie couldn't suppress a smile.

In her room, she half expected to see Jasper waiting for her and was glad when he wasn't. He'd arranged her things nicely, but the empty bed on the other wall made the room feel stark. She collapsed onto her bed and heard a crinkle. Sitting up, she found a note:

> *Amélie,*
> *Your audition is in five days. But if you're not ready, I'll understand.*
> *I'd like to see you. You need only call.*
> *As to that, I've had a telephone installed here.*
> *My home number is:*
> *SEG5107*
> *My office number is:*
> *GUT6838*
> *Please don't hesitate to call me. For anything.*
> *Take care of yourself, sweetheart.*
> *J—*

She clutched the note to her tender heart.

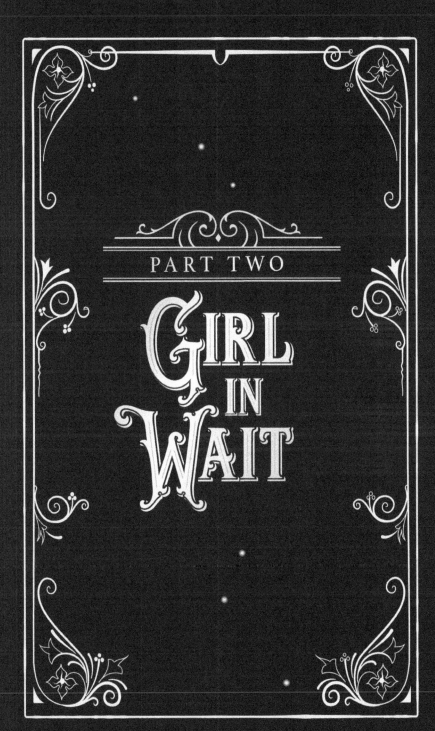

PART TWO

GIRL IN WAIT

17

A telephone.

The next day, Amélie stood before the peculiar wooden box with the cord and the horn. The other women crowded around her.

"To think, you can pick up the horn and hear another's voice from across town as clear as if he were standing beside you," Claire said.

"It's a receiver," Zara, a wiry, tawny-skinned girl, said.

Amélie cradled the receiver to her ear, and they all leaned in as if waiting for it to bite or shock her. "Has anyone ever made a telephone call?"

They shook their heads.

"Who would I call? No one I know has a telephone," Mireille, a wide-hipped strawberry-blonde, said. "Go ahead, Amélie. You have his number. He wants you to call him."

She had his number—*two* numbers. Had, for some

120

reason, already memorized them as if they were lines from a poem she recited.

"Oh, Amélie." Mireille slapped the back of her hand to her forehead and feigned a swoon. "He can't get on a day without hearing your voice."

"I think it's romantic," Claire said, her almond eyes going dreamy.

"Go on," Zara urged. "He's expecting your call. Don't you want to make a telephone call? I do. Le Fauborg, indeed. Does he have a cock as big as his purse? I'll call him for you."

Jasper did, but Amélie wasn't about to tell anyone that bit of news. She did, however, want very much to make a telephone call. But she liked that he'd given her a way to contact him, then left her alone. It felt like freedom. More importantly, it felt like respect.

They heard a gasp and turned to see Madame Pelletier bounding toward them with a glare.

"You're a lazy lot. All of you. Now get back to work, or I'll throw you all out before I throw out this telephone."

Amélie fell easily back into the laundry routine. Early morning deliveries, sorting and darning, washing and bluing, starching and mangling, drying and ironing. Then starting all over again. The other women expressed their sympathy for Léo's death, but it was tempered by their worries that Amélie herself might be sick, and she overheard whispered resentments about her special treatment in being allowed back.

So, she kept her head down and worked longer and harder to prove herself fit. After all, it wouldn't be for long, she reasoned. Soon enough she'd be employed down the hill on de Clichy. Perhaps she'd get a garret with some of the other performers.

Just like that, she began planning for her new life as a full-time performer. No longer would she have to stumble into Le Chat Noir, exhausted from a grueling week of work at the washhouse, to sing a wasted set in front of a meager crowd on Sunday nights. With her audition looming and her friendship with Jasper, it seemed more possible every day.

When the phone rang that Thursday evening, the sound was so peculiar and out of place, the Virgin Mary may as well have jumped out of the Bible and danced the cancan while flinging her celebrated blue cloak around. Everyone rushed to the wooden box, staring wide-eyed at it and Amélie. Surely it was for her. No one else knew anyone with a telephone.

"You say *hello*," Zara instructed as Amélie stared at it.

"'A-llo?'" Mireille asked.

"Hell o. With an H. It's a special greeting just for the telephone. You put the receiver to your ear and say *hello* just there." Zara indicated the tiny open mouth fixed to the box.

"How do you know that?" Claire asked. The phone still stridently rang.

"I read it somewhere," Zara replied.

"You read it somewhere," Madame Pelletier said, stalking in. "That's a fine thing, seeing as how you can't read." She flicked her hands in a shooing motion. "All of you get. Haven't you anything better to do than to stand around like idiots?"

"I can read, madame," Zara insisted as she and Mireille and Claire shuffled reluctantly away.

"A-llo-o," Madame Pelletier answered in a high, syrupy voice. "Why yes, of course she's here, Monsieur Degrailly." She spoke so loudly into the phone she nearly hollered. The women couldn't suppress their laughter.

"Here, dear, it's for you." She handed the receiver to Amélie.

"You needn't yell into it as if you're trying to reach him across town," Zara instructed.

The laundry madame scowled. "Move along. Get. This is not for the likes of you, you sluts."

"H-hello?" Amélie said.

"Hello, Amélie." Jasper's voice crackled through the line with such happy intensity she took a deep, satisfied breath and felt her body relaxing into him as if he were there.

At first, she'd been so relieved to be away from his and Aubrey's scrabbling, so happy to focus on the tiny minutiae of her tiny life, that she'd all but convinced herself she was better off without him. But as the days wore on and no call came, a call she'd very much expected, she realized she missed him. Perhaps, smart man that he was, he'd done it on purpose.

"Jasper."

"Is this your first time using a telephone?"

"Y-yes."

"You've taken to it. There's nothing to it, you see?"

She did. The idea of it was more peculiar than actually using it.

"I was just calling to see if you were ready for your audition tomorrow."

"I think so." There was no thinking. She'd been preparing for this audition since first hearing of the new dance hall to open just a few blocks from the washhouse. "Yes," she amended. "I'll be ready."

"Good. Good. Fair warning—Charles can be difficult."

"'Difficult'? Charles Zidler is a performer's manager. Everyone knows it. I'm not worried."

"Yes. But he's very discriminating about who he takes on. Sometimes he's a mite too fussy. Any small thing—a misstep, a trill in your voice, the wrong look—could dampen his interest. Even in the best performers."

Incredulous, Amélie exhaled sharply. There was no mistaking— Jasper was preparing her to be cut. For some reason, she hadn't imagined this. She'd assumed that an acquaintance with Degrailly or Zidler would give her a leg up. Not make an already difficult dream more difficult. Now that she considered his deepening interest in her, she didn't know why she hadn't.

"But you're a voice of reason."

"I'm only one half of the partnership, and he has a better eye for talent than I. I tend to defer to him, and he's been happy to overrule me at times."

"Do you often disagree?"

"Not often."

"Do *you* think I'm good enough?" She felt defensive, and the hostility in her voice betrayed it.

"I think you're a better singer than almost anyone I've ever heard, including Fidès Devriès. But dancing is just as important. Can you dance?"

"I can dance."

"We'll see tomorrow, won't we?"

Yes, they would see, she thought indignantly. Amélie was no stranger to proving grounds. She came into her own when faced with defying expectations. She would defy theirs.

"Plan to spend the week's end with me when it's done."

The audacity of this man! He'd just insinuated she wasn't good enough, then promised an arousing week's end in bed to cushion the blow.

"I don't think so."

"Of course you will."

"I don't know. We need to talk about it."

"And we will. Over dinner."

"Jasper."

"Amélie." There was a pause. "Pack a bag. I'll see you tomorrow, darling."

She exhaled on his click.

18

*L*ate the next morning, Jasper stood in Daphne's apartment, trying to collect his thoughts while his beautiful lover sprawled naked on a chaise longue.

"Would you mind terribly putting on a robe?"

She rolled her eyes as she slunk off the chaise. "Since when did you become so provincial?" She slid into a petal-pink silk robe. "Or is it that you'd rather unwrap me like a present?" She secured the bow and gave him a wink.

"Not today. We need to talk." He sat and indicated she do the same.

"This is boring when I already know what you're going to say. So provincial and so predictable."

"How was Nice?"

"The flower market was tight and fashionable as always. But, honestly, it was a dump without you."

Daphne could be catty in an amusing way. She was

the best fun in these public places where the goal was to see and be seen. The flower market in Nice was a perfect complement to that. Like her, on the surface it seemed lovely and uncomplicated, but too often, ugly and bewildering words lay behind pretty posied hands.

"Well, you may have to get on without me, then. If you already know what I'm going to say, then you know I'm here to part ways. Romantically, that is. I hope we can continue to be friends."

Daphne pursed her lips as she thought. "The girl in the Salon. If I hadn't come along, you'd have given her my champagne, your handkerchief, your heart…"

"Yes."

"Why? I don't mind if you see her alongside me. I see Christian and Albert and Edouard besides you. The more the merrier, I say."

He smiled, then sighed. "You're a good sort."

"I'm not a good sort. I'm a good fuck. And so pleasingly submissive you hadn't the first clue how to dominate in bed until you found me. Why do we need to stop? Is the Salon girl so jealous? Bring her into our bed sport. I don't mind in the slightest."

There again that intoxicating visual. Now that it played in his mind, he couldn't get it out. Finally, he sighed again.

"I don't know that she's jealous. She's… different."

"Not in the scene, you mean."

"No, but—"

"Jasper, darling"—she knelt at his feet—"we both know you won't be happy with a girl like that. Why do you torture yourself?"

"She's not in the scene, but she's definitely submissive."

"There you have it. If she's submissive, then we can play together. Bring her to Chez Christiane, and we'll find a nice room."

"I don't feel like I need the scene with her. I can't explain it. It's only that I feel… differently toward her."

"Love?" She lingered over the word as if licking it with her tongue.

"No," he said so quickly and easily Daphne's eyes widened with knowing.

She paused for a long moment, as if taking it all in. Finally, she said, "How about one more go? We'll give each other a proper send-off. I'm going to miss you," she whined as if only just realizing she was losing him.

Jasper stood to leave and placed a kiss on her forehead. "I'm sure it would be special, but I can't."

Daphne pouted as she walked him to the door. "Don't tell the other boys, but you're my favorite."

He kissed her one last time, a good and lasting kiss. Then he pressed his forehead to hers. "I promise you I will, the next time I see them."

Daphne stood in the doorway with her arms folded across her chest. "She must really be something."

That afternoon, Jasper sat with Charles in the empty dance hall. Faux archways, red velvet swags, and dozens of towering mirrors had been brought into the space since they'd last waited for Amélie. Chandeliers that resembled a set of giant goblets leaned on the floor like unused tops waiting to be hung. In a dull cacophony in the background, workmen pounded and hoisted and hollered. The piano player strolled his fingers in waves up and down the keys, the notes falling like a fine rain of pitch.

Then Jasper heard the squeak of a door opening and the soft, determined clack of lady's pumps on the hardwood. He looked at his watch and smiled to himself. Three minutes to four. Perfect.

With regal poise, as if this were her realm and she the queen, Amélie strode toward them in the sapphire silk evening gown she'd worn at the opera. Her long hair styled high, she had subtle color on the apples of her cheeks, and she'd rouged her lips a shocking shade of red that drew his eye.

"Monsieur Zidler."

Charles's eyes danced with intrigue over every part of her before returning to those rouged lips, his muttonchops curling up to his ears.

"I've heard an awful lot about you, monsieur. I'm so appreciative of this chance to audition for you." She extended a hand.

"All good things, I hope, my dear."

Jasper's gaze was riveted on Charles's lips as he kissed Amélie's hand, lingering a beat too long.

"All good things," she assured him while smoothly pulling her hand away. Amélie turned to Jasper with a confident and calculating smile. "Monsieur Degrailly. A pleasure to see you again."

"Yes." His voice sounded rougher and smaller than normal.

"Jasper tells me he saw you sing at Le Chat," Charles said. "That your voice is a revolution."

"A revelation," Jasper corrected.

"He's being kind," Amélie said. "But I feel confident."

"Well, good. Good. We're considering a cast of performers," Charles explained. "Regular players who can dance and sing and act. We'll weave in and out of storylines as productions are written. As of right now, there is no planned favorite for this stage. But she may emerge as her talents prove."

Amélie nodded and seemed satisfied.

"The audition," Charles continued, "consists of three parts—a song to be performed, the cancan to be danced, and finally, you'll pair me in a dance. I trust you have a song prepared. Perhaps our piano player already knows it." He indicated the man at the piano.

"I have a song." She shrugged out of her cape and pulled out some sheets of music. "I don't think he knows it, but it's easy enough to accompany."

"Very well," Charles said, and he and Jasper sat.

Jasper didn't know what he'd imagined. If Amélie would be white as a sheet or trembling. Somehow he'd known she wouldn't be. Yet this woman... A calm fell over her as she straightened and strode confidently to the piano. She showed such poise as she spoke with the pianist and bustled her skirt. This was a woman who owned a dream and would own any person who stood in the way of it. It sent a small tremor through him.

Then he peered more closely. She didn't have her respectable, flowy knickers on, but sheer and tight ruffled bloomers and petticoats. How high was she going to ruck that skirt? He took a calming breath as she climbed onto the stage with her shoulders back and her head held high.

A brilliant limelight came on, shining into her face and lighting her dark hair and peachy skin against the deep-blue dress. The cut gems and beads sewn into her bodice made her sparkle. She was breathtaking on that stage, and he could've sworn he heard Charles take in a breath.

"She's stunning," the director said.

"Yes," Jasper replied with the slightest hint of a possessive growl in his tone.

Amélie's hand came up to her brow.

"Can you see all right?" Charles asked. He knew very well performers couldn't see much of anything when that spotlight shone on them. But that was hardly the point. The audience could see them. *That* was the point.

"Well enough," she replied in a satin tone that echoed in the space.

"Whenever you're ready, then."

Amélie looked to the piano player, and a workman coughed in the distance. The scraping and shuffling stopped.

The song began in delicate, almost sweetly romantic chords, then danced into an elegant waltz. Jasper turned to Charles and gave him a questioning look. Charles appeared to search his mind, then shook his head. They'd never heard this song before.

When Amélie opened her mouth to sing, her voice dipped and climbed masterfully, just like a dance. That stage, this place, everyone in the room, was hers. She held them in the palm of her hand as she sang:

"I understand your distress
Dear lover
And I yield to your wishes
Make me your mistress

We are far from moderation
And further yet from sadness
I long only for the precious moment
When we will be happy
I want you…"

Like a matched set, Jasper and Charles sat forward, mouths agape. Jasper felt hot. Felt all his blood rushing to his cock. Out of the corner of his eye—for he couldn't take his eyes off her—he saw Charles squirm, then cross one leg over the other. "Je te veux." *I want you*. Now he knew the reason for the rouged lips. She was seducing them, and they were enraptured. It was the most base and beautiful thing he'd ever heard.

What Amélie was doing was exactly what he and Charles had envisioned for the place. For months, they'd imagined and planned and built and hoped. Then she'd walked onto that stage and become the embodiment of all of it. It was stunning. And terrifying.

He heard Charles's clapping before he realized the song had ended. With a soft, satisfied smile, she took a gentle bow.

"An unusual song, Mademoiselle Audet," Jasper said tightly.

"Yes," Charles agreed. "Wherever did you find it?"

"Are you familiar with Monsieur Satie?"

"Erik," Jasper said. "He composes at Le Chat. He wrote that for you?"

"He didn't write it for *me*. It's something he's been working on. I've sung it for him a few times, and when I asked him if I might use it for my audition, he agreed. 'Je te veux.' Did you like it?"

"I loved it," Charles said.

"It's scandalous," Jasper said at the same time.

"That's why I loved it." Charles clapped him on the shoulder.

When the pianist started in on Offenbach's "Infernal Galop," Amélie slipped seamlessly into a dancer. The beautiful legs Jasper had promised Charles were on full display as she shook her skirt and kicked her legs high. Though she was obviously a skilled dancer, it wasn't a particularly inventive routine. But the cancan wasn't known for its originality anymore. It was an opportunity for a man to see some pretty leg in the midst of a provocative dance.

The men in that dance hall were getting a good look. Jasper couldn't stand it. He thought the song bad enough. But adding to that her willingness to kick up her skirts, he felt his whole body going red with possessiveness and anger. Her performance began to fade out as he envisioned pulling her skirt down, throwing her cape around her, and escorting her from the hall. Did she really expect him to recommend her for any position in this place? This planned den of decadence with a sumptuous suite in the adjoining tower set aside for liaisons between performers and patrons? She'd have to be mad, or he would surely go mad trying to manage her night after night. He couldn't do it. He was only capable of so much.

Charles stood as the dance ended, clapping and strolling toward the stage. "Very nice. Very nice, indeed. Only one last part. Paired dancing with a gentleman. After all, we plan to make our patrons feel special, and waltzing with one of our stars would make them feel very special."

"I'll do it," Jasper said.

Charles looked back at him with a frown. He'd always done the paired dancing. "Are you sure? I'm more than happy—"

"Quite."

Amélie came toward him with rosy cheeks, her chest rising and falling as she caught her breath. She unbustled her skirt and stepped into him. Their arms high and boxed, he folded his hands around her and held her decorously as the pianist began Waldteufel's "The Skater's Waltz." As the sprightly song played, he could see their reflection in all the mirrors, a proper and handsome couple smiling politely and gliding effortlessly around the dance floor. But inside, he simmered, and when he finally met her gaze, she smirked.

"How am I doing, Monsieur Degrailly?"

"I think you know very well how you're doing, Mademoiselle Audet." He gritted his teeth. Why, when he finally had her in his arms, was he getting even angrier?

"Is something the matter?"

She was too satisfied. Too calm. It made him incensed.

"No," he replied tersely. All he could hear was that gorgeous voice scaling the walls of the place. All he could see were those rouged lips wrapped around those scandalous words. And… something else. Not to mention her skirt flung so high that with her sheer bloomers, one could almost see her sex.

"Are you certain?" she pressed.

"Yes. Why?"

"Because it looks as if you're going to grind your teeth to dust."

After glancing again at Charles, Jasper said, "I think you've had your fun leading me around by the nose. But as soon as this audition is over"—he whispered—"and it almost is, then it's my turn."

The song ended, and Amélie seemed reluctant to let go. It was Jasper who now smiled in satisfaction.

Charles clapped as he walked toward them. "Well done. Well done, you two. Degrailly, I had no idea you were such a fine dancer."

"Yes, well, Mademoiselle Audet is easy for me to lead."

Jasper and Amélie exchanged a look.

"We have some decisions to make in the coming weeks," Charles continued, seemingly oblivious to the tension between them. "I couldn't find your vocal range, mademoiselle. Are you a—"

"A contralto," Jasper said. He knew a contralto would be less likely to be cast as a lead and her voice was smoky enough to pass.

"A mezzo-soprano, monsieur," she corrected with narrowed eyes. "With a very broad range."

"Oh, yes. Good. And I'm not aware you're in the demimonde. Are you known by a stage name? This Belle Étoile that you go by at Le Chat?"

"No, monsieur. I'm not in the demimonde. Under any name."

19

"Are we done here?" Jasper addressed Zidler while he continued to look at Amélie.

To almost anyone, he would have appeared bored, but she knew better. He carefully masked the frustration she'd piqued while they danced.

"I think we are." Zidler kissed her hands. "Very impressive, my dear. We'll be in touch."

"I thank you very much, monsieur."

Just like that, the table tipped to Jasper. They both knew it, and the satisfaction that grew on his face gave her a chill. She wasn't certain if it was fear or something else.

Amélie made it onto the street before she felt a hand snake around her arm.

"Where's your bag?" Jasper asked as he signaled for his carriage.

"I didn't pack a bag. I thought it best I return home."

But when the carriage pulled up, Jasper held fast to

her as Louis opened the door.

Jasper indicated the interior. "I insist."

Amélie hesitated, looking first to Louis then to Jasper, who nodded.

When they sat in the roomy carriage, she sensed his penetrating gaze on her, and the space between them seemed to shrink. She was still warm from the audition and felt her body growing hotter still with anticipation. The carriage didn't stop on rue Ravignan. She hadn't imagined it would. Still, she pressed her face to the window as if somehow that would place her outside instead of in.

"Come here."

Again she hesitated. How was it she could feel so confident, so brave, so determined, when it came to virtually every other aspect of her life, yet with Jasper, a look, the subtle command in his voice, and something else intangible were all it took and she melted?

She looked at him. By the rigid lines of his jaw and body she knew he was tense. Still, he wore a beautiful mask for what was behind it.

"You don't plan on casting me."

"Why do you say that?"

"You're preparing me to be cut. You didn't like the song."

"Oh, I liked the song. 'Make me your mistress.' I loved it. Charles loved it. You sang it knowing we would."

She looked out the window again.

"It isn't up to me," he said. "Not entirely. Now come here." He patted the bench next to him. When she still didn't move, he said, "Would you rather sit beside me or kneel in front of me?"

Just the idea of it made her shudder with arousal. She closed her eyes and swallowed.

I can't keep doing this. He'll run over me. Worse, I'll lay down for him to do it.

"I don't think we should see each other anymore."

He leaned forward to catch her gaze. "You don't think that. Not even close. In fact, I think you want to see me so badly you're frightened of it."

They exchanged a knowing look.

"We want different things," she said.

"We want the exact same things." He sat beside her. "The only difference is I can admit it and you can't."

Jasper slid a hand around her nape and kissed her. Amélie tried to brace herself against it, but the determined play of his tongue over her lips made her soften and open. When she relaxed, he opened her cape and brushed a soft trail of wet kisses along her jaw and down her neck. The warmth of his breath, the smell and feel of him… Her head fell back, and she gripped his thigh, brushing his hard arousal.

"You do that to me," he said in a rough voice. He took her hand, wrapped it around his sex, and squeezed.

A hand slipped under her skirt and tugged on her bloomers. "You might as well be naked in these."

"Next time I will be, then."

"Perish the thought." He groped her sex. "This is mine. I'll not have anyone else seeing it."

He slid a finger into her heavy, engorged sex, and she cried out as she gripped his arm. He thrust two fingers in and out, then pulled out and grazed his nails lightly over her tingling outer lips.

"Oh, this pretty cunt is so wet. All for me. Isn't it?"

She was so aroused her body shook and her breasts grew tight. The weight of all her fears and the final futility of their relationship seemed to fade to a pinprick when compared to what she needed right then.

"Jasper."

"Is this mine?" He squeezed the tense little button above her sex, then two fingers pressed back inside.

"Please."

"No," he said in his teasing lilt. "That's not an answer."

"Please stop, or I'll come."

He held her face, and she opened her lust-lidded eyes. "Do you belong to Talac or me?"

"I belong to myself."

Jasper gave her a smile, both lecherous and pleased. "Tonight, then. Will you give yourself to me tonight?"

She couldn't say yes, and she couldn't say no. She was in agony.

The carriage came to a stop, and Jasper returned to his bench and fixed himself. "You're being very naughty tonight, sweet girl."

Amélie sat in a plush, high-back chair clad only in her bloomers. Her wrists were bound near the back of her neck, thrusting her breasts up. Her legs were slung wide over the arms of the chair and bound by the ankles to the back lower legs.

Jasper had brought her into his apartment, stripped and bound her like this, caressed and licked and played until she was on the edge of her release, then walked away.

Now he strolled back in with a taunting grin on his face.

"How are you doing?"

"Fine. This is a very comfortable chair. I could sit here like this all night." His third time returning, she'd likely been there an hour or more.

"Mm, good." He pressed light kisses along her collarbone and around the outside of a breast along her ribcage. "You may."

It tickled, and she squirmed.

He threaded fingers through her hair, massaging her scalp. She moaned. "You're so defiant. It boils my blood."

He produced a pair of scissors and snipped once in the air. Then he crouched between her legs. "What. Are. These?" He snapped her bloomers.

"Bloo. Mers," she mimicked, then winked.

He cupped her face. "Oh, sweetheart," he whispered, looking and breathing as if in awe, "you're going to get it." Then he returned her wink.

Pulling her bloomers away from her legs, he cut up and up, first one leg, then the next and through the waistband.

"What are you doing? I need those."

"For all your cancan dancing at the washhouse? Lift your bottom."

She did, and he pulled the decimated bloomers from her. He tied one, then two, then three strips around her eyes until she couldn't see, then she heard him walk away.

"Jasper?"

Met with silence, she sighed.

From the lighting in the room to her clothing and hair, if she was bound or free, what she could see and hear and feel, the delicate balance of pain and pleasure—he seemed to take great pleasure in manipulating every tiny detail of their time together. He controlled her with the most magical sleight of hand. Because never in her life had she wanted to be controlled. And yet in that dark, naked, and raw place that didn't seem to exist except when they were together, she wanted to be controlled by *him*. It was as if she'd never really known arousal—overripe and so sweet—until she'd given herself to Jasper Degrailly.

It was so unnerving because it made her feel weak and wanton in a world that naturally assumed she was. She'd always hated that assumption. Railed against it in her moving to Paris, in her singing, in loving Aubrey and in leaving him. With both hands, she'd been grasping at what little power and control she had, and with Jasper, she gave it away.

Poof.

He made her a puddle on the floor. And she wanted it.

"Jasper?"

"I promised there'd be dessert," he said when he finally returned.

"Did you make it yourself just now?"

He *tsk*ed. "I'm shaking my head at you. Amélie, Amélie, Amélie."

"Jasper, Jasper, Jasper."

"Shall we get started, then? You seem to be itching for a good thrashing. And I'm just game enough to give you one."

"Why do you like this?" she asked. Perhaps the blindfold made her fearless. She could finally ask a question she worried made her look small. But at times like these, it seemed the only thing she wanted to know.

"'This'?" he asked.

"You know what I mean."

"I do. It's only that I think you're the first person to ever ask me without condemnation at the heart of it." He paused, then chortled. "It isn't that I'm damaged somehow. I'm not depraved or a brute."

"I didn't think that."

"Yes, you did. Most everyone does."

He was right—she had.

"It's a tedious story," he continued. "I won't bore you with it."

"Tell me. Please. I want to know."

"One day I may. Now open your mouth."

She did.

"Bite down."

"Are you going to remove a bullet?"

She felt his face an inch from hers, his fingertips skimming over her lips. "I love that wise mouth. Now bite down."

She bit into a type of stiff leather rod. "What is it?" she mumbled around it.

"Patience, little one."

Amélie flinched. Looking many a man in the eye since she'd achieved her full height at sixteen, she hadn't been referred to as *little* in nearly a decade. If anything, there were taunts about her ungainly height. Always by men and women who were small. Still, they hurt.

"You are little to me," he whispered as if he knew exactly where her thoughts had strayed.

The heated blush of gratefulness rushed into her cheeks.

She felt the pulse of his presence nearby, but he made no sound. As time stretched, she could feel his perusal as well as any hands or mouth on her skin. More so because her body, the cool bumps on her skin, seemed to reach for him.

She tried to remain still. But the effort made her so keenly aware of her body that she couldn't help but shift and squirm. Her fingers moved. Her toes.

"Easy," he purred. "Just relax."

Occasionally she caught the soft clink of silver on fine porcelain. Suddenly his gentle hand caressed a breast.

"Mm, you're doing so well. Very good." He pressed a light kiss to her breast. "Are you comfortable still? Nod once for yes."

She nodded once.

"Good."

He pulled the rod from her mouth, ran the back of his hand down her cheek, and kissed her, his tongue sliding in so that she tasted sweet cream. As he did this, he played with her nipples, pinching and pulling, running over them up and down with his fingers until they felt hard and tight. He pressed a tender kiss to each as he slid a finger into her engorged sex, and she moaned.

"Mm, nice. You're like a sunflower that leans toward my sunlight, do you know that? I should buy you some yellow. Yes, I think so. Some warm, pretty yellow." He took a deep breath and exhaled. "Are you ready? Nod once for yes."

She nodded once.

Then she heard a whistle slice through the air, heard a smack, then immediately felt a sharp sting on a nipple so jarring she tensed and cried out.

"Shh, Amélie. Not a sound. I know you can do it."

She bit her lip and whimpered.

A leather keeper, varying in no particular rhythm or intensity, smacked between her breasts. It stung, and she curled into herself as much as she could, but her bonds left little room to move. Ten stinging smacks, then suddenly a hand so tender she flinched.

"Easy." He brushed over one breast, then the other. "It's all right."

When the keeper smacked again, she was confused. Twelve strikes this time, then more caressing. After a round of eight more, she heard the riding crop clatter to the floor and saw her blindfold removed.

Jasper crouched before her, peering up at her, studying her with some intensity while he dragged his thumbs over her tingling nipples.

"Did that hurt?"

She hesitated, then nodded.

"What was that? I couldn't hear you."

"Yes. At first."

"I'm so sorry, Amélie," he said in the low and lilting honey tone he used when he wasn't sorry. He pressed a tender kiss to each nipple, rubbing gently, licking, suckling. He seemed to pull a line that went straight to her core. Then he pressed a finger into her full and wet sex.

"What's this?" Slowly he pumped his finger in and out.

"You know," she bit plaintively.

"Yes." He untied her.

He slid his hands along her inner thighs, directing without words that she keep them right where they were, slung wide over the plush arms. But her hands he brought to her sex.

"Touch yourself."

She slid two fingers around her nerve that felt three times its size and squeezed. She moaned and relaxed, closing her eyes as she squeezed and swirled around it. Pressing two fingers deep inside her core, she pushed up and up, closer and closer. That she did it at Jasper's direction, *for him*, made the sweet edge of the pleasure even sweeter.

Then she felt the warmth of his breath, looked down and saw him a mere inch from her sex, his eyes wide in the soft light of the darkened room.

"Are you getting close?"

"Yes."

"Good girl. Now get closer still without going over."

Instinctively she shook her head. "I'm almost there."

"No. You're close, but you're not quite there."

"I think I know my own body."

He looked into her eyes sharply, almost derisively. "But not quite as well as I do. Isn't that right?"

She wanted to say no, but she knew good and well he was right.

"I-I'm there. I'm going to come."

Jasper just stared at her, not a flinch or a sound.

"I'm going to come, Jasper. I am."

But the more frantic she sounded, the more ridiculous it was. Because, of course, she wouldn't come until he said. She'd given him that right alongside him taking it. It was so wrong yet somehow natural. She hated it and didn't question it.

"Jasper."

He pulled her hands from her sex and stood. Threading his fingers through her hair, he held her still while he opened his trousers and pulled her to his cock. When she took him deep in her mouth, he groaned and widened his stance, and she moaned, licking from base to tip.

"Ah, you're so good at this."

"Mm." She loved driving him crazy like this. With his cock in her mouth, for these small moments, *she* was in control of *his* pleasure. And she *was* good at it.

Without conscious thought, she slid a hand to her dripping core and began to work herself right alongside him. But he slapped her hand away.

"No. It's my turn, you hungry girl." There was the slightest hint of breathiness in his dark tone. He was close.

Just as she felt his cock getting impossibly bigger in her mouth, he pulled out and picked her up, throwing her down on the bed. Then he breathed warmly and wetly on her core and began pressing kisses, far too softly, all around her sex. So close to where she wanted him to be and not nearly close enough.

He licked down the crease where her leg met her sex and just alongside the outside of her swollen lips.

"God, Jasper, please."

She shook as she begged and grabbed his head to move him where she needed him. But he wouldn't budge.

"Lift your bottom."

She did, and he pushed her hands under her cheeks.

"Hold on right there, and don't you dare think about moving them, or I'll tie you to the bed and leave you there while I go to the club for a drink."

She whimpered. "Please."

"Shh. I know." He returned to her sex, one finger finally pushing slowly inside as she moaned.

Her body shook with the strain, and she rolled her head back and forth as one finger became two and his tongue finally licked her nerve.

"Oh, God."

When he pulled away, she grabbed for him. "No, please." After shedding his clothes, he took her hands in one of his, crawled up her body, and finally slid his cock slowly inside her.

"I'm going to come."

"No. Wait for me." He thrust hard, then harder and harder. "I know you can do it."

"No. I can't. I need to come. Please let me come."

"Almost there."

And she knew he could come just then or pull away and darn a pair of socks. That was the unreal nature of his exquisite control. Desperately she pulled back from the precipice, her toe on the edge, until finally, mercifully, he said it:

"Come."

They crashed over the edge together. Christ, was there anything more beautiful than that death?

20

$\mathcal{S}$unday afternoon Jasper and Amélie rode in his carriage.

"Where are we going?" she asked, peering out the window.

"You'll see."

She looked at him and furrowed her brow. "Why do you look so satisfied? Like the cat who stole the cream."

He smiled in that sly way that revealed nothing.

If Jasper looked satisfied, it was only because he was. Amélie was real. A woman of such substance beyond her beauty: the strength she showed to beat back against the world that would crush her, her remarkable talent, and though her mind was not ready to acknowledge it, the way her body leaned so exquisitely toward submission in the bedroom. She was so real as to be unreal, as if God had crafted his perfect woman. Yet he certainly wasn't worthy of it.

The crowded Paris center opened up to the pastoral

eastern edge of the city. Soon enough they rode up to a hôtel particulier of buff stone under a slate-gray mansard. But instead of stopping at the front entryway courtyard, the carriage wended around toward the stables.

"What are we doing?"

"You can't guess by now?"

She wore the black riding habit, matching top hat, and blush stock he'd presented her to wear.

"I think I can. I only wonder why it seems we're stealing onto this estate when we might have made our presence known properly."

"We might have done that. But this is my sister's home, and she understands I don't want to put them out."

"You mean discretion."

"Exactly. My parents' estate isn't far from here. One word and they would be here to greet us when we returned from our ride, and I'm not ready to scare you off just yet."

"I don't frighten easily."

"Good." The door to the carriage opened, and they climbed out. "Just remember you said that when one day you meet them."

When they entered the stable, Amélie's eyes flew wide and her mouth fell open. "This is your sister's? A stable fit for Louis XIV."

It *was* grand. Jasper took a moment to consider it with fresh eyes—the vaulted brick-barreled ceiling, an unending row of deep mahogany stalls and iron fixtures, and freshly swept cobblestone floors.

"Thank you, mademoiselle," Marie-Louise said, walking toward them. His oldest sister was five years his senior, but somehow she held on to the youth she'd once spent recklessly.

After Jasper introduced them, Marie-Louise appraised Amélie skeptically. Then she showed them to a groom who saddled two thoroughbreds, a large black nearly seventeen hands tall and a leaner bay at fifteen.

Amélie climbed onto the bay with an ease that belied her station, and Jasper couldn't help but shake his head. Marie-Louise walked with them out to the paddock.

"I trust I won't be seeing you when you return."

"Likely not," Jasper replied.

"It was nice to meet you, mademoiselle," Marie-Louise said, lifting a measured smile to Amélie. "Perhaps we'll see you again soon."

"Perhaps. And thank you for the generous use of your stable, madame. It was a pleasure to meet you."

They cantered for a while. Amélie's face was filled with wonder, her smile an easy one. She sat the bay with a facility and grace that shouldn't have surprised Jasper.

"You're a natural, Amélie." He reined into a walk beside her.

She looked at him almost absently, then pulled a tendril of hair from her lip. "I am not. And it's no false modesty, I assure you."

"How did you come to it?"

She slowed some, and her eyes grew distant. "My father was in the cavalry. He used to say he sat a horse better than he did anything else. But that wasn't true. He loved my maman and me well."

She hurried on as her voice grew tremulous.

"He put me on a horse before I was out of napkins, and I was terrified. She was so big and powerful and unwieldy I couldn't see her beauty. But he wrapped his sturdy arms around me, and all my trembling stopped. I'd never felt so safe in all my life. And so loved."

She sniffed and wiped at an eye, then took a big breath and turned back to him with a sparkling smile.

"Race you to the break in the trees."

Then she slapped her horse and took off.

Jasper was so shocked at the turn—she'd felt, finally, like a bird in his hand, only to slip from his grasp—that he sat momentarily stunned. His heart in his throat with terror, he kicked his heels and sent his horse after her. He could feel the stallion move fluidly beneath him; a gentle knee was all he needed. So, he bent into Fitz Roy and said, "You can take her, boy."

His blood coursed through his body with the terrible adrenaline of fear. But he felt like he hovered out of his body. In his mind, he was at her horse, taking the reins, cursing and spitting and making colorful promises about her colorful backside. All the while, he scanned her path. The bay knew the way, but she didn't. No matter how deft, anything could happen, and at her speed… He cringed to think of it and whispered, "Come on, come on, come on."

Finally, she shot through the tree break, slowed, and turned with a triumphant smile.

"I won," she called even as he slowed and jumped off his black.

"Get down. Right now, Amélie."

"Are you a poor loser?" Chuckling, she dismounted the bay.

Without thought, he bent into her, throwing her over his shoulder. He landed a hard smack on her bottom as he strode with purpose, trying desperately to cool his anger.

"Ow! That really hurt."

"You could have been thrown and hurt or worse."

"But I wasn't. So, let me down. Where are you taking me? My hat!"

He glanced back to see her top hat fall behind them, but he kept walking.

"How much farther? This hurts."

Finally, he laid her down in a field of lavender just beginning to bloom. Her mouth fell open, and she gasped as her hair came loose from her bun.

"The smell."

Amélie lay in her own world, completely oblivious to his anger that still simmered. All the while, he took deep breaths until he felt her hand on his arm.

"Are you so upset?"

"You're skilled on a horse, but you don't know this countryside. A subtle dip in the turf and…" He couldn't finish.

She sat up and brushed a gloved hand over his brow, her eyes flitting all over his face. Then she rested her head on his shoulder. "You really were alarmed."

Jasper pressed her back into the bed of lavender, her sable hair and black habit stark against the cool and soft flowers and pale green stems. For a long moment, he simply looked at her, her flushed cheeks, furrowed brow, and worried chocolate eyes.

He might've lost her. Suddenly he knew he didn't want to lose her. Ever. He never wanted to let her go. His heart beat faster, but it wasn't fear.

When she opened her mouth, he kissed her. It wasn't small or tender. He propped his arms beside her head, pressed his body into hers, and slid his tongue in deep.

For some minutes, his tongue mimicked the grinding he did with his cock. He felt overcome with a heady rush of emotions—the intimacy he'd felt during her story, the fear during the race, the cold sluice of relief at the race's end, the heat of anger when he spanked her, and finally the vulnerability of his realization. Now she was under him, there was only flaring desire.

He slid a hand, burrowing through the layers of her underthings, to her wet sex and pushed two fingers deep inside. She moaned.

Opening his trousers, he pulled out his cock and thrust inside her with no warning.

"Jasper."

She was wet but not completely ready. And so damn tight. He couldn't wait. He had to be buried inside her. He fucked her as if he were still running that race, still hoping to overtake and punish her. He wanted desperately to bind her to him so there would be no her without him. For long moments, he thrust deeper and deeper, but it wasn't enough.

"Put your legs around me."

She immediately obeyed like the good girl she was, and he wiped her wild hair from her brow. "Look at me." She did, just as he thrust a finger deep into her mouth. "Get that wet. Nice and wet." He pulsed his finger in her mouth to the same rhythm he fucked her with his cock, then pulled it out. "There you go." He brought his finger to her bottom. "Eyes on me." Then he slid it in.

She tensed and gripped his cock so hard, he nearly came right then. Her breath was high and tight, and her eyes were wide.

"Relax. Easy now. Can you feel me inside you?" He flexed his cock and wiggled his finger.

"Yes."

"Good. Because from now on, I want you to feel me everywhere inside you." Then he thrust his tongue into her mouth and fucked her hard for long minutes, all the while feeling his release tingling in his balls, until they came.

"Are you all right?" he asked when he finally pulled away from her.

"Fine."

"I didn't think... I... Are you certain?" He held her cheek and studied her. Skin glistening and cheeks flushed, lips rosy and plump from being kissed, hair tangled in the lavender, Jasper had never seen her more beautiful. Maybe he had never seen a more beautiful sight.

"I'm fine. Better than fine. Believe me." She gave him a soft smile of reassurance.

He fell back down, resting his head on her belly. She combed lulling fingertips through his hair. At length they lay there, the low hum of summer life buzzing around them and cotton-ball clouds drifting overhead.

Then she began to sing—"Au clair de la lune." He couldn't remember the last time he'd heard that lullaby. Perhaps thirty years ago. The last words he heard before he drifted off to sleep:

"Open your door to me
For the love of God..."

21

On Friday, the true heat of the summer settled over Paris. To make matters worse, in the washhouse, it was ironing day. Four irons for four hands thudded dully against linen while four more waited on the stove.

Amélie listed in the heat. Like the rest of the women, she stood barefoot, dressed only in her chemise, knickers, and corset. The doors and windows were flung wide to catch any breeze. Still, ash from the constantly burning firewood floated in the air, and it held a sour crispness that seared her lungs and made her eyes water.

On these particularly hot days, where the conditions outside met the same inside, wine vendors rolled their carts along the street, ready to offer the ladies a drink. And the men, too, who hovered nearby for just a glimpse of a glistening and scantily-clad laundress.

So, when Amélie heard a man's muffled voice at the door, it barely registered in her mind until Madame

Pelletier appeared at the door to the ironing room.

"Amélie, there's a man here who wishes a word with you."

Amélie blinked and rubbed her eyes. "A man?"

Jasper would have called first, and she'd only said goodbye to him the night before. The other women tittered, and Madame Pelletier shot them a quelling look.

"Not Monsieur Degrailly. Come on. Be quick about it," she said when Amélie was slow to set her iron down. "And you might want to grab a shawl and some shoes. You look like something the cat coughed up."

"Thank you, madame," Amélie said sarcastically.

"You're welcome, dear," the laundry mistress returned archly.

Amélie found Aubrey in a smart suit tailored to fit and his chestnut hair tamed as if he'd taken a comb through it.

"Aubrey." He looked so handsome and debonair her hands flew to her hair, smoothing wayward strands, and she wrapped her shawl tighter.

He smiled softly. It was almost tentative, even nervous. "Amélie."

Madame Pelletier narrowed her beady eyes at them. "She's not off until five. You've got ten minutes." She turned away mumbling. "Five," she scoffed. "A waste of good hours is what that is."

Aubrey led the way out onto the busy street, and she sucked in a fresh breath.

"You told me to stay away, and I've honored that. But—"

"It's fine." She touched his arm. "Really. Is everything all right? With Daan?"

"Everything's fine."

A wine vendor offered them each a glass of burgundy, and Aubrey reached for his wallet, but she waved it away. "I don't have much time."

"Right." He stopped and looked at the wine vendor, at passersby, at anyone but Amélie. Finally, his eyes climbed to hers. "Would you have dinner with me?"

She shook her head. "I don't think—"

"I know you're still seeing him. It's not about that. Well, not entirely, that is. I have some news, and I'd like to talk with you about it. At length, if possible." When she hesitated, he said, "Just a friendly dinner for now."

"I have another hour of work. Then I need to freshen up."

"I'll come back."

Two hours later, Amélie sat woodenly at dinner with Aubrey. Never had she felt so uncomfortable with him. He knew she was still seeing Jasper, but that didn't mean very much. *For now* still ran through her mind. But she forced a smile when he seemed so illuminated by something.

"You look… good," he said.

"So do you. I never thought I'd see you looking so bourgeois."

He put a dramatic hand to his chest and smiled proudly. "I hope I haven't sold out for too little."

"Have you sold out?" she asked after the waitress took their order.

"I don't think so." He leaned toward her. "But I'm curious to hear what you think. After all, you know me better than anyone." He paused. "I've accepted a commission, and you were the first person I thought of."

"What is it?"

"Well, for lack of a better word, they'll essentially be advertisements. Posters. For the dance hall reopening this fall."

"On de Clichy?"

"The very same. The owner commissioned me to do a series of posters. Dancing girls and such. I know it seems like a step backward for me, but it doesn't feel that way. His vision for the place—"

"His?" Amélie's mind raced. Why would Jasper commission Aubrey for this? It didn't make any sense.

"Monsieur Zidler."

"Zidler." She exhaled a breath she hadn't realized she'd been holding. "I just auditioned for him."

"You did?" He squeezed her hand excitedly. "You didn't tell me you were going to audition. How did it go?"

"I don't know. Fine, I think. It was only this Friday last, and I haven't heard anything yet."

"No. No. Of course you haven't. Not yet. He's finalizing his list as we speak. But soon, I should think."

"Right." She took a large gulp of her wine.

"This is even better. Because he's certain to choose you. He'd be a fool not to. And I… Well, hear me out before you say no. I was wondering—well, hoping—you wouldn't mind being my muse for these posters."

She shook her head. "I told you—"

"I know what you've said." He scooted his chair closer to her and took her hands. "I know. Believe me"—he sighed—"I'm trying to get past it because there couldn't be anyone who embodies my style the way you do. But this is different."

"How? It doesn't seem any different to me. Do you think I like working in that laundry? It's terrible. I hate it. But I don't want to drop my dress in every atelier in Montmartre. You know that. And if I'm exclusively your figure model, then I might as well be kept again."

"I would keep myself, Aubrey. And I will. Soon. When I'm cast, I'll run so fast from that washhouse it won't even remain in my memory."

"If you feel like you need to stay in the washhouse for now, you can. I spoke with the madame. She told me your hours have been reduced. I know you have time in the evenings and when the week ends. I could pay you handsomely, and you wouldn't have to drop your dress. Not for me or anyone. Best of all, you could be the face of the Moulin Rouge. Isn't that what you want?"

It *was* different because it was exactly what Amélie wanted. Another proper source of income. She wouldn't be naked, she wouldn't be Aubrey's, and she wouldn't be kept. It was too difficult for her to refuse, and he knew it. Yet Jasper would certainly protest. At devoting any of her meager free time to someone else. Worse, that someone else would be her ex who'd made it clear he wanted her back.

"I need to think about it."

"Of course. Yes. Take some time. But not too much time. He

wants the posters up by the end of the summer."

"He. Not *they?*"

"Pardon?"

"Nothing."

22

hat Sunday, Jasper and Amélie strolled arm in arm through the leafy lanes of Saint-Cloud. The air hung so warm and ripe it seemed to hum with its own electric life. But they were shrouded from the searing sun by canopies of majestic oak and chestnut trees and towering cones of yew trees standing guard over the former royal residence.

"I'd no idea they still held festivals here," Jasper said.

"I'm sure they're not as grand as when Monsieur presided over the château. But these grounds beg for a fair, don't you think? I suppose it was only natural the people started them up again."

The Château de Saint-Cloud was once a decadent retreat for the Bourbon kings. Le Fauborg had ridden brilliantly decorated boats down the Seine to enjoy concerts or plays or masquerades, any excuse for an elaborate fête. A favorite of Marie Antoinette and Napoleon, sadly it was occupied, then torched by Prussian forces in 1871. Now its once-great château lay abandoned.

Yet amidst the wandering orangerie and rose gardens of the ruined royal château, there now stood a country fair. Food stands and wine wagons. Challenges such as smashing plaster figures with clay pellets and amusements such as donkey rides. There were conjurers and jugglers and peepshows. Slippery-handed children wielding frogs gave chase to others who squealed and dashed off. More children blew into mirlitons while fathers in their frock coats and mothers in red-ribboned bonnets stared after them with glassy eyes and tired smiles.

Jasper took it all in with some confusion. He'd proposed a day at the Exposition Universelle, promising all sorts of never-before-seen delights. He'd cajoled and pressed and all but insisted. Yet in the end, Amélie had been relentless, finally convincing him it was her turn to decide how they would pass their Sunday. Saint-Cloud's garden fairs, she stressed, were where bohemian Paris spent its Sundays.

But he saw scant little evidence of that. Rather it seemed the very picture of bourgeois French life. It made him wonder if there wasn't an earnest longing somewhere in Amélie's heart for just that. Worse, it made him wonder if there wasn't a longing in his own heart for that.

Then he caught the sweet smells of almond and sugar and vanilla as they approached a macaron stand. Row upon row of cream-filled cookies in yellows and pinks, bright blues and creamy whites, sat handsomely displayed at just the right height for a child's eyes. A waiflike boy of perhaps seven pleaded and pointed and yanked on his mother's skirt while she shook her head with implacable firmness.

Jasper paused. The boy was gaunt and looked like he hadn't had a decent meal in some time, let alone a sweet treat.

He approached the stand.

"Two bags, please."

The baker loaded the brown bags, then proudly handed them over when Jasper gave him his sous.

"I'd no idea you had such an affinity for macarons," Amélie said.

"I don't," Jasper replied even as he opened a bag and popped a cookie in his mouth.

At his offer to share, she shook her head. Then he strode over to the boy and his mother.

"Would you care for these?"

"No, thank you, monsieur. We couldn't possibly take them."

Red-faced, the boy beamed and bounced, pleading for his mother to reconsider.

"Pity," Jasper said. "It seems my lady doesn't care for them. And now I find I'm embarrassed. You'd be doing me a great favor if you would consent to take them."

The woman exhaled and gave Jasper a cynical look, then she smiled.

"I thank you, monsieur. You're too kind." She accepted the bags and handed one macaron to her son. "Auguste, what do you say to the man?"

"I thank you, monsieur," he mumbled through a mouthful of macaron with a bright smile in his eyes. "Thank you very much."

When Jasper returned to Amélie, she said, "If you'd simply bought them for her, she wouldn't have accepted them."

"The working poor have their pride. Do they not?"

"Especially the working poor."

Jasper replied with a soft nod.

"You're kind."

Her voice held a note. He couldn't tell if it was an indictment or a compliment.

"Are you surprised?"

After a pause, she replied, "No."

A short time later, they stopped at an archery stand. At the conductor's urging, Amélie picked up an arrow and bow and nocked it.

"Can you hit your mark?" Amélie taunted Jasper.

"Can you?"

With fluid grace, she took a stance, narrowed her gaze, and let go. The arrow cleaved cleanly through the air, piercing the bullseye with a dull thunk.

"Ha!" she shouted with childlike glee. "I'm awful at archery."

Shamelessly she crowed and jostled Jasper even as he picked up his own bow and arrow. He took his stance, determined to show her, then nocked his bow and narrowed his gaze.

"Amélie!"

"How good to see you!"

At that voice and the sounds of hugging and kissing, Jasper flinched and let go. The arrow sailed embarrassingly wide.

Aubrey whistled. "You missed your mark there, Degrailly."

Jasper glanced at Aubrey and a man he didn't recognize. A man who seemed entirely too familiar with Amélie. Grinding his teeth, Jasper handed the bow back to the conductor with an accusing glare, as if the poor man were responsible for Jasper's own inadequacies.

After Aubrey introduced his friend to Jasper, he said, "I never fancied I'd find you here, Degrailly."

"I was just thinking the same."

"Oh? Amélie and I spent many happy Sundays here, didn't we?"

Aubrey looked as if he might lace an arm around her waist until Amélie moved to stand next to Jasper. But that small triumph wasn't enough to arrest the humiliation growing inside.

Why did she bring me here? Surely it wasn't to throw her former lover in my face. Did she know he'd be here?

Jasper scrutinized the pair of them—the way they held their bodies around each other, how they looked at one another or didn't. Were they hiding something? He knew, as men know other men, that Aubrey wanted her back. And no matter what Amélie had said, *could* say, Jasper wondered if she didn't still hold a tenderness for the artist. After all, Jasper could admit the man was not unhandsome. He wore the mantle of his success with an allure that could have drawn most women. And she had loved him once. Jasper knew exactly what it was to love beyond all sense. Despite every effort or intention, to be drawn inexorably back to that one love.

Just then he realized how absent that pull was. For the first time in so many years, since meeting Joselin all those years ago in school. Here, now, he felt himself free. And desperate to win someone else. Amélie's heart, her hand, every piece of her. It was the most bewildering and exhilarating and terrifying feeling he could remember.

Aubrey and Amélie and their friend Didi shared a laugh about something. Conductors called out, enticing fairgoers to play and eat. And children screamed in delight. But it all faded in the light of Jasper's hope and fear. Could it truly be possible he was finally falling out of love with Joselin and falling in love with Amélie?

"When will you decide?" Still stunned, Jasper didn't respond, and Aubrey tried again. "Degrailly. When will you decide?"

"Pardon me?"

"On your cast for the Moulin Rouge. Much as it pains me to say, you'll find no one better than Amélie."

"Ah, yes. Monsieur Zidler will be deciding in these next few weeks."

"You have no say?"

"On these matters, I defer to my partner. He has a better sense for the entertainment."

"For what do you have a better sense, monsieur?"

Jasper smiled tightly. He knew the answer he wanted to say, the first one that always came to mind. But much as it is a talent, and it is a talent to grow money, it would be the last thing to silence the artist. And more than anything, he wanted to silence the man and move on.

"Value. I know a precious thing when I see it. When I see it, I go after it. And when I have it, I don't let it go. Now if you'll excuse us. Good day to you, messieurs." He threaded his arm through Amélie's and walked on.

Trying desperately to calm his rioting emotions, Jasper walked steadily down the busy lanes. He could sense Amélie, even with her long legs, hustling to keep up, but he didn't care. He would get as far away from Aubrey Talac as he could while he still had some control.

"Where are we going?" she asked.

Jasper took longer and longer strides until all the people and noises of the fair had faded into the distance. Finally, he slowed when he came to the razed château.

Blackened and crumbling and open to the elements, at first glance it appeared a sad and stripped skeleton of a once-great house. Still, greenery burst through gaping windows and climbed up fading murals while tall grasses flowered sweetly amongst the rubble. It remained an eerily determined beauty despite the ugly scars.

"Will they tear it down?" Amélie asked.

"I think so."

After a pause, she said, "Pity."

"Why do you say that? It's merely an ugly reminder of what's been lost. Better to tear it down. Get rid of it altogether."

"So the people can forget?"

"The people, it seems, have long memories for things as they never were. Better to move on. Newer is better. Come."

Jasper threaded his fingers through hers and dragged her to a trellis gazebo all but covered in climbing vines. Weaving them through an archway, he pulled her in behind him, then looked at her squarely.

"I'd no idea he'd be here," she said, sensing the mire of his thoughts.

"Didn't you?"

"Of course not. It was merely by chance. Yes, we used to come here. But not every Sunday. Hardly. Once, maybe twice a summer."

When he said nothing, she continued.

"I love the grounds. Even the sad château. And all the people and amusements. It always seemed like a good place. Especially for people who struggle. To have a day, a special place that once belonged only to the rich, where we can set aside our cares and feel free. I guess it was too much for me to expect you'd understand."

"Do you still love him?"

"No."

Amélie had paused, only for a second, but that was enough. Jasper felt a small kernel of pain in his chest.

"Tell me the truth."

She took a long, deep breath and sighed.

"He was my first love, Jasper. Sometimes I wonder if I'll always love him. Just as you'll always love Madame Travers. You and I, we're not meant to love as others do."

The pain in his chest bloomed.

"You're right."

Vibrating with what exactly, he wasn't sure, slowly Jasper leaned into Amélie. But when she moved her lips to his, he kissed the corner of her mouth instead. They stood only a hair apart. The slightest nudge and he would be pressed to her. Still he held back. Breathing the heady citrus-and-musk scent unique to her. Watching a vein on her neck pulse. Her tongue gliding over her lower lip. Chest rising and falling under the ruffled blueberry bodice.

In the distance he could hear children shriek and laugh, the rising din of the fair's conductors calling out, a triumphant shout of a winner. Yet in this earthy, vine-shrouded gazebo they were in their own world.

"Turn around."

Her eyes went wide, and her mouth moved as if to question him. Then a blush spread across her cheeks and chest, and she did as he asked.

His hands skated down her arms until his fingers laced through hers. He dragged a wet line of kisses along her nape and up to her ear. Licked and suckled the lobe leisurely as her breath hitched.

"What are you doing?"

"Keep a lookout."

"Not here."

"Yes here."

She tried to turn around, but he held fast to her hands.

"We're in the middle of the fair," she hissed. "Anyone can stroll by. Families. Children, Jasper."

"Then you'd better be quiet."

He urged her forward and wrapped her fingers around a viny arch.

"Don't let go. Whatever I do."

"What are you going to do?" There was panic in her voice.

Jasper spared a final glance through the vines toward the fair. In truth, they were a good distance away from the crowds, and though the trellis gazebo might once have been open to exposure, the tangle of weeds and crawling vines meant they were all but hidden unless one was deliberately searching through them.

When he lifted her skirt, Amélie gasped and tried to pull it back down. "No!"

Jasper merely put her hands back on the trellis and held her tight. "Shh. Quiet now and keep your hands here, or I'll bind and gag you."

He felt her breath coming in jagged bursts when he bent again to lift her skirt. "Tell me how you don't want me. How you don't want this."

"Not like this," she whispered breathily.

When he slid fingers into her knickers and found her wet sex, he *tsk*ed, and she whimpered.

"No? I think this may be the wettest cunny I've ever felt. I think you want it exactly like this."

Deliberately teasing, he dragged his fingernails lightly over her sex, up and down, carefully avoiding the button of nerves on top. At length he did this, feeling her shake and gasp, hearing her mewl and whimper. She was torturing him. The least he could do was torture her back.

He felt heady with his control when he knelt and breathed her in.

"No," she said in a strangled whisper.

"Shh. I want a taste."

With the same deliberate teasing as he'd done with his fingers, he now dragged up and down and delved lightly inside with his tongue. All the while, she breathed and sagged and whined. For as close as he got, and he made certain to get very close, never did he touch those nerves that held the secret to her release.

"Please," she finally managed.

"So polite, my sweet girl." He pulled back and tenderly caressed and kissed her bottom. "What do you want?"

"Let me come, please, monsieur."

"Do you think you've earned it?" he asked, pressing a kiss to her ear and opening his trousers.

"Yes."

"I don't think so."

With that, he thrust inside her, and she squeaked trying to strangle her cry. He clapped a hand over her mouth and began to fuck her, thrusting hard and deep, punishing her like she was punishing him.

For long minutes, he pounded mercilessly inside her. But none of it arrested his anger and humiliation, his deep longing for her that never seemed to abate.

A child ran past the gazebo, and he stilled, his heart pounding as hard as his cock. Another child and still another followed, taunting and shouting and laughing. Then a mother called out.

"Remy! Jules! Eddie! Don't wander so far. Get back here."

With each word, the woman sounded closer and closer, and Amélie trembled. Soon there were sounds of boys racing past the gazebo in the other direction and fading again into the distance.

Somehow the abrupt stop at the crest of his release and the heightened fear of being discovered had made him harder. When Jasper drove inside Amélie again, it didn't take much to bring him to the edge.

Hastily he pulled out. "On your knees."

She obeyed like the perfect submissive she was and took him in her mouth. Ten strokes was all it took, and she swallowed him down.

He combed his fingers through her hair as she cleaned him. "Good girl." She was rosy-cheeked and desperate.

When he put his cock back in his trousers, she stood with pleading in her eyes.

"Did you want something?"

"Yes, Monsieur Degrailly. And you know exactly what it is."

He wanted her so much, wanted to give her whatever she desired, but he wanted to hold on to his control more. As if somehow his manhood rested in that space.

He ran a hand through his hair. "Pity."

When he moved around her to the archway, she grabbed his hand.

"After all that, and now you're leaving me like this?"

"We don't always get what we want. Do we?"

She exhaled in a huff. Her cheeks, if possible, flooded with even more redness. "As soon as I have a moment alone, I'll see to myself."

Jasper held her cheek tenderly, tauntingly. "No, you won't."

Amélie stood gape-mouthed.

"You may not want to give me this." He put his hand over her heart. Then he cupped her sex and whispered, "But you need to give me this."

The very next day, Jasper sat in the Grand Café with Maxime Tasse. Paperwork, mostly ledgers, blanketed the table between their plates.

"What is this all about?" Max asked. When Jasper was slow to respond, he shook his head and sighed. Jasper's dearest friend since their days at university, he managed far more than Jasper's finances. "What does she want now?"

The honey-haired, blue-eyed charmer routinely wore a smile, except when faced with Joselin Travers's demands of his friend.

"This isn't about Jos," Jasper replied, fixing his gaze on his finger tracing around the lip of a glass.

"Oh? Good." Max sat up and began to gather his papers. "Then you can say no."

Jasper finally looked at Max and shook his head. "Tell me there's enough for me to renovate that apartment on Saint-Dominique."

"Are you moving?"

"It's not for me."

"Then no."

"Come on."

"What do you want with another apartment?"

Again feeling so embarrassed he couldn't meet his friend's gaze, he folded and refolded his napkin as he uttered, "I need to get her away from him. Out of Montmartre, at least."

"Who do you know in Montmartre?"

Jasper looked at Max, his mouth open to answer, but he could scarcely admit the truth to himself, let alone his friend.

"That singer you brought to the opera? Is she that talented in bed?"

"It's more than that. Much more."

"What are you saying? After all these years pining over Joselin, now you've lost your heart to a showgirl?"

"No… I don't know."

Later that afternoon, Jasper sat with Charles in his office.

"Aubrey Talac. That's the artist you commissioned to do the posters," Jasper said.

"Is there a problem?"

Jasper exhaled and scrubbed his hands down his face.

"We agreed we weren't going to use your ex-wife. A little too on the nose there. And anyway, she isn't really our style."

"This isn't about Joselin."

"What's it about, then? He was on a very small list of finalists we agreed upon. You told me to choose, and I chose." Without an explanation from Jasper, Charles continued, "Talac is a rising star, and everyone knows it. His stylized depiction of the female form is sensual, graceful, and very modern. The epitome of what we want. Isn't it? Sensual and modern? We must be avant-garde. With our shows. With our lights. Even with our posters. To have Talac painting them. It's a coup. And you know it."

"Isn't there anyone else on this list you like as much?"

"For the Moulin Rouge? Frankly, no. And anyway, it's done. I offered him the commission, and he's accepted it."

Jasper stared out the window. His private affairs were crowding into his business interests, and he couldn't see clearly for either of them. Charles was right. Talac was the perfect painter for their posters. And yet when he thought of the artist, he couldn't see the art. Only the man who wanted Amélie and would take her from him if given half a chance.

"What's going on with you these days?" Charles pressed. "First you arrange not one but two auditions for a girl who would be perfect for us, then tell me to shelve her."

"Are you going to cut her?"

"I don't want to, but you seem tortured by the prospect of me casting her. And despite my best attempts, I find I like you."

They exchanged bland smiles.

"I'm eager to cast her, but I haven't made up my mind. Honestly, we need her vocal range. Any halfway decent dancer can dance the cancan. But we need someone with her presence. She's a star. And, besides that, exquisite."

"She is," Jasper acknowledged tightly.

"She's not in the demimonde, and that's a very real problem."

"How big of a problem?"

"Less of one if she stood in the back as a chorus girl. But even if I put her there initially, I don't see her staying. Do you?"

"No."

"No. So it's a problem." After a pause, he asked, "Will she consider it? She didn't show any inclina—"

"No. She won't. And I won't allow it either."

Charles looked at him for a long moment, then sighed. "It seems you're doing a little bit more than dallying with this girl."

Jasper merely looked at him, unwilling to acknowledge anything.

"When do you leave for Deauville?" Charles asked.

"Are you trying to get rid of me?"

"Yes."

"I'm long overdue. The season ended more than a week ago, and my mother's chomping at the bit to see me there."

"'The season.' Right. I forget le gratin has its social calendar. Why don't you go? The sooner the better."

"And leave you here to make all the decisions?"

"Naturally."

They exchanged tight, amused smiles.

"This girl, whatever she is to you, is messing with your head, and that's messing with my baby." Charles sat forward and pressed a finger to Jasper's desk. "It must come off. It will. A partner, silent or otherwise, with his head in his cock will not fuck it up." He stood. "Go. I'll see you in September."

"I won't be gone that long."

"Perhaps you might find someone new to fix your attentions on so you can focus on the Moulin Rouge."

"We'll be in touch," Jasper said as they shook hands.

"Certainly."

"And you'll let me know what you decide on the final cast list before you tell anyone."

"I will."

Two nights later, Jasper lay naked and spent with Amélie in his arms.

"Tomorrow I need to go away for a while."

"Where are you going?" She turned to look at him.

"My family's summer home in Deauville. I need to make an appearance."

Her face fell into contemplation. "Your 'family's summer home in Deauville.'" She chortled. "You need to 'make an appearance.' Of course you do." She sounded incredulous and taunting.

"What?"

"Nothing. It's good. Better than good. Actually, it's perfect. I needed to take some time for myself. A break is just what we need."

"A break? I didn't mean that at all, darling. Though they're a pretty den of vipers, they're my family. I need to go. I go every year. It's expected of me, and expectations are very important in my set. I won't be gone long."

"No. It's fine. Really."

"I would be happy to bring you. I would love it. But you insist on staying and working at that shithouse."

She scowled at him, and he exhaled.

"I meant you insist on working." She seemed to need some reassurance, so he straddled her and slid his fingers through hers, pressing her hands down near her head. "I'm typically gone through the end of August. But I think I would miss you too much."

"Do you think so?" she taunted sarcastically.

He tipped his head and pretended to think. "I might."

She rolled her eyes.

"I planned on returning within a month." He kissed an ear and began sucking on the lobe.

"And don't forget your investments," she said.

"The Moulin Rouge."

"That, too, I suppose. When will he finalize the cast list?"

"He's close. I should think you'll know within the next few weeks."

"While you're away."

He nodded, and they looked at each other a long moment.

"You should go," she finally said. "Have a good time with your family."

"Your mother. In Rouen. Do you ever see her?"

"It's been more than a year. Since before I began singing at Le Chat. I can take the train on a Sunday. But it won't surprise you to know the madame hates it any time we're away."

"And your mother never gets down here?"

"No. She's suffered from prolonged bouts of melancholy ever since my father died. She was so cheery before. Now she's… unpredictable."

"You have something to occupy you while I'm gone?"

She paused—far too long, he thought—so he gently held her face and searched for the truth in her eyes.

"I worry about leaving you here with your friend gone."

"Go. Have a good time with your den-of-vipers family. Don't worry about me. I'm sure I can find something to amuse myself."

"Not as amusing as me."

"Never."

23

*O*nce again Amélie stood before the sweet stone-
and-brick house on Cortot, considering it with
trepidation. Before the door, she hesitated, poised
to knock, but couldn't quite bring herself to do it. She hadn't
told Jasper, and she knew why. Yet she wasn't doing anything
wrong. Unreasonably, he wouldn't see it that way.

After she knocked, the door opened, and Aubrey
stood before her as the rakish artist he was. Flowy linen
shirt and too-tight trousers, worn and paint-smudged.
Loved. His shoulder-length chestnut hair was down and
thrown wildly over to one side. His beard was unkempt
as if an afterthought. But she knew better. Everything
about Aubrey's appearance was deliberate.

His dark eyes lit warmly all over her, as if he were
imagining her in a different state.

"I was worried you might change your mind." She
shook her head, and he threw the door wide. "Come on in."

The attic was once again restored to an artist's

studio. The smell of turpentine clung to the air. But all Amélie could see was how it had looked when she'd been there last. She felt a pang in her chest. Had it only been a few weeks? She'd felt so wrung out by her grief during that week that when it was over, she'd moved on with a sense of finality that hadn't allowed more tears. Now she felt them burning her eyes and wiped furiously at the corners.

A hand slid around her waist as Aubrey dropped his chin on her shoulder. "You miss her."

She nodded. "I worry there are some days I don't think of her. And I don't know how that could be. It seems like a betrayal or something. Just to move on. How are you? How's he holding up?"

"I'm fine. Daan still seems to be in a daze sometimes. By the way, you're still not his favorite person. He's not around as much these days. I think he's seeing someone. But he won't tell me."

"That's probably good. That he's seeing someone."

They stood for another moment like that, too close.

"I'm so glad we're doing this. You have no idea." He pulled away to look at her. "Your bath is ready. I hope you don't mind—I used what you left behind."

In the bathroom, she stared at her things and smelled the fragrant rose salts steaming up from the water. That he kept them, the familiarity of it all, should have felt wrong, but it didn't.

"Is this all right?" he asked eagerly. She knew he was anxious to use whatever light he could for the day.

"It's fine. I won't be long."

Aubrey closed the door, and she considered the key, then turned it. When she slid into the tub, she slid easily back into her memories.

The sun fell just right, casting the room in a peachy-yellow light. She was sleepy, always so sleepy, it seemed, when she slid into the hot water. When they'd been together, they were always up half the night, talking and making love with the exuberance of new lovers who had endless things to talk about and endless touches to explore.

Aubrey sat in only his trousers, his tall and lean frame hunched over a sketch. His face furrowed in concentration as he bit his lip, his hand stabbing in great fluid strokes. He always sketched in a manic frenzy, as if by some compulsion he had to. He flicked a glance over his pad and winked.

With a great sigh, he dropped his pad and slunk to the tub. He dipped his charcoaled fingers in the water and bent to give her a kiss.

"I'm dirty," he said, his hands sliding down her belly to her sex.

She chuckled. "That isn't the soap."

When he pulled back, he glanced from her eyes to her lips and back. "How did I get so lucky?"

He'd been so tender in the beginning. So giving. It was dangerous to think back on it. Even in her memory, it held a rose-colored hue. Why had she bathed here? It had been a compromise. Aubrey wanted her to stay.

When she finally felt the washhouse sufficiently scrubbed from her body, she quickly got out and dried. In her reflection in the mirror, she saw her skin glowing from the salts she'd left behind and was glad she'd decided to bathe here. Then she looked all over for a robe and couldn't find one.

"Aubrey!" she called out the door. "A robe, please."

"Sorry," he said when he brought one, his eyes dancing quickly over her bare skin.

Returning to the attic, she saw her red damask, her sapphire silk, and her gold brocade gowns hanging over a changing screen. She felt unclean at the thought of wearing the red or sapphire for Aubrey.

"I prefer the gold brocade from Le Chat," Aubrey said, to which she immediately agreed. "How did you get the miser to part with it?"

"I promised he could dock my pay as insurance against any damage."

"Very clever. If you just get dressed, I thought I could sketch in some framework while your hair dries."

He was anxious. She couldn't remember him so excited to work. Never at this early morning hour. As she dressed, she wondered if it was the exposure of the posters or working with her that so compelled him. When she bustled her skirt, she decided it was the exposure.

After all, Aubrey had a love affair with himself that equaled the one he'd had with her.

She emerged from behind the screen to see him propped against a stool, a knee bent and a bare foot resting on a rung. He smiled softly. "This is right, you posing for me." He came to her, brushed her damp hair away from her face with tender, familiar fingers, and considered her face. "Do you think rouge is necessary? On your lips or cheeks?"

"I don't know. Do you?"

"How would you propose to put some color on those cheeks?"

She tipped her head and gave him a scolding look.

"What? I'm painting a dancer." He shook his head. "You're so saucy. Get your mind out of the gutter."

"*My* mind."

She looked at the piano. Even tinny and terrible, it was better than nothing. "Do you think Daan would be willing to play the 'Galop' for me?"

Aubrey called Daan, who greeted Amélie grudgingly.

"You look well," he said, a hint of condemnation in his tone.

"So do you." Though his sandy hair was askew and he still had sleep in his eyes. She hugged him and whispered, "I miss her very much."

Daan's eyes filled with tears. He gave a great sigh and shook his head. "I'm all alone without her."

"You're not alone," Amélie said. "Will you let me be your friend?"

"Will you come around more?" Daan looked between Amélie and Aubrey.

"Perhaps. Let's start with this, and we'll see."

Daan's small nod seemed to be the end of his anger. He sat at the bench and said, "The lady wishes the 'Galop'?"

Daan played, Amélie danced, and Aubrey sketched. Soon enough they bantered and laughed as they always had. Aubrey showed them his canvases, shared his ideas, and asked their advice. Daan cooked, and they ate in the shade of the garden. Soon these friend-souls fell easily back into their harmony.

The sun went down, and they were well into their third bottle of chianti when Amélie felt Aubrey's searching gaze on her.

"What?"

He propped an elbow on the table between them, his head in his hand. "You were magnificent today."

"You're drunk."

Daan flicked glances between Aubrey and Amélie and yawned. "I'm going to turn in."

Amélie reached for him. "What? No. It's early." She'd been in a drunken languor and hadn't realized how much she needed Daan to sit easily between them.

"It's past ten," Daan said, clearing the now-cold leftovers from the table.

"Is it? I need to go home. Let me help you."

"No. I've got it." Daan glanced again at Aubrey, then Amélie. "I'll see you tomorrow."

When Daan went into the kitchen, Aubrey followed Amélie as she collected her things.

"I didn't realize it was so late."

"Stay." Aubrey searched for her gaze and held her arm. "This is silly. You'll only be here first thing in the morning. And I've got your old bed made up for you."

"I really should go." She went to the door, and Aubrey blocked her path.

"It's not safe for you to be walking the streets after dark."

"It's only a few blocks."

"Still."

She stared at him until he finally moved.

"Thank you. I'll be back first thing in the morning." Aubrey followed her onto the street. "What are you doing?"

"Walking you back."

She paused. It was only a few blocks, but an escort wouldn't go amiss. "All right."

He looped an arm properly through hers, and they wended their way back to Ravignan. At the washhouse, he shifted his feet.

"Does he know what you're doing?"

She looked at him, and his dark eyes were so hopeful.

"No."

Aubrey took her hands in his and dragged his thumbs softly over them. "Why haven't you told him?"

"Honestly, I don't know."

He nodded, then turned a hand over and dropped coins into it.

"What's this?"

"Your payment. A first payment. I told you, this isn't simply a favor to me. It's good money. And this is yours."

Amélie stared at the francs in the soft gaslight. It was good money. And hers. Did it seem more beautiful somehow? She held it over her heart.

"Thank you."

He shook his head. "Thank *you*. You're helping me, it's true, but you deserve more than you have. I only wanted to give it to you. At least with this, I can do something true and right."

He reached to smooth a tendril of hair behind her ear. Something he'd done a hundred times when she was his. Something he'd done earlier that day. Now it felt more intimate, and he was hesitant, his hand slow and unsure. Then it fell on her shoulder and squeezed.

"I'll see you tomorrow," he said.

When Amélie fell into her bed, she exhaled as if it would release all the tender memories she had of Aubrey. Then she retrieved Jasper's note. She missed him. That was all this was. He felt so far away, so particularly out of reach in Deauville. What did they do there, he and his family, all summer?

24

*L*ife at Château Sainte-Clare, the Degrailly family's summer home in the Norman countryside, was the same people and pretensions moved north six hours by train. It was a daily grind of one social engagement after another, so well suited to the pursuit of leisure and so distancing from his entrepreneurial pursuits in Paris that it never took long to wear away at Jasper.

At ten, he strolled with his family along the plage de Deauville, the sole purpose of which was to be seen being seen. After returning home for luncheon at half past eleven, in the afternoon there was inevitably a charity bazaar, art exhibit, or garden party. If there wasn't, they rode through groomed trails on their hundred-acre lands or lazed in the intricate topiary gardens amidst fragrant herbs, vegetables, and flowers. At four o'clock, they attended low tea—any respectable member of le gratin was an ardent Anglophile—whether hosting it or paying a call on friends or acquaintances. In the evening, they dressed for dinner. And still more, there were balls and house parties to attend, sometimes lasting for weeks.

One day at luncheon three weeks into his stay, Jasper's mother Eleanor made an announcement.

"The Traverses are coming tonight for dinner."

"Pardon me?" Jasper said, clearing his throat.

"A few days ago, I ran into Joselin and her mother at la plage. Did I not tell you?"

"No. You didn't."

"I do believe she's looking lovelier and fitter than I've ever seen. Though she might consider wearing her hats lower before the sun warms her skin too much."

"Tonight?" Jasper prompted.

He loved his mother in a breezy way and had learned early on that her inanities masked a deep-seated desire to control far more than appearances.

"Yes. Tonight works for them, and it works for us." Ellen, brittle yet somehow still intimidating, gave him her trademark placid look that allowed for no refusal.

"I look forward to it."

"I knew you would." Ellen gave a satisfied smile, then took a hearty sip of chardonnay.

Whenever the Traverses and the Degraillys were in residence nearby, it was expected they share a dinner. Still, to say convention had been strained at the first dinner after Jasper and Joselin's divorce would've been a supreme understatement. Lurid details of aberrant sexual behavior had colored ladies' cheeks along with enough alcohol to sink a ship. Brittle smiles were plastered on faces while gazes flitted everywhere but to each other.

"I've heard a rumor that unfortunate business with Monsieur Durand may be at an end," his mother continued.

"'Unfortunate business'?"

"Their affair. For all her dabbling in painting and... other such things…"

Leaving her son for another man, such things, Jasper thought.

"Joselin is a reasonable woman."

"Do you think so?" Jasper swallowed his skepticism with his glass of wine.

"Yes. And the good news is she may finally be ready to return."

Ellen, like her son, had always assumed the estranged pair would reconcile and made certain to insinuate it as often as she could. Together they'd entertained a conspiration pour l'amour, hoping one day it would bear fruit.

Marie-Thérèse chuckled. "I wouldn't get your hopes up, Maman."

But Ellen Degrailly lived comfortably in her own delusions. She was still respectably married, though she lived encamped on the other side of her husband's life. No matter that some of her children had caused some scandals in their youth, not to mention Jasper's scurrilous divorce in recent years, she still thought herself a good mother. After all, didn't she have a daughter in the religious life?

"Why is that, dear?" Ellen asked.

"Jas is seeing someone," Marie-Thérèse said.

"Madame Kohl?" Ellen said. "She's a trifle. Jasper can have all he wants of liaisons with pretty widows as long as he doesn't get them enceinte or give them too much of our money."

Our money. That's rich, Jasper thought. There'd be no Degrailly family money were it not for his desperate decision to convert some of their residences into luxury hotels.

"Not Madame Kohl," Marie-Louise said.

"I thank you ladies to keep out of my affairs." Jasper pierced them with a quelling look. "Is Charlie still harming small animals?" he asked Marie-Thérèse.

"You're terrible. He isn't doing anything of the sort."

"And you, poussin?" he said to Marie-Louise. "Is Marie-Rose still having her night terrors? She really should see a doctor."

"It was a phase. She's well beyond it now. And I do wish you'd quit calling me 'little chicken,' little brother."

"Huh," Jasper said sarcastically. "So, there are things that would be better left unsaid."

"What affairs?" Ellen asked. She could easily pocket her children's squabbling for other matters of greater importance.

"An enchanting mademoiselle," Marie-Thérèse said.

"A demimondaine," Ellen pronounced confidently.

"No," Marie-Louis said. "Not a demimondaine. A very beautiful and *marriageable* young woman." His sisters sat back, triumphant in their coveted knowledge.

Jasper could feel his mother's piercing gaze directed at him. Like a bird of prey, she could pick her children's bones clean.

"Marriageable? Who's this, Jasper?"

That evening, Jasper, along with Marie-Louise, Marie-Thérèse, their husbands, and their mother and father, mingled with Joselin and her family over cocktails in the drawing room. His middle sister, Marie-Élise, rarely visited their holiday homes. Her family's wealth burdened her conscience the way others were burdened by poverty, as if it were an injustice.

Ellen made the rounds of the room with Jasper's father, Hector, on the other side. His mother loved to entertain and wouldn't allow a petty thing like marital estrangement to dampen her enthusiasm. This, after all, was where she wielded the Degrailly family persona like a tool she loved to sharpen. Yet she would sooner cut one with it than have to acknowledge it was paper-thin.

The hour had been light and easy when Jasper finally cornered Joselin. After sharing a warm embrace and exchanging some banalities, his mind went blank when he came to what he'd always punished himself to ask.

But for the first time since hearing his wife was having an affair with his own estate manager, Jasper found he no longer cared. He'd been in a fight with the man, all but openly acknowledged, for Joselin's heart. For far too long he'd been far too interested in every move

Martin and Joselin made. Now he found he could wish them well. As he realized it, it rocked him to his core. Who was he if not the man waiting for Jos to love him again?

These dinners, always filled with such tenuous hope, seemed suddenly boring.

"Where is your Monsieur Durand?"

"In Paris. Last I heard." Joselin's smile was etched in glass.

"Last you heard?"

At length she stared into the middle distance until finally saying, "I don't think we're going to make it. He isn't right for me. Not in the way you always were." She paused. "I don't know what I was thinking when I insisted we divorce. It's the worst decision I ever made. Can you ever bring yourself to forgive me?"

Jasper sat in stunned silence. There were many things Joselin had said, particularly in the beginning, that felt warm and real and vulnerable. This was the most heartfelt sentiment of all. It stirred something in him. A remembrance of how it was or how it might have been.

When he didn't respond right away, Joselin took a delicate sip from her glass.

"I miss you, Jas. I really miss you. Do you miss me?"

Only weeks ago, he would have given anything to hear her say those words. Now they fell with a lifeless thud between them.

He stared, mouth ajar, having no idea what to say.

She smiled sweetly. "I see I've stunned you. That's understandable, I suppose. We can go for a walk after dinner." She stroked his cheek, a move he was utterly aware everyone could see. A move *she* was certainly aware everyone could see. But it felt wrong. His stomach churned with just how wrong it felt.

He pulled her hand down, perhaps a little too roughly. "We'll talk after dinner."

Then he knew, as much as he'd felt it at Saint-Cloud, now he was certain. Seeing Joselin, hearing her profession, it was clarifying. A gift. Finally, he could have what he's wanted most these past three years.

And he no longer wanted it. He wanted one woman. And it wasn't the woman standing before him.

All through dinner, a dinner he'd struggled to eat, he'd tried to harness his thoughts. Now they walked in the shrub maze of the garden, the heady scent of zinnias and cornflowers carried on the cooling breeze.

"I'm sorry. About you and Martin."

"You're sorry."

"Yes."

"That's kind of you."

"It also happens to be the truth."

"'The truth.' I thought you'd be happy I'm coming back to you. Because I am, Jas. I'm ready."

Her declaration hung between them as they walked. Somehow, as much as he'd wanted it, he could never have conceived of being in this position. Now he was, it felt completely foreign, as if he hadn't the proper language.

"I'm sorry about you and Martin because… I don't think we're a fit like I once did."

He continued on the path until realizing she wasn't behind him. "Jos?"

She stood frozen, her face pained in the torchlights lining the paths. "Not a fit?" she finally said when her eyes fell on his. "I don't understand."

He went back to her side. "You moved on, and I have, too. I'm sorry, but I'm not in love with you anymore." Now he'd said it out loud, it felt genuine and true. And the truth was he wasn't sorry in the least.

"The figure model? That's why you haven't entreated on my behalf." She grimaced. "You've fallen in love with her."

"That isn't important." He took her arm tenderly.

"It is to me." She yanked her arm away, huffed, and strode further into the garden at a fast clip.

"Jos, wait."

"She isn't good enough for you," Joselin finally said when she stopped. "She's not like us, Jas. She could never be like us." Her mouth fell open, and her eyes flew wide. "She's like you. She has your peculiar perversions. And that's really what you want. Isn't it? A woman you can hurt and control."

"No."

"Yes," she hissed. "Yes, it is."

"I don't mean to hurt you. I'm sorry."

She shook her head for some moments.

"You can't hurt me. You're too pathetic to hurt me. What a deviant you are. How could I have ever thought to love someone like you?"

Joselin stalked off, leaving Jasper standing in her wake. Joy bloomed in his heart as he thought.

Who am I if not the man waiting for Jos to love me?

The flames from the path lights danced harder and burned brighter. The air smelled sweeter, and the nighttime songs of birds and cicadas trilled more beautifully. He put a hand to his mouth in grateful awe.

Who was he? Finally free to love someone else.

25

The summer days at Cortot were some of the happiest Amélie had passed in a long time. In the mornings, they applied themselves to their crafts. By late afternoon, they succumbed to hunger and thirst. The evenings were a tired stupor of roasts and sauces and wine and stories and laughter. Amélie had never dined so well at Cortot. Aubrey had clearly made a name for himself and lived better as a result.

Still, there came those moments when the words and laughter died and she saw the space where Léo had been. She'd remember how much Léo had wanted them to return and feel a pang of regret. Daan or Aubrey would nod or smile, and what passed between them seemed to be enough until, inevitably, stories and laughter would return. Eventually it didn't feel like a betrayal—moving on. It felt like Léo's hand was there.

But Amélie missed Jasper. He'd written twice. Long letters filled with lighthearted musings that reminded her how much she missed his wit:

> *...Madame de la Cour insists on presenting her papillon wherever she goes. Much to our delight, he seems desperate to mate at all times with candlesticks, vases, chair legs—even legs of the human variety. The poor boy is the most wanton dog I've ever seen, and everyone can see it but the madame herself, who carries on eating and drinking and talking as if precious André weren't madly rogering the plant stand. Of course, her garden party is the most well attended of the season. We all flock there to get dead-drunk in the afternoon and stare goggle-eyed at the madame's obtuseness, so tight-lipped we're bloody for fear of being the first one to burst out in guffaws. Once the dog starts in, I can scarcely meet Thérèse's eyes or I'll break. Would you believe me if I said it's the highlight of the season...?*

In the simple accounting of his days, Jasper included a list of events so carefully groomed in their refinement—the Deauville Ladies Auxiliary Charity Flower Show, horse races at the Hippodrome, the Rochefort's annual garden party, the Hachettes' annual ball—it fed Amélie's doubts about the two of them. What could he want with her when she didn't belong in that world? Until he signed off:

> *...I don't know who's worse off—poor little André or me. Because I miss you, my darling, and can't wait to return. More than you can possibly know...*

Amélie missed Jasper's stirring touch, too. For more than a year, she'd ignored her body and become the instrument Madame Pelletier thought she was. Yet Jasper, with merely a look or a promise, not to mention his skilled hands and mouth, made her feel charged, so attuned to her body and its needs that it seemed always to be on her mind.

Late one night in the garden, fingers slid into hers as she sat. She regarded them as if they were curious things. Perhaps she'd had too much to drink. Because she missed the tender touch of a hand in hand. Strong arms that wrapped around her, held her close, and made her feel safe. The warmth of a man behind her as she drifted off to sleep.

She jolted out of her daze and found Aubrey's tender smile fixed upon her.

"You look like you could fall over right there."

"I suppose I'm tired." She rubbed her eyes and took a deep breath. "Best get going, then."

She had collected her things to leave when Aubrey slid an arm through hers and directed her toward the stairs.

"Stay."

She shook her head.

"You belong here."

She shook her head more emphatically.

"What's the harm? You've been very devoted. Very good. I've been very good. I think we can handle our urges for a night so you don't have to trudge back to that house. Unless you're worried you can't."

His hair had long since come loose from its ponytail and fell softly on his shoulders. She'd always loved his hair. His beard was born of laziness and unkempt, yet still it made him more handsome than the smooth-chinned boy he appeared without it. His dark eyes could sometimes appear menacing, except when they were warm pools as they were now.

"Do you have urges?" she teased.

"Do you not?"

"Not for you."

"Not for me. Right. Then it should be easy to suppress them when he's so far away."

"It is."

"So, what's the problem?"

Limply she let him urge her to her old bedroom. When she slumped onto the bed, she felt again like she was betraying Jasper. She hadn't, of course. But would she tell him she'd modeled for Aubrey while he was away? When he saw those posters, he would know. Would she tell him about all the time she'd spent at Cortot? Or that she'd spent the night? Would she tell him she still found her ex so damnably alluring? No. She wouldn't tell him that.

A soft knock sounded at the door.

She glanced at it and realized with alarm it was unlocked.

"Amélie?" Aubrey whispered. "Are you still awake?"

Her voice caught in her throat. If she gave any answer at all, he would come in. From that part inside, that insecure, diminishing part of herself, came a reminder that what she had with Jasper was a lark and wouldn't last. He loved his ex-wife and could never love her as she wanted. And she did want to be loved. Aubrey loved her. He would cherish her. If only she allowed it.

Heart beating loudly in her chest, she went to the door... only to hear his footsteps pad away. She exhaled in relief, then locked the door.

The next night, Amélie closed the door of the washhouse and shuffled sleepily to the stairs.

"What are you doing with that one, girl?" Madame Pelletier asked.

Jolted right out of her skin, Amélie slapped a hand to her chest. "Oh, madame, you scared me."

It had been late when Aubrey escorted her home from Le Chat Noir, and the house had always been asleep by then.

"What are you doing?" Madame Pelletier pressed. Certainly the madame's interest was a financial one. She'd never cared who her girls saw as long as they could work.

"Coming home from the club like I do every Sunday night."

With accusing eyes, Madame Pelletier approached, crowding Amélie. "Not with that one, you don't. Does Monsieur Degrailly know?"

"I fail to see how that's any of your business."

"It *is* my business. When it affects my business, it is my business."

"Monsieur Talac is an old friend."

"An old friend who's been coming around altogether too much."

"I'm helping him with a project is all."

"A project." She arched a dubious brow. "What kind of help? The kind that keeps you away at the week's end. Keeps you *overnight*. I know you didn't come back last night. The kind that puts you in his bed? What would Monsieur Degrailly say to that?"

"Has he set you to spy on me?"

"Would you mind if I did? What would he say about these things?"

"All but the last are harmless. And the last isn't true. So, yes, I would mind. Now if you'll excuse me, I'm tired."

"Monsieur Degrailly is a reasonable man."

Reasonable? She doesn't know Jasper.

"I daresay kinder than most," Madame Pelletier continued. "If what you're doing is harmless, like you say, then you should have no problem telling him."

26

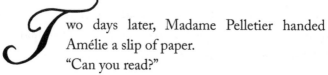

wo days later, Madame Pelletier handed Amélie a slip of paper.

"Can you read?"

"Yes, madame," Amélie said. Why did she insist all her girls were ignorant when she knew otherwise? She opened the telegram:

DEAREST AMÉLIE – (STOP) –
JASPER DEGRAILLY TO RETURN ON SEVENTEENTH JULY – (STOP) – JOIN ME FOR DINNER THAT EVENING AT THE JOCKEY CLUB – (STOP) – I WILL SEND LOUIS WITH THE CARRIAGE AT SEVEN – (STOP) – WEAR THE DRESS AND THINGS HE PROVIDES – (STOP) – HOW I HAVE MISSED YOU – (STOP) – PHONE CALL FORTHCOMING
JASPER S. DEGRAILLY   11:17AM

Amélie felt a physical relief flood through her heart and pressed the telegram to her chest.

"Good news, I hope," the madame said.

"Tell me you didn't read it."

The madame pursed her lips and walked away.

Amélie still felt conspicuous in the Jockey Club. No less now for what she wore, an eye-catching evening dress of peacock-blue lace and sweeping emerald-green silk. She didn't see Jasper in the Grand Café, and her anticipation heightened everything.

"Monsieur Degrailly?" she inquired.

"He's running behind by a few minutes. In the meantime, may I show you to your table?"

But instead of being shown into the dining room, she was brought to a private suite up on the first floor. She'd planned to order her customary Syrah, but the nervousness she felt for the evening, what she had to tell Jasper, made her reach for something stronger.

"Absinthe, please."

"Very good."

Her eyes kept drifting to the door. It would be just like him to keep her waiting on purpose. She watched the waiter place the slotted spoon and sugar cube, watched as he poured water over the sugar, making the chartreuse spirit cloudy and tempering the bitterness. She was just taking her first sip of the sharp licorice drink when Jasper finally strolled through the door looking even more beautiful than she remembered. Despite his ruddy complexion, his skin was sun-kissed and his eyes and smile bright.

"Sweetheart."

He cupped her nape firmly and kissed her, his tongue sweeping in as if to reclaim what was his. Her latent arousal flared. When he pulled back, he scrutinized her face, then he stepped back to range down her dress.

"This is a gorgeous dress. *You* are gorgeous. How is it you became even more beautiful while I was away? I didn't think it possible."

He kissed her again, his hunger only slightly dimmed from the first.

"I see you're starting with sterner stuff." He indicated her drink. "I hope that bodes well for the evening."

Jasper ordered the same, and when the waiter poured it, he sent him away until he was called for. After taking a sip, he sat back and looked at her, his eyes filled with desire. He appraised her for some time, then his eyes finally found hers again.

"Are you hungry?"

Amélie was buzzed. With spirits and nervousness and pure lust. She shook her head, and a lecherous smile played at the corners of his mouth.

"Did you follow my explicit directions?"

"Yes, monsieur."

He crooked a finger. "Stand just here." He turned his chair, indicating the space in front of him.

She did.

"Pull up your skirt. Slowly."

She did, revealing her black-stockinged legs sans petticoat and knickers.

"Very good, Amélie. I see you haven't forgotten how to obey me."

"No." She went to lower her skirt.

"Keep it up for me." He took her in at his leisure, his slow, deliberate perusal making her blood pool at her sex. "How do you feel like this?"

"Naked. Exposed. Shameful. Needy."

"Mm." His eyes found hers. "I like that. I want you needy for me. That makes me happy. And you want to make me happy, don't you?"

"Yes."

"Good. Now lift up your chemise and show me what's mine."

Her breath left her, and she felt her sex bead with arousal as she lifted her chemise and spread her puffy lips open. His eyes flared, and he licked his lips.

"Come closer." He spread his legs, pressed his face to her sex, and took a deep breath. He moaned. "Oh, God, I've missed this." He pressed a soft kiss to her mound and stood, moving their drinks. "Lay back. Keep your dress up and relax."

She did, and he slid his tongue into her slit with a low moan. "Mm. I've thought of nothing but this for a month. Promenades and garden parties and balls and all I could think of was this."

Slowly, torturously, he moved his tongue up and down in long laps. In and out in deep, pulsing thrusts. Swirling around her nerve, nipping and sucking. Then starting over again. All the while, her breathing grew faint as her arousal climbed up and up. She grabbed his head, but he pulled her hands away.

"No," he said in his lusty lilt. "Lace your fingers together and put them behind your neck."

"I need to come, Jasper."

"I know." His voice was so tender and understanding. "But not yet. You'll come when I say, won't you?"

"No!" she whimpered as he pulled back, pressing too-light kisses all around her sex, outside her heavy lips, where her legs met her core.

"What do you need? This?" He slid two fingers deep into her sex. It was so good. Close but not enough.

"Yes." She moaned. "More."

"More?"

"More, please, monsieur."

"Oh, good girl," he murmured into her slit, his tongue flicking gently. "I love this new polite woman. So respectful. So desperate."

"Yes."

Faintly she registered sounds of rustling clothing, then she felt his cock slide into her to the hilt. There was a small bite of pain at the tightness, but it felt incredible. She moaned and opened her eyes to see him above her.

"Is that what you need?"

"Yes. Oh, God, yes, Jasper." He stilled inside her, and she began to rock.

An arrogant smile spread across his face as he held her hips. "No.

I've waited too long for this to let you take us there." He cupped her face preciously and said, "Relax, greedy girl." He pulled out and thrust back in with agonizing slowness. "Easy now. I'm right here."

She whimpered and took a deep breath as he began to pulse deliberately, torturously inside her.

"I'm close. So close."

"Not yet, Amélie."

As if her fingernails were on the ledge, she pulled back even as the telltale tingling crackled in her sex.

"Please, Jasper. Please, please, please."

"Almost. You're so good. So perfect for me." He picked up the pace and began pistoning inside her as she clawed at the tablecloth.

"That's it. Come."

"Yes?"

"Yes."

And with that, her arousal crested. The tingling flooded her sex and up her spine, making her whole body shake as her sex squeezed and squeezed and squeezed his cock. With a guttural groan, he climaxed moments behind her.

Finally, she relaxed back on the table and opened her eyes to see him smiling. When he kissed her, she tasted the sweet tartness of herself on his lips.

"I've missed you," he said. "So much."

They righted themselves and ordered dinner. Amélie listened as Jasper recounted his time in Deauville—the endless parade of events that constituted le gratin's social calendar in summer, who was there. "Marie-Thérèse and Marie-Louise send their greetings." More about his family. "My father is a scoundrel. And my mother does the only thing she can do—she avoids him, and she drinks."

"Doesn't every son feel that way about his father at some point?"

"No. And even if they did, they wouldn't always be fair. In this case, *scoundrel* is the kindest word I can think of."

"What's he done that's so terrible?"

"Many things. But to give you a white-lace example, do you

remember when I told you my father had made some bad investments?"

"Yes."

"One of those was with my ex-wife's family's money. So desperate were they to regain the wealth that came with their social standing, they gave him nearly all their money. Then he lost it. Oh, but he kindly returned a small portion."

"My God."

"Yes. He was *not* allowed at the wedding."

"Your father was not at your wedding?"

He shook his head.

"I'm so sorry."

"I'm not. I despise the man."

All this time spent on Jasper's summer and Amélie remained conspicuously silent about hers. She didn't want their happy reunion to end and feared it would when she told him about Cortot. But he didn't seem to notice. In fact, he fidgeted with his silverware, which wasn't at all like him. And grew quieter, his gaze directed everywhere in the suite but on her.

"Is there something the matter?" she finally asked.

He smiled so softly it felt like a warning shot, and her body tightened.

"Come here." He settled onto the plush eggplant sofa. The suite was a mix of mahogany, dark velvets, and gold trim.

She went to sit beside him, but he relaxed into a corner and urged her to rest back against his chest. He wrapped his arms around her so that she couldn't look into his eyes without twisting uncomfortably.

"What is it?"

He exhaled. "He didn't cast you."

The words were so ill-matched to where her own mind was that at first she didn't register them. "Pardon me?"

"Charles. He didn't cast you for the Moulin Rouge. I'm so sorry."

She felt it first in her throat, a pain that spread down to her chest, burning her up. Her whole body felt hot, and she blinked, seeing black spots. Her dream, her plans, everything seemed to tilt on its axis. She thought she was going to be sick and tried to sit up, but he held fast to her.

"Let me up, Jasper."

When he did, she pressed herself to a far wall and looked at him, his head and body slumped.

"Did you do this?"

"Of course not." He went to stand, but she put a hard hand up.

"No. Stay right where you are."

He sat back down.

"Look me in the eye and tell me you didn't cut me. *You.*"

Unflinching, he looked at her. "I didn't cut you."

"I don't believe you."

He stood and slowly approached.

"No. Don't come any closer."

He shook his head and caged her in with his arms. "I'm not going to do that, sweetheart. That's the last thing I'm going to do."

Amélie felt tears filling her eyes and angrily wiped them away. "I don't... believe you!" She glared at him. "Now move. I'm leaving."

"You're not leaving. Not like this." When she tried to duck under his arms, he pressed his body to hers. "Ah-ah-ah. No. I understand you're upset. But don't shoot the poor messenger."

"Tell me you're not happy," she said, staring at the floor.

He gripped her chin, urging her to look at him. "I'm not happy."

"I don't believe you. You didn't want me to perform on that stage. As soon as you began feeling something for me, you couldn't conceive of it. Tell me I'm wrong."

"I want to protect you, it's true. I'm not going to lie or apologize. Those women sell their bodies. The song and dance is merely pretty foreplay. But you're good. Better than any woman we've seen. We'd be foolish not to cast you. But when I left, the decision rested entirely in Charles's hands."

"Why wouldn't he cast me then, if I'm so much better than the others, if not for your reservations?"

"I don't know for sure, but I can guess."

She looked at him, waiting.

"You're not in the demimonde, and I don't want you to be. *You* don't want to be. The only one who did, who needed you to be, is Charles."

"So that's it, then. No matter my talent, I need to be a demimondaine if I want to perform."

27

mélie slumped in her dressing room at Le Chat. While her dress maid, Penny, a caramel-haired, golden-eyed girl of fifteen, loosened her stays and chattered happily about Amélie's performance—"Another great one, as always."—Amélie's gaze fell despairingly over the meager space. Once there was a time when this gig and this dressing room had been everything. A lifeline that breathed needed air into her dreams. Now, lit by the dull patina of her heartbreak, it was small and spare and shabby.

Days strung into weeks, and still she couldn't get over her dashed dream of performing at the Moulin Rouge. Somehow she managed to wake and work and sing. And Jasper was being so tender in his gifts and calls that it made her crazed and made it impossible to place the blame solely on him.

So, she cursed the demimonde.

Those grandes horizontales, their boldness and

ingenuity, easy virtue and glittering prominence. They made her feel like a prude, like a provincial who found herself when looking down her nose on people and things she didn't understand. But she was an artist, wasn't she? Someone who prayed to the religion of truth and beauty and art for art's sake. Wasn't she? In truth, she didn't know anymore.

And some moments, when she felt so low, so low and so lost like this one, she just wanted to let herself be held by Jasper. Wanted to leave Le Chat and Ravignan and Montmartre and never look back. She was all but certain if she let him, Jasper would sweep her away from all of it—her aching back and aching heart. And the awful struggle of wanting something so impossible sometimes it seemed to live on the other side of the moon. So dark and distant, as if she were never meant to see it.

She hugged herself. Oh, how she wanted Jasper to hold her.

Just then there came a knock on the door.

"Belle Étoile?" Salis said. "You have a visitor. Are you decent?"

Amélie's heart wept for joy. Perhaps it was meant to be. If Jasper came for her now, she would run away from all of it and never look back. Sliding into a robe, she wiped an errant tear from her cheek and stood.

"I'm ready."

The ethereal blonde who entered was quite possibly the last person Amélie had expected to see.

"Madame Travers."

"You remember me."

The woman's face and tone were inscrutable, and Amélie indicated for Penny to leave with Salis. "I remember you," she said once the door closed.

"The Salon. You complimented my nudes. Though they were so small and pitiful. So inconsequential there, all tucked away. Not too close to the real artists."

Amélie didn't know Jasper's ex-wife save for their brief meeting at the vernissage. There she'd seemed brittle, and now she seemed nervous. Yet the more she considered the woman, the tighter and more hostile she appeared. What would such a madame of le gratin want with her? And at this place and hour?

"Can I help you with something, madame?"

Amélie indicated the sofa, and Joselin sat rigidly. With the woman's butter-blonde hair and the blush that rouged her cheeks, her features, her form, even her manners and speech, seemed angelic. Although they were both tall and lithe, Amélie appeared to be as different from Joselin Travers in coloring and class and manners as night was from day.

What can Jasper possibly see in me?

While Joselin peered around the room distractedly, on closer inspection, Amélie discovered she had one eye of cornflower-blue and the other a mocha-brown. Never had she seen someone with two different eye colors before. It lent some unexpected mystery and weight to her.

"He didn't ask you to pose for me, did he?"

"Pardon me?"

"My husband."

Amélie bristled. "Your husband?"

Madame Travers squirmed in her seat and pinched her lips. "My *ex*-husband." She'd said this last as if it were distasteful.

"He didn't, madame."

"And now I know why."

"Why?"

"He's…" She paused and swallowed, then shook her head. "We saw each other. In Deauville."

"You saw each other."

"We always do." The blonde smiled slyly, and in that moment, Amélie could see cool flint in one eye and crackling challenge in the other. "Even after the divorce we… well, we can't seem to stay away from each other. You understand how that is. Artists and their muses."

The implication was clear. Amélie's chest burned in indignation. She could feel her cheeks flooding with warmth. Her mind raced to contain every caustic, childish, embarrassing thing she might say.

"Is this what you came all the way over here to tell me? Late on a Sunday night? That Jasper's still in love with you? I already knew that, madame. In fact, I wouldn't be with him if he weren't."

This was only partially true and mostly in the beginning. She merely clung to the notion now as her last brace against Jasper. Still, what Joselin said made Amélie seethe. Made her feel like a visitor in her own room while the blonde had command of it. Joselin's tight smile said she knew this very well.

"How modern and broad-minded you are, then," Madame Travers said.

"Yes, well, we artist types."

"We're not unalike, you and I, are we?"

"We're nothing alike, madame."

Joselin's eyes scanned around the room.

"There isn't something you want more than anything?" She paused. "I can help you with that."

"Why would you help me? And how?"

Joselin gave her a pleased smile. "Jasper and I travel in the same set, you see. He knows people. I know those people, too. As to why, there's something I want more than anything. And you can help me with that."

"How could I help you?"

It was nothing more than a reflex, really. A curiosity, mostly. Amélie had little doubt Joselin Travers knew people who could help her. But she couldn't possibly be considering helping this woman who delighted in throwing Jasper in her face.

"I want you to pose for me."

"What?" Amélie chortled. "You've got to be joking."

"I'm quite serious."

"Nude."

"Naturally."

"I'm flattered, but no, madame. For many reasons. But primarily because I'm not a figure model. I had no wish to be then, and I still don't."

"But for the right inducement, you might consider anything."

"No. And you don't know me very well if you think that."

"Don't be too hasty. I could pay you handsomely, mademoiselle."

"With Jasper's money. His wife and his lover. What a neat trick that would be."

Joselin smiled tightly.

"You wouldn't have to work for quite some time. You could focus on your dreams. Of being on the stage. Far grander than this one. I know as many people as Jasper. More even. And different. Think about it."

"There's nothing for me to think about. Now if you've had your say, it's getting late. I must get home."

"That's right. A blanchisseuse must start her day before the sun comes up, does she not? What a dreary and hard-worn life." She *tsk*ed. "It's a shame such a talent as you should be so confined for want of coin… when you don't need to be."

28

*J*uly turned to August, and Jasper still hadn't seen Amélie. When he'd finally let her go, she'd stormed out of the Jockey Club saying she didn't want to see him. That she needed some time to think. He hadn't wanted to acquiesce. No matter what she thought, it wasn't his fault.

The first week, she hadn't accepted his calls. So, he'd sent her gifts—dresses and underthings and jewels. All of which she returned. Then he sent her flowers—roses and daisies and sunflowers. Whether or not she kept those he didn't know. But he liked imagining her receiving something from him.

Max had raised a brow at the flood of gifts but smirked good naturedly and kept his mouth shut.

The second week, she finally answered his call.

"Stop this molesting of me. I told you I needed some time."

"And I've respected it. To a degree. Have I shown up

at your doorstep? No. But it doesn't stop me from wanting to hear your voice. To see how you're doing. How are you doing?"

"You're impossible, Jasper." She disconnected the call.

Three days later when she answered his call, her voice sounded small and tremulous, as if her angry fever had broken.

"I'm coming to see you."

"No."

"Darling."

"I'm not ready." She paused. "I'm not ready."

She sounded lost and heartbroken. It broke Jasper's heart. Even if he could convince Charles to cast her, she would still have to face, night after night, the same fate she condemned.

She'd said she needed time. But with the sadness in her voice, it became harder and harder to restrain himself. First Léonie and now this. She needed to allow people to help her. She didn't need to face the harshness of the world alone always.

Just then, Charles walked into Jasper's office with a bright smile.

"I'm seeing a circus." The man plunked down in a chair, his hands framed in the air in front of him as if presenting his idea in a picture.

"That must be tricky."

Zidler guffawed.

"Good afternoon, Charles," Jasper said sourly.

He was torn. He knew why the man didn't cast Amélie and, on the one hand, didn't blame him. But he'd hurt the woman Jasper cared for deeply. So, on the other hand, he did.

"Still in a foul mood, I see. Well, I have something that'll cheer you up." Charles reached for a leather tube he'd brought and slid the curled paper out. Then he cleared some space on Jasper's desk and unrolled it.

The first thing Jasper saw was Amélie. She gripped the gold brocade from Le Chat Noir high to reveal her shapely long legs encased in seductive black stockings leading up to scandalous bare thigh. Her midnight-brown hair fell loose and whipped wildly with two fat red roses thrust into it. Her cheeks were flushed, and her gaze, though off-center for the viewer, was directed outward. All this against a background of blue that swirled and changed from indigo to cerulean, then faded out at the edge. Rounded over the top were the words "Moulin Rouge" in a ripe, red font, and running straight under her feet, "Le Diamant."

"Isn't it beautiful?" Charles asked. "It's even better than I imagined."

But Jasper couldn't hear any of it. Because the next thing he saw was red. He ran hot with rage, his mind racing in confusion, trying to imagine a scenario, any scenario, in which Amélie had not betrayed him.

He was angry at everyone just then. Charles for commissioning Talac. Talac for painting Amélie. Amélie for posing for him. God only knew what else. All of them seemingly oblivious to what Jasper might want.

"Talac painted this," he said when he finally found his voice again.

"It's a color lithograph. But yes."

"He received the commission, and then he began."

"I assume so. Why?"

"'The Diamond.'"

"I love it! It says our girls are sparkling jewels. Only the richest and most beautiful money can buy. We're on our way, Jasper." Charles clapped him on the back, oblivious to his distress. "With posters like these, girls like these, a singular spectacle, the Moulin Rouge will be the brightest star in all Paris. No. The world."

Charles had always had grand visions, but he failed to see what was happening in front of his face.

"This is undoubtedly Mademoiselle Audet."

Charles peered more closely at the poster. "Huh. It is a strong resemblance, I grant you."

"It's more than a resemblance."

Charles scratched his chin. "If that's really so, it's unfortunate."

Jasper glared at his partner's obtuseness.

"Well, there isn't anything we can do about it now. You didn't want me to cast her. It's done."

"What do you mean, *I* didn't want you to cast her? The decision was yours."

"You're joking, right?" They stared hard at each other across Jasper's desk. "You would have chewed your head right from your neck in frustration if I'd done so. See there—you're gritting your teeth even now as you try to hold in your denial. But we both know it's true."

When Jasper didn't respond, Charles pressed on, "No question, she's a talent. I was sorry to cut her. Very sorry. But you haven't been very silent in this silent partnership. Not for a while. You would see her managed one way, and I may manage her a different way. Could you have tolerated that? You needn't answer that, because the answer is no, and we both know it.

"Demimondaine or not, she would still have to deal with her nightly requests. *You* would have to deal with her nightly requests. Perhaps she becomes a star and a proper courtesan and you share her with other gentlemen of means or rank or both."

Jasper felt his anger turn from red to white-hot.

"Or she leaves her dreams behind," Charles continued, "and you become a proper little bourgeois family. But the pair of you need to make some decisions."

"There has to be another way. Can't we simply say she's not for sale?"

"Is she a woman of independent means?"

"You know she isn't."

"Then that's a question you need to ask her."

29

Madame Pelletier beckoned Amélie, and she left the washing, closing the door behind her.

"Monsieur Degrailly called."

"Yes, madame."

"He's sending a package. He wants you to wear it."

Amélie shook her head. "Send it back."

"He insists."

"I'll not see him again, madame."

"This time he sounded determined. He's sending a carriage for you at seven, and you should be on it."

"I'll not."

Just then, the phone rang. Only ringing once, perhaps twice, a week, it was still jarring.

Madame Pelletier narrowed her eyes at Amélie and stalked to answer it.

"Yes, she's right here, monsieur."

Amélie shook her head, and the laundry mistress

covered the receiver. "Who do you think I am? Have me confused with someone else, do you? I'm not your secretary. If you say no to that man, you'll say no for yourself."

The madame thrust the transmitter at Amélie, and she reluctantly took it.

"Monsieur Degrailly."

"Have you gotten the package?"

"Not yet. But I'll not accept it. I don't want to see you ever again. I don't want any dresses or flowers. I don't want anything from you."

"You'll see me tonight."

"Jasper—"

"Perhaps it'll be the last night, but you'll see me tonight. We have something to discuss. It's important. And I'll not take no for an answer."

His tone was low and menacing. Disturbingly different from how tender it had been over recent days and weeks.

"Fine. Tonight. But that'll be the end."

"Fine."

The call disconnected with an alarming click, and Amélie shuddered. She didn't know why she should be upset with Jasper for seeing his ex-wife in Deauville. She knew he loved her still. They'd promised each other what was between them was a lark. Yet all she felt was righteous anger, and all she wanted to do was hold on to it.

As soon as the transmitter was back on its hook, the madame returned.

"Your Monsieur D doesn't strike me as a very forgiving man. If you've crossed him—and I've no doubt you have, you idiot—you might think very carefully about how you tread."

"It's I who's not forgiving him, madame."

"What's he done, then? Slink around behind your back as you've done to him?"

"I never cheated on him."

"I wonder if he'd see it that way. Are you committed to each other to the exclusion of all others? I wonder if a man such as he can be.

Sometimes I wonder if any man can be."

When Amélie merely stood there with her mouth agape in wondering, the madame continued, "Men come in all shapes and sizes. All manner of needs and expectations. But they all have their egotism, which needs to be stroked as good as their cocks. Better so.

"For some reason I fail to see, he holds a tenderness for you. And believe me, you could do a far sight worse than to keep that man happy."

"You don't know what he's done, madame."

"Perhaps I don't. Then again, perhaps you don't."

When the package arrived, Amélie opened yet another dress box to see a black satin dinner dress embroidered with glass beads from bodice to toe. Blood-red satin accents at the lapels, cuffs, and skirt panels. With deep colors and the beads so tightly laid it almost appeared to be a knight's chain mail. It seemed more of a sculpture than a dress, and the madame, who insinuated herself into the opening of the package, gasped.

"That is the most unusual dress I've ever seen. Oh, heavens, I was right. You're not nearly worthy of the man."

"Thank you, madame," Amélie said sarcastically.

"You're welcome, dear," the madame replied in earnest. "You're so welcome." She slapped her arm affectionately, then walked away.

The carriage arrived at precisely seven, and though Amélie was cleaned and coiffed and wearing the unusual dress that seemed to hug her curves like a second skin, she hesitated. Though she had no right to be—they'd never committed exclusively to one another—she still harbored petulant outrage over him. First cutting her from the Moulin Rouge, then dallying with his ex-wife while on holiday. Every time she thought of him, she wanted to rake her fingernails down his face, then slam a door in it. Still, something felt different about his insistence. Something had changed.

For the month while she'd held Jasper at bay, trying to reconcile her dashed hope with his role in it—whatever that was she still wasn't certain—she'd felt firmly in control. He'd behaved like a man who cared but also carried a measure of guilt. It had been easy to hold him back if he was the cause of her hurt. And after Madame Travers's visit, easier still.

But this seemed different. He no longer behaved like he was afraid. And that made her afraid.

Louis stood by the carriage door, waiting. They'd exchanged a glance. He knew she was there.

"Go on," Madame Pelletier urged. "Best see what he wants before he loses all patience with you."

She stepped out, and Louis opened the door. "Mademoiselle."

Distracted by acknowledging Louis, Amélie was nearly inside the carriage before she saw Jasper.

"I was beginning to wonder if you were coming out."

Her heart jolted in surprise, and instead of sinking into the squab beside him, she sat across from him.

"Monsieur." She exhaled. "I didn't know you were coming."

Striking in a black suit with a snow-white dress shirt and red ascot, he appeared to be relaxed back into the seat, but Amélie knew better. Tension radiated in the set of his shoulders and the churning of his jaw, even in his swimming sage eyes.

He didn't respond, merely looked at her while the carriage proceeded on. After some moments trying to meet his gaze, she looked out the window.

"Where are we going?"

"My apartment. Sophie's preparing us a late dinner."

Amélie nodded. She could feel the anger from his unflinching gaze touching her from across the benches. So, she tried to return it in kind. As tension filled the carriage, the silence became almost suffocating.

"Is something the matter?" she finally asked, looking at him boldly.

"You could say that."

"What is it? You've condemned me already, I see. You're punishing me when it's I who should be punishing you. I might as well know what for."

"Punishing you? Is that what people are calling it these days?

When a man sends his girl a dress nearly as striking as she. Insists she accompany him to dinner. That's a punishment, is it?"

"You know what I mean. Your manner is hard. I might even go so far as to say accusatory. And I'm not your girl."

He leaned forward. "Of what might I accuse you? And you are mine. At least I thought you were."

"I can't imagine." That was a lie. She was beginning to imagine exactly why he might be angry.

"Then there will be a surprise at dinner."

At Jasper's apartment, Amélie looked nervously everywhere. Try as she might to hold on to her anger, all she could think about was what he might be planning. In the formal dining room, there were two elegant place settings, one on the end, and the other to its right. Candles were lit, making light bounce off the crystal goblets filled with a merlot liquid. And a draped easel.

"Are you hungry?" He held an arm out in invitation.

"Not really." Her stomach was in knots with anticipation.

"Then let's start with the exhibit. A private piece. For now."

When Jasper removed the drape to reveal Aubrey's first completed poster, Amélie felt a peculiar mix of emotions. Guilt burned in her chest and cheeks, though she railed at her mind and heart for that. Jasper had obviously been entertaining himself with Madame Travers, likely laughing at her while they lay in bed.

But immediately on the heels of that, breathless awe. She'd seen Aubrey's sketches. Marveled at his delicate hand on the limestone, as if he were both sculpting and sketching. But to see the finished work on a poster, it was truly beautiful. And to think it could be recreated again and again. Lithography, he'd promised, would revolutionize the art world. Now she was certain it would.

Amélie felt an arm snake around her waist.

"I see you're admiring your lover's work." He handed her a goblet and took a sip from his own.

She pulled away. "He isn't my lover, Jasper. No matter what you may think, this proves nothing."

"'Proves nothing.' Interesting choice of words. Those are the words of a guilty person."

"Then let me try different words." She stiffened her spine and turned to him, meeting his gaze. "Aubrey isn't my lover. He hasn't been since well before you and I met."

"But you posed for him. And you didn't think it important for me to know. If there wasn't anything to hide, why couldn't you tell me?"

"Honestly? I expected you might make assumptions that were unfounded. You've proven me right. And I could very well ask the same of you. Have you anything to tell me of your holiday in Deauville? If we can't trust each other, then we have a problem."

"It isn't that I don't trust you. I make assumptions because I know men. It's clear he wants you back. Tell me I'm wrong."

"Are we seeing each other to the exclusion of all others? We never said. I don't know that you've parted ways with Madame Kohl. And I know you're still seeing Madame Travers. This was a lark. Remember?"

"You didn't answer my question."

"You didn't answer mine."

They stared at each other for a long moment.

"Why did you pose for him?"

"I didn't do it to hurt you."

"But you knew it would."

"I needed to do it." She paused. "Nearly two years ago, Aubrey used me, made me beholden to him, and took away my choices. When he offered me this, I didn't want to at first. I thought he was using me again—"

"He did use you—"

She put a hand up to silence him. "I needed to make my peace with Cortot. I needed to feel like more than the dirty work of hardened hands. I kept my clothes on, and I danced. He offered me a chance to be the face of the Moulin Rouge." Her voice broke as she felt shame burning in her nose and eyes. "And I needed the money. You haven't any idea what that's like.

"You can't possibly imagine what it's like to be measured from the moment you're born and found lacking. For what? A birthright I didn't have? A sex I didn't have?

"I don't get to choose. Not like you. So, don't tell me what I should and shouldn't do when my life's choices are so meager they can be held in the palm of my hand. And *still* I have been honorable. To you when you were not so to me. But most importantly, to myself."

She set her goblet on the table and strode to the front door. "I'd like to go home now. I'll return this dress in the morning."

The measured thud of his shoes fell on the parquet. Closer and closer.

"Are you done?" he asked from right behind her.

"I've said my piece."

He came around in front of her and leaned against the door, his face inscrutable.

"Your modeling—are you done with the modeling?"

"Nearly. I go in case he may need touch ups."

"When do you see him? Are you alone with him?"

"Mostly at week's end. Daan is customarily around. He plays the piano for me while I sing and dance."

Jasper straightened and approached. Amélie's arms were folded as tight as a fist across her chest. She needed the armor of that chain-mail dress.

"I'm not going to stand here and lie to you and say that I'm perfectly all right with you modeling for him when I'm not. He would use you and take you from me if given half the chance." He cupped her neck and urged her chin up. "I won't let that happen."

She opened her mouth to protest, but he pressed a thumb to her lips and a finger to his. "Shh. You've had your say. It's my turn now. I trust you. You invite trust with both hands. You're the most honorable person I have ever known. It's him I don't trust.

"You may think he's being noble, being a friend to you, giving you this opportunity. Perhaps he's doing all that. But if he's doing anything, he's also calculating how best to win you back. The compliment of a well-earned coin is only one way.

"And as for the other thing, this stopped being a lark for me some time ago. I've ended my affair with Daphne, and I've told Joselin I no longer have the feelings I once had."

Amélie was struck dumb. Indeed, her mouth fell open to speak—Jasper's declaration seemed to require it—but she couldn't think what to say.

"What? She told me you saw each other in Deauville."

"She told you? When did you see Joselin?"

"This Sunday last. She came to see me at Le Chat. To preen over how you still love each other. How you saw each other on holiday. How you can't seem to stay away from each other, apparently. All this and then she asked me to pose for her."

"What? You're not posing for her, are you? She's back in Paris? I don't understand. She usually spends the whole summer in Deauville."

"Perhaps she missed you."

"She doesn't miss me, Amélie. She's angry with me. And jealous, obviously. Yes, we saw each other in Deauville. We always do. As a matter of course. Even after the divorce. My mother has been conspiring to get us back together. Until recently, I was happy to let her.

"Our families had dinner. Only the once. And she was so pleased to tell me she was finally ready to come back to me. But I told her I'd moved on. That I don't love her anymore. And I meant it."

"What does that mean?" Amélie finally managed. "I-I thought that this was… That is to say, I assumed you were incapable of… of deeper feelings."

Jasper pressed a chaste kiss to her forehead. "I thought so, too."

This wasn't right. One of them had to feel a casual attachment, and increasingly she knew it wasn't her. She was falling for him. *Had* fallen for him. She had relied upon him to be the disinterested party. To be resolute in his indifference. But if he cared for her deeply…

"I need to go." She pulled from his grasp and reached for the door.

"Where do you think you're going? I tell you I care deeply for you, and this is your cue to leave? No. We need to talk about this."

"There isn't anything to discuss, Jasper. I told you in the beginning that I couldn't fall for you. That I get easily distracted. Nothing has changed. I can't focus on my dreams if I'm comfortable in bed with you."

"Perhaps your dreams aren't so important, then," he asserted angrily as she walked away.

His charge felt like a physical slap, and she froze as if holding her injured self. Slowly she turned back to see him glaring at her.

"If you're as easily distracted from them as you say," he continued, "perhaps they're not worth very much. Perhaps they're really an excuse for you to avoid loving someone who may one day not be there. And then suddenly you're a five-year-old girl again whose whole world has changed."

Amélie felt a pain in her heart, both old and raw. She shook her head. "How dare you say that to me? When you know, *you know*, they mean everything to me?"

"I'll tell you what I know." Jasper folded his arms across his chest and leaned into the doorframe. "I know your body responds to me like it can't imagine responding to anyone else. I know you care for me. More than you're willing to admit. And I know that terrifies you.

"Someday you might wake up and find that loving me is just as important as being on stage. Then what will you be forced to admit? That you're not in control. That someone else might influence your steps. Let me help you. Let me save you all that. Because you're already there. You're already there, and I'm already there."

"I'm not."

"You are. I already live here." He placed a hand over her heart. "That frightens you because you want me to. And, happy coincidence, so do I. So, let's dispense with all this."

She shook her head and kept shaking it over and over again, feeling a dam of emotion rising in her throat and nose and eyes, threatening to break.

"Have you ever loved someone more than your own life," she finally uttered, "and one day he was simply gone? Forever?"

"Yes."

His answer was immediate and unflinching.

"This isn't the same."

"I'm not talking about Joselin."

Her mouth fell open as she stared at his inscrutable face.

She turned for the stairs. "I won't love like that again. My heart can't take it. Don't you see?"

"What I see is a woman grasping at every ounce of control she can, thinking somehow she can govern away all fear, all heartbreak, all loss. And in the meantime, she's losing every chance at joy just trying to hold on."

Tears welled in Amélie's eyes even as she shook her head.

"You're wrong. You couldn't be more wrong. And I'm going to prove it."

30

The next morning, Jasper stood anxiously in Joselin's foyer, waiting to be announced.

He'd passed a frustrated, angry, and sleepless night. Amélie was the most infuriating, beautiful, stubborn, captivating, strong, and utterly decent woman he'd ever known. If only she were obedient. No. That wasn't true, for he wouldn't care for her as much if she were. If only he could bring her to heel *some*times. He would take it. What a triumph that would be.

He felt certain about what he'd said. That she cared for him deeply. That he felt the same had made her bolt like a skittish horse.

"Madame Travers will see you now, monsieur."

The butler showed him to the breakfast room, where the spaniel Bijou leapt from Joselin's lap to greet him.

"So, this is how the light falls in this room at this hour," Jasper began, picking up the dog. "I'd no idea you ate breakfast."

Joselin regarded him with a hooded glance while slathering jam on her bread. "It's customarily done at this hour."

"Oh, I know it's customarily done. I just didn't think you bothered with it."

"I bother with a lot of things you don't know about."

"I know you do. That's why I'm here."

Jasper took a seat with the dog on his lap, poured himself some coffee, and helped himself to some sausages.

"Would you care for some breakfast?" Joselin smiled into her cup.

Jasper fed the dog a sausage.

"You spoil her," she said.

"I like spoiling those who love me. It's a pesky habit I refuse to break."

They exchanged taunting smiles.

"I could ask why you're back in Paris so soon," he said, "but I already know the answer."

"She's a pretty girl, Jasper."

"No, she isn't. She's beautiful, and you know it."

Joselin scanned *Le Figaro* and pursed her lips. "It seems there's another murder in Whitechapel that might be Leather Apron's doing. How gruesome."

Jasper grimaced. "Ghoulish reading for breakfast. Don't change the subject, Jos. What were you doing there? You'd no right to visit her."

Joselin appraised him squarely and folded her hands before her. "I'd no right? You're setting me aside for another woman. I've every right to know who she is."

"*I'm* setting *you* aside? I? You'll pardon me, but I think you have that backward." When Joselin didn't speak, he continued. "Have I slipped through time? Is it three years ago and we're ending our relationship? Again? No.

"You were pleased to set me out like a naughty puppy on the back step. Happy to feed me scraps while I waited eagerly and begged." He fed the dog another sausage. "The pity is I did. Waited and begged and hoped. I think you like me like that. You like men like that. Half men who don't know their head from their backside but for what a woman may tell them."

Joselin had the good grace to blush with an arch smile.

"I'll not be that man for you any longer. Not for anyone." He downed his coffee, set the dog down, and stood. "You'll not pay a visit to Amélie Audet ever again, Jos."

"Is she such a child, then? She can't make her own decisions or have her own say? I didn't think you a man for half women either."

"Don't mistake my instructions for her weakness. She's more of a woman than I've ever known."

They exchanged glares.

"But I know you. You're cutting and small when you want to be. And she's far too honorable to meet you measure for measure. Don't you dare mistake that for weakness. She's anything but."

As he walked out the door, he called back, "She's not posing for you."

"You might let her decide for herself," she replied as the door closed.

Not an hour later, Jasper stood on rue Cortot banging determinedly. He wasn't entirely sure what he would say. He might commiserate with Talac, for now he had some idea how the man felt. Jasper had thought him a cur for having Amélie and losing her. Now, it seemed, he was the cur.

He banged again.

"All right. All right. I'm coming."

The door swung open, and there stood Talac in only a pair of trousers, undone at that. His long hair spun wildly in all directions. Noting his visitor, the artist sniffed and scratched his beard. "Have you come to punch me? I haven't even had my breakfast yet."

Talac turned to go into the house, and Jasper followed. What did she see in the artist? More to the point, what did she see in *him*? They were nothing alike. Not physically, not in manner, nor profession. Amélic had called him an entrepreneur with the smallest hint of a sneer, for derision was the pervading view of businessmen in bohemian

Montmartre. Oh, the artists acknowledged the need for patronage. Not a one of them would look askance at a commission. But commercial enterprise couldn't hold a candle to truth and beauty and art for art's sake.

"Why should I punch you, Monsieur Talac?"

The artist lit the stove and began preparing coffee. "Why should you punch me? Your ladylove posed for me, and you only just found out."

"The first poster was"—Jasper hated to admit it—"good."

Talac made a point of turning back to him with a smug smile.

"All right, it was impressive. You know it."

"Yes." He paused. "Because of her."

"Well, you're going to have to find a way to get on without her. She can't be your muse."

"With all due respect," Talac began in a tone that dripped with disrespect, "you haven't any right to say that. An artist has his muse, and no one, not even a jealous rival, can say otherwise."

"Are we rivals?"

"You tell me."

Jasper nodded, as much to himself as to Talac.

"She can't be your model."

"I think you should let Amélie decide that. She's perfectly capable of making up her own mind."

"I don't need to tell you, monsieur, she's stubborn to the point of blindness. Her pride won't always allow her to make the right decisions. That's why I'm here."

"Oh? Now this is interesting. In what way can Jasper Degrailly be in my debt? I'd be much in demand in this district and beyond with your favor in my pocket."

Talac handed Jasper a coffee and sat down with his own. Jasper looked at the coffee, then at Talac. Skimming a knuckle across his lips, Jasper considered.

"When you're done with this contract, you'll leave her alone."

Talac chuckled breathily. "She and I are friends, monsieur. Devoted. Friends."

"She wasn't so devoted when she left you."

"She came back, didn't she?"

"I think you made her an offer a woman in her position couldn't very well refuse."

"She could have. As you say, her pride can make her stubborn beyond sense."

"Still, I'm told you had no association with her for more than a year."

"That was her wish, monsieur. And whether you believe it or not, I've tried to honor it. Though I love her and missed her terribly."

"You don't love her. If you did, you wouldn't have run her down the way you did."

"I was a hurt and heartbroken man when I did that. You would know something about that, wouldn't you? Being hurt and broken."

As the arrogant artist knew it would, the last dig made Jasper seethe. If he were hot-tempered, he might have been tempted to hurt Talac.

"You're a despicable man who cares only for himself. You don't love her. I don't think I've ever seen a man more self-interested than you."

"You would know. Wouldn't you?" The artist took a sip of his coffee. "Does Amélie know you're here? She might be curious to know."

Jasper's smile was filled with malice.

"Is this where you punch me?" Talac asked.

"You seem awfully interested in that, monsieur."

"It would certainly make things easier for me. A small hurt from your puny arm and she would come running to me."

"Do you refuse to give up your interest in Amélie?" Jasper asked.

Aubrey pressed a dramatic hand above his heart, and his eyes twinkled. "The heart wants what the heart wants."

Jasper stood to leave. "If we're to be rivals, monsieur, I should tell you now—I don't lose."

As soon as the carriage stopped at Ravignan, Jasper alighted with a bounce in his step. Madame Pelletier answered his knock and collected Amélie, who regarded him with a jaundiced eye.

"Have you forgotten your clothes, mademoiselle?" She was clad only in her chemise, knickers, and corset. "Dare I hope you're seducing me?" He looked at her glistening décolletage as her chest heaved up and down, then glanced at Madame Pelletier. "If you'll excuse us, madame."

The madame narrowed her eyes and pursed her lips, clearly biting down a caustic remark. In only a short time, he'd become familiar with her sharp tongue.

"Fine and well. But I don't pay her to entertain gentlemen callers."

Jasper merely raised a brow in warning, and the woman left.

"What are you doing here? If I didn't make myself clear last night, I don't want to see you anymore."

"I was in the neighborhood. I do have business interests in the district."

"What do you want? I need to get back to my ironing. The other girls won't think very much of me if they must do my work while I stand around talking to you."

"Fair enough. I'll just cut to the heart of it, then. You did make yourself clear last night. Now I need to make myself clear." He rested a hand on her shoulder. She tensed but didn't pull away, so he skated a thumb near the hollow of her neck until he could feel her pulse.

"I know you're scared. Being with me, *loving me*, scares you more than any fear you've ever known. Because it's more real and more right than anything you've ever known. More tenuous, too. To love another person is the most complete act of faith one can demonstrate.

"But I'm not afraid. We were meant to be together, you and I. I'm more certain of that than anything I've ever known. What we have is no common thing. And I'll do whatever it takes for as long as it takes until one day you know it, too."

31

"This is a pleasant surprise," Aubrey said when he opened the door to Amélie the next evening. "Come in. Come in. We were just sitting down to dinner."

She followed him to the back garden, her nerves flaring up. Ever since leaving Jasper's apartment, Amélie had been feeling sorry for herself. She wasn't meant for a love affair right now. Jasper could say whatever he wanted—her dreams were not excuses. He could do whatever he liked. She certainly couldn't stop him. That would make it more difficult, of course. Because she seemed incapable of resisting him. On that point, he was correct. And he would press it to his advantage at every turn.

But she had to pick her head up. Had to move on from the immense disappointment of not being cast at the Moulin Rouge. There were other dance halls, other theatres, other cabarets. Her rash decision to leave Cortot had thrust her in the unwilling position of having no place to go and little money. So, when she'd found a position that included room and board, however lowly and grueling but good, honest work, she'd taken it.

She wasn't in that desperate position anymore. She could look beyond Montmartre. She would. What better place than the current bright star on the entertainment landscape, certain to be the biggest rival to the Moulin Rouge? But she needed a way in.

They ate and chatted about a new piece Daan was working on, then chided him about the mysterious affair he was having. Finally, Amélie could bear it no longer. She looked at Aubrey.

"Are you still friendly with Monsieur Marchand?"

A flash of satisfaction blazed across Aubrey's face that he immediately snuffed out.

"Yes. Why do you ask?"

Amélie exhaled, then took a sip of her wine. "Would you mind terribly putting in a word for me? I want to audition for him."

"What happened with the Moulin Rouge?"

He tried to appear sincere in his concern but couldn't quite pull it off. This was the selfish man she'd left. One who'd cared very little for her dreams when the pursuit of them supplanted him. She'd all but forgotten that Aubrey when she modeled for him.

"I wasn't cast."

"What?" Daan shook his head. "They're mad not to. Well, good riddance to them. You'll go on to be a star somewhere else. What better place than Folies Bergère?"

"I thought the same."

"It's a fine idea, birdie," Aubrey said.

Birdie. Whenever that casual endearment slipped out it said more about Aubrey and his disdain for Amélie's singing than he realized.

"But Folies Bergère," he continued. "It's so far away. Where will you live? How will you get there day after day? Have you thought this through?"

She'd done nothing but since she decided on it. The Folies Bergère sat in the ninth district, not far from the opera house and where Jasper's office was. Too close to him and more than a mile from the washhouse. Yet the Élysée was really the only other dance hall of note in Montmartre, and it looked and felt its age. She couldn't wait around for another dance hall to open nearby. And if the Moulin Rouge was the success Zidler promised it would be, no others would dare. Once she'd set her mind on the newest, brightest, and best, there weren't many others that would do.

The Folies Bergère had been around for twenty years but was still a beating heart, lively and entertaining. She could find an audience there. She would. Yet she needed to take things one step at a time.

"I have thought about it," she said. "It's a walk that could take close to half an hour."

"Late at night or in the still-dark hours of the morning," Aubrey added. "That doesn't seem safe."

"Nearly every day I walk the streets of Paris during those hours. And with the burden of a heavy basket besides. I would give anything to take that same walk limp and flushed and happy from singing and dancing. Besides, thanks to you, I have some money now I can put toward an apartment closer to the hall. Maybe I might find a room with another performer. Or Penny.

"I'll think about that when I'm cast. For now, I need an audition."

"You're really determined to do this," Aubrey said in a tone that spoke more to his doubts than his confidence.

Why was it that men could not imagine a woman feeling passion for anything other than marrying and having babies? She might have actually felt something for those things if the bonds of convention hadn't required her to.

"Yes. I am."

Not three days later, she received word from Aubrey that Marchand would see her for an audition set for ten days hence. Aubrey might have dragged his feet and let her stew in her obligation, but he didn't. For that small kindness, and the far greater one of calling on his friend, she was eternally grateful.

For the first time since that night in early July when Jasper had told her of Zidler's decision, she felt a measure of hope. Getting a coveted audition demanded the right associations. But doing well in one relied upon her talents alone. About those she had little doubt.

In the meantime, it seemed now that she and Jasper were no longer officially seeing each other, she saw him more than ever. He stopped by the washhouse on a near-daily basis, always under the guise of checking on his laundry investment. But no one was under any illusion he wanted anything other than Amélie. Yet the comedy of it—"Oh, Mademoiselle Audet," said in such surprise, as if he had no idea she worked there, "what a pleasure it is to see you. You're looking well, as always."— was so damn endearing. She gritted her teeth even as she hid a smile, for always when she heard the distinctive tread of his boots, when he came around the corner into a room, when their eyes met, she felt that singular current that seemed only to exist between them.

Beyond his frequent visits, Jasper did nothing more to insinuate himself into Amélie's life. On the rare days he didn't come by, she was disappointed. Too often her mind wandered to him. What he was doing and who he was seeing. And his heartbreaking revelation. If not Madame Travers, who had he loved more than his own life and lost?

She could lie to herself, but there was no use. She missed him.

When Amélie walked into the Folies Bergère for her audition, it had been more than two months since she'd done the same at the Moulin Rouge. She would sing the same song and dance the same dance, but everything about this audition felt different.

In the first place, it felt illicit. She was auditioning for Jasper's rival and found no small satisfaction in that. Despite his assurance that the decision, in the end, had been entirely Zidler's, she couldn't help but feel that Jasper had affected it. Fair or not, she still blamed him in part for not being cast. She should have felt justified by this step, and she did to some degree. But she also couldn't help feeling like it was a betrayal.

In the second place, this was a theatre, not a dance hall. There was a grand stage before a sea of seats on the main floor and a horseshoe of them wrapping around on the second and third. When it opened twenty years before, the Folies Bergère had been designed as an opera house for the prevailing light entertainment of the day—the opéra comique.

And in the third, Monsieur Marchand didn't seem interested in the least in meeting her. She was directed around him by an imperious assistant.

"Just there." The lanky young man directed her to the stage.

After handing her music to the pianist, she climbed the iron stairs and walked out on stage. This time there was no blinding limelight, but the warm glow of gaslight flickering all along the edge of the stage. She could see Marchand, a man who seemed to be so interested in his own chest Amélie thought he could be asleep. This only made her more nervous, for in auditions she was always a little nervous at first, no matter her confidence.

Then she began to sing "Je te veux." It happened as it always happened in auditions—when she got a few bars in, her nerves dissolved. And in their place, a strength and clarity that knocked the pitch clean and made her voice resound in the space. She felt the provocative words reach right to Marchand as if they gripped his lapels and shook him. Indeed, he looked up suddenly, then sat up, adjusting his spectacles and stroking his long, chestnut beard.

Her satisfaction infused her, sending her confidence and voice soaring. If she closed her eyes, she could see the seats filled with people, could sense the other actors around her, could see her name on the marquee. It felt so right she wondered why she hadn't considered auditioning there earlier. Then she remembered Aubrey's smug smile and knew why. But this feeling was worth an ounce of his satisfaction. She would see a dozen, a hundred such smiles if she could feel this feeling every night.

Marchand seemed pleasant enough when at the end of the audition they were formally introduced. By a stroke of luck, there was an opening in the chorus line, and he would inform her of his decision in the coming days. This he said as his eyes mentally peeled the gold brocade from her body. She ignored his lecherous regard, reasoning that she couldn't keep playing the wide-eyed provincial. If there were games to be played to secure her dreams, she would play to win.

When Amélie left the audition, she had a foolish notion that took her to La Madeleine. She'd been raised in her mother's one true church. If Maria wasn't praying to the Holy Trinity, she consecrated herself to the Virgin Mother or the communion of saints. It seemed there was a saint for everything, which was why Amélie stood here in this neoclassical church inspired by Rome's temples.

A faint smell of burnt sandalwood and cedar incense hung in the air as she treaded softly through the mostly empty church. Past towering columns, under lapis domes and intricate frescoes, she finally found the painting and offertory of Saint Rita, the patron saint of desperate causes. Most of the artists Amélie knew tended to disparage religious faith. After all, there was no better religion than truth and beauty and art for art's sake. But, for some reason, kneeling here before this small painting had taken on its own religious following. The cynical bohemians believed in Saint Rita because she believed in them.

After lighting a candle, Amélie knelt and clasped her hands, but she hadn't any idea what to say. She wiped her glistening brow, shifted and looked around, then glanced at the painting, feeling as if Saint Rita herself were growing anxious with her. Finally, she cleared her throat.

"You'll have to forgive me. I-I haven't done this in some time." Again she looked at the painting of the nun with the stigmata on her forehead kneeling before a crucifix. "Madame, saint of the impossible, if you might sway Monsieur Marchand's mind to cast me at Folies Bergère, I'd be forever grateful. Give me the courage to hope. To remain steadfast." She paused as Jasper's sun-kissed face and sage eyes swam to the fore.

"And help me to love him… or let him go."

32

"**W**hy, look who it is," Mireille said, peering out the window with a smirk.

On this Friday, it had been a full week since her audition, and every day that passed, Amélie grew more and more anxious for word.

Feigning indifference, she strolled to the window and peeked out to see Jasper alight from his carriage carrying lavender posies. She exhaled. It had been three days since he'd come by, and no matter that she spurned his advances, she looked forward to his visits. As if sensing her watching him, he stopped on the front walk, looked up to her window, and gave her a sunny smile. She waved. How he made her heart leap.

Moments later, he came into the washroom, bowing and kissing hands and gifting flowers from one girl to the next like Don Giovanni himself. All the while, the sour, round ghoul of Madame Pelletier and her pursed lips trailed behind.

"They're not off for another quarter hour, monsieur."

"I'm happy to wait, madame. I hope I'm not disturbing you overmuch."

The madame stood stock-still, her eyes blinking rapidly, her mouth opening and closing like a landed fish. The women snickered. They all loved to see someone, anyone, put the laundry mistress in her place. Rarely was she struck dumb, but by Jasper—her generous benefactor, she liked to call him as if they were lovers and she a kept woman—she routinely was.

"Oh, well…" Her head bobbed as if on a spring. "No. It's your laundry, too, I suppose. You can do whatever you like."

"I thank you, madame." He handed her a posy. "I didn't need your permission. But to have it makes the sun shine brighter."

Madame Pelletier blushed as she pressed the posy to her nose. Then, as if remembering herself, she frowned and cast narrowed eyes at the women. "Don't think you can just drop your things where you stand simply because a handsome man hands you some flowers. Finish up." When they hesitated, she flapped her hands at them. "Go on, you lot, finish up."

They looked to Jasper, who nodded.

The madame propped her hands on her hips and glared. "Mind you, quit your looking at him. I gave you the positions. It's I who puts a roof over your heads and I who can put you out. There's more what needs to be done yet. Now finish up. Then you can flit off, lazy as you please."

When Jasper stepped up to Amélie, she accepted the posy with a polite curtsy. "Thank you, kind monsieur."

He stepped into her space as if he belonged, and the lavender between them reminded her of that sweet day riding at Marie-Louise's.

"Have dinner with me."

She started to shake her head.

"One dinner. Completely innocent."

"Things are rarely innocent with you."

"An innocent dinner and a decadent dessert, then. Look me in the eye and tell me you don't want it."

She shook her head.

"You have to eat," he continued. "And I know you want to come." His eyebrow arched with the double entendre. "Admit it. You miss me." He brushed the back of his knuckles slowly up and down her arm, and the nerve endings there crackled to life. Then he leaned in, so provocatively the other women would be sure to notice, and whispered, "You think my patience with you is limitless. It's not. Tell me you'd like me to move on. That I should go back to Daphne. Or half the women in this city who would be only too happy to be with me. Is that what you want?"

Her body vibrated with his closeness. Begged him to be closer still. The alarm of him actually leaving her alone was a potent threat, and he knew it. Her heart clutched in fear. She knew she was being selfish.

"You know that isn't what I want," she said, looking at her feet. "You've backed me into a corner, it seems."

He urged her to look at him. "I'd like to back you into a corner." He tipped his head to one. "That one looks good for a start. Would you like that?" He whispered wetly, "Would you like me to take you against that wall while the others, unable to help themselves, stand gape-mouthed and panting as they watch?"

The mere press of his body and promise in his words made her sink into her arousal. "No."

"Good." He pulled back. "I don't need to put on a show. Now finish up here and get changed. I'll be happy to wait." He turned for the door. "A dinner dress would be appropriate. And pack a bag."

In her room, she scrubbed her skin pink and surveyed her dresses. The worn powder-blue one hung on the end. Compared to the rich ones beside it, a stark reminder of her life before Jasper. When she'd first met him, it had been her best. Now it seemed merely pale and serviceable. Her gaze floated to a Neptune-green and black silk dress. The drape and beads, the black jeweled embroidery over the green bodice. Everything about it made her long to wear it. But something in this moment made her feel like choosing a dress meant far more than a dress. Nothing short of giving in to her heart's desire. She wanted it and was terrified of it in the same breath.

A short time later, she found Jasper in the drawing room. He stood, his eyes feasting on every inch of her and a smile threatening to break wide on his face.

"That dress. I knew when I saw that green—not quite emerald and not teal either—and that black. You are a rare beauty, my pearl. Come."

At the carriage, he stopped. "Where's your bag?"

"Might we take this one small step of dinner? Just for tonight?"

Then she caught sight of Aubrey over Jasper's shoulder. The madame considered any correspondence that should arrive at the washhouse hers to read merely because she owned the place on the address. Amélie couldn't have Madame Pelletier informing Jasper of her audition. So, she'd given Marchand the address on Cortot and asked Aubrey to bring word.

Her heart leapt into her throat, hoping for the right answer— *pray God it's yes.* Their eyes met, and he smiled and waved. Then his face fell as he saw Jasper.

Amélie pleaded with her eyes for him to turn around before Jasper saw. But it was too late. Jasper turned and spied Aubrey.

"Monsieur Talac." His tone was incensed.

"Monsieur Degrailly."

They appraised one another, the two men, so different in their work and dress but so striking in their charisma and sexual magnetism.

"You came by to visit Mademoiselle Audet," Jasper observed.

"Yes," Aubrey admitted.

"Do you visit her often?"

"No. I was very nearby is all. I thought I'd pay her a visit."

Jasper seemed to scrutinize Aubrey for a long moment. "Well, here she is," he said as if presenting the gift of her that was only his to bestow.

Amélie stepped around Jasper. "Thank you for coming by."

Aubrey turned to leave, and Amélie felt alarm and a frantic need to know the answer, whatever it was, despite Jasper's presence.

"I do hope all the news at Cortot is good."

Slowly Aubrey turned. His smile was soft, his eyes distant.

Her heart fell into her gut.

"It is."

"It is?" Exhilaration thrilled through her body. She wanted to leap and shout and dance, wanted to kick the washhouse front, wanted to kick the carriage, wanted to hug Jasper and Louis, Aubrey, anyone. Then a moment of doubt gripped her. "You're certain, then. It's good."

"Yes. The news is good."

Her happiness threatened to burst. She couldn't remember when last she'd felt such pure joy. "That's good to hear. So good."

Aubrey bowed with taunting formality. "Monsieur Degrailly, always a pleasure."

"I wish I could say the same, Monsieur Talac."

Jasper glowered at Amélie as they wended out of the district. The atmosphere in the carriage felt like a tomb compared to the elation she'd felt on the front walk.

"Where are we going?"

"The Jockey Club."

She nodded and tried to meet his gaze in challenge, then found she couldn't be bothered to care about challenging him or anything else in that moment. She was happy and deserved to feel every bit of it. Her life was about to change, and when Jasper found out, whether or not they could continue their affair, whether or not he wanted to, that would be the test.

"What's going through that head of yours?" he finally asked.

"I'm happy." She pulled her gaze from the city streets to look at him.

He gave her a sardonic grin. "Were you so happy to see him, then?"

Yes, she thought, but certainly couldn't tell him why. "Do we need to speak about Aubrey?"

Jasper leaned forward. "You tell me. Are you seeing the both of us? After I told you I severed my ties with Daphne and Jos, would you do this to me?"

Amélie knew exactly how it looked. She could explain his worries away easily with the truth. But that may solve one problem while igniting another even worse. And she felt too joyous with the news about becoming a performer at the Folies Bergère to have to defend it right now.

"I'm not seeing either of you."

"If you'd like to lead someone around by the nose, it won't be me." He looked at her with exhaustion and wisdom far beyond her years in his eyes. Then he leaned back, brought a hand to his mouth, and peered out the window for long moments. "You must choose."

At the Jockey Club, they were shown to a private suite. Jasper ordered two fingers of whiskey, a single malt he adored from Ireland, splashed over a single fat cube of ice that only the wealthy could afford in the heat of August. When Amélie ordered the same, he raised a brow.

They sat across the suite, staring at each other as they drank. After some time, Jasper set his glass down and sat back.

"Take off your dress."

She looked to the door. "Aren't we going to eat?"

"Yes," he replied as he locked the door. "Now take off your dress."

She could've used his help. He knew it and didn't offer. And for some reason, that made her arousal, always humming when she was around him, tick up a notch. His gaze never left her as she struggled to loosen her laces and remove the bodice, then the skirt.

When she stood before him in her underthings, he said, "Now the rest."

She didn't move. Neither did he. They stared at each other for what felt like endless moments. But when he gave her an order, her skin pulled into aching goosebumps and all her blood seemed to pool in her core so that she had little choice but to obey. Her eyes slid to her chest as she untied her bustle and loosened her corset.

"Stockings, too," he added when she would have left them on. "Everything."

Finally, she stood before him in the raw. His gaze slid slowly and deliberately over every inch of her, then came back to her eyes. He sat back, his jaw rigid and body coiled tight. He was about as relaxed as a cat about to pounce.

"Now you're as naked as I've been for the last few weeks. That ends tonight."

"Jasper—"

He put a finger to his lips. "No talking." He shook his head. "Come here."

She did.

"Turn around."

She did. She felt his warm breath on her bottom, but he didn't kiss her. Didn't touch her. Didn't do anything so much as she could tell. And the anticipation heightened everything. Made her fingers fidget and her breath hitch. He was masterful at doing nothing and making her wait.

"Relax these busy fingers." He took her hand and massaged each finger, then kissed them.

After doing the same to the other hand, he pulled them behind her and looped something, likely his tie, around her wrists, tying them tightly. Then he stood.

"Good?" he asked, his mouth at her ear.

She nodded.

"Good."

Then she felt what was almost certainly the ice cube pressed to her nape along with the warm, skating breath of his mouth. She gasped.

"Shh." He drew the cube down her spine. She tried to arch away, but he only grabbed her breasts and pulled her back. "You've been very cold to me, sweetheart." Water trickled down her spine and into her bottom. "And I've let you."

After moving her tied hands, he rubbed the ice where her back met the curve of her bottom, then came around to her front. He held the ice between his teeth, his smile like a sneer. "Not anymore," he said.

He pulled her hair loose from its bun and arranged it around her breasts. Then he drew the cube deliberately around her right breast, circling at the edge, then drawing in toward the puckered areola and pebble-hard nipple. After doing the same to the other, he trailed a line down her belly, then knelt and pressed what remained of the ice into her sex with his tongue. It was no more than a tiny nugget, still it felt piercing cold. She bit her lip to hold in her gasp.

"Melt that ice for me."

Then he all but attacked her nerve, licking and sucking, swirling around it and nibbling on it. Too soon, the jarring cold that had arrested her arousal became heat. Her sex grew fuller and heavier as he thrust a finger deep inside.

"I'm going to come," she said, putting her hands on his head.

"Easy. Just relax."

"No. I'm going to come, Jasper."

"No, you're not. Not until I say."

The doorknob was tried.

"Someone's here," she said.

"Are you close?"

"Yes."

"Very close?"

"Yes, yes, yes."

He stood, holding her nape and kissing her hard. She tasted herself on him as he slid his tongue in, fucking her mouth, then pulling back.

"What?" She stared gape-mouthed at him. "Are you just going to leave me like this? Frustrated? Again?"

"Are you frustrated?"

"You know I am."

"Now you know how I feel."

Jasper dressed her, and they ate dinner, exchanging banal small talk. All the while, her sex was a heavy mass of flared nerves. When she squirmed in her seat, his arrogant eyes slid to her.

After their dessert cups were taken away, he put his napkin on the table.

"Come here." He indicated his lap, and she straddled him and sat. He smiled sweetly, almost tentatively, and laced fingers through her hair, which she had left down. Slid his hands down her arms and skimmed over her breasts. Slid up her neck and cradled her face. He seemed anxious as he marked her.

"I love this body and this hair. This beautiful face with these pot-of-chocolate eyes. How you beg and submit. How you want me to hurt you and hold you. Make you cry and make you come." His hand slid to her heart. "And more importantly, the woman inside. I think you know how I feel about her." He stared at her for an interminable length of time, then finally he swallowed.

His eyes were glassy, face flushed, and voice tight when he said, "But I'm done."

You could have felled Amélie with a feather. That was the furthest thing from what she'd anticipated he'd say.

"Somehow it's finally come to me. I suppose I should be grateful to you in a way for finally making me see." But his bitter tone belied his words. "I can't go on chasing after women who won't or don't return my affections. I won't. I'm worth more than that. And I suspect you know it, too."

She could feel pain flooding up from her heart, a thick weight in her throat, a tingling in her nose, and a burning in her eyes. She could barely steady her voice to speak.

"Are you saying goodbye to me? For good?"

Jasper stared into the middle distance as if in deliberation. Finally, his resigned eyes tipped to hers.

"Yes."

By the thinnest thread, Amélie held in her heartache. Sharing the carriage on the way to Jasper's apartment. Through his insistence that Louis bring her home. While he stood at the open carriage door for the longest beat. Finally, he gave a curt nod and a doleful smile.

"I hope you find everything your heart desires."

Somehow she nodded, though it was the last thing she wanted to do.

Just as soon as the door closed, she wrapped her arms around herself and fell into open sobs. Only a few hours before, she'd been flying higher than she'd ever been in her whole life. Finally, she felt her dreams of performing in the palm of her hand. For so long she'd convinced herself it was all that mattered. If she forsook her home and friends and lovers, it was nothing compared to what she might gain, who she might become.

To believe in herself. To be in the daily hunt. To be steadfast in the face of fear and doubts and rejection. To strive when others settled. She hadn't chosen her sex or her voice, nor the feeling she had when she stepped on stage. She couldn't ignore how it ignited her. That meant something.

Now suddenly it all seemed like a universe of striving had shrunk down to a grain of sand. She hadn't just fallen for Jasper—she'd fallen in love with him. Only now that he'd ended their affair, all her fragmented feelings for him had become crystallized. If her dreams were the sun, he was the moon, moving her as steadily as the tides. She wanted them both. *Needed* them both.

33

"What are you doing tonight?" Charles asked as he strode into Jasper's office.

"Dinner with Madame Kohl."

"Cancel. You're joining me for dinner. And a show."

Jasper exhaled dramatically. Charles had been relentless in trying to distract him from his doldrums since he'd broken up with Amélie. Daphne and Max, too. They'd all succeeded as flies might at a picnic—annoying enough to fix one's attention on but not nearly as delicious as the meal. Jasper had been dining with relish on melancholy and self-doubt for a month.

He hadn't intended on breaking up with Amélie that night. In fact, when she'd finally agreed to go to dinner with him, he'd planned on effecting a full reconciliation. But when Talac arrived and Jasper saw her unconcealed joy at seeing him, it was too much. Suddenly he could see himself clearly in a way he hadn't before. Yet again he'd become a man chasing after a woman who wanted

235

someone else. How it had happened or why didn't matter. He simply wouldn't be that man. Never again. Jasper didn't like to lose. To Talac or anyone. Still, he had to gather the crumbs of his pride.

The very next day, he'd contacted Madame Pelletier and told her he was withdrawing all but his financial interest in the laundry. Beyond an annual financial report, he had no interest whatsoever in any of the goings on at her establishment. Then he closed the accounts he'd opened for Amélie at the House of Worth and Fashion House. Finally, because he seemed to be charging full bore into self-flagellation, he went to Deauville to endure his mother's and sisters' prying for the rest of the summer.

He'd been back in the city less than a week when he ran into Daphne at Chez Christiane. She'd wagged a finger at him in gentle chiding, then welcomed him back with open arms.

"A show," Jasper said with an edge of skepticism.

"A new girl is bringing down the house at the Folies. Their nightly receipts have shown a marked uptick."

He sat forward. "Really?"

If anything could bring him back to life, it was his interest in the Moulin Rouge. A new act at their biggest rival less than a month before opening night? It would stir his blood to poach her. *Finally.* Something might stir his blood.

"Let's have a look at this girl."

When they walked up to the theatre on rue Richer, Jasper glanced absently at the second story, a front entirely of windows that always called to his mind a cage. Distracted for a moment, he didn't realize Charles had stopped until he was through the front door. Jasper glanced back and saw Charles fixed on something.

"What is it?"

It was a poster almost certainly of Amélie, the strokes and shades so similar to their own poster of her. The main differences were that this one splashed the name "Folies Bergère" in rounded, dripping red over the top, the name at her feet "Fleur de Lotus," and the ensemble she wore was a scandalous daisy-yellow corset and wisps of all-but-sheer yellow fabric that revealed her legs nearly to her sex.

It was difficult to grasp the tethers of all his feelings in that moment. Arousal definitely. It was like a pistol shot, and his blood raced to his cock. But anger, too. For her. For him. For so many reasons he couldn't decide which mattered most.

For a month he'd tried desperately to forget her. Put her out of his life and mind and heart, like locking the door and swallowing the key. Now it seemed like he was pressed against that bulging door, that he had been all that time and was running out of strength.

"What is she thinking? Did you know about this?" Jasper asked.

Charles merely looked at him and walked into the theatre.

Jasper's eyes scanned for her everywhere, his mind crawling with questions. *Does she work here every day? What about the washhouse? Where does she live?* He didn't want to imagine with whom she might live. When he'd ended his overt interest in the laundry, he was glad. What did he want with a laundry—when he specialized in hospitality investments—but the singular one that employed her? Now he cursed his petulance. And, along with it, everything he didn't know.

Distracted by his musings, he wandered under the chandeliers and towering palms of the indoor garden. Somehow Charles, with his charismatic showmanship—he was famous for complimenting with the right hand while taking the coat off your back with the left—had managed to charm seats from someone right near the main stage.

"My source wasn't leading me astray," Charles grumbled as they sat at a table in the garden for the preshow entertainment. "Look how crowded this place is."

Yet Jasper wasn't looking *at* the crowd so much as looking *through* it. For her.

"Sit. Have a drink. Your edginess is making me edgy, and I don't wear that well. Frowning makes my jowls sag."

"Who can tell with your muttonchops?"

"Why do you think I wear them?"

Jasper sat and swallowed a whole glass of whiskey.

Charles *tsk*ed and waved a hand for a waitress. "I've never known you to abuse such good whiskey."

When another was placed before Jasper, he sipped gracefully as he always did.

"There now, calm down. You're behaving like a scraggly pup I can't arrest no matter my grip on your neck."

Jasper shook his head as he finally looked around. "There are too many people here."

"On that we agree. Can we look at this as a simple poaching, or is your head in your cock?"

Jasper narrowed his eyes at him while Charles rolled his.

"You young whelps are so predictable."

"I'm hardly young."

"No? Then start acting your age." Charles drank and eyed the crowd. "Perhaps it's finally time you settled down. Married and had a few young ones. My Betta has been a positively righteous influence upon me. She's consecrated herself to seeing me right in the eyes of Almighty God."

"Really? And has she made much progress in that endeavor?"

"Hardly, as you well know." Charles winked. "But simply knowing there's someone seeing to my eternal soul, no matter that it isn't me, helps me to sleep at night."

"No matter in whose bed you're sleeping?"

Charles made an amusing attempt at shock. "Yes."

The first attraction, and the most popular in their preshow, was the dames de petite vertu. They marched two by two around the garden, faces painted white, eyes smudged in blue, and lips rouged in red. Breasts thrust out over corsets tied so tight it was a wonder they could breathe. They parted the panting crowd of men, who stepped aside but a moment to let them pass, then rushed back like water, mouths agape and eyes fixed.

Two years before, Marchand had debuted the "Place aux jeunes" revue, changing the artistic direction of the Folies Bergère into a hedonist's paradise.

"Place for young people, indeed," Charles said. "You'd have to be half dead with your cock in a vise to be able to ignore that."

Jasper bristled with distaste as he searched continually for Amélie's face. He felt all but certain she wouldn't be among those ladies—the poster out front was reserved for performers on the main stage. If he were being honest with himself, he was a hypocrite. He and Charles planned to offer similar entertainments. Yet, and this was a most important distinction he clung to, the Moulin Rouge would be top-shelf. Nothing but the most high-class entertainment for his most high-class clientele. Not something so rude and base and obvious as this.

There was something so unsubtle about selling sex, like a heavy-handed smith hammering iron. But selling seduction, like the deft hand of a potter in turning clay, now *that* was an art form. They intended to be masters of their craft.

After the ladies made their turns, like show horses prancing around a circle, the patrons moved in a wave of turned interest toward the main theatre.

The show began with a pantomime troupe. Then a brother act doing high-flying acrobatics. Next an orchestra accompanied a ballet pantomime followed by an intermission wherein a musical entertainment of gypsy women performed in the entrance garden for the imbibing crowd. After intermission was a sister chanteuses act. Another ballet, then a monocyclist, yet another pantomime until finally, *finally*, the lights dimmed for the last act.

Jasper was as keen as he'd ever been, his body tight and eyes desperate. The whole program he'd been absently rubbing his thumb over the name "Fleur de Lotus" there at the end of his program declaring her in fat, bold print. She'd star in a ballet pantomime accompanied by a full orchestra. That was all he cared about, to the exclusion of the rest of the show. In truth, he'd hardly seen any of it, the blur of flying, leaping, singing, and performing lost in the *ooh*s and *aah*s of the leering and leaning crowd.

Now he fixed his attention on a dim limelight illuminating what appeared to be a brown, bubbling pool in the middle of the stage.

"I suppose if she's the lotus flower, then that's supposed to be mud," he said to Charles.

"I suppose," Charles agreed.

"Don't tell me she's going to slime around in that, or I will leap on the stage and remove her myself."

Charles studied him, his brow furrowed. "I suspect, in your state of mind, you might do just that." He leaned in. "Perish the thought, Degrailly. Whatever she does on that stage, whatever you do, do *not* embarrass me. And if you care for her at all, you won't embarrass her either. You think about that and hold your seat."

The orchestra started in with a sprightly, almost-delicate song as the light grew bolder and brighter. Jasper made out cable that appeared to be fixed to the ceiling and somehow slid through the pool. Then a snow-white cocoon pierced the center of the pool, tipping the pool back.

"Will she have mud all over her?" Jasper asked.

"My source says it's chocolate."

Jasper gritted his teeth. "That's worse."

Steadily the cocoon, untouched by the chocolate, rose until it hovered above the stage by a good ten feet. Then it flowered open to reveal the most exquisite woman Jasper had ever seen. Amélie sat comfortably on a swing in the daisy-yellow corset and diaphanous layered skirt that fell in a train behind and in front revealed her shapely legs crossed seductively. Her dark hair was styled partially up in a half chignon with the rest falling in soft waves. Her make-up was subtle but for her bold, red lips.

"My God," he exclaimed under his breath. "She's a queen. A goddess."

Amélie scanned the audience with a placid, inscrutable look until her eyes fell on Jasper's, and she paused. Her mouth fell open as their gazes held.

Then his heart plummeted as she tipped dangerously to one side, one hand holding the cable between her legs, the other out as if to embrace the whole audience, and she began to slide over the crowd as they fell back in their chairs, *ooh*ing and *aah*ing at the beautiful woman swinging directly overhead. All the while, she crooned about a lost love. "Come back to me," she sang. "I'm yours, my lover."

The orchestra leaned into a crescendo as her voice soared through the theatre to a climax. When the song ended, it was like a petal falling, an eerie silence in the midst of that crowd. She collapsed back from the swing as if dead, and the crowd rushed to its feet in a collective gasp. But subtly, she held on tight with those exquisite legs. And for a moment, just a moment, there was that same unreal quiet. Then thunderous applause.

Every man in that theatre wanted to claim her while Jasper couldn't breathe for the pain in his chest. It felt so immense it ached in his throat and made his eyes water. Scarcely could he hear the applause or see anything but for her. He felt himself riven in two. One half of him wanted her more than his next breath. And the other half knew he had to walk away.

34

mélie's heart raced as she rushed through the narrow warrens backstage. Somehow in that faceless crowd, she'd seen Jasper like a beacon on a black shore. If she knew him at all, if he'd come to watch her, he would come for her. As politely as she could, she accepted the kind compliments and backslaps from her fellow performers while she moved swiftly to her dressing room.

She closed the door just as she saw Marchand charging down the hallway toward her, cradling two massive bouquets of roses in his arms.

"Help me, Penny, quickly. I need to hurry on home tonight," she urged her dress maid.

Then came Marchand's distinctive *rat-a-tat-tat-tat* knock. "Are you decent?"

"No. And I'm afraid I must be getting along home now."

"Now? Why the rush? May I come in?"

Amélie rolled her eyes and flew behind her screen as Penny let the director into the room.

"Another excellent performance as always." Marchand handed the roses to Penny and flopped down on a sofa. "My dear, you are as reliable as the sun and far more brilliant."

"Thank you." Amélie finished donning her dress in record time and emerged from behind the screen to secure her pumps.

"Why are you rushing off?" He pointed to the flowers. "The comte is asking for you. You should see his face. It's all lit up like a child's. When he talks about you…"

"That's very sweet." Amélie turned to her mirror to remove her makeup. No time, she decided and stood. "But I really must be going."

Marchand stood between her and the door. "What is this, puppet? You're no shy maiden. He's harmless and quite influential and not bad looking, as you well know. His personality may be somewhat lacking. But what he lacks in good humor, he has in other ways." He leaned in and put a hand around his mouth conspiratorially. "The ladies say he's quite adept in bed sport. And how long has it been since you've had your bell rung? One dinner. What can it hurt?"

She exhaled. She'd been delivering excuses to the persistent man for weeks. "Tomorrow. If he comes by tomorrow, I'll be happy to share a dinner with him after the show."

"Will you really? You promise?"

"Just dinner, Edouard. Make sure he knows that."

"Just dinner," Marchand affirmed. "I'll make it as clear as… well, very clear."

She grabbed her cloak and opened her door to see Archer Bonnin, the Comte de Beaumont, smiling down at her like a buffoon.

"My Fleur, what can I say but that your beauty and grace on that stage do not do justice to how radiant you are standing before me?"

Somehow he always said, "What can I say?" then went on to say the most inane things. He was an ardent pursuer, she could give him that, and not unhandsome. As tall as Jasper with chestnut hair, caramel eyes, and a full muttonchop beard. Though twice her age, it didn't seem to faze him. He was well kept, recently widowed, and on the prowl for a new light-of-love. Whether he was as influential as his name implied, she couldn't say. But despite his title, influence, and appearance, he was almost certainly the most comically inept man she had ever known. Beyond that, he knew very well her name, yet insisted on calling her Fleur.

Amélie went to slide around him, but he was an imposing man.

"Dare I hope you've agreed to come to dinner with me?"

She looked back at Marchand with pleading eyes, then quickly scanned the hallways. They were emptying out. Marchand strode out to the comte with his arms out in fawning. "Comte, let's have a drink."

When Amélie finally managed to slip out the backstage door, she peered up and down rue Saulnier and, satisfied that it appeared quiet, began to walk home. She'd taken perhaps ten strides when someone stepped into her path.

"My dear."

She swallowed a scream and stepped back.

Charles Zidler stepped into the warm gaslight that illuminated his features. "I'm sorry I startled you. I assure you that wasn't my intent. Are you all right?"

"You scared me out of my skin, monsieur."

The Whitechapel Murderer hadn't been captured and hadn't struck in months. Rumors swirled he'd fled England for the Continent. No woman, especially any unaccompanied woman on a dark street, was safe.

"But, other than that, yes, I'm all right." She scanned the narrow street.

"He isn't with me."

"But he was there."

"Yes." He paused. "That was quite a performance, mademoiselle."

"Thank you. I suppose you couldn't wait for me backstage."

"No."

She nodded. "You made a mistake when you cut me in July. Now if you'll excuse me, it's getting late. I should be getting home."

"A mistake. I did indeed. May I escort you? I have a proposition for you." He indicated a carriage. "I'd like to discuss it." When she hesitated, he said, "Please."

In the carriage, they sat regarding each other evenly. Now that she considered the director without nerves, his cheeks were rosy and his bottle-glass-blue eyes were kind.

"You're a star, Mademoiselle Audet. I knew it this summer."

"And you didn't cast me, so what's changed?"

"You're a shrewd woman. I think you know."

"I think I do."

"Come to work for me," he said, leaning forward.

"You have your cast. And you open in two weeks, I hear."

He flicked his hand in dismissal. "We'll work the bugs out before you grace the stage. I've no doubt you'll carve your own place. It'll be a spectacle, your unveiling."

"Why should I desert the man who gave me my first chance for a man who's merely offering me a second chance?"

Zidler smiled an admiring smile. "People make mistakes. We do one thing when we know we should do another. But who are we if we're unwilling to fix them? Unwilling to give people second chances?"

She stared at him for a long minute. "Why didn't he come with you?"

"He wanted to. Believe me he wanted to. He came to the theatre tonight not knowing you were here."

"But you knew."

"I saw the poster. Before tonight." He put his head down as if deep in thought. "When we were first partners, we'd all but agreed on a silent partnership. He would front the money and le Fauborg while I would be the director. I don't work very well with full partners. But somehow we do. We both care about this endeavor. Equally. That's why he agreed only moments ago to sign a proper agreement of silent partnership. So that I may manage you, mademoiselle."

"Why would he do that, monsieur? Unless he's moved on…"

Amélie peered at Zidler with her heart in her throat. The heady rush of seeing Jasper tonight had made her heart race. Wretchedly, she wanted him now more than ever.

But the director's soft smile gave away nothing.

"He doesn't give up control easily," she said. "You don't know him very well if you think he will."

"We want you to work for us. And he's willing to have a lesser voice to make that happen."

"Marchand gave me a chance, and he's making me a star."

"Give us a chance—give *me* a chance—and I'll make you a bigger one."

Amélie shook her head.

"The Folies is all about the girls, increasingly naked girls."

"And you won't be?"

"It may seem a subtle difference."

"Marchand doesn't require me to be a demimondaine."

"Because he has his dames. And that's something we can negotiate."

She shook her head again.

"Tell me you weren't entertaining any admirers while I was waiting for you."

She looked away.

"Aha! What's his name? A general, a count, or a duke?"

She wouldn't look at him.

"You can leave him behind, whomever he is, for a while anyway. Has Marchand increased your pay since you became a headliner? I'll double whatever he's paying. I've no doubt it's not nearly enough."

"Double my pay? Why would you do that?"

In truth, her pay was paltry, but it was just enough to scrape by as a performer, and a performer was all she wanted to be.

"As I said, you're a star. You should be treated like one. And I can give you your own furnished apartment right near the theatre."

She shook her head in astonishment. She couldn't turn this down, could she?

"You'll be a star wherever you go. The only difference is the stage. At the Moulin Rouge, you'll be on the brightest in Paris. Maybe even the world. The choice is yours."

Finally, she looked at him squarely.

"Say yes, mademoiselle."

PART THREE

GIRL IN ROUGE

35

Opéra, Paris
Sept. 22, 1889

*A*mélie watched as Monsieur Zidler's carriage drove away from her building. After looking to make certain she was alone, she leapt into the air with a shriek of joy. Wildly she danced and wept and shouted and laughed, exclaiming, "Yes! Yes! Yes!" and hugging herself for want of anyone else to hug. All the while, her heart beat in a mad tattoo, and she felt her blood singing in her veins.

A month before, she'd barely had a few hours of exhilaration after Aubrey's news, and hidden at that, before Jasper ended their affair. For some days, she'd been so devastated by her heartbreak it felt difficult to grasp her achievement.

Then only too soon, Marchand had made her feel like boot scrapings, like a clod who couldn't dance, a crow who couldn't sing. When he wasn't working her to exhaustion, he paused to tell her she was too fat or too thin, that she'd scarcely amount to much. That he was the soul of kindness in offering her any position at all. That she should be grateful. And made certain she knew exactly how.

Until she'd begun to draw people into the Folies Bergère. Then he'd cossetted her like a babe or preened with pride or both. She was no stranger to pompous managers and directors, not unaccustomed to ridicule and abuse. And perhaps Zidler would be just like Marchand. Maybe even worse.

But tonight he'd made her feel more talented, more wanted, than any person had ever made her feel. Any person, that was, save one.

At that, Amélie felt her heart burn. Jasper had come. His face in the crowd had been more beautiful than in her memory. A subtle look of wonder or desire or pride. Perhaps even love.

He'd come just shy of professing his love for her that night. She knew he had loved her. And she'd loved him. Still loved him. If she took the position at the Moulin Rouge, would it be better or worse? Would she see him more? Or would it be like Zidler had intimated? Would he make certain he wasn't around?

What am I doing? Somehow I'm allowing yet another triumph to be clouded by Jasper.

In her tiny garret tucked into the roof of a building, Amélie found Penny.

"Where've you been?" the girl asked. "You should've been back well before me. I was getting worried. No telling who's on the streets at this hour. Leather Apron, perhaps."

"I've made it, Pen." Amélie clutched a hand before her mouth, suppressing another squeal. "The Moulin Rouge. They want me."

"The Moulin Rouge? I thought… I thought they had their cast."

"I thought so, too. But they came to the show tonight."

"Monsieur Degrailly. He came to see you?"

"He came to *poach* me. Monsieur Zidler. He found me outside the theatre and made me an offer. Can you believe it? Me. He wants me."

"What kind of offer?"

Amélie took Penny's hands. "He wants to make me a star. Says he'll increase my pay and furnish me with an apartment near the Moulin Rouge."

"Just like that?"

"You make it sound ludicrous. That he would want me. When it's been me who's increased ticket sales at the Folies. Marchand would never admit it, but we all know it's true."

"It's not like that, and you know it. I don't doubt you. I've never doubted you. But what about Monsieur Degrailly?"

"H-he wasn't with him. Zidler made an arrangement with him to step back from their partnership to allow me to have my place."

"He did? Why would he do that? Unless he…"

Amélie pulled the girl into her arms, smothering the thought.

"This isn't about him."

But Penny pulled back and gave her a scolding look. She was too clever by half… and knew very well how Amélie's heart still ached for Jasper.

"You're sure to see him again. At the Moulin Rouge. No matter what Monsieur Zidler said. No matter what Monsieur Degrailly arranged. No matter what you think, you'll be even closer to him. Do you want that?"

After the pair readied to go to sleep, Amélie crawled into bed beside Penny, and for the first time since moving into her precious little garret, the meager mattress felt unforgiving. Penny's breathing evened while Amélie peered up at the sloped ceiling, unable to quiet her mind.

Seeing Jasper's florid face, so beautiful, in the audience. Zidler's astonishing offer. How could she say no? And finally her little dress maid's prediction, so astute for one so young.

You'll be even closer to him. Do you want that?

The easy answer was yes. But her heart… She didn't know if she could bear it.

The very next day, with shaking hands, Amélie opened a package from Charles Zidler. In it was a contract with Zidler Productions bearing details and amounts so staggering she could scarcely believe it held her name. Not only did it double her pay, as promised, it also contained a tidy signing bonus, the address of her new apartment on de Clichy, and a rehearsal schedule to start two days hence. All this and a promise of a year's employment with an opportunity to renegotiate these terms year after year. And there at the bottom, her name—Amélie Álvarez Audet.

The dream of performing on the brightest stage in Paris lay in the palm of her hand. Her heart was so full it burned in her throat and welled in her eyes. She swallowed but couldn't blink back the tears. They fell fat on the page as she signed it with a flourish. There was no going back now.

And, apparently, no time.

Before the day was out, she'd quit the Folies, much to Marchand's indignant protestations. He called them mad, her a no-talent hack. They were snakes, she a vamp. But none of his sweet pleadings—and in the end he had pled—could change her mind. The Folies would try, but somehow Amélie was as certain as Jasper and Monsieur Zidler that the Moulin Rouge would be a show palace without equal.

And after breaking the lease on her garret on rue la Fayette, Amélie moved with Penny into a well-appointed apartment in the turret of the gothic tower adjoining the Moulin Rouge. Yet all the while, and despite the heady thrill she lived on, Jasper was never far from her thoughts. From the moment she set foot on de Clichy, whenever a carriage came to a stop outside, she wandered to her turret window, looking hopefully for him. But he never appeared.

Amélie's heart beat so loudly when she walked into the Moulin Rouge she could feel it pulsing in her ears. Three months had passed since that fateful audition. Now it seemed nearly everything was in its place. Curtains and mirrors were hung. Chairs were stacked, and tables lay waiting to be set. It smelled faintly of new wood and lemon polish.

All of it lit by a stunning array of glowing electric chandeliers, wall sconces, and stage lights. Everything about the dance hall felt new and decadent and exciting.

Chorus lines of performers huddled together, stretching and chatting and laughing. When she sidled amongst them, they stopped to peer at her askance.

"Good morning."

For what seemed like endless moments, they continued to stare, their appraising gazes skating all over her, saying nothing, doing nothing. A blush of self-doubt crept up her chest and into her cheeks.

Finally, a buxom blonde straightened and strolled to her.

"So, you're the new girl. From Folies."

Amélie felt a yearning to be small just then, wishing she could hide from the condemnation in the woman's voice. Everything within her wanted to shrink. Wanted meekly to reply yes. To degrade her worth to fit in.

So instead, she mustered all the confidence and courage she could and straightened. Towering above the blonde by nearly half a foot, she jutted her chin and looked down at the woman.

"I just want a chance to find my place here."

The disapproval on the blonde's face and in her posture broke, and a tiny glint of admiration shone in her eyes. She extended her hand.

"I'm Gisèle. But everyone calls me Gigi. Have you stretched?"

"Not yet."

"Better do it, then." Gigi proceeded toward the stage, and the other performers followed. "Try to keep up."

But for a short break for lunch, they sang and danced, cued each other and called out their lines, well into the afternoon. All that time, Amélie received no accommodation for joining late. She danced two steps behind, sang three notes behind, staggering and sweating and cursing.

By the end of the day, when the other performers were packing up and planning their nights, she heard one of them whisper, "Zidler's folie," to which others chortled.

Amélie sagged, near tears, feeling as pitiful as she'd looked.

What am I doing here? I'm a laughingstock.

Indeed, when a door squeaked open, she heard a cackle floating outside the hall and knew instinctively it was about her. She would be the butt of their jokes if she couldn't master the numbers.

Measured boot treads fell on the dance floor, approaching her.

"Monsieur," the performers called out as they passed.

For the first time since walking into the dance hall that morning, Amélie's nerve endings crackled to life, wondering if, hoping that Jasper had finally come. Beyond mastering her performances so she wasn't humiliated, all she could think of was how badly she wanted to see him. He would hold her and reassure her how talented she was. Make her cede her fears along with her control. How she wanted to submit. Just once more.

But it was Zidler who approached, and her heart plummeted. What was wrong with her that she couldn't arrest the terrible longing she felt for Jasper? Still? He'd obviously moved on. She must, too.

Yet that led to the most provocative question of all—what was wrong with her that she couldn't be content? Most people lived their whole lives wanting to love something as she loved performing. Wanting to achieve something so impossible as she had. But still to want more, to continue to grasp for something out of reach, felt as natural as breathing. Would she never be truly happy?

Jasper's words echoed back.

Perhaps they're really an excuse for you to avoid loving someone who may one day not be there. And then suddenly you're a five-year-old girl again whose whole world has changed.

Then she knew, and it resonated like a sonorous bell inside her:

You can't lose happiness you don't have.

"You survived your first day," the director said, interrupting her thoughts.

Amélie gave Zidler a soft smile. "Barely, monsieur. I'm afraid you've made a poor investment in me."

"Were you so awful, then? Performing songs you knew not a note of, dances you knew not a step of, lines you knew not a word of?"

Chagrined, she nodded.

"You insult me, mademoiselle."

She opened her mouth to protest.

"Oh, I know you don't mean to. Only consider this: if I trust you know what you're doing, you might trust I know what *I'm* doing."

"Touché."

"Now, then. You, my chick, will give them an encore. More singular and seductive than any audience has ever seen."

A month later, Amélie's heart raced as Penny helped her into her final costume and Madame Lefebvre—the pinch-faced stage mother—fit a silvery white wig over her hair. She could barely hear herself think with the thunderous claps and chants in the background for Diamant, Diamant, Diamant. But Amélie didn't care. She felt exhilaration the like of which, in all her imaginings, had never been this good.

After that first day, she'd gone early and stayed late for every rehearsal. At first so she wouldn't be an embarrassment. Then so she'd be on par with all the rest. Finally, so she would surpass them and earn the praise and investment Zidler had lavished on her.

She was no one's idiot. No one's clod. No one's *folie*. But most important of all, somehow she had to find a way to banish the nighttime of her fears. Amélie would be happy—unreservedly, unashamedly happy. So, she'd set out to prove she didn't need anything more. Nor any*one*.

It would start tonight, stitching together one triumph after another until she wore a shroud of success so golden she'd be lit by the light of it. No one else, certainly no man, no matter how alluring, could take it from her. At any rate, it wouldn't be Jasper. As Zidler promised, he'd completely absented himself from the business. Amélie hadn't seen him since that night at the Folies Bergère, knew nothing of him and promised herself she didn't care. He was out of her life. And she was happy.

Tonight, at long last, she'd performed at the Moulin Rouge. Sang and danced, kicked and climbed and soared. Over the crowd, into the crowd. Eyes were wide and mouths agape. Men panted and women delighted, hanging on her every note and step. Leaning and calling and clapping for more. And here how modern it all was. With the bright, electric lights, it felt like a new world was dawning. And she right in the middle of it. Her heart felt like it would burst right out of her chest with joy.

Zidler had insisted on an encore from her, something seductive, in red. But Amélie had a different idea. It would be, she promised, entirely unexpected. While he loved his idea, he loved the unexpected even more. He wasn't certain of her plan when she'd explained it, but the new sheet music had arrived for the altered version of the iconic song only a week before, and in rehearsals she'd held the hall enrapt.

He poked his bewhiskered head in the room. "It's time, chick." In a few short weeks, Amélie had come to understand this tight, singsong chiding was the director barely restrained. And in truth, his cheeks were flushed as if all his spinning energy and tension had flooded there.

"Just a minute, gov," Madame Lefebvre scolded. She shoved pins into the wig, securing it so tightly there was scarcely any notion Amélie had sable hair only minutes before. "There," the stage mother finally pronounced, stepping back with a smile of pride.

Amélie stood and regarded herself in the mirror. Her unusual hair and that distinctive dress. But for her brown eyes and the blush on her cheeks, she didn't know the woman staring back at her. A small, triumphant smile lit her face, then she turned for the stage.

36

*J*asper snaked his way through the crowd. Nearing midnight, rivers of champagne had been flowing for hours. Everyone, it seemed, was loose and loud and uninhibited. Eating and drinking and, most importantly, spending money. Just as he and Charles had imagined. Friends and acquaintances barked his name and clapped him on the back. Wanted to buy him a drink. Wanted him to stay so they could fawn over him. He acknowledged them all with a warm smile and a demure nod but kept walking. He had to get closer for the encore. He had to.

Daphne called for him to slow down, to settle down. She knew him too well. She'd welcomed him back to their play, just as keen to submit to his ravenous appetite as he was to dominate her. For the past couple months, he'd played and fucked and experimented, visiting Chez Christiane as frequently as he had in the beginning. Sometimes he had more than one woman in a night.

Sometimes he had more than one woman in a scene. All of it was good, so good. But never quite good enough.

He gripped Daphne's hand tighter, pulling her along. But in truth, from the moment Amélie had appeared, he was lost for anyone else.

Jasper had known that night at Folies she was a star. Her soaring voice and seductive body. That commanding presence and incomparable beauty. She deserved to be on the Moulin Rouge stage. Bitterly he'd made that unthinkable arrangement with Charles. It broke his heart, but if he could give her every dream she'd ever had, he would do it.

Suddenly all the lights in the theatre went out, and there was a collective gasp. Charles's insistence on electric lights was paying off. Half their patrons came simply to experience the unreal bright lights. When they stayed out, there were murmurings and tipsy giggles. The crowd pressed all around him and felt like a swarm of bees buzzing. They knew, *hoped,* something was afoot.

Then one light appeared near the ceiling of the stage. A cut diamond amidst black, it looked like a star. For an unbearably charged moment, that determined star shone. Then a spray of lights, some big and some small, staggered and bunched, a constellation of stars, blinked on, and there were *ooh*s and *aah*s in wonder. An incandescent masterpiece, the crowd stared owl-eyed and gape-mouthed in astonishment.

That alone might've been enough for an encore, to send them off with the night sky on their lips—until a limelight shone on a woman perched on a crescent moon. She wore a sleek, gray gown so light it was almost white with an over-robe of tulle embroidered in intricate crystal moons and sprays of stars. Her hair was piled high atop her head in a softly swirled pompadour, but he'd never seen the like of the color—an unearthly silvery white.

For a moment he was as stunned as the rest of the crowd. She was a woman and a diamond in one. And then she began to sing:

"By the light of the moon,
My friend Pierrot,

Lend me a quill,
To write a word.
My candle is dead,
I have no light left.
Open your door to me,
For the love of God..."

"Au clair de la lune." But the simple French folk song, an utterly common lullaby used for a century to sing French babies to sleep, had never been sung like this. She poured it slow and sticky like honey and so inexplicably arousing that the hive of the crowd stood mesmerized.

Jasper's feet bumped against the stage, and when he looked back up at the woman in the moon, she was looking at him. In that silvery white, Amélie had transformed herself for the crowd. But the song she sang to all the men panting beside him and the packed house beyond—a song about a girl who was cold because her fire has gone out, who sought the help of a boy whose fire burned brightly but refused her—she sang only for him.

When finally she hit the last note, the volume that had pierced the place fell off a cliff. In its place hung a note small and pure, then it arced into nothing like a falling star. No one dared take a breath. Then it was gone. For a stunned beat, there was nothing, then the crowd roared and whistled and clapped. A tired, old song sung a thousand times, a million even, and she'd remade it. Just like performing itself. Like light itself. It was being remade here in this performance palace. And in one night, she'd made herself its unrivaled star.

"Lune, Lune, Lune," the crowd chanted as the moon descended.

Amélie gracefully slipped off and strolled downstage as roses rained down on her. Mere feet from him she paused and took a deep bow. When Amélie finally stood, she was looking at Jasper. In her eyes shone a childlike twinkle and a glassy well of tears. It filled his heart to see her so happy. But it broke it, too. She stood so close he could have reached out and touched her. Yet she'd never seemed so far away.

Moments later, Jasper once again dragged a reluctant Daphne behind him, this time through the labyrinthine backstage.

"Wouldn't you like to meet her again after such a performance?"

"Of course. But everyone in the hall wants to meet her. The line of well-wishers…"

"Nonsense. And I know the owner." He stopped to wink at her, then carried on. But she pulled her hand from his grasp and stopped.

"Would you have me pick up the pieces again? Is it not bad enough you don't love me? Must I constantly be reminded?"

Jasper stopped cold. "We don't love each other, darling. That isn't how we are. Right?"

Daphne gave him a rueful grin and shook her head. "You break my heart a hundred ways every day."

"A hundred every day. That seems… dramatic."

"Don't patronize me." She pulled her hand away and turned to leave.

"Daphne—"

"I'm too sober for this."

"Are you really upset?"

"Are you really so obtuse, Jasper? You of all people should know that arrangements and intentions mean nothing when faced with a heart's desire."

After all the things Jasper had been stunned by on this night, this was one he never could've imagined. All this time he'd thought Daphne as carefree as a hummingbird, happy to flit amongst her garden of men, sipping from their nectar whenever she pleased.

"Have I been careless? Or are you assuming?"

"Both, of course. That's why I like you still."

He felt wretched and held her cheek tenderly. "I mean only to congratulate her. As her employer. I may not be her director, but I still sign her checks. You would agree I'm bound to encourage my performers. I won't be but a moment. I'll come and find you."

"You're lying. And to yourself, which is worse. If you see her, you'll never be able to let her go."

This, finally, gave him pause. Was it possible Jasper could only be content chasing after women who didn't love him? *Couldn't* love him. What was wrong with him that he only sought unattainable women? Here stood Daphne—amusing, beautiful, submissive, professing her love to him—and he couldn't summon more than fondness. It couldn't be the chase. The older he got, the more pathetic it felt. Amélie could never be his when she belonged to everyone else. He should take the angelic blonde's hand and not look back.

"I won't be long," he croaked in an embarrassed whisper.

As he imagined, the hallway to Amélie's dressing room was packed. A crush of men in top hat and tails waited eagerly with bouquets of roses. Jasper, like an idiot, held nothing. He'd not planned to visit her in her dressing room. He'd not planned to allow her to see him at all.

These past weeks, after learning of her early arrivals and late stays to rehearse, he'd sometimes come. Hiding in the shadows. Watching as she struggled and worked to master her craft. That he wanted her body there was no doubt. But he admired and respected her, too. Those were stirrings infinitely rarer.

Jasper would congratulate her. Some chaste busses on the cheeks in greeting. That would be all. Then he'd find Daphne, and together they'd get drunk or high or both.

He excused himself as he threaded through the line to the front. Then he saw him. Monsieur Talac stood in a formal evening suit as fine as any man's in that line. His hair was neatly clubbed, and a blood-red bouquet of roses spilled from his arms. He made a suitor as dashing as any man in that line. And, Amélie claimed, her forever love.

Jasper felt his heart break. Again.

What am I doing?

He could convince himself all he wanted. That it was to be a chaste congratulations from her employer and nothing more. But he wasn't a complete fool. In his heart, he knew exactly what he wanted in coming to see her. For her to belong to him.

His chest burned when he turned on a heel and left.

When Jasper returned to the dance hall, he apologized profusely to Daphne. Told her she was right and that he'd changed his mind. That he was grateful for her patience. Then he ordered an absinthe and proceeded to get drunk. Rarely did he allow himself to lose control. But on this night, it seemed the only necessary thing.

By the time Amélie emerged from her dressing room with Talac and the others lapping at her heels, Jasper simmered with unchecked longing. There she was, like a cool goddess of the night, wearing a sleek, black after-performance gown. White opera gloves highlighted her silvery-white wig, and smooth satin hugged every curve. She was both elegant and base. And more beautiful than any woman had a right to be. Their eyes met.

Jasper tipped his hat to her, then held her gaze as he kissed Daphne's neck. The smile that had lit Amélie's face turned into a rigid line, and she crisply turned away.

Good. You've made your choice and I've made mine.

For more than an hour, it went on like this. Jasper with Daphne and Amélie with every man, save him. She smiled and leaned in, placed an affectionate hand on an arm and whispered coyly. Decorously sipped from each glass handed to her and made a warm study of each admirer, all the while laughing overloud and blushing overmuch. She may have played the prudish provincial with him, but with these tongue-wagging suitors, she radiated the consummate seductress.

Periodically she made certain to catch Jasper's eye and smirk. He hated her taunting and wanted to spank her bottom so hard his hand itched.

Finally, when he couldn't stand Amélie's shameless display any longer, he turned to Daphne. "Let's go to La Bête."

"Do you mean it?" Daphne brimmed with excitement. "Will you try it?"

"Why not?"

Moments later, they climbed a spiral staircase in the leg of the giant elephant he and Charles had secured only days before from the Exposition when it closed. Soon they entered a room in the belly of the beast. Limned with a musky maple-syrup haze, it was lit by the twilight glow of low lamps. Suggestive nudes hung on the walls. Men and women in an opium languor sprawled on low-slung velvet divans next to tables bearing silver-engraved bowls and pipes. Belly dancers in beaded bedlehs swiveled and gyrated amongst it all.

"There's one that's free," Daphne said, pointing to a plum divan.

Once they sat, one of the hostesses prepared their pipe. Jasper watched as the tiny bead of opium swelled over the flame, then was rolled and worked into the hole in the pipe bowl.

After a few inhalations of the pipe, Jasper reclined back on the divan and peered up at the draped ceiling. He felt... nothing. No high, as some described it. No languor either. Instead he fixed his gaze on a hanging lamp and wondered when he would finally be able to forget Amélie.

As time passed, Jasper declined more pulls of the pipe, drinking a mild Indian tea instead. All the while, Daphne continued to smoke. That was yet another good quality about her. She had a keen curiosity about life that held no judgment.

Not for the first time, he wondered why it was he couldn't love her. It would be so much easier. Jasper looked at Daphne and found her dazed and slack-jawed. Perhaps that was it. She was too easy to intoxicate.

Eventually, whether it was the pulls he took or the potent air in the room, Jasper began to feel faint perspiration on his skin and his muscles relaxing. He felt a floating numbness, a sort of disconnection from his limbs and mind, when he sensed a terrible lure at the door.

37

Amélie peered through the smoky haze of La Bête. Luckily this was Zidler's last prescribed stop for her for the night. The adrenaline and champagne she'd been floating on had begun to fade nearly an hour before. But it had taken that long merely to say her goodnights.

Now as she stood in the decadent room, she calculated the least amount of time and the least she must do to satisfy her director's edict.

For now, my chick, I'll keep the wolves at bay, if only you'll promise to lavish as much attention on my patrons as I require. A visit, a word, a dance with you, and they'll be ours.

All she could think now was how much she wanted to crawl into bed. How her head and feet ached from the bright lights and all that dancing. And how her heart ached.

She could claim to Zidler, and did, that "Au clair de la lune" was simply part of an artistic vision. But the greater truth was what she'd found when she saw Jasper there in the crowd, peering at her with such wide-open admiration it had made her heart flutter. She'd sung it to him. *For* him. Then he'd so callously flaunted his mistress as if he were happy to have moved on.

Across the smoky room, a man stood and put himself to rights. When he strolled toward her, she saw it was Jasper.

"Lune." There was something in his tone, not quite taunting and not quite admiration.

Amélie smiled tightly, trying to brace herself against the flood of feelings that surged to the surface.

This man she loved. More than she'd loved Aubrey. More than she'd loved anyone, she was certain now. She could hear herself saying the words, her heart beating so fast in her tight chest.

If she could have gone back to that night at the suite, she would have explained there was no competition. No one else for her. There never could be. But like an idiot, she'd been stunned. Then so hurt she'd curled into herself as she'd always done. Humiliated and flailing, she'd gotten indignant. Then gotten hard. Fortified, she'd stiffened her spine. Told herself to move on. To take control wherever she could. However she could. Here and now, she knew it wasn't enough. Not nearly. It was all filigree—pretty fretwork but completely useless.

"Monsieur," she managed.

"I must be high."

"High?"

"I didn't think I'd see you again tonight. Care for a smoke?" He indicated a pipe.

"No. I thank you. It's getting late. I only wanted to make an appearance and say…"

Those mesmerizing green eyes skated all over her, stripping her.

"What did you want to say?"

"Monsieur?"

"You said you wanted to make an appearance and say… what?"

She was so unsettled by her desire she hadn't any clue what to say. "I need some air."

Moments later, Amélie tripped up winding stairs to an arched and gilded Indian gazebo that sat atop the great elephant. The November night air was bracing, and she wrapped her arms around herself.

Scarcely a minute passed to think about him when suddenly she heard his boots scraping toward her. Then his warm coat fell around her shoulders. His familiar scent—faint citrus and chamomile and tobacco now mixed with a smoky vanilla-and-maple sweetness.

"I seem to recall a time not so many months ago," Jasper began, "when we looked out over Paris together. When you were chilled and I gave you my coat. Do you remember?"

Amélie's heart beat so hard in her throat she didn't trust her voice, so she merely nodded.

Just as he had that night at the Sacré-Coeur, he stood behind her, placing his hands neatly beside hers on the railing. The message— "If I could, I would wrap myself around you."—was the same and so unsubtle her knees wobbled.

"You were magnificent tonight. I knew you would be."

"I thank you, monsieur. For your faith in me. For hiring me. I know you didn't want to."

Jasper stepped back and chortled, then broke into open laughter. It sounded tinged with madness, and Amélie turned to see his face contorted in pain.

"I don't get to have what I want. We both know that."

"What do you want?"

His mouth fell open, and though Amélie waited, he said nothing.

"Where's Madame Kohl?"

"Madame Kohl?" He glanced back at the stairs. "Passed out in La Bête. And your Monsieur Talac? I saw him waiting outside your dressing room."

"How could you know that unless you were outside my dressing room, too?"

He didn't deny it. The cold smile on his face said enough.

"It's getting late," she said. "I'm tired. It's time for me to find my bed."

"I'll walk you."

"I thank you, but you needn't bother. I'm quite close."

"Just there," he said, pointing to the turret. "I know."

For some reason, Amélie was struck by his knowledge and was going to ask him how he knew. Then she remembered whom she was talking to.

With all the patrons still in the garden, wide-eyed and eager to stop her to chat, it took them another half hour just to walk from the foot of the elephant to her apartment in the gothic tower next door.

There they stopped outside her door.

"I thank you, monsieur. For your escort. For your coat." She handed it back to him.

"If La Bête will be your last stop each night, we should see about making you another way home. An elevated walkway, perhaps. Something secret so your admirers don't get any salacious ideas."

"You give me too much credit. Tonight was merely something new. In that spectacular night sky and original costume, Gigi could've sung it just as well."

"You don't believe that. I certainly don't."

Under hooded eyes, she gave him a grateful smile.

"It's late for your return to Saint-Germain."

"Dare I hope you're inviting me to spend the night?"

More than anything, she wanted to. Wished they could go back to that night in the suite and instead of ending their affair, he... She hated to think it because a part of her wanted it so much.

"No," she replied instead.

"You needn't worry." He stepped daringly into her space, and she didn't step back. "I'm spending the night here."

"H-here?"

"In the tower. One floor below."

"I see."

After a long pause in which they exchanged a ripe gaze, he leaned in, and she sagged gratefully until he stopped his lips a breath from hers and said, "Do you think, if I put you on your knees and made you beg so sweetly, you'd be my good girl and love me?"

Yes.

Amélie wanted to scream it and swallowed the hardened ball of it that had suddenly lodged in her throat. She felt she'd said exactly that in the dance hall. She wanted him so much she felt all her blood rushing to her core. Wanted him so much she felt on the verge of weeping.

Then a hard, chiding voice—the one that spoke to her fears and guarded her heart—howled in her head, reminding her how Jasper had hurt her. How she was over him. That she wasn't weak. Wouldn't be submissive. Not a plaything for him or anyone. If she could reign over the brightest stage in Paris, she could rein in her unruly heart.

He cupped her chin and put a thumb on her lips, then slowly, so excruciatingly slowly, opened them until her mouth gaped wide. Like a stupid lamb, she let him. From pure instinct or a flaring desire. It was a strangely claiming gesture. So strange and so arousing.

"You needn't say anything." He smiled, so sly and pleased it made her ashamed. "I already have your answer."

She wrenched his hand away and turned to unlock her door.

"I know what you're going to do." There was such taunting in his tone she turned to glare at him. "And I'm going to enjoy very much imagining it."

He blew her a kiss and winked, and when she slammed the door behind her, she heard him chuckle. Fuming, she stalked to her bedroom, racing to strip. Because, of course, he was right about that, too.

Night after night, Amélie performed. For her admirers, she became Lune. Posing for another poster that would be splashed all over town. Owning that stage as she'd always dreamed. The more she did it, the more word of her spread through Paris, the more applause and praise fell like rain, the more she knew a swelling pride in herself. All those years, all that struggle and heartbreak when it seemed only she believed in herself, now it seemed they all believed.

And no matter that he fielded the requests, Charles never asked her to spend a night or even a special dinner with a favored suitor. This, too, was part of her growing allure. Being as cool and distant as the moon itself.

After that first night, Aubrey never returned. Perhaps he saw, at long last, that he didn't have a chance to own Amélie as he'd always wanted. That she would never need him as he'd wanted. And as he'd sketched her for the new posters, the savage bite in his tone where there wasn't one before made her know, finally, she could let him go.

Jasper, however, was another matter. After his taunting and her desire that night, Amélie steeled herself against him. He came infrequently. But when he did, he acted on her like a magnetic force, drawing her eyes to him whenever they shared the same space. Her mind whenever they didn't. Not, she was determined, her body. And especially not her heart.

Never did she allow herself to be alone with him. Never did she allow herself to feel anything but benevolent gratitude for him. Because even as she felt Paris clamoring for more, even as she felt that stage was hers, she knew if she allowed herself, too easily she could belong to him.

Then who would she be?

"Are you ready to entertain your admirers, mademoiselle?" Charles asked one night in her dressing room.

Amélie peered a final time in the mirror. Her cheeks were still flushed from the rush of performing that never seemed to abate no matter how many nights or weeks she did it.

"As I'll ever be." She stood, giving her director a resigned smile.

He chuckled and stood, smacking the stack of calling cards on his thigh. When he opened the door, Amélie's heart fell into her gut.

"My Fleur! What am I saying? Lune."

The Comte de Beaumont stepped grandly into the space, filling it with his tall frame, his arm full of roses, and a look of such triumph, as if he'd just crested an impossible summit.

Archer Bonnin closed the door behind him and wagged a finger at Amélie. "You've been a very naughty girl, haven't you?"

If Jasper had said those words, Amélie would have been weak-kneed and panting for more. But coming from the comte, she felt a very different visceral reaction—disgust and indignance.

"You promised me a meal," he continued, "and then I come 'round the next night only to find you gone."

Amélie glanced at her director. Zidler appeared resigned and could only shrug.

"And Monsieur Marchand was distressingly unhelpful, the bitter man. He lost his star, and he looked to all and sundry like he'd swallowed a lemon." He chortled. "Poor wretch. He's been positively tight-lipped and white-knuckled. Now I see why."

The comte clapped Zidler on the back. "They're calling this den of decadence a 'performance palace.' How right they are." He handed Amélie the bouquet. "And you its queen."

The easily three dozen roses and various other leaves and flowers that made up the garish bouquet dwarfed her, and Penny moved smoothly to take them.

"Comte," Zidler began, "would you be so kind as to gift us with your presence for a drink in a few moments?" The director's tone dripped with adulation.

Archer looked from him to Amélie as if calculating the arrangement.

"I'd be happy to." The comte gave Amélie's hand a lingering kiss. It was all she could do not to yank it away. "And, of course, I plan to collect on that dinner, mademoiselle. Dare I hope you're famished?"

Over the comte's shoulder, Zidler went bug-eyed with a look of such desperate pleading.

"I might be feeling peckish."

After Charles managed to send the comte away with the most honeyed words about how flattered they were by his attendance and interest, he closed the door, giving Amélie a stern look.

"No."

"Chick, he is your problem."

"No, Charles."

"Yes."

"But you're so deft in dealing with these matters. What's one more?"

"Did you, in fact, promise a meal to this man?"

Amélie swallowed hard and uttered, "Yes."

Zidler threw up his hands. "The only thing to do is honor it and move on. One dinner. What can it hurt?"

"But my allure. You said it yourself—my reputation as untouchable is adding to our mystique."

Zidler winced and thought. Finally, he drew in a deep breath.

"Perhaps he can be persuaded, if he is to realize this dinner, to be discreet?"

"Do you know him to be a discreet man?"

They exchanged a despairing look.

"Perhaps he might be put off for a night. Maybe he'd consider some negotiations? After all, that may only add to his fascination."

38

*D*ays later, Charles strolled into Jasper's office and slumped into a chair. His usually sunny demeanor was gone, and in its place was a look of misery. The director slapped his gloves on a thigh and stared out the window at the lightly falling snow.

"Charles?" Jasper finally prompted.

"We have a problem."

"What's the matter?"

The director finally looked at him. "It seems that unfortunate business out of St. Petersburg has made its way here."

"You mean the influenza epidemic?"

"The very same."

"Poor souls. What are we to do with that?"

"Well, the new wisdom is that it isn't caused by bad air so much as contact with exposed persons. A new prescription is to avoid crowded places."

"Like the Moulin Rouge." They exchanged an

uncomfortable look. "What would you have us do? Close down? For days? Weeks? For what? A few unfortunate cases?"

"A few can only lead to more. Would you have us ignore the advice?"

Jasper considered this for a long moment.

"When they begin to close down the museums, we'll follow suit. But no sooner. We don't want to spread panic."

"Of course."

Charles looked again out the window, dragging his hand along his lips pensively.

"For the record," the director said, "before I tell you this next bit, I'd just like to say that we'll be fine either way."

"Mm-hm."

"And I'm perfectly capable of handling it myself."

"Of course."

"I just thought another perspective might be helpful here."

"For God's sake, what is it? It can't be worse than influenza."

"Are you familiar with the Comte de Beaumont?"

"Yes. We travel in similar circles. His wife is…"

"Newly deceased. Yes. And no children. He fancies himself a randy bachelor again."

"No harm in that. Though he must be going on fifty."

"He's well preserved and not hideous to look upon."

"No indeed. Is he on the prowl for a new lover? I'm sorry to disappoint you, but I don't swing that way."

Charles threw his head back and laughed.

"He *is* on the prowl and has his sights set on someone we hold dear. I'll give you one guess."

Instantly Jasper grew cold.

"No."

"I haven't told you anything yet."

"I thought you weren't requiring that of her."

Charles sighed. "It's only that the man followed her from Folies." He went on to explain all that Amélie had told him. About the comte's dogged interest. His visit backstage. And vow to collect on the dinner she'd promised.

"We agree that her dismissal of her suitors has added to her allure." Jasper nodded.

"But when I tried to enter into some discreet negotiations with the man, well, he upped the ante."

Jasper sat forward and arched a warning brow.

"He wants to court her. He's willing to be discreet for now, but he wants her, and his discretion has its limits. It'll be no chaste arrangement."

Jasper had known this day would come. Amélie couldn't be hidden. Her talent, her presence, her beauty—she called to men like a siren. Of course the comte wanted her. Talac wanted her. He wanted her. It was maddening.

Jasper sat back. "No. There's your answer. What more?"

"Jasper—"

"What? Does she want him?"

"Of course not."

"And we'll not force her. So that's the end of it."

"He's offering us a lot of money. It's really rather obscene." Charles appeared misty-eyed with awe.

"We don't need his money."

"*You* don't need his money. I, on the other hand, could always use more money."

"How much?" Jasper pulled out his bank book.

"How much?"

"How much money do you need?"

"What do you mean, man?"

"He's offering you money to court Amélie. I'm offering you money so she doesn't have to."

"Don't be absurd. I'm not taking any money from you." Charles sat forward, peering at Jasper's bank book. "Well, if you have some to spare, it wouldn't go amiss."

Jasper arched a brow with his pen poised, and Charles batted his hand in the air.

"We knew she'd have to face this eventually. *She* knew she'd have to face it. I'm telling her. And we'll let her decide." Charles strode to the door.

Jasper knew a raw panic. He didn't believe Amélie would give herself to the comte, no matter how much the man offered. But then again, she might decide that out of all the unsavory arrangements she might be forced to make in her position, it was the least offensive. He couldn't bear the risk.

"What if she were married?"

Charles turned and arched a cynical brow.

"What if she were purple?" the director asked. "What if she were a German opera singer? Or a high-flying trapeze artist? She isn't married. That's very much the point."

"Can you persuade her to see me privately?"

"You know very well she won't. And I must respect that."

"If you care about her as you claim—"

"You offend me."

"If you do, then you'll arrange to let me see her. Alone."

Zidler took a long breath. "It won't be the entire solution."

"It'll help. Especially in the beginning. Leave the rest to her."

"This can only end badly."

"You have too little faith in me."

"Precisely so." Zidler drew in another exaggerated breath, then sighed with resignation. "The pair of you will be my ruin. You know that, right?"

"Where would you be without my money and her talent?"

The director looked at the ceiling, dramatically pretending to give this some thought.

"You owe us, Charles."

"She won't agree to your proposal."

"You leave that to me."

39

Amélie turned the key in its lock and sagged inside her door with a relieved sigh. Every night since the Comte de Beaumont had first appeared in her dressing room, she looked at Charles with dread when he sorted through her calling cards.

The comte had returned twice since, each time with another garish bouquet and ardent kisses for her hand. He wormed himself right beside her wherever she stood. Ingratiated himself, fetching her drinks and fawning over her every word. Whispered innuendos and laughed conspiratorially, as if they shared something the others didn't.

Periodically she looked at Charles and found the director smiling kindly at her. She knew of the arrangement the comte wanted, and knew that he promised her and the Moulin Rouge an astonishing amount of money. So that her disgust at all of it was matched only by her guilt. Charles would never make her do it. So, she knew she must.

But more than all of it, Léonie had returned. In recent nights, Amélie's dreams had replayed that long-ago education on the steps of the Notre Dame de Lorette. In her earliest days in Montmartre, when Amélie was a green eighteen-year-old, wide-eyed and determined, proud and stumbling, Léo had slapped her with a harsh lesson she'd conveniently forgotten:

Performers in Paris sell. Their performances, their shows, their theatres. Escape, diversion, sex. Themselves. They sell. It's for you to decide whether you want to sell yourself cheaply or be celebrated.

Little matter that over time, Amélie had convinced Léo she was worth more than selling herself to perform. For now, if there were any clearer sign than that recurring dream, she didn't know.

Amélie would have to become the comte's lover, was nearly resigned to it. If she could have told her younger self anything, it would have been of this inevitable crossroads. She'd have told that determined girl on those church steps, casting blindly for a way into the city and its game, not to shrink from it or despair it. But to own it however she could. She'd explain with kindness and sympathy that performers—*women*—must prostitute themselves for their art. It wasn't fair, of course. But what of life was fair?

Amélie strolled into her apartment.

"Penny?"

The girl always left a lamp burning, but tonight the room lay in conspicuous darkness. As Amélie stopped to turn the lamp on, inexplicably she felt a small shiver of fear.

It's probably nothing. Penny forgot.

She walked to her dress maid's room.

"Sorry to wake you, Pen, but I need your help." She turned on a lamp to find the room deserted and the bed neatly made.

Now that small shiver grew to a skittering down her spine. Her heartbeat notched higher, and the taste of metal flooded her mouth.

In her own room, Amélie felt a foreboding darkness. She couldn't say why, but she felt with near certainty there was someone in the room.

Yet that was impossible. Two others held the key to her apartment. Neither would have turned it over without her express permission.

"Is someone there?"

Desperately, she grabbed for her lamp and turned it on. Light flooded the charming circular room in an amber glow.

"Jasper?"

In regal frockcoat and ascot, he reclined on her chaise.

Amélie swallowed a relieved cry as she slapped a hand to her chest. "What are you doing here? Where's Penny? H-how did you get in here?"

He held up a key.

"I-is that—? That doesn't belong to you."

"Why is that, I wonder?" He stood and approached.

"What do you wonder?"

What was wrong with her that she couldn't keep a thought in her head. But she knew exactly what was wrong with her. Jasper was here, in her bedroom. And he looked so right in the space.

"Why I don't have my own key to this apartment. This apartment. In this tower. That I own."

He stopped before her, his breath whispering across her forehead. Then his fingers slid to the edges of her wig.

"I'm here to speak with Amélie. Not Lune. Take this off."

His tone was thick and dark like molasses and brooked no denials. So, without conscious thought, her fingers flew to obey him, pulling desperately at the crown of pins securing the white wig. When finally she pulled it off, she turned to him, her fingers smoothing her wig-smashed mane of hair.

"Better," he said.

When his fingers fell on the stays of her bodice, she gasped and pulled away from him.

"What are you doing here, Jasper?"

"If you need someone to maid you, I'm happy to help."

"I can do it myself." But she made no move to undress. Instead, she held herself, building a distance between them. For her breath and for her own sanity.

"Yes. Amélie Audet can do it all by herself."

"I meant here. In my apartment. What are you doing here?"

"You haven't been seeing your Monsieur Talac."

"Neither have I seen you with Madame Kohl."

"Why do we speak of these two, I wonder?"

Amélie's mouth fell open as she thought. Finally, she uttered, "It's convenient, I suppose."

"And this, between us, it isn't convenient. Is it?"

She felt a building warmth in her breast and shook her head.

"It seems I stand in a long line of men who wish only to love you."

"No."

"No?"

"They don't love me. They want a piece of me. That's different."

"Too true. And this between us. It's rare."

Her heart beat so hard she could hear it pulsing in her ears. But she could say nothing.

Again he approached, moving into her space and backing her against the wall. She was trapped with him, and her breasts and core tightened.

"Some months ago, I allowed myself to forget who I was—a man who knows a thing of value and goes after it. And when he has it, doesn't let go.

"That August night I was… jealous and petty. I wanted to hurt you like you hurt me. But I forgot who you are, too—a woman who turns her pain into a flame. Who remakes herself in the ruins of that fire. Stronger and more beautiful than ever."

His praise was bighearted and sweeping. And, Amélie felt with a certainty, sincere. Her heart felt so full to bursting it actually ached.

"You're not seeing Monsieur Talac, are you?"

"No. Not since long before I met you."

"You told me you loved him. That you'd always love him."

"Now I know differently. I loved him, yes. My feelings were all so new and heady. It felt like the first taste of something so sweet because it was. But I'm not certain he ever really loved me. He put me on a pedestal. If he could have sculpted me, he would have. That's admiration. Worship, even. But not love. And what I feel for him now, it's no more than a fleeting fondness for what we once shared."

"When did you realize all this?"

Jasper's voice was tight, and his face contorted into a look of such pain that Amélie hesitated, then finally sighed. "After you ended our affair."

Jasper's face collapsed and froze. After an agonizing moment where Amélie wanted to wrap her arms around him to comfort him, he looked unflinchingly into her eyes.

"Marry me, Amélie. Tomorrow. First thing."

"Marry?" She let out an astonished breath. Her heart soared with joy and hope. This was something she could never have conceived from him. But so hasty. She wanted to be swept away by her longing, by the romance of it. Yet something just didn't add up.

"We can find a justice who would ignore procedure for a little coin. And then… then we could go away together for a nice, long honeymoon."

Amélie held his cheeks tenderly. "This is all so sudden. This takes some thinking. We haven't been together in so long. And you know I can't do anything right now. Not when the show has only been running for five weeks. Perhaps at the Christmas break we can—"

"No." Jasper took her hands and kissed them. "It has to be done right now. Tell me you don't love me. Tell me you don't want to spend the rest of your life with me."

But for Amélie, a warning sounded, and her heart slammed shut at those words:

It has to be done right now.

She pulled away from him and crossed the room with an angry huff. "This is about the comte."

"No."

But he'd paused, and the sweet hopefulness she'd felt only moments before now sank like a lead weight in her gut. She screwed balled fists into her eyes, cursing the tears that threatened.

"Of course it is. Charles told you. You don't want to marry me; you just don't want anyone else to have me. That's it."

"You know how I feel about you."

"Get out. Leave the key and get out."

"I'm not doing that."

"I said get out!'"

"No." He shook his head and prowled toward her. "I won't do this with you anymore. All this hurt and childish pride when we love each other."

"I don't love you."

"Yes, you do."

"I don't need you to fix this for me, Jasper. You can't keep me from every suitor who asks for me. You said it yourself. Don't you remember? Don't be narrow to suit something that doesn't serve me. For a woman in my position, what he's offering me is the world." Amélie tasted the bitter bile of his haunting words. "Isn't that right?"

Jasper stepped back with a chagrined look on his face, then shook his head. "I didn't know you, then. You were an enthralling painting and a very talented singer. But you're no courtesan."

"You would have me trade the comte's bed for yours?"

"Yes."

"And what of the next man?"

"Yes."

Amélie felt such a painful longing to submit that it prickled in her nose and welled in her eyes. But it warred with an equally painful feeling of betrayal. Marriage to him would only be a mercenary convenience. She shook her head and looked away.

"We need our entertainment to be entertaining." Her voice broke as she said it. "That's why women take to the stage. Remember?"

"If you're going to throw my words back in my face, here are yours: the expectations are changing."

"Not fast enough, Jasper. I'm sorry. More than you know."

"You'll be a slave to them but not to me? Is that it?"

Amélie slumped. The fatigue of all of it suddenly drained the life out of her. She sank onto her bed, feeling as if her heart were breaking all over again. "Please leave."

Jasper stepped before her and stood like that, in her space, for a terrible moment of anticipation. Then she felt his hand wrap around her neck. It wasn't tight and certainly wouldn't bruise. But she felt the deep ache of it, how utterly claiming a gesture it was. He tipped her head back, and she looked up into his beautiful eyes and the subtle promise on his lips. All she felt was despair.

"We're not done with this, sweetheart." He pressed a chaste kiss on the tip of her nose and turned to leave, placing the key on a table. "Not even close."

The next night, Amélie stood at her apartment door, trying fruitlessly to get her key into the lock. She'd had a terrible night. It was by far her worst performance since she'd started at the Moulin Rouge. Perhaps her worst performance ever.

The night before, she'd cried herself to sleep, then woke hard and fierce. She'd passed the performance like that, cutting the air with her sharp notes and stilted dancing. During the set changes, Charles had bobbed like a panicked bird, chirping his need for an explanation. But the worse she got, the worse she got. And by the end of the night, she felt panic at her own haplessness.

Afterward, she barely tolerated her courtiers. As the minutes dragged on, she drank like a teamster and spoke like a shrew. Now this.

She stabbed the key into the hole, jiggling and cursing. Maybe she was drunk. That was a distinct possibility. She'd hidden her embarrassment behind the green fairy. More than one, which was never a good idea.

"Penny?"

Amélie knocked, but there was no answer.

"Pen." She pressed her mouth to the door. "There's something wrong with my key. I-I can't get it into the lock. Can you open the door, please?"

Still no answer.

She pressed her forehead to the door and slumped. Then she stepped back, hollered, and knocked. "Penny! Wake up! You need to open this door! I'm locked out!"

An envelope was pushed under the door with Amélie's name on it.

"I know you're there, you coward," she fumed as she reached for it. "I've had a terrible night and am in no mood for this, Pen. Please, just open the door." She opened the weighty envelope, and a new key fell into her palm as her eyes landed on the familiar hand:

> *Dearest Amélie,*
> *Enclosed is the key to your new apartment.*
> *Just downstairs.*
> *Be a dear and don't bother Penny any more tonight.*
> *She needs her sleep.*
> *Yours,*
> *Jasper*

Of course she ignored him. Pricked at his audacity, Amélie knocked and pleaded for some moments, going from perturbed to full-blown anger.

"Why do you help him?"

In a flash of fury, she was down the stairs before this new apartment door. She paused, then pressed her ear to the door. She heard nothing and wasn't even sure what she anticipated.

This suite, Amélie knew, Jasper and Charles had designed for affaires d'amour between stars and patrons. In the weeks she'd been here, it had been used, sometimes as it was designed, and sometimes by Jasper or Charles if they stayed late. But she knew it exclusively from the outside. By the stained-glass lancet windows that called to mind a Gothic cathedral.

Whatever or whomever was on the other side of the door, she had to face it. The anger that had spurred her only moments before seemed to have drained away. Now she wanted nothing more than to find a bed and forget this whole day.

Amélie raised her fist to knock, then put the key in the lock instead. If it was to be her apartment, she wouldn't knock.

The lock turned easily, and when the door creaked open, she peered tentatively into the darkened space until the door was pulled from her grasp.

"You are stubborn."

Jasper took her by the hand, drawing her into the cavernous space marked by vaulted, arched ceilings and the play of lit candelabras, tall like sentries posted against murals of stained glass.

"And disobedient." He sat her down on an ornate four-poster bed. "I specifically wrote you not to bother your poor dress maid. And there you were, hollering at her like a harpy."

"You had no right to conspire with her. I can only imagine how you bribed her. With what or how much. She has stars in her eyes, that girl, and is easily persuaded. You men think you may—"

Jasper pressed a rude finger to her lips. Despite that it caused a frisson of desire to zing to her core, Amélie slapped it away.

"That's another thing," he said, urging her to meet his penetrating gaze. "From now on, I won't be held to account for all mankind. You condemn all men as calloused and cruel, eager to lord our authority over weak women, when you refuse to see how much we need you. How we'd worship you if only you'd let us."

He bent so he was only a breath from her and gazed intently into her eyes.

"I'm not all men. I want only to be one man—your Master."

Jasper turned to stoke a fire Amélie only now noticed. He tended to it carefully, deliberately placing another log, turning and blowing until it blazed cheerily again in the dark space. All the while, he spoke.

"That arrangement isn't for society to bless or condemn. It isn't for their salacious whispers built on ignorance and envy. It's for us alone. If only you can abandon yourself to it."

Then he sat in an embroidered Louis XV chair and studied her. At his intense perusal, which he knew unnerved her, she glanced away and swallowed.

"Look at me."

She felt a crackle of contest and met his gaze, jutting her chin and straightening her spine. He smiled slyly as for a long moment they held a challenge between them.

Finally, she found her voice. "This is all so neat for you."

He furrowed his brow and leaned forward, resting his elbows on his knees. She couldn't tell if he was keen or taunting.

"When you haven't a notion what it's like for me," she continued.

"Tell me."

"What?"

"Tell me. What it's like. For you."

Her mouth fell open. *Where to begin?*

When she didn't respond, he continued. "You're happy to tell me what you want. Who you'll be and what you'll own. This is me telling you what I want. Who I'll be and what I'll own.

"What I won't be is implicated in all your frustrations. I won't be made to answer for how the world sees you or what they expect of you. I won't. This here, between us, that's what I own."

Faintly, Amélie shook her head. She couldn't say why. Only that it terrified her to accede to him. Still more, it terrified her how much she wanted to.

"Now take off that wig."

The unyielding tone in his voice marked her like a whip, made her squirm and her breath hitch. Shaky with arousal, she slid her fingers to her scalp and pulled pins.

When she removed it, he pointed to a faceless bust on a vanity.

"Every night when you come home, you'll remove that first thing."

"Home?"

"For now, this is your home."

"Here with you?"

He nodded.

Amélie strode to the vanity and placed the wig on the bust, then peered at herself in the mirror to make sure she was still there. Her brown hair was sweaty and lifeless. Her face, tired and resigned. She could still feel a flair of fight within her. But the part of her that wanted to let go seemed weightier, stronger still somehow.

"Take off your dress."

The words, his implacable tone, it raced around her nipples and made her sex clench.

She blinked and stretched her neck. A slow reach and hold. To the right, then to the left. She forked fingers through her hair. It felt luxurious, like giving light and air to a strangled thing. And she massaged her scalp for some moments. It wasn't exactly disobedience, but it wasn't compliance either.

"You already have a punishment coming," he said as if sensing the direction of her thoughts. "For your earlier disobedience." A pause. "For so many things I don't know where to begin. But I will. And I'll delight in it."

Awkwardly Amélie reached for her bodice stays.

"I'm only doing this because I'm dying for sleep. Not because you told me to."

The fire crackled and popped, and Jasper chortled.

"I know, naughty girl. I love that about you."

Finally, her black satin gown fell in a rustle at her feet.

"You'll place it there."

Jasper pointed to a series of trunks and wardrobes that held all her things.

"What about Penny?" she asked, putting her dress away.

"What about Penny? She can still see to your things in the morning and help you get ready for your performances in the evening. But at night, with me, you're mine alone. Now the rest of it."

Amélie paused. She hadn't been naked with anyone, save her dress maid, in months. Not a man and certainly not one content to strip her in all ways as Jasper was.

"I haven't agreed to anything. I'll not marry you to save you the inconvenience of the Comte de Beaumont."

"Do what I asked."

Once again, she did. But only, she told herself, because she was tired and could just as well sleep naked.

"Come here, my beautiful girl."

There was something in his tone, something unique to him with her, that made her stomach flip. Ever since her father's passing, she'd wanted fiercely to be taken seriously, to feel the weight of maturity. And, as she grew up, to be seen as a woman, competent and strong. But with Jasper alone, when he called her *girl*, there was something clenched in her belly that unfurled. As if in that moment, she needn't hold on so tight. He'd hold on for her and care for her. It filled her heart and flooded her sex. It made no sense but for the fact it felt so good. She wanted to let go.

Nervously she began playing with her fingers as she walked to him.

When she stood before him at the fire, he took her hands, massaging them tenderly. He'd seen her flitting fingers. He saw everything.

"Are you warm enough?"

Amélie peered at the fire. The room was warm. The hearth warmer still. And yet she felt chilled by her apprehension.

"Yes," she uttered.

"Good." Jasper spread his legs. "Now bend over my lap."

Stark humiliation flooded into her cheeks. No matter that she'd been talentless tonight, she was still a talented performer. Held sway in Paris's premier performance palace.

"Don't think. Just do it. Here with me, you'll turn off that ripe, firing mind and feel. Now bend over my lap. Head near the floor, bottom high."

With a whimper, she did it.

"Have you ever been spanked before, my love?" Sweetly his hand landed on her bottom and began softly rubbing.

Amélie could scarcely catch her breath. She swallowed. "When I was a girl," she uttered. "A brat."

"Mm-hm."

Then his hand fell hard, harder than she'd imagined. It hurt. Terribly. And she flinched and cried out. After ten punishing strokes, he rubbed her bottom sweetly again.

"Shh. It's all right, my precious pet. You're all right."

"That hurt."

"It's supposed to."

Without warning, his hand fell hard again. Five. Ten. Twenty. When that round was done, his tender hand caressed softly again. And though she felt the wetness of her tears on her cheeks, she felt something else in her core even more. A heaviness and heat he stoked as deliberately as he'd done the fire in the hearth.

She was panting with want when his hard hand fell again. Ten. Fifteen.

"Jasper, please."

This time when he caressed her, a finger slid into her crack down to her sex.

"Mm. You like this, I think."

Then she felt his finger at her core slide unerringly inside.

"Oh, your cunny's so wet for me."

Amélie began to whimper. At the shame of it and how desperate she was for more. Jasper's finger slid too slowly, too tentatively, into her. He was anything but tentative, so she knew it was a deliberate taunt. It was agonizing, the slow slide of that one finger just inside her. Not pressing the spot that led to her release. Just a slow, cruel slide.

"Jasper, please."

"Please what, my love?"

"I need to come. Please."

She knew she was begging and didn't care. All these months, no matter how she saw to herself, she had never been this close to something this good.

"And you'd like my permission, is that it?"

She was stunned by what she'd given him so naturally and after so much time. Immediately she bolted from his lap. But before she could stalk indignantly away, he grasped her wrist and pulled her to straddle him. There she sat, naked, aroused, incensed. And there he sat, clothed, hard, delighted.

His hands encircled her waist, then carefully stroked up, caressing her breasts and weighing them.

"Look at me."

Always Amélie had carried herself with her head up and met people's gazes. But with Jasper, she tucked her gaze neatly away. It was as if he alone looked intently and saw all of her. She didn't want anyone to see all of her.

He took her nape and pulled her to him, kissing lightly at first, searching, opening, then delving deeper. Their tongues tangled for long moments, and she remembered the silk of his lips. How hard and soft they were. How expert. How patient, as if he didn't need her. Didn't need their kisses. Though the hardened sex through his trousers told her otherwise.

She felt limp and even more desperate, if that were possible. This was the embrace she wanted to crawl into and never come out of.

Deftly he caressed a nipple as they kissed, twirling, pulling, bringing her to the edge and keeping her there.

After some time, she managed to wrench her lips away. She told herself she needed to breathe. Needed to calm down. But his lips blazed a trail down her chin and neck, then into the hollow of her collarbone. When he went to cup a breast and take it into his mouth, Amélie gasped and pushed away. She stumbled to stand.

"What are we doing?" she asked.

"I thought you knew."

Now he stood and began removing his clothes, stalking her across the wide-open space as each item was discarded.

At the bed, Jasper held out a hand. "Come here."

Amélie shook her head.

"Yes, sweetheart. You know you want to. Your cunny's so wet for me. Only for me. Isn't that right?"

Amélie felt such painful humiliation at that truth. Why could she not be strong with him? She closed her eyes and shook her head. It was a pathetic denial. They both knew it.

Then he threaded his fingers through hers, guiding her.

"You want me to lead, don't you? Here in this room, just you and me. You need me to, don't you?"

She felt the pressing weight of humiliation with just how much she wanted him to lead her and faintly shook her head.

"Lie down on your back. Hands above your head."

No sooner had she complied than black rope, as thick as her pinky and smooth as silk, was laced around her wrists, tying them to the headboard.

"I would mark every inch of your body if you cried for more. But with your show, I won't make them too tight. Try them. Can you get out?"

She pulled and found them knotted fast. "I can't get out."

"I'll just have to find other ways to mark you."

Then a handkerchief was tied over her eyes.

"Can you see?"

She shook her head.

"Words, pet."

"No, monsieur."

"I like that." Tenderly he traced fingers down her cheek. "How polite you are for me, sweet girl." There was an excruciating pause where she listened desperately for any clue to his next step. "Are you scared?"

His lips had whispered over hers, his warm breath skating over her face and neck.

She was scared but still found it difficult to admit the truth to him. So, she did a ridiculous shake and nod. Suitably, he chuckled.

"I see."

Then he drew a slow, splayed hand from her neck down her torso and wrenched her legs wide and back.

"Keep them open for me, or I'll bind them, too."

Helplessly she nodded. She wanted to. It seemed like the only right thing with him. Obeying.

She felt him ease his body over hers. Then he began to play and kiss and caress. At her ears, along her jaw, down her neck and arms. Along her wrists and down her legs. Fingers and nails, teeth and tongue. He dragged his touch along nearly every inch of her. Bit hard and licked softly. Making her skin pucker and bead. Making her rock and beg, pant and moan. Making her bite her lip and cry out. Still never did he touch her breasts or sex. And somehow they felt more alive with need for the want of him than they ever had.

Then she felt cool air. His body coming off her. His weight shifting on the bed. She felt panicky with need until she heard him stroking himself, then felt a splash on her breasts and belly.

"W-what? What did you do?"

That was, of course, ridiculous. She knew exactly what he'd done. She was stunned.

"Jasper?"

His cum-laden fingers were at her mouth, thrusting deeply inside.

"Suckle me sweetly."

Angry and helpless and aroused, for long minutes she did, taking and sucking and swallowing him until he was satisfied. Then the handkerchief was removed and the fire banked. Finally, he untied her and wrapped himself around her.

"Sweet dreams. You did very well tonight. I'm so proud of you. So pleased."

Amélie lay looking up at the arched ceiling. It appeared to be reaching into the sky—didn't it know it was only designed to go so high? Too soon Jasper settled into sleep, and his breathing grew even. But all the while, she seethed.

40

*J*asper woke slowly, delighting in a satiated languor he'd not felt in months. He opened his eyes to see midmorning light pouring through the stained glass. Astonished, he blinked again and again.

How many hours did I sleep? he wondered. And so deeply he could scarcely remember feeling so rested and restored. Then he remembered.

Beside him the bed was empty, though he found it still warm. Sitting up, he scanned the apartment. He almost called for Amélie to return to bed. She didn't need to report to work until eight that night. And he could certainly take a much-deserved day off. Something told him to slip quietly off the bed and go look for her.

Jasper found Amélie sitting naked on the floor of the bathroom. Her long legs were bent, knees to nipples. One arm braced on the floor at her bottom, the other threaded between her legs. Her head rested back against the wall. Her waist-length hair was sexily sleep-tousled.

Her eyes were closed, her cheeks flushed, and her mouth open.

He didn't need to see her fingers to know exactly what they were doing. And it was the most beautiful sight. He could have been irritated to find her seeing to herself. But he wasn't. Rather amused. And definitely aroused.

Jasper *tsk*ed and crouched before her. Amélie flinched, opening her eyes.

"J-Jasper... I..."

She pulled her guilty fingers away, but he drew them back.

"Shh, love. Relax. It's all right."

With his finger leading hers, they traced slowly around and around her nerve, so plump with arousal.

"Is this what you need? Poor thing. Did I leave you wanting last night? Now you're seeing to yourself as if this belongs to you"—he slid their fingers deep inside her, and she moaned—"when we both know it's mine to do with as I please. Is that about the state of it?"

After one deep thrust, he pulsed their fingers once, twice, a shallow tease to her sex, then pulled out and tasted her.

"Mm."

Then he stood and offered his hand. She peered up at him with panic in her eyes.

"Are you going to leave me like this? On the edge? For how long?"

He pulled her up and collected her in his arms. Smoothing her hair out of the way, he tenderly stroked her shoulders and breathed into the shell of her ear.

"That's for you to decide."

"Me?"

"When you decide to submit to me, you may have your release."

She stepped back in a huff, mouth agape and cheeks red with indignation. After staring and blinking at him for a long moment, she said, "You know you're an expert lover, but I'm not so desperate as all that. I don't need you to come to my release."

"No indeed. But tell me this, had I not found you, would you have brought yourself there? Hiding in the bathroom? Biting your lip?"

"Yes."

He arched a brow—because she'd hesitated, just a beat. "Are you so certain, then?"

Amélie stalked to a wardrobe and grabbed her chemise.

"What do you think you're doing?" Jasper snatched her chemise away before she could put it on.

"I'm done with this. This whole arrangement I didn't agree to."

"No."

"You won't respect me. And I can't love a man who doesn't respect me. I must respect myself."

"What?"

"This isn't about love, Jasper. I thought it was. I told myself you couldn't love anyone but her, but I was wrong. It's about respect."

"What are you talking about?"

"Madame Travers. You respect her... more than anyone... because she wouldn't submit to you."

"Is that what you think?"

"I know."

"You don't know anything."

"You expect me to love you and submit to you completely. But if I do, then I'm lost. You'll think less of me."

"No."

"You don't think you will."

"You forfeit so easily, then? I never imagined you as someone who would stalk off the field of play when it was a challenge. Are you so weak, Amélie? So afraid?"

She froze and gave him a steely gaze that sent sparks. He smiled triumphantly.

Jasper brought Amélie back to bed and sat beside her.

"You have all the power in the world right here, right now," he said. "Look me in the eye and tell me you don't want this."

Her mouth fell open to speak, but struggle lay behind her eyes as her chest rose and fell and a blush of arousal bloomed across her skin.

After a patient wait, he whispered, "And now the power is mine."

Then he tied her wrists to her knees and splayed her legs. "Beautiful. Can you keep these open, or must I tie them, too?"

"For your puny ministrations, I can manage to keep them open."

He chuckled and gave her an arch grin. "Oh, love, you're in such trouble."

Then he drew a riding crop from under the bed and smacked her sex.

Amélie slammed her legs closed and screamed, arching off the bed.

"Too much?" he taunted after she caught her breath.

She clenched her jaw and shook her head.

Tenderly he caressed her cheek. "Ah, so good."

Then he flicked the crop again, not as hard, but still she closed her legs and cried out.

"Snap your fingers if you want me to stop," Jasper said as he shoved a handkerchief in her mouth and tied her knees open. "There. Now you may cry and struggle all you like."

He brought the crop down ten times in quick succession, and she arched and cried and moaned. Then he pulled the handkerchief from her mouth and sat. With a petal-soft touch, he stroked the ribbons of her sex, stirring the warmth growing there.

"Are you all right?"

She bit her lip and, after a pause, nodded.

Again he put the handkerchief in her mouth and used the crop on her sex. Five times, then caressing. Ten and more tender touches. When he removed the handkerchief after the fifth round, he gave her a glass of water, then kissed her sweetly on her forehead, her nose, her lips. All the while, he whispered, "Shh, it's all right, pet. You're all right. Just relax now."

Jasper sat beside her, an arm spanning her waist as he studied her. Amélie quivered like a plucked string, her skin ablaze with arousal, her mouth open as she raced to catch her breath, and her eyes wide.

"Are you all right?"

She nodded.

He arched a brow in prompting.

"Yes, monsieur."

Gently he petted her sex. "What do you feel here?"

"It's tender."

"Mm-hm. And what else?"

"I-it's hot. So hot. Burning. And so full." After a pause, she uttered, "It's so good."

"Yes. It is. And that heat, that fullness, is it laced with anything else, perhaps?"

Amélie closed her eyes, and a tear fell, which Jasper swiftly smoothed away. "Need," she uttered breathlessly, shamefully. "I need it. I love it."

"Yes." He held her core and leaned over her, his gaze flitting all over her face. "And it's all right that you need it like this. That you love it. Isn't it?"

She looked away, out the storybook stained glass to the wide world outside as if by magic she could transport herself there. And he knew he'd pushed her as far as he could go for now.

"It's all right. You did beautifully."

Jasper pressed a soft kiss to her sex and untied her knees.

"Would you like me to fuck your mouth, or would you prefer to take me to my release?"

She glared at him, but it was half-hearted.

"Such a choice, monsieur."

"But a choice nonetheless."

When she didn't answer after a long moment, he climbed up her body and pressed his rock-hard arousal to her lips. Squeezing a bead of precum out, he dragged it along her lips, painting them. As if by instinct or submission, perhaps both—at the moment, he didn't care—she looked up at him with those pot-of-chocolate eyes and opened wide.

Sliding slowly inside her hot mouth, he groaned in relief. This torturing of her was torturing him, too. He wanted her to come so badly. Even more than he wanted to himself. But for now, she took him expertly in her mouth, licked and sucked. Dropping her jaw and bottoming her tongue, she even managed to take him deep into her throat. He moaned and shuddered with the exquisite tightness. Massaged the column of her neck that held him so snugly. All the while she kept her gaze locked on him. Such a sweetly submissive thing to do.

What a goddess she is.

For long moments, he fought himself, wanting to come and wanting to hold back. When finally the tingling in his balls became unbearable, he crested. As he pulsed inside her, Amélie gagged, and Jasper wiped the tears falling down her cheeks. Still, she swallowed him down.

After she tenderly cleaned his cocked, he wrapped himself around her and pressed a lingering kiss to her ear.

"You'll be the death of me."

∽⌒∽

That evening Jasper sat in the Grand Café with Max. They'd shared dinner and small talk, eating around the real meal now at hand.

"You look like shit," his friend observed.

"Thank you." Jasper tipped his glass to Max and took a hearty sip. He'd drained a couple of stiff drinks already and was finally feeling detached from the sharp edge of his frustrations.

"A showgirl?" Max said. "She's nothing."

"She's not." Jasper felt the heat of anger rising in his chest. "Don't ever say that to me again. She's as far away from nothing as I've ever known."

Max threw his hands up in surrender and sat back. At length he sipped his drink and studied Jasper, then finally shook his head.

"Why do you do this to yourself? She's beautiful, I grant you. But beauty fades."

"Her greater beauty lies on the inside, I promise you."

"No matter. She's not worth all this." He paused. "I thought you realized something important in August—how you don't need to chase after the two women in Paris who don't want you when a dozen and more do.

"You ended it—and you were right to. And now this? She has you by the balls just like Joselin."

"No. This is different. Jos was trying to crush me, but Amélie... she loves me."

Max shook his head. "You can seduce her all you want... The attraction between you two... The sex... I understand it's captivating. You didn't have that with Madame Kohl. You never had it with Joselin. Maybe you've never had it before. But is that love?"

Jasper leaned forward, piercing his friend with an unwavering gaze. "Au clair de la lune."

"A lucky break. She sings every red-blooded Parisian man to sleep each night. It's genius, I'll give her that."

"She sang it for me, Max. When we went riding at Marie-Louise's she sang it to me. 'Open your door to me for the love of God...' I'm telling you, she loves me, and she sang that song to get me back."

"And now that you're panting at her door?"

"She's just afraid to let me love her. I need to convince her is all."

Max raised a glass with a dubious smirk. "I hope for all our sakes you succeed."

41

mélie stood in her dressing room as Penny helped her into her final gown. Every tug and hook and tie made her feel rattled, like she was coming out of her skin. Every corset felt like a harness, every necklace, a collar. She'd never felt more alive to touch and so suffocated by it at the same time.

And her sex rang like a bell that wouldn't stop. Every step she took, she was certain it drew everyone's eye to her. Somehow they knew what a shameless wanton she was.

All evening she'd performed like the desperate coquette she felt she was. Charles was so manic with delight he tripped following her during one of her costume changes. She hoped that if she put all that unquenched desire into her performing, it would abate. Instead, the crowd had fed on her hunger and given it back in return.

Now as she climbed carefully onto the crescent moon for her final song, she felt almost mad with need.

As she was lowered into place, the stars blinked on, one after another, and for those brief moments, before the limelight shone on her, she could see the crowd.

There Jasper stood, front and center. Claiming the premier space in her audience as he was doing over her mind and body. And, she had to reluctantly admit, her heart.

You'll be the death of me.

It'd been a strangely dramatic thing for him to say. Particularly since it was she who'd been worked and denied.

How long can she hold out? If, after only one day, his determined seduction had left her this scattered, it wouldn't be very long. A part of her wondered why she even bothered to resist him. Clearly she wanted his touch, *needed* it. Was it respect, as she claimed? Partly. Surely. Of course, she needed to respect herself. Her pride told her he was probably using her. That he'd tire of her. That he'd weaken her.

Yet she knew her beating heart, so wrapped up in emotion, was the most fragile of all. She couldn't rely on it and certainly couldn't follow it. Forget being the death of him. *She'd* never survive *him* if she gave in.

Then the blinding limelight rendered Amélie all alone on that moon. In its gentle lap, divorced from all those faces in the packed hall, all her scattered thoughts and fears shrank into nothing. What bloomed in their place—pure voice.

That she'd known all her life. In the dew of her childhood when anything had seemed possible. When she'd first sat that horse with her papa and his warm embrace had chased away all her fears. And after he was gone, when nothing had seemed real. When her mother faded away. When her papa's boots remained by the door, a wound that would never be allowed to heal.

Her voice had remained. It was the only love that mattered. The only love she needed. It would never abandon her. And now she lifted it with love.

A week passed. Each night, Amélie came to work to give a lust-laden performance that was the talk of the town. Some suggested she'd taken a mysterious lover. Or that she was high. Or both. She didn't care what they said. Nor did Charles. They only knew the crowds clamored to get in.

In the early morning hours, she returned to Jasper's relentless seduction. Deliberately he roused her, whether with the kiss of a crop or his own tender kisses. He battered her senses, flayed her body and mind, and spoke all the soft, reassuring words that tore down the wall around her heart.

Now she posed on her knees and elbows in bed, her bottom high and head resting in the cradle of her arms, while he used his mouth on her sex and turned and pulsed two fingers deep inside her. Two nights before, he'd begun doing this, fucking her with anything but him. As he'd known it would, it had turned her arousal on a knife's edge. She lost her breath and mind with the wanting.

"What do you want from me?"

"Mm. You know what I want."

"Please." She begged and cried, feeling the shameful wetness on her cheeks and fingers. "I can't take it anymore, Jasper. What do you want me to say? I'll say anything."

Suddenly he pulled away, and she jerked up. "No, please."

"Shh. Relax." Gently he pressed her head back down to the bed and stroked her bottom. Then he wrapped his naked body around hers. She could feel his sex, so big and erect, brush near the mouth of hers. It was so teasingly close she shuddered and whimpered.

"Are you ready to submit to me?"

Night after night he'd brought her to the brink and teased her with those words. Somehow, she'd been able to resist. She knew defeat would be bliss. But tonight she no longer cared why that would be bad.

"*Yes. More. Please. Master.* These are the words I want to hear from you. Because they're the truth. And because you want to say them to me. You *need* to say them to me."

This was true. In Jasper's constellation of control, Amélie felt freer, more fully herself, happier than she'd ever been. She could take on the world and all its unfairness, performing, any stage; she could be strong, *dominating* even, everywhere else. If only she could submit to him.

"Why do you insist on doing this to me?"

He pulled in a long, slow breath, then dragged his hands along her ribs and up her back. At length he petted and caressed her in long, languid strokes. While he did, he spoke.

"We had a baby. He didn't come easily. It took years. When he finally came"—Jasper shook his head and kept shaking it for long moments—"he was so tiny," he continued, his voice tight and strained with emotion. "So perfect. But there was something wrong with his heart, they said. I'm haunted now by his blue lips."

Jasper stopped caressing Amélie and wrapped his arms tightly around her. His hold felt so desperate and so vulnerable.

"I'm convinced there's nothing worse than watching your beloved wife, catatonic, helplessly rocking your cherished child until he slips away. I never knew you could survive such pain." He paused. "Sometimes the heartbreak is so devastating it seems impossible for it to go on beating, but somehow it does.

"Joselin sank into a fugue of despair. She was angry, at me or God, probably both. For months she carried on, heartbroken one minute and enraged the next. I tried to comfort her as best I could, but she wouldn't even allow me to touch her, much less hold her or love her. It was only then I discovered how much I needed to touch her. How much I needed to touch and be touched."

He loosened his hold and began to stroke her body again with so much reverence.

"The more I tried, the more she pulled away. Finally, she implored me to seek physical solace elsewhere. So, I did. Marie-Louise brought me to Chez Christiane that first night. It was there I saw a woman give herself over to a man, not merely for sex, but for submission. It didn't seem perverse or cruel but strangely right. That scene lit something inside me that wouldn't be extinguished until I tried it.

"When I first bound and spanked a woman, I discovered it wasn't about controlling her, nor a free hand to hurt and humiliate, but a vulnerability and frailty that took my breath away. Together we went to a place where pretense and affectation were stripped away. In my society world, then married to Jos, I could never fathom such a place existed. It felt at once so honest and real and exhilarating; the more I did it, the more I wanted it.

"I wanted it so much with Joselin. I thought if I could just love her like that, I could get her back. That together we could heal that terrible loss. We could mend everything. Perhaps I pushed too hard, bound her too tight or spanked her too hard. I was so clumsy and eager then. But she wouldn't let go. And the more I tried, the more she despised me for it.

"She refused to go to that beautiful, vulnerable place for me. *With* me. You will. Because you're brave. Braver than anyone I've ever known."

Jasper pressed a tender kiss to her spine and stilled. At length Amélie felt nothing but the soft warmth of his slow breaths in and out, her own heartache at his raw revelation, and a breathless awe at the beautiful, vulnerable place he'd just brought her to.

"Yes." The utterance was so small it barely constituted speech.

"What was that?"

"Yes, Master. Please. Let me submit to you."

She heard him take in a deep breath, then let out a long sigh. Whether it was one of satisfaction or relief she didn't care.

He dragged the head of his cock along the thick petals of her sex, and she squirmed to get closer. For long moments he did this, building and building.

"Will you come the moment I finally get inside you?"

"Yes."

He chuckled, actually chuckled, at the desperate honesty in her voice.

"But you'll wait. Won't you? For me."

"Why must you tease me after all this?"

"Why indeed?"

Then slowly he slid in. At the exquisite penetration, his largeness and hardness in her tight sex, she arched and cried.

"Shh, pet. It's all right. I've got you."

With one hand, he threaded fingers through her hair and pulled, biting her neck where it met her shoulder, then claiming her mouth. And with the other, he held her body tighter. His embrace, like a straitjacket, was strangely comforting. Then a wet kiss fell on her nape as he began to pump sweetly insider her. Harder and deeper but exquisitely controlled.

"I need to come. Please let me come."

"I know, sweetheart. I know. I want you to come. I do. Just hold on a little bit longer."

"Why? Please. I-I can't, Jasper. Please."

She became insensate, whimpering and pleading. Finally, after what seemed like an endless time, she felt him grow impossibly bigger inside her.

"You'll marry me."

"No."

"Come."

"What?" She'd been so desperate to hear those words that when she finally did, they seemed too small for her need.

"Come, love."

Blissfully, she did.

42

The next day Jasper sat in his office, punch-drunk with his success. Finally, Amélie was his. Of course, weak with orgiastic need, she'd said no to his assertion about marriage. But it was a feeble denial, and that was a minor inconvenience he'd soon remedy.

His first stop after he'd left their love nest was to Lucien Gaillard. The jeweler, fresh from his prize at the Exposition Universelle, worked in animal motifs and intricate gold design that was ushering in a new style. There Jasper had commissioned an engagement ring along with a number of other handsome pieces, including a choker he was particularly excited to see complete.

In his hand now was an engagement announcement he'd written and rewritten half a dozen times. But pathetically, he realized he had yet to meet Amélie's mother, let alone get the consent required. And perhaps he should choose a wedding date first.

Jasper was just contemplating his schedule in the coming weeks when Charles knocked and entered. The director strode to Jasper's desk, shucked his damp cape, flinging raindrops everywhere, and sat.

"How long has it been since we've seen the sun?" Charles asked.

For days the city had been wrapped in a misery of fog and sleet that showed no signs of let up.

Charles looked speculatively over Jasper. "You seem pleased."

"I'll give you one guess why." Jasper smiled like the cat who stole the cream.

Charles shook his head and slapped down a wilted copy of *Le Temps* on Jasper's desk. The headline above the fold in bold print read "The Great Dread."

"We have to close."

Jasper took the paper and began reading—the infection rates, the makeshift tent hospitals springing up in hospital courtyards across the city, the alarming daily death rates.

"Postal service is slowing; schools are closing for lack of teachers. They're even calling on medical students for lack of doctors. Did you hear every doctor at Hôtel-Dieu has fallen ill? Every one. We must close."

"And the museums?"

"Any day now. But we must lead the Rive Gauche in this matter. The infection rates in Montmartre are far higher than on Saint-Germain."

"We have our final performance before Christmas in three nights."

"It must be sooner. I worry for our performers. Don't you?"

Jasper narrowed an offended brow.

"And it must be longer than two nights," Charles added.

"What are you thinking?"

"Perhaps we could reopen on 31st December to ring in the new year."

"We'll lose a lot of money."

"Two hundred more dead this past week alone. The Magasin du Louvre has closed. Butcher shops are closing because cooks are afraid of buying infected meats. The silk weavers in Lyon have had to close down after succumbing to the contagion, and now our womenfolk aren't buying any clothes for fear of infected fabrics. Shops, factories, schools. Commerce in this city is grinding to a halt. We'll survive a week with the stage dark."

"And leave our performers and servers without pay at Christmas? The very time when they need it most? I can't stomach it."

"It's not ideal, I know. But perhaps we could split the difference. We can't very well pay them for work they won't do. Still, we could give them their bonuses. It's small, but it's something."

Jasper nodded. "Tomorrow, then. That should give us enough time to announce the change. And having our final performance the Saturday before Christmas, well, it doesn't appear as if we're succumbing to hysteria."

Charles nodded. Still, he appeared contemplative.

"What is it?" Jasper asked.

"Frankly, I think it best we leave the city until this blows over."

Jasper pointed at the screaming headline. "They're trying to sell newspapers, Charles."

"Still, this illness, it strikes grand dukes and pot boys alike. And for some reason, it seems to strike the young and hale among us the hardest. Those are the ones who don't seem to survive it. Don't you go to Monaco to be with your family for the holidays? You really should go."

"I want to be with Amélie."

"Take her with you. But the pair of you should leave."

"Are you and Betta leaving?"

"Now we've agreed on tomorrow night, I'll go to the train station straightaway to get our tickets out on Sunday."

"Do you really believe it that serious?"

After a pause, Charles shrugged. "Why risk it?"

Charles left the paper behind, perhaps deliberately, and Jasper set about reading it. Too soon it was clear, in the midst of his seduction of Amélie, he'd been blissfully unaware that a true influenza epidemic was sweeping across Paris and the world.

Swiftly he began making plans. First, he decided on the date of 1st, February for their wedding. For the practical reason that he was divorced and not annulled from his marriage to Joselin, it would have to be a simple mayoral marriage for now. As to that, he was chagrined to realize he hadn't any idea whether Amélie would object to a mayoral marriage without the formal religious one to follow. Once again, that consent from Amélie's very Catholic mother niggled him. Civil or religious, her hand on the proper documents was required for both.

Then he proceeded to write a series of notes. The first to Max. As his pen hovered over the paper, he realized this may be a touchy topic. At their last dinner Max hadn't particularly championed them. And now Jasper had to call on him to make the trip to Rouen on their behalf. In the end, he'd chosen his words carefully, thankful that Max, an attorney and devout Catholic, would make the first intercession with Madame Audet.

The second was a telegram to his own mother, already ensconced at Villa Beausoleil for the winter. Hector and Ellen Degrailly would welcome the news of their son's engagement to a showgirl as warmly as they would a dread virus. Still, Jasper had little concern for their consents, for he had the greatest leverage over them all—money.

He sent his secretary to Max's office, on to the telegraph office, and finally to the train station. Then he spent the remainder of the afternoon polishing the engagement announcement.

By the time he climbed into his carriage to go to Amélie's apartment, he was feeling confident he could persuade her.

43

mélie was fuming and confronted Jasper as he walked in the door.

"Is it true?"

"Is what true, darling?"

When he tried to kiss her, she shrugged away, leaving him with his arm out and his lips puckered stupidly.

"You're closing the Moulin Rouge."

"Only for ten days."

"Only? And how will we be paid if we can't work?"

Jasper stoked the fire and turned back to embrace her, but she was feeling prickly with her anger and again shrank away from his touch.

"You'll be fine, my love."

"And what of the others? How shall they eat? It's Christmas, Jasper."

"I know. I know it's Christmas." Now he held her shoulders and wouldn't let go. Again, this tight hold, it calmed her somehow. "But this influenza, it's serious,

Amélie. More serious than I imagined. The numbers in this district alone, they're some of the worst in the city. I know you must think me and Charles heartless. When the truth is I don't know if I could live with myself if we contributed to the contagion."

"How do you contribute to it? It's bad air. There isn't anything any of us can do to prevent that. But the show must go on. If only to lift the spirits of the people here."

"I thought the same. But some medical experts don't believe it's bad air but germs passed from person to person. If they're right, then the crowds here, they're a recipe for disaster."

"Germs? Passing from person to person? You make it sound like croque-mitaines. A ghost story."

"More than six hundred at the Magasin du Louvre have fallen ill. Six hundred in one dry-goods shop alone. And yet no one in the shops next to it. Tell me, can bad air be so selective?"

"There must be something to this germ theory, as they're calling it. We must wash our hands. Routinely. And avoid touching our eyes and nose. And lips."

"We can't touch? You're scaring me now."

"Would you miss it? If we couldn't touch?"

Amélie rolled her eyes and turned away.

"We can touch." Jasper pulled her back and kissed her. "I don't mean to alarm you. I only want you to know it is serious. We didn't make this decision lightly. Now come." He led her to the chairs by the fire. "We've so much to discuss."

When they sat, he handed her a piece of paper. As she read, Amélie felt a burning ball of indignation light in her chest. This was the very thing her fearful voice had warned her about.

"You have us engaged." Her hand was shaky as she held up the paper. "Getting married on 1st February."

"Of course I'd like your thoughts before I submit it."

"Would you? You'd like my thoughts."

Jasper sat back with an amused smile he couldn't hide.

"I suppose I should say how kind you are to ask me, monsieur—if

I want to marry you. Since you've asked, twice now, and both times I've said no. I can see why your enfeebled mind might think we're engaged." She peered at the fire. "I've half a mind to toss this in the flames."

Jasper chuckled and steepled fingers before him. "Do it."

"Would serve you right."

"Do it."

She did.

For a single second that seemed to last forever, his eyes flew wide and his jaw dropped. Then he scooped her up and landed three hard smacks on her bottom before carrying her to the bed.

"I can't believe you did that," he said, leering at her before taking her lips in a kiss.

For an endless age, they kissed and scratched and rolled around in their layers of clothes.

"You're impossible, Jasper," she said once they finally pulled apart. "I've consented to be your lover, but we can't marry."

"Why?"

"Why? Am I the only one who cares for your reputation? Marriage to me would turn you into a laughingstock. The last heir to the great House of Foix-Grailly marrying a showgirl? It can't be. We can be lovers. But a proper marriage, it would ruin your family. I won't do that. I won't be held responsible for that."

"If we don't marry, you'll ruin me. Would you be held responsible for that?"

"Your mother—what am I saying?—*my* mother will never consent to it."

"You leave that to me."

"It isn't so simple."

"We love each other. That's all that matters."

"Do we love each other?"

"Yes," he replied without equivocation. "I love you, Amélie. I'm *in* love with you. I've been in anguish, all these months, believing you don't love me as I love you. Believing you loved Talac. Believing I would never have the woman who held my heart.

"I promise you this is not some fit of jealousy over the comte. It's only that his proposal urged me to make the one I've been wanting to make now for months.

"And I've already made the proper marriage. The one that suited my family. In the end, it nearly ruined me.

"But you, you're my heart. More than my heart. My home. I want to be where you are. Where your eyes land in a crowded room. Where your feet land at the end of each day. Make no mistake, it isn't you who must be worthy of me, but me who must be worthy of you. The strongest person I know, so strong she isn't afraid to be soft when I need it—and I do need it. It's you I want."

Amélie lay below Jasper, her cheeks flushed and her lips bruised and ajar. This was exactly what she'd been longing to hear all these months. She could deny it. Or tell herself that her dreams mattered more to her than romance. But this felt like everything.

Bravely she whispered the longing in her heart, "I want to say yes." A lump wedged in her throat and tears welled in her eyes. "I do. But I'm afraid if I love you like that, I'll lose you."

Jasper tenderly smoothed her hair off her cheek and kissed her. "You'll never lose me. I promise."

Then they proceeded to make love. Softly. Sweetly. With no rope, no taunts, and no pain. No more pushing, no more fighting, and no more negotiating. There was nothing whatsoever left to prove. Only love.

Afterwards, Jasper held Amélie in his arms.

"It took me all afternoon to write that announcement you burned."

She chuckled. "Serves you right. You were too presumptuous."

"I choose to think it was confidence."

"If it took you all afternoon, you should remember some of it."

"Oh, I forgot—I bought us tickets to leave for Monaco on Sunday."

"What?"

"Charles thinks it best to leave the city. He and Betta are leaving on Sunday, too."

"Monaco. Why do we go there?"

"My family winters there. I want to introduce you. Influenza is merely a good excuse."

"I barely consented to marry you not a half hour ago. I'm not ready to meet your family yet. I can't be what they want for you. They'll hate me."

"It isn't up to them. And you've met Marie-Thérèse and Marie-Louise. It'll be fine. It's so beautiful there this time of year. Not this cold and gloom."

Amélie could feel her cowardice churning like acid in the pit of her stomach and sighed. "I can't. Not yet. Can't we just stay here? We'll wash our hands. We'll wash every part of ourselves. Then we'll get dirty and do it all over again."

"You have to meet my mother eventually."

A stark feeling of terror raced through her. "And you my mother. I'm afraid she may not approve of you either. Older and divorced."

"We'll deal with that. We'll deal with all of it in its turn. For now, you've agreed to be my wife." He kissed her, then gazed at her with a look of love. "My wife."

⁘

Days later, Amélie studied the sprawling Christmas village on Jasper's drawing-room sofa table. Then sighed and moved the bakery, adjusting the church and the café.

"A crèche, you said." Jasper slid his arms around her waist and nuzzled her nape.

"A proper one," she teased.

"And where's the baby Jesus?"

Maddeningly he played with her breasts through her layers of clothes and licked a line along her nape.

"Not arrived yet, of course. But he'll go just there." She pointed at an intricately painted stable.

"Ah, yes. There's the manger tucked away there by the smithy."

His fingers dipped into the lace at her bodice. "This dress seems disturbingly tight. Perhaps you should take it off. I think you need some air."

Amélie felt the heat of embarrassment and looked around for Bertie. The butler had been in and out all day, striding industriously into one room after another to bedeck Jasper's apartment in sprays of evergreens and holly, to hang mistletoe and set the Yule log. He and Sophie, busy in the kitchen preparing for the réveillon, were readying to leave for the rest of the week, and five days' worth of care and keeping was being finished. The heady smells of greens and roasting chestnuts, braised goose and caramelized nuts, filled the air. Outside, the fog, which had blanketed the city for more than a week, had given way to a light snow so that Jasper's stark, modern apartment had been transformed into a cheery Christmas home.

"Can you manage to restrain yourself until after we return from mass?" she whispered, peeling his determined fingers away.

"Must we go? Neither one of us is particularly devout."

"That's expressly why we must go. To remind ourselves who we are."

At midnight they knelt in La Madeleine, when a single candle was lit in the eerie darkness. The tiny flame was passed, one to another, lighting face after face with a golden glow. One row after another, going back and back, the light grew until the neoclassical church was lit with a thousand flickering stars, each one held in a hopeful Parisian hand. Then they began to pray.

After the mass was over, Jasper turned to go.

"I'll be right there," Amélie said.

"Where are you going?"

"I won't be long. Just a moment."

As crowds filed out of the church, she strode to the painting of Saint Rita.

"Madame."

Amélie stared at the painting of the nun with the stigmata on her forehead who stared soulfully up at a crucifix. The moment seemed charged with a strange anticipation and she waited expectantly.

Finally she whispered, "I must thank you for interceding on my behalf. I know it was probably rather luck. And hard work. Likely both. But if you had a hand in my happiness, I thank you."

A knot lodged in her throat, and instantly she felt ridiculous. Hurriedly she lit a candle and glanced again at the woman in the painting.

"For the next one, madame."

She turned to see Jasper hovering.

"What was that all about?"

"Nothing."

He held out his hand. "Let's go home, then."

She took his hand, then glanced back at the woman, feeling strangely as if they shared a conspiracy.

"Yes. Let's go home."

∽

Touch, light and playful, skated up the valley of Amélie's belly.

"Mm." Slowly waking, she shifted amidst the mound of blankets.

Fingers spider-walked around her breasts. Lips kissed her nipples.

"Mm, Jasper, do you never stop?"

"It isn't Jasper," Jasper said in a comically disguised voice. Then he kissed her jaw.

"Who is it then?"

"Bertie. Come to relight the fire."

She chuckled, and he took her lips with his, giving her a slow, cherishing kiss. As he did, a strange weight, somehow delicate and substantial, cool and warm, was dragged tauntingly up her body.

Amélie opened her eyes to see Jasper's pleased face hovering over hers. And dangling from his hand, a choker.

"What?"

Mouth ajar, she sat up. Her fingers shook as they fell over the fourteen strands of freshwater pearls linked by five columns of diamonds.

"Merry Christmas, my love. It isn't nearly what you deserve. But it's a start."

"It's too much. I can't wear this. I'll be too afraid."

"You'll wear this and more. You must."

He bit the turn where her neck met her shoulder hard until she felt the sharp bite of pain and clenched her core. "I need to mark you," he said, then tenderly licked the grooves his teeth made. "Now let me see it on."

Turning, Amélie lifted her hair and surveyed the carnage from the night before. They'd returned from mass to see the dining room set properly for the all-night feast. But instead they'd regarded each other with hunger in their eyes. After stripping and making love before the fire in the drawing room, they'd enjoyed each course as they'd enjoyed each other, then slept in the makeshift bed they'd made with mountains of blankets and pillows.

Now the bed of ice that held the oysters was a silver bowl of water and a lonely ramekin of mignonette. A plate of skin and bones was all that remained of Sophie's chestnut goose. Half-eaten bowls of caramelized nuts and dried fruits, glazed tarts and powdery cakes, lay about. Empty crystal goblets that hours before held wine and Bénédictine held only the midmorning light in their facets.

When the clasp was secured and Jasper's fingers fell away, Amélie instinctively put a protective hand over the cool choker. It lay heavily on her neck and made her feel, as she suspected was his purpose, owned. Wrapped in a cloud of down, still half-drunk from the night before—*the year before!*—it was difficult to fathom just how much her life had changed.

"How does it look?" she asked.

"Beautiful. Even better than I imagined."

"I don't know how to thank you."

She thought of all of it. The sexual enlightenment. How he took her and made her let go. Perhaps no man could make her let go like he did. And how she wanted to. The Moulin Rouge. The auditions. Stepping back from his position there so she could have her place. All the chances he'd given her. All the love he gave her. He wouldn't let her content herself with her fears.

"You already have."

Amélie peeled off the blanket to go to the bedroom when Jasper took her hand.

"I need to get your present."

"Don't you want to check your boots first?" With an impish grin he indicated the fireplace. Two pairs of boots lay neatly in front of it.

She crawled to hers and found a clementine in the first. When she reached in the next, she rolled her eyes at him and pulled out a belt.

"It seems you've been naughty," he said as he peeled her clementine. "Père Fouettard made a visit instead of Père Noël."

"Would that be a present for you or for me?"

"Both, naturally. Look in that one."

"I already did. You're peeling what I got."

"Look again."

This time Amélie reached her hand further and found a small box. She pulled it out and it lay in her palm for a long moment.

Jasper wrapped an arm around her waist and rested his head on her shoulder. "Open it."

Inside, perched on blue velvet, was a ring. A brilliant round diamond lay nestled in a rectangular bed of smaller diamonds crisscrossed by square sapphires.

Her heartbeat kicked higher, and her mouth went dry.

"This is too beautiful," she uttered breathlessly.

"Not nearly as beautiful as you."

She meant the ring, of course. And also his generosity. The choker. The gluttonous spread. The finest clothes. But more his devotion. This beautiful man loved her. Desperately she loved him, too.

"You will marry me on 1st February, won't you?" he said, sliding the ring on.

And even though her warning voice screamed loudly again that this happiness was too perfect, that it couldn't last, she nodded.

The next morning, Amélie's eyes blinked open to see Jasper tying his tie. She looked around. The light was shrouded so she couldn't tell if it was early yet or if it was cloudy outside. She rubbed her eyes. The more she performed, the more she'd settled happily into being a night owl. But Jasper was never one to sleep in.

"Why are you so bright-eyed?" she asked, swallowing a yawn.

"I thought I'd get to the markets early. Avoid some of the crowd."

"The markets? Why do you go there?"

"Sophie left me a list of items and markets to tide us over while she and Bertie are away." He kissed her forehead. "It's still early, yet. Go back to sleep. I won't be long."

Amélie still felt tired, and the room beyond her covers seemed cold. So, she settled back in and closed her eyes. Just as she did, an inexplicable panic seized her chest.

"Jasper!" She flung the covers back and shrugged into her robe and slippers. She hissed—it was even colder than she thought.

"Yes?" He turned back from the door. "Did you need me to pick up something for you?"

"No, I…" She went to her dressing room and flung open a wardrobe. "I'll come with you."

"Don't be ridiculous. I'm ready to leave. I'll be right back."

"No! No, no. I should come."

She couldn't say why, but there was something inside her, a terrible foreboding, that this sweet time was merely an idyll. That it wouldn't last. Somehow she knew if Jasper were out of her sight, then something would happen to him. She didn't know what exactly. Could have been anything. And everything.

Frantically she rifled through her day dresses—with Jasper's generosity, the collection was growing by the day—yanked out a suitable one, then sat to pull on her knickers.

"What are you doing?" He clapped a hand to her forehead. "Are you feeling all right?"

"Of course I'm all right." He was babying her, and she slapped his hand away unduly hard. "I just want to come with you, is all."

Jasper took her shoulders and bent to peer into her eyes. "I'm going 'round the corner for milk and eggs. Maybe some other things. I'll be gone an hour or two. And it's snowing. Wet and miserable. What is this all about?"

"Nothing." She felt ridiculous just then. Like the baby she'd been determined not to be just a moment before. But the fear she felt scaled her heart like a living, breathing thing. She knew it was absurd and still couldn't arrest it. "I just... thought you might like some company is all."

"I'd rather return to my warm fiancée in our warm bed." He tipped his head to their bed. "Now get back in there before I tie you to the bed, spank you raw, then leave your rosy bottom exposed so it's the first sight I see when I walk in. Tell me you wouldn't like that, you saucy minx."

Something in his voice, the tone of his control, it soothed that panicked demon climbing inside her. She exhaled a grateful sigh.

Then with a raised brow and an arch grin, she said, "I wouldn't like that, monsieur."

He took her chin and held her gaze with his. "You're such a bad girl, lying to me like that. What shall I do with you?"

⁓

As promised, he'd tied her down and spanked her raw. Until her bottom burned and her cheeks were wet with tears. Then he'd left her exposed. As hot as she was, as humiliated as she was, she was even more aroused.

By the time he walked out the door, promising to be back soon, she was giggling. And so needy for his touch she scarcely remembered that desperate, childlike fear.

Yet as time wore on, past the time when she assumed he'd be back, she began to worry again. At first it was simply the memory of the fear. Then she began to doubt her mind on time itself. Finally, she began to test her restraints. Not tight but unrelenting.

What if something happened to him? she wondered. What if her fear had been a healthy foreboding to which she should've listened more carefully? What if he'd tripped on the slick streets? Hit his head and was bleeding somewhere? What if he was beaten and robbed? What if he needed her help and she couldn't get out?

By the time she heard his key in the lock, her mind and heart were racing. At the sound of his familiar footfalls, she sighed and whimpered with relief. She listened as he threw down his keys. Walked into the kitchen for some moments. Then headed for their bedroom.

By the time he entered their room, she was so embarrassed by her irrational fears she tried to wipe her tear-wet cheeks on her pillow and tried to hide her face.

Amélie felt the bed depress beside her and a hand smooth over her bottom. She hissed and clenched at his cool hand.

"Easy, sweet girl. Does this still hurt?"

His tone, like a mouthful of honey, was so soothing she felt a hitch in her throat.

"No, monsieur."

Jasper smoothed her hair back from her face. "Look at me, Amélie." Then his eyes scrutinized every feature. "What's the matter?"

"You were gone so long I thought something happened to you. I was worried." She knew how that sounded and bit her lip. "So worried."

His brow furrowed. "I wasn't gone long."

"Yes, you were."

"Are you telling me I don't know time?"

"No, but—"

"Yes, you are. That's exactly what you're telling me. That I'm not capable. That something could happen to me at the market 'round the corner."

"Anything could happen."

"But it didn't.

"But it could have."

"But it didn't." He pinched her bottom. "You can't go on planning for that day, or you'll be miserable. And you'll make me miserable, too. All the joy in the world isn't rationed. It doesn't only belong to some. Or only for a short time. It belongs to all of us. The heartbreak is we don't realize it until it's gone.   So, while we love each other, while we're happy, let go of your fears. Or, better yet, give them to me."

Her cheeks burned. Finally, she nodded.

44

$\mathscr{J}$asper sat at his desk, reading the telegram he'd picked up the day before when he'd gone out for "milk and eggs."

JASPER – (STOP) –
MADAME AUDET WILL NOT CONSENT
– (STOP) – UNLESS YOU SEEK AN
ANNULMENT – (STOP) – COMMENCED
CHURCH PROCEEDINGS ON YOUR
BEHALF – (STOP) – SHE REQUIRES A
MEETING – (STOP) – MADAME AUDET
TO ARRIVE 27 DEC. – (STOP) – PHONE
CALL FORTHCOMING
MAXIME D. TASSE   *1:23PM*

Their romantic idyll would soon be over. He'd not told Amélie yet. In truth, he was almost completely in the dark about how she felt about her mother, if this would be a happy reunion or something else entirely. He suspected the latter. What he did know was that mothers were a particularly tricky business. And his reputation wouldn't help matters.

Moments later, he carried a tray into their bedroom bearing tea, lemon, and honey. He rested it on the bedside table and smoothed Amélie's hair from her face.

"Love," he whispered. "I need to go out."

"Mm?"

"I've brought your tea. I'm afraid I could be some hours."

Amélie cleared her throat. She sat up, her brow knitting.

"Are you feeling all right?"

She pressed measuring fingers to a temple. "A small headache."

"Too much Bénédictine."

"Too much everything."

"Back to sleep with you, then. I'm afraid I'll be gone much of the day."

"What? Where are you going?"

"Work calls. But I'll be back to collect you for dinner."

"Must you work during the holiday? I thought, I hoped, we'd have this week for ourselves."

"I did, too. But something's come up. And it's urgent I see to it."

Amélie grimaced and sank back into the pillows.

"Are you sure you're all right? I could call Dr. Rioux in to have a look at you."

"I'm fine. Perfectly fine. I've only just woken up. Let me come to my senses a moment."

Jasper paused. She looked tired. But his pressing need to meet Madame Audet's train convinced him that was all it was.

The train screeched into the station wrapped in a skirt of steam. As passengers spilled out, Jasper felt how awkward he looked, holding a sign that read: *M. Audet*. He realized he hadn't a clue if the woman could even read, much less what she looked like. But he knew, of course, she was Brazilian. Perhaps she would have Amélie's dark hair and chocolate eyes. Or perhaps Amélie had more the look of her father.

Just then a woman stepped off the train who left no doubt. The same sable hair and eyes, the same peachy complexion, even the very same features, though lined with age, the woman was the picture of Amélie in twenty years. She wore a modest day dress and a forbidding countenance. Still it was plain the stunning young woman she'd been. Jasper tossed the ridiculous sign in a bin and strolled to her.

"Madame Audet."

He was the picture of chivalry and wealth. Still, she narrowed her eyes skeptically. "Monsieur Degrailly, I presume."

Her accent, even after so many years in France, was distinct, like she held a babbling brook in her mouth. Though her clothes were far simpler than his, she held herself as regally as he. As regally as anyone he'd seen. Perhaps it was this steel spine that was Amélie's greatest inheritance from the woman.

Once he saw her settled in the finest suite of one of his hotels, they sat for lunch.

"You want to marry my daughter."

Jasper nearly choked at her abruptness. It was amusingly refreshing and so familiar.

"Yes."

"Why?"

"Pardon me?"

"It's a simple question, monsieur. You want to marry my daughter. I'd like to know why."

Jasper sat back and adjusted his napkin. Then a fork. "I could give you a dozen reasons. And they'd all sound sweet. But the sincerest answer is that I love her."

"Love?"

A flash of pain blazed across the woman's face, then was snuffed out. Jasper realized, then, how the lines on her face caressed sad eyes and a downturned mouth. How it wasn't simply lines or age, but that anguish was burying her.

"Love," he repeated. Not ironically. Yet here was a woman who would not be swayed by love. On the contrary.

"You needn't marry her to love her."

This woman was nothing like he'd expected. Just like, he realized, her daughter. He wanted to dislike her. Could feel it growing instinctively inside. Yet there was something shrewd about her he couldn't help but admire.

"No, madame. You're right about that. There are many men who would love your daughter. I suspect you know very well how beauty intoxicates men."

Her flashing eyes settled on his. "How should I know that?"

"Have you never looked in a mirror?" He smiled tauntingly. "You know you're beautiful. The question is why you think it bad."

"It isn't real and only leads to foolish things. Evil things."

"Evil. Is that why you've hidden away? Would you have your daughter hide away?"

"I want what any mother wants—for her child to be happy."

"Then you should consent to our marriage."

"You make her happy, do you?"

"I do. And beyond love, I should add I would cherish and respect her. If there's any more proof, it's that I could keep her as my lover, but I want more than that."

"More. Yes."

Still, she sounded displeased or skeptical. Both.

"You surprise me, madame."

"Do I?"

"I thought you a devout Catholic. A more traditional woman."

"I am. But my daughter isn't."

They exchanged an assessing look. Then it was her turn to adjust her napkin. She pursed her lips, then licked them.

"Have you seen that scandalous painting?" Her voice was thready with unshed emotion. Maria continued to fret with her service and worry her mouth. "She bared herself for anyone's eyes." She sounded sickened by it and for long moments couldn't manage to meet his eyes.

Jasper felt a rush of indignation on Amélie's behalf that thickened in his throat. No matter what he wanted to say, he needed to tread lightly here.

"It's a beautiful painting, madame."

"It's vulgar," she spat. "All her life I felt I didn't know my own daughter. Born of my body, my face reflected back at me, yet still she was a stranger. But that painting. When I saw that, I knew I would never know her."

The bitterness was palpable. Clearly her sadness had swallowed her whole.

"I understand she had no wish for that painting to be seen."

"What did she expect? She takes up with an artist. Bares herself to him. Gives herself to him? She was terribly naïve."

Jasper looked at Maria, wishing desperately he could say, *And whose fault is that?* She looked back at him as if she knew the nature of his thoughts.

"On a small list of people I despise completely," he began, "Aubrey Talac is near the top. And yet I'll say this for the man: he's a gifted artist. Any man in his position would have been negligent not to capture Amélie like that. It's easily one of the most beautiful paintings the Salon has seen in the past decade."

"Of course you would say that, monsieur. You sell sex."

"Desire, madame. The two are very different."

For some reason, this shut the woman up. She buttered her bread and took a bite with great relish.

"I would add, your daughter"—for some reason, he felt a compulsion to remind her of that—"she's so much more than that painting."

Maria regarded him for a long time as if considering it. The pain of something, losing her husband, losing her daughter, losing her joy, all of it etched on her beautiful face.

"I can't say she'll make you a good wife."

"Why is that?"

"She cares only for herself." Maria paused in contemplation. "And despite my tutoring, she has no facility, no interest whatever, for the home arts."

"Is that the measure of a good wife?"

Maria stared at him as if puzzled. "Yes, monsieur. The only measure."

"Then she'll be a poor wife to me, indeed."

Hours later, Jasper returned to his apartment.

"Are you ready, sweetheart? I have a surprise for you."

In the bedroom, he found Amélie sprawled listlessly on a chaise. She was dressed and coiffed for the evening, but her mouth was ajar and her skin was pale with a distressing sheen.

"Don't," she swallowed. "Don't come any closer."

He stroked her cheeks. "My God, you're burning up."

"I'm so sorry, Jasper. This is all my fault. We should've gone to Monaco like you wanted."

"Yes."

It was all he could muster. Because he was incensed. They should've gone to Monaco. He should've insisted. But he'd been so happy at their reunion he would've given her anything. When she was well, he'd roast her bottom for it.

"I ache all over." She sighed, and a tear fell down her cheek. "And my head. It's never hurt this much. It feels like it's going to burst." She paused. Every word, every breath seemed a great labor. "You mustn't get anywhere near me, Jasper. I won't have you catching it."

"Too late for that, my love."

He tried to be light-hearted and reassuring. But he felt a terror seize his heart like he'd never known before. All the dread headlines ran through his mind. And the death rates.

"You'll be fine. Let's get you back in bed."

Jasper helped her out of her dress. All the while, she held herself tight, her movements bracing. She winced and grimaced and panted, her eyes closed and her brow knit in pain. Never had he wanted to touch someone more and less than now.

"What about the surprise?" she asked as she slid into bed.

"What?"

"The surprise?"

"Another time. It'll keep. Just rest." He kissed her forehead and ran soothing fingers over her brow. "You'll feel better in no time."

At his desk, he wrote notes to Bertie and Sophie, explaining that Amélie was sick and imploring them to stay away. Another to Dr. Rioux asking him to come as soon as he could. And a final one to Madame Audet, begging her forgiveness and understanding.

He tiptoed into the bedroom to explain he was going out for a bit but found Amélie fast asleep. Her features were colorless and her mouth was open. Her brow, even in sleep, was furrowed—against how great a pain he could only imagine.

"Just rest. I'll be back soon."

At the door to his apartment he posted a grim sign: "En quarantaine."

On the street, Jasper paid a boy handsomely to deliver his notes. And promised him a good deal more if he returned with responses. The boy dashed off, eager to do his bidding. At the pharmacy, Jasper grabbed some ether lozenges and when he couldn't find the tonic, asked.

"All out, monsieur. We expect a new shipment in a week."

"A week? I need it now."

"You and everyone else in the city. I'm sorry. No one can keep it in stock. I'm surprised we had any ether."

"You don't anymore." Jasper took out his money.

He returned to his apartment to hear Amélie struggling through a wheezing cough and shuddered, grateful he'd bought all the ether lozenges he could find.

Filling a glass with water, his hands shaky with fear, he reminded himself Amélie would recover. That his worry was unnecessary. Yes, an alarming number had sickened and succumbed, but a still greater number sickened and survived. For now, he would live in a hell of waiting with the fickle flu.

"Here, love," he said as cheerily as he could. "I've a lozenge for that cough."

Amélie regarded him with glassy eyes. She seemed barely awake, taking a drink and sinking back into the pillows to suck. "Thank you," she uttered. "You should go."

"I'm not going anywhere."

A knock sounded at the front door. Jasper immediately bristled at the dismissal of his warning sign. Then he remembered the boy returning with messages and strode to answer it.

A louder knock came. "Coming. Coming, boy. Hold your horses." But it wasn't the boy. "Madame? Did you not get my note?"

Madame Audet strode into the space without invitation, and Jasper hesitantly closed the door.

"I got your note, and I saw your sign." She removed her gloves and coat. "But I must see her. Especially if she isn't well."

"It isn't safe, madame."

"Is it safe for you?"

He had no answer to that, and she raised her eyes, looking for direction.

"At the end of that hall."

Like a boy trailing his governess, Jasper followed closely on her heels. Meekly he said, "You won't stress her unduly."

Maria almost certainly heard him but didn't respond.

He hung back by the door as Maria sat and soothed her daughter's forehead.

"Maman?"

Every time Amélie spoke, her voice seemed to get weaker and weaker. From the first, that strong voice had chilled him to the bone. Now the anemic frailness made him sick with dread.

The errand boy from the street arrived soon after, and Jasper sent him immediately out again to scour the city for tonic and ether. These simple pharmaceuticals were all he knew, and his ignorance made him feel helpless.

When a knock sounded at the front door, Jasper jolted awake. He blinked, trying to focus, and the knock sounded again. The midnight-dark outside confirmed he'd fallen asleep and had slept several hours. Amélie had been sleeping fitfully with Maria attending her, and he'd felt like an interloper. So, he'd relaxed on a sofa in his drawing room. Now stiff and feeling monstrous, he stumbled to the door to give whomever dared a tongue-lashing only to find the mole-faced Dr. Rioux with his black bag.

"Doctor, thank God. Come in, come in. Where have you been?" The room suddenly spun, and he pressed fingers to his head.

"Are you all right, son?" The doctor doffed his coat and sat Jasper down.

"Fine. Fine. I fell asleep on the sofa and woke quickly is all."

"Are you certain? I've a remedy we should use on you. It claims to arrest the flu before it takes hold. If you've been exposed…"

"I said I'm fine. It's my fiancée. She's fevered and can scarcely breathe. Come, she's right this way."

They found Amélie asleep, her forehead slick with sweat, her skin drawn, her breathing heavy and wet. Maria slept in a chaise drawn adjacent to the bed, her hand resting on Amélie's bed. Jasper left the doctor to perform his exam, pacing up and down the hallway for what felt like endless minutes.

His fear made him tired and his fatigue, punchy. Jasper wanted desperately to do and fix. It was all he knew. Not doing anything, not fixing anything, not having the faintest clue how, made him ache. It felt like every bone in his body hurt with his worry.

Finally, the doctor emerged. "It's almost certainly influenza."

"But you're not certain? It could be something else? A mild cold, perhaps."

"I'm as certain as I can be, monsieur. She has influenza."

Jasper put a hand before his mouth. The confirmation felt like a death sentence.

"It seems serious now. It grips hard and fast. The fever and aches and catarrh rage, then dissipate as quickly as they came. Inside of a week, she could be as well as always."

"She's always been healthy."

"That's good. That's very good." Dr. Rioux took Jasper's arm and led him back into the drawing room. "But I'm worried about you."

"I'm fine."

"If you don't mind me saying, monsieur, you don't look well at all." The doctor opened his bag and drew out a rubber ball with a nozzle on one end. "If you've been together these last many days, you're almost certainly infected yourself. We should start you on this carbolic."

"Treat Amélie with it."

"The madame has one for her daughter. But you should begin this treatment, too. My friend in London swears it's a miracle cure."

"What about her? You must attend to my fiancée for right now, or you can leave and I can find someone else."

"Jasper, I can see you're frightened. I intend to do everything I can for her. When she's awake, we'll set about creating a Turkish bath for her. I've peppermint oil and menthol. And we'll use the carbolic, too. I'll do everything I know to do. I promise you. But you'll not help her by falling sick beside her. I fear you're already there."

Jasper went again to check on Amélie and found her unchanged. As he hovered, he felt the madame's gaze on him and turned. Slumped in a chaise, her lids heavy, Maria appeared asleep herself but for those keen brown eyes assessing him. For a long moment, moved only by the heavy thunk of the clock and Amélie's labored breathing, they stared at each other, saying everything and nothing. *This girl is mine,* they said. And, *I have her.*

Finally, Jasper could no longer ignore the heat that had been building in his body for hours. Heat and aches and such devastating fatigue. A pressure in his head that made his eyes water, his cheeks hurt, and his teeth lance his jaw with pain if they scarcely brushed each other.

As sick as he'd ever felt, he nodded lamely to Madame Audet and stumbled into the room next door. Immediately Dr. Rioux was there, shouldering him into his nightclothes, then into bed. Though his nose felt blocked and he said as much, he relented and inhaled

Rioux's miracle cure. Sucking desperately on an ether lozenge for his throat gone so thick and rough he could scarcely bear to swallow, he drifted off to sleep.

45

mélie woke slowly, laboriously, like climbing up through a viscous fog. She opened her eyes and winced against the hazy early-morning light. Blinking to steady her gaze, she examined her arms and the lawn chemise that clung to them. Somehow she felt both heavy and light, rested and drained. Warm but not hot. Then she remembered.

The debilitating aches and heat that had ravaged her were gone. The fluid swimming in her lungs gone but for a slight wheeze that wrenched a hearty cough. The congestion in her nose also mercifully relieved.

Peeling her covers back, she sat up intending to find Jasper when the room spun and she sank back with an exhausted sigh.

"Don't try to get up. You'll be as weak as a newborn colt."

Maria Audet's hollow-eyed face appeared.

"Maman?" Amélie blinked again and again, trying

to clear her mind. "Is that really you? Wh-what are you doing here?"

"I come to Paris to treat with my daughter and her intended only to find you stricken with influenza."

Then it occurred to Amélie how peculiar it was Jasper wasn't by her side.

"Where is he?"

Maria gave her a rueful grin.

"Where, Maman?"

"In the next room."

Though she wanted to fly, her limbs were indeed weak as she staggered to stand and don a robe. In the spare bedroom, a man with a pinched face and a black coat stood with a satisfied sigh.

"Ah, there you are." He introduced himself, then insisted she take his chair. "So much improved. I'm heartily glad to see it, mademoiselle. You gave us quite a scare."

But she barely regarded the man when her gaze crawled eagerly over Jasper lying in bed. He lay so still, his eyes were closed, and his features were such a sick pallor of grayish-white that her heart lodged in her throat. It was all she could do to keep from screaming.

"He isn't…?"

"He sleeps. But it's fitful. He isn't well."

"He has influenza?"

"As you did. I can't tell you what a relief it is to see you so clear-eyed, awake and on your feet. This apartment has been in an agony of nursing and waiting all these days. And praying." He nodded to Maria.

"How long has it been?"

"It's 1st January. Good year and good health to you, mademoiselle! At least I can say that now with some confidence."

Images faded in and out, of broth and vapor and a steamy bath. Of days and nights. "First January," Amélie echoed, unable to believe it. "The Moulin Rouge."

"Reopened last night. Monsieur Zidler was here briefly on Monday. We're keeping him updated. He'll be so pleased to hear you're awake."

Looking again at Jasper, she said, "How long has he been like this?"

"I put him to bed in the early hours of the morning of 28th December. Only, I might add, after seeing you cared for."

Amélie tenderly threaded her fingers through Jasper's. His hand was so limp and lifeless. He seemed too far away, nearly beyond her reach. She felt a sob and hitched a breath, then fell into a wracking cough.

"Come back to bed now," Maria said.

Her mother, nursing her now. Caring for her now. Amélie felt a peevish flare of indignation. "I'm staying right here. He needs me."

"Your mother's right, mademoiselle. You've only just awakened from a severe illness and need more rest. The last thing we want is for you to relapse into fever. That's the last thing *he* would want for you."

As he surely knew it would, the doctor's last point convinced her.

"I'll rest, but I won't leave his side. Won't you bring the chaise in here, please?"

Her mother and the doctor regarded each other.

"What's the harm? I can rest just as well on the chaise. I want to be with him."

Just then Bertie entered bearing the chaise in his arms with Sophie trailing behind. The housekeeper's eyes were glassy with unshed tears.

"Thank heaven you're awake. We've held a constant vigil for you both."

As soon as the chaise was placed, Amélie felt a deep weakness gnaw at her. Sinking gratefully into it, she took Jasper's hand again.

"When will he wake, doctor?"

"It's difficult to say. I hope that if his symptoms took hold a half day or so after yours, perhaps we might see him begin to recover this evening or tomorrow morning."

For now, that satisfied her. Amélie succumbed to sleep still clutching Jasper's warm hand.

Days later, Amélie held Jasper's lifeless hand to her cheek, stroking it and kissing it. After each nap, she'd woken feeling more recovered than she had before she slept. She took baths and took air. Sophie had cleaned her room and freshened her linens. And just this morning, she'd donned a dress for the first time in a week. In nearly every way, she felt increasingly herself. But her heart, strained with constant worry, felt wrung dry inside her chest.

"Why doesn't he wake, doctor? It's been two days now and no sign of a change."

Dr. Rioux wore a grim countenance on his haggard face and shook his head.

"I can't say. The human body is unique from person to person. He fights the illness, just as you did. And we're doing all we can, treating him as well as we treated you. But the fever refuses to break. Instead, it spikes. And his lungs are so full. I'm afraid I—"

"What?" Amélie's tone was like a whip crack as she stood, glowering and shaking her head. "You can't be afraid, doctor. *I'm* afraid. You're not allowed. Do you understand?"

He put gentling hands up. "I mean only to say, mademoiselle, that I feel now, given all this time with no marked improvement, I'm afraid I must classify his condition as grave. For the sake of his family, you must send a telegram to Monaco. They should come. While there's still time."

"'While there's still time'?" She felt shrieky and unhinged. "What does that mean, 'While there's still time'?"

But she knew exactly what it meant.

Amélie studied Jasper. His blanched and lifeless face. How much flesh he'd lost in only a week. His chest still rose and fell, but the wet and wheezing sound… Suddenly she was transported back to that attic. To the lifeless hand in hers. To her lioness friend whom she couldn't help but love breathing her flooded last breaths.

Then Jasper had been there for her. Though she'd claimed she didn't want it, didn't need it, he'd cared for her. And made her see that accepting his help wasn't weak but deliverance.

Then she remembered his recent admonishment:

Let go of your fears. Or, better yet, give them to me.

A red-hot rage seized Amélie, and she hissed in Jasper's ear, "You can't die, monsieur. You can't make me love you, then leave me behind."

Tears welled in her eyes, and she furiously wiped them away.

"I laid myself bare for you, Jasper. You required it. You wouldn't accept anything less. And now you think you can just leave me here? Bare and begging? No." She shook her head maniacally. "No."

She knew she was behaving like a harridan. Knew she burdened his breaths. And in his condition, her venom-filled anger made no sense. So, abruptly, she left in search of Bertie. With him, she deliberated over the wording of the telegram. She wrote Jasper's family of his grave condition and invited them to come. The family he'd described as a pretty den of vipers.

And why not Madame Travers? Of course she should be informed. Madame Kohl and Monsieur Tasse, too. All these people who either rivaled her or despised her. Let them all come. They couldn't possibly hate Amélie more than she hated herself.

Jasper lay on his deathbed because of her.

He'd wanted to go to Monaco. To leave the city and its plague behind. But she'd been a craven coward. Confident enough to sing and seduce half the city yet too afraid to meet her future mother-in-law. She deserved all of this. Maybe not losing Jasper. But everything else. All the people, all the scorn to come.

When the notes had been written, she watched anxiously as Bertie donned his coat. Then they exchanged a nod, and he left.

"Chick."

Amélie jolted awake. Sitting beside Jasper's bed, she'd fallen asleep with her head on top of his chest and now looked up to see Charles. When his mournful eyes met hers, she broke. For the first time since waking to find Jasper so gravely ill, she let go and cried.

The director threw his arms open, wrapping her in a bear hug that made her feel truly safe and cared for for the first time in days. When her hitched sobs fell into a wheezing cough, he let go.

"There now. Sit. You're still sick, little one."

Amélie did feel little just then. Like a five-year-old in desperate search of comfort.

"Who is this?" Maria asked. Her mother had remained hovering all this time. But for whispering over her rosary, saying and doing very little.

Amélie made the introductions.

"Your mother." Charles decorously took Maria's hand and kissed it. Still, he lingered too long, his mouth ajar.

Amélie knew her mother—though she hid behind modest dresses and a forbidding face—was stunning. Even in her middle forties, she still made men gape and stutter. Her mother's beauty had once been a source of great pride for Amélie when she was a girl. For then it had been far more than perfect features and form. There was something else, incalculable to a girl, that she understood very well now as a woman. There are some who have an allure that goes far beyond features and form. In Maria it had radiated from within, and Amélie's father had been proud of it, too.

But after he'd died, after the suitable mourning period had been observed, men had come to call. Maria Audet turned into a sour scold, railing against men and love.

How cruel was fate that they must rely on this bitter woman to deliver her consent to their true love match?

A short time later, Monsieur Tasse arrived. After speaking with Charles and exchanging a familiar greeting with her mother, he looked gravely at Amélie.

"Jasper sent me to Rouen on your behalf," he explained.

"Of course. Yes. I thank you for that, monsieur."

"How fortuitous she's here for you now."

Amélie could only nod.

"May I see him?"

"Of course."

After Amélie led Max into the room, she turned for the door.

"You needn't go, mademoiselle."

"I'll just be outside."

Half an hour passed before Max emerged from the room, his cheeks flushed and his eyes red. He took a seat beside her. "I don't know if this is the right time. Right now it feels like there is no right time. I don't know if you've seen it, but if you haven't"—he withdraw a clipping from *Le Temps* and gave it to her. "He labored over every word."

Amélie held their engagement announcement.

"At times I haven't felt the warmest toward you, mademoiselle. You must know that."

"You had good reason, monsieur. I don't blame you."

"Still, whatever happens, I wanted to be sure you knew that *I know* he loves you very much. That it could only take an incredible woman to inspire him to believe in love again. A real and true love, that is. Like yours. For that, I'm grateful to you."

Again her eyes welled with tears. "He will live, monsieur. Surely."

After a pause he said, "Yes. He's strong." Again he paused, and for such a long moment, Amélie thought he planned to leave. "If, however, the worst should happen, you need only call on me."

In her throat lay a ball of such unrelenting tears that Amélie couldn't speak. She merely nodded. This was too unreal to bear.

He can't be dying.

46

*T*he next morning, when a knock sounded with the time nearing noon, Amélie knew the Degrailly family had arrived.

Heart racing, she stood, smoothing the day dress she'd chosen—a somber and elegant deep-peacock silk— then nodded for Bertie to open the door. It had occurred to her more than once the terrible irony of meeting Jasper's mother in this way. If they'd gone to Monaco as Jasper had planned, they might've avoided this. The embarrassment of it needled her as she listened to the growing din of voices in the foyer and braced herself.

Marie-Thérèse and Marie-Louise sought her first, wrapping her in warm embraces. Then a regal older couple entered—he with black hair gone white at the temples and a handlebar mustache and she bird-thin with strawberry-blonde hair shot through with threads of gray.

"Mademoiselle," the man said.

Jasper's sisters performed the introductions. Amélie had expected Jasper's parents' disdain or their disapproval of her. Anything of distaste or displeasure. But it wasn't so much that as indifference. Eleanor Degrailly wanted only one thing—to see her son.

Amélie left Jasper's family at his worn bedside and returned to the drawing room to find Madame Travers waiting. Of course she would come with them. She had been family to him until only a few years ago.

The two women straightened and exchanged appraising looks. When last they'd seen each other, Jasper's ex-wife had asked Amélie to pose nude for her. There had been slyness and taunting then. Now Madame Travers's face was drawn and her lips pulled into a tight line. Here was the distaste and disapproval.

At least she'd waited until this morning. If she'd arrived the night before, she would have found Amélie with Madame Kohl. His fiancée and his former mistress. But Madame Kohl had wisely come when there were fewer people about. She'd not stayed long, slipping in and out with wide, red-rimmed eyes and tender words of gratitude for their friendship.

"What happened?" Madame Travers asked. The accusing tone in her voice and the implication were clear.

"He fell ill. We *both* fell ill."

"Yet here you are, standing before me. Perhaps pale but more or less recovered. Why is he there and you here?"

"I wish I could trade places with him, madame. If not for you, then for me and my breaking heart."

At this, Madame Travers cackled mirthlessly.

"I don't know why I'm recovering while he still suffers," Amélie added.

Madame Travers shook her head. The look on her face was one of barely tamped rage. "Why didn't you come to Monaco as he telegrammed? I'd no wish to see the two of you together, but it would've been better than this."

"We should've come." That was all she said. What more could she say when it was her fault, after all?

"Is he truly dying?"

Amélie stood with her mouth hanging open to speak for what felt like an interminable moment. She didn't want to speak the truth. She couldn't.

"I don't know."

Then Ellen emerged and sought Bertie.

"Send for a priest."

Bertie looked at Amélie, and belatedly Ellen did, too.

"Now."

Amélie darted into Jasper's room and pushed around the doctor, who hovered over his patient.

"It can't be that bad."

"I'm afraid so," the doctor confirmed. "His pulse has gone weak."

Amélie felt a terror burn in her chest and saw the room dim all around her.

This can't be happening. He can't be dying.

Numb with fear, she strode from the bedroom and found her mother standing by Madame Degrailly and Bertie. When her mother's gaze fell on her, she nodded, urging. Lamely Amélie nodded.

"I'll fetch him right away." The butler bowed and reached for his coat.

A short time later, Jasper's mysterious third sister arrived. Marie-Élise wore the distinctive white, winged wimple over the severe blue-gray habit characteristic of her order—the Daughters of Charity. Regarding Amélie, the sister appeared as starched and uncomfortable as her uniform. Amélie felt the heat of her condemnation.

Then Maria appeared, bearing her rosary in one hand and the other hand outstretched to greet the sister. For the first time, Amélie knew true relief to have her pious mother there, for in the next moment, Madame Travers appeared, exchanging a warm embrace with Marie-Élise.

"Thank God you've come," Madame Travers said to Marie-Élise. "We need your prayers now more than ever."

"Of course," Marie-Élise replied. "How good you came. It's only right his wife should be here for him now. I knew you'd not abandon him."

"Never," Madame Travers agreed.

The pair glanced at Amélie, then strolled arm in arm back to Jasper's room. Maria looked at her. It appeared she might say something. Whether comforting or condemning, Amélie couldn't guess by the inscrutable look on her face. But then she, too, turned and walked away without a word.

In that moment, Amélie had never felt more alone in all her life. Wandering to Jasper's room, she hovered in the doorway, staring at the women who attended him, the weary doctor in one corner and the stone-faced man consigned to the other.

Already Amélie felt Jasper no longer belonged to her, if he ever had. By dint of will, somehow she remained standing when all she wanted to do was collapse into a heap and sob.

When the priest appeared, solemnly kissing his crucifix and smiling ruefully, she wanted to bar him from the room. Childishly press her hands to the frame and scream for him to get out. Implore the doctor to do something, anything but the woefully inadequate vigil he'd been waging. She wanted to send his family from the apartment. Her mother, too. Anyone who wasn't the two of them, who didn't live or love inside their woven world.

When the priest began, her mother suddenly appeared and drew Amélie into the room. Like the rest of them, Amélie sank to her knees, and horrified, her heart in her throat and her head screaming no, she watched as the priest performed the last rites.

It was then she knew, and it struck her like a blade to the heart— finally she understood her mother. How she had rested their whole world on Captain Rafe's shoulders. And when he'd died, she had, too. Amélie had been unforgiving in that pure way of a child. Now it was painfully clear.

If Jasper dies, he'll take me with him. They don't give out this kind of soul-giving love twice in a lifetime. He was the beginning of me. This will be the end.

Jasper lay beside her, his face beaming with satisfaction. He dragged a delicate finger around a stray lock of her hair, smoothing it from her face.

"Are you lonely in all your hiding away, Amélie?"

"What are you talking about?" She chuckled with the certainty of blissful ignorance. "I sing before a packed house every night. I'm not hiding."

"Are you sure about that?"

Amélie jerked awake. She'd fallen asleep on a sofa in the drawing room. Now she saw night had fallen while she slept. But for the constant thunk of the hall clock, the apartment lay eerily quiet. She stretched, then went for Jasper's room. The dream, the feeling of Jasper with her, had been so vivid she tried to remember if it was a memory or something she'd conjured whole cloth.

She found Jasper's room surprisingly empty. Only her mother remained, lying on the chaise.

"It's a miracle. Surely God interceded. The doctor pronounced he's sleeping peacefully and his temperature's fallen," Maria explained with a reassuring smile. "They've gone to their hotel. The doctor, too. Gone home to see his family. They'll be back first thing in the morning."

Her mother vacated the chaise.

"Would you like to sit with him?"

Amélie felt a grateful flood of relief at hearing they'd all left for the time being. For these precious midnight hours, he would be hers.

All through the night, Jasper's fever played with her hopes and fears, peaking one hour, then plummeting the next. Meanwhile, his chest carried on in an agonized rhythm. Sometimes he opened his eyes and appeared to see clearly, giving wings to her prayers. And other times his lungs sounded so full she dreaded any moment might be his last.

Sometime later Amélie woke. There Jasper lay, as still as death, save for his chest that continued its agonizing climb and fall. And with it, her faith. She peered into the shrouded room, soft early-morning light drawing it into relief. Then she spied her mother slouched in a chair.

"Come now to bed." Maria urged Amélie back to her bedroom, neglected for so many days. Tucking her into the warm, clean bed, her mother said, "You need proper sleep. For the days to come."

～～

"Wake up, Amélie. Have you fallen asleep, my beautiful girl?"

"Mm." Amélie felt sated and heavy. "Tired. So tired."

"Have I worn you out?" There was impish delight in Jasper's tone, and she smiled.

"You know you have."

She felt his hand skate up her spine, followed shortly by his mouth, dragging wet kisses.

"Wake up."

"Why? Can't I just sleep for a bit more? Go on touching me if you must, monsieur. I don't mind."

"No, my love. I need to go."

Amélie woke to midday sun bursting around the curtains, lighting golden bars of dust in the air. The room seemed rosy and hopeful, and she felt so rested and reinvigorated that for a brief moment she simply luxuriated in stretching. Then with alarming clarity, she remembered Jasper's desperate condition and threw back the covers to reach for her robe.

In her frantic race, she struggled to get her arm in a sleeve, and at the door, still turning a sleeve outside right, she heard the sniffles and the crying. Shrill terror raced through her as she pressed her ear to the door.

"I can't believe it. He was improving. Wasn't he?"

"It's a deadly flu."

"But it was only the flu. The flu. He can't be gone. He was so young and healthy. He had 'round-the-clock care. Every advantage. What good are money and power if it can't help you when you need it?"

"Everyone's different. You saw. Some recover."

"And some don't."

More gentle sobs.

"They were getting married."

"Such a beautiful couple. Do you think they really loved each other?"

"I just can't believe he's dead."

Amélie lost her breath and felt an ache so deep in her heart she knew it was breaking. Limp fingers and her heavy head fell onto the door. She blinked—once, twice. And breathed—in, out. Her gaze followed her fingertips, dragging down the mahogany door. Her mind continued to work. She could still move, still touch, still feel. How was it possible? Then she remembered Jasper's now-prescient words.

I never knew you could survive such pain. Sometimes the heartbreak is so devastating it seems impossible for it to go on beating, but somehow it does.

Amélie swallowed and tasted metal. Then spun on a wobbly heel and stared at the cheery room that suddenly didn't seem real. Nothing seemed real.

Jasper—dead.

And where was she when he'd struggled to take his last breaths? Sleeping comfortably in their bed. She'd never forgive herself. Then a flood of memories rushed through her mind and heart.

You're the most beautiful woman here. And if you know it, they will, too.

Tonight I live to serve you. And the only thing you need do is let go.

You're my heart. More than my heart. My home. I want to be where you are.

Amélie's eyes welled with tears. She sucked desperately for a breath as her chest hitched and hitched and hitched. Finally, she wrapped her arms around herself, slid to the floor, and sobbed.

A knock sounded at the door behind her, and she jolted. She couldn't answer. She could scarcely stop crying to breathe. Another knock, this time more determined.

"Amélie?" Marie-Thérèse asked.

She couldn't stop crying, and she couldn't catch her breath to answer.

Finally, she managed. "I'll be out in a minute."

That was a lie. She never wanted to leave this lying room, this dying room, ever again. She'd sit in the sunny space and go stupid catching whirls of dust on bars of light. Anything if it meant she didn't have to say goodbye to Jasper.

Another knock sounded.

"Amélie." This time her mother. "May I come in?"

"No, I—no. I'll come out. I just…" She paused and shook her head and mopped the rivulets of tears that wouldn't stop coming.

"I'm coming in."

Amélie scrambled to stand and wipe away her tears even as the door opened. She hated the sight of her mother just then. Finally, they were in a unique position to understand each other, and that was the last thing Amélie wanted. She'd have rather anything else than losing the love of her life to understand her mother.

"Would you please give me a moment?"

Unable to face Maria or anyone, Amélie wandered to a window and peered out on the sunny day. People walked up and down the street as if the world hadn't stopped turning. She hated that sun and those people.

"You're crying," her mother said. "Finally. This is good."

Amélie's mouth fell open to scream, but everything that tumbled through her mind would have ruined what little remained between them. Instead she imagined scratching her mother's perpetually mourning face, carving deep grooves right into it. She felt so hot and tight with her anger, she forced herself to stay rooted by the window, or she'd do exactly that.

"A good cry?" she finally managed to strangle out. "Is there such a thing?"

Perhaps Maria sensed her daughter's anger when she took a tentative step toward her. "Yes. Sometimes it's the only thing."

"For you, perhaps. Not for me. I'm not a child anymore. It's too late for you to console me. I just want to be left alone."

"You should see him."

"I'm not ready." She paused. "I'm not ready."

After a pregnant pause in which the weight of the room seemed to surround them, Maria said, "You're right. You're no longer a child. You'll come when you're ready."

Amélie nodded.

When she heard the door latch, she fell back into her sobs. She cried until her head ached and her eyes burned. Cried until her cutting memories of Jasper were blunted enough to take a breath. Cried until she no longer wanted to stand. Yet somehow she knew this was a moment when standing mattered the most. Finally, she lifted a heavy-lidded gaze to a misfit bar of light pressed against the wall.

Never. No, Jasper. I can't.

Amélie stumbled to a mirror and peered at herself. Her robe hung crooked, her hair stood on end, and her face and neck were swollen and marked by livid red splotches. For the elegant people who would have been her family, for Madame Travers and the doctor, for her mother, for any of them, she might try to compose herself. Might try to wait until any evidence of her broken heart wasn't etched on her face.

Somehow she also knew she could understand her mother, even forgive her mother, without becoming her mother. Not only that, she must. In another hour, perhaps in another minute, she'd likely collapse into more sobs. But now she must begin the painful process of letting go. If Jasper could lose a son and a wife and go on to live and love, somehow she must do the same. If he'd taught her anything, if he'd *given* her anything, perhaps it was this most of all.

Amélie dragged a hapless hand through her hair and retied her robe. Her hands shook as she reached for the knob and slowly turned it, the growing weight of dread pressing on her chest. The door clicked open, and she saw his sisters' soft and sad faces. No one said a word. There didn't seem a need.

When she drifted into Jasper's room, but for the renewed presence of the doctor and Madame Degrailly, it seemed strangely undisturbed from when she'd left it early that morning.

"Might I…?" There was a frog in her throat, and she cleared it. "Might I be alone with him, please?"

"Of course," Dr. Rioux replied.

Madame Degrailly dabbed at her nose with a handkerchief and finally glanced at her. Then she reluctantly stood and filed out.

Amélie's gaze fell everywhere—the table, the lamp, the blankets, the window, the wall coverings—until finally she sank into the chaise and looked at Jasper. He appeared so still, as if he were merely a wax figure of himself. As if he'd never been a living thing. But his color, it wasn't a sick grayish-white.

Then she saw it.

"Doctor!" She flew to the door and wrenched it open. "Doctor, he's breathing."

Dr. Rioux strode into the room and pressed his stethoscope to Jasper's chest. "Yes?" He sounded puzzled by her observation.

"H-he's breathing. If he's breathing, he can't be dead."

Amélie peered at everyone who hovered in the doorway.

"Of course not. In fact, he's had some steady hours of improvement. I dare say I think his fever's finally broken. Why did you think he was dead?"

Amélie staggered, thunderstruck. She stared, mouth ajar, at the women in the doorway until finally finding her voice.

"They said he was dead. I heard them in my room when I was readying to come out. They—they said he was so young and healthy. He'd 'round-the-clock care. And… and soon he was to be married. They couldn't believe he succumbed to the flu. Didn't you say that?"

Gape-mouthed, Marie-Thérèse stepped forward. "Oh, mademoiselle, I'm so sorry you heard that. I hate to imagine how you felt."

"You don't want to know, madame!" Amélie cried.

"We were speaking of the Duke of Clarence," Marie-Thérèse said.

"The Duke of Clarence?" Amélie asked.

Jasper's sisters and Madame Travers, practically everyone in the room, nodded.

"It was he who died of the flu. We just received the shocking news a short time ago."

"Queen Victoria's grandson. *Not* Jasper."

Again it seemed everyone nodded.

Amélie didn't know what to feel—a soaring relief, anger at them, or embarrassment at herself for the misunderstanding. Her mind began to spin, and, in truth, she felt a little light-headed at the sudden change.

"May I please be alone with him?"

Once again, the room emptied. Amélie shut the door on Madame Degrailly's objection and strode to Jasper. She pressed a hand to his forehead and found it cooled, almost normal. Without the cloud of grief, now she could see his color was no longer a sickly grayish-white because it held a hint of healthy pink. She took his hand and kissed it, unable to suppress a sob. Then she sank to the chaise beside him, rested her head on the bed, and cried.

"If I must wait," Jasper began, his voice wan and wheezy, "until you stop crying over me and start singing to me"—he paused to drag in a desperate breath—"I fear I'll be in bed 'til May."

Amélie's mouth fell open when she found Jasper looking at her clear-eyed and with a soft smile. After a stunned moment, when still more tears burned and welled in her eyes, she threaded her fingers through his, pressed kisses all over his hand, and stroked it along her cheek.

"I'll sing. I'll do whatever you want."

"Good of you to remember."

Amélie cupped Jasper's face and kissed and cried and laughed and cried, raining kisses and tears all over him.

47

One month later...

*J*asper looked at Max and checked his watch again. Now fifteen minutes past the hour, he winced and blushed with embarrassment. He caught Charles stroking his beard. The director mouthed, "Performers," then shrugged indifferently. Glancing at his mother, Jasper found her countenance as flat as a millpond. But he knew better. Ellen Degrailly could seethe like a gentle breeze.

By contrast, his father smirked in open satisfaction. After being cut from his son's first wedding, a society one and entirely uneventful, attending this one by way of dangling his consent over Jasper appeared to be his greatest delight. In fact, it seemed Hector Degrailly could barely keep himself from falling into open guffaws. At least Jasper's sisters appeared sympathetic and suitably uncomfortable. He felt the heat of embarrassment crawling up his neck. This was increasingly growing into the single most humiliating moment of his life.

At twenty minutes past, the judge sighed. "If she doesn't appear within the next ten minutes, I'm afraid we'll have to reschedule. I'm sorry."

"Of course," Jasper uttered.

But by now his embarrassment was turning into anger. He knew what they were waiting for. *Whom* they were waiting for. And it wasn't Amélie.

As the long hand crept slowly toward half past, Jasper closed his eyes and envisioned meting out every painful punishment he could imagine. But that, even he knew, was entirely inappropriate. To think such things of his mother-in-law. If she would ever *be* his mother-in-law. That was a pity. For if ever a woman begged to be taken in hand, it was Maria Audet.

Finally, Amélie rushed in with a great exhalation. Penny, holding her train, trailed behind. But Jasper's relief was tempered by the reassurance he desperately needed. He craned his neck to see behind her, but Madame Audet wasn't with her, and he knew she was in town. His heart sank as he tried to catch Amélie's gaze while she shucked her muff and cape with an inscrutable expression on her face. Was it embarrassment or devastation?

Amélie sidled up to Jasper wearing the ivory silk brocade they'd chosen. And though it was modest with its pearl buttons and lace at the sleeves, she made a most stunning bride. Then she smoothed back a tendril that had come loose from her pompadour and gave him a beatific smile.

"Is she coming?" he asked.

"No."

"Are we—"

Amélie looked at the judge. "I'm so sorry I'm late."

Jasper whispered, "Do you have the form?"

"No," Amélie replied.

"But—"

She grasped his hand tightly and gave him a reassuring smile. "I filed it. That's what took me so long."

Jasper felt a lump of relief burrow into his throat. "She signed it.

Your mother actually signed it. Then why isn't she here?"

Amélie stared meaningfully at him and whispered, "Her name is scrawled on the form."

"Her name…" Then he realized what she'd done and felt a panic so real he glanced around to see if anyone could see it on his face. "Have you…?"

Amélie indicated the bouquet Jasper held for her, and he handed it over.

"What have you done?"

While the wedding ceremony was intimate—and rushed—at their wedding reception, Jasper and Amélie played host to what seemed like all of Tout-Paris. The moneymakers and their mistresses. The artists and the inventors. Performers and patrons. Old money and new. They all came.

At Jasper's grandest hotel, champagne flowed from fountains while guests dined on a dozen courses. Consommé and oysters and quail, liver mousse pâté and American crayfish and new asparagus. Finally finished off with Bénédictine rosé and bonbons and fruit.

The marriage was scandalous, of course. Not the handsome gentleman romancing the beautiful showgirl. That was a love story as old as time itself. But the business of marriage in Paris, that had nothing whatsoever to do with love. At its heart, cold calculation. What woman from which family with how much of a dowry. It was an arrangement for trusts and traditions and titles. For family and children. It wasn't for love.

So, when the only remaining heir to the once-great House of Foix-Grailly married a laundress-cum-singer, it made more tongues wag than the rumors of how they carried on in the bedroom. For that was merely sport. But marriage, that was blood sport.

Even on their wedding day, the vultures circled. Aubrey Talac attended because he would always be an artist in search of an investor. Joselin for much the same reason. And also because she would always be in attendance at the grandest fêtes. No matter if the day burnished her great defeat. Even the Comte de Beaumont attended, strutting and laughing and circling. Always circling. And why not? For life and love in the world's incandescent capital were fickle things.

But as happy as Jasper felt, and he felt it to the depth and breadth of him, one woman on the edge of the crowded ballroom drew his eye. He tried to put her out of his mind. Still, the more he tried, the less he found he could.

Finally, his curiosity overcame him. He excused himself from Amélie's side and wove politely through the crowd. Plucking a glass of champagne from a tray, he followed her even as she turned for the street.

"Madame, please wait."

Maria stopped.

"Why do you come to your daughter's wedding reception like this? Hiding yourself away and in mourning dress."

Shrouded entirely in black, Maria Audet hid her face behind a black lace mantilla.

"A grieving woman disappears in a crowd, and I didn't want anyone to see me."

"You didn't want your daughter to see you."

"She's resourceful, my daughter."

"She is that."

"I could write a letter of challenge. They could easily compare the signatures."

"You could do that. But you won't."

"You wonder why I didn't give my consent."

"Yes."

Maria Audet nodded and carried on nodding as if in contemplation.

"From the moment she first kicked inside me, my willful daughter has delighted in provoking me. I say up; she says down. I say pray; she says play. I say Rouen; she says Paris. But instead of tempering her enthusiasms, my disapproval has turned her into someone I recognize all too well. A girl who fled her simple world for a great love.

"I know she thinks me a terrible mother, and she's probably right.

But I can't help wanting to spare her the heartbreak that's almost certain to come. Though she thinks me bitter and small, I want only to protect her, monsieur."

Maria looked Jasper plainly in the eye.

"I believe you mean to protect her," Jasper said.

He turned and caught a glimpse of Amélie laughing with some of the Moulin Rouge performers.

"We're not so different, madame. I once tried to love her by protecting her. It doesn't work. And I nearly lost her."

He paused again to admire Amélie. The way her hand fell on her friend's arm. The way her eyes lit up. The way her lips caressed the rim of her glass. Until her gaze ranged the room and met his.

"Do we understand each other?" he asked.

"We do."

48

*H*ours later, Amélie slumped against the bed in their hotel suite. Her feet ached from standing, her chest from an unforgiving corset, her cheeks from smiling, her head from too much champagne. And still amidst all those aches, when she caught Jasper's soft smile, it all felt like a chimera.

"Why do you hold yourself like that?" He bent forward, resting his elbows on his thighs as he was wont to do when making a study of her. "All the way across the room with your arms wrapped around your middle. Girding yourself from me. What's the matter?"

She looked down, then loosened her arms straitjacketing her waist. "I don't know."

In truth, she didn't. The whole day had been a blur.

All morning she'd spent on the edge of her breath, begging her mother, arguing with her, pleading with her to sign the consent form. From the moment Maria had arrived in town the day before still undecided, at breakfast this morning, over lunch while Penny fixed her hair and helped her into her dress. Through all the reasonable arguments, emotional pleas, and venomous threats. Nothing, it seemed, would ever be easy.

Yet from the heady moment it occurred to Amélie she could forge her mother's signature, while she waited, her heart pounding so loudly in her chest she was certain everyone could hear the lie, when finally a simple nod from a commune clerk signaled she would marry Jasper Degrailly, every true and terrible thing had fled.

Through the short ceremony, her voice whispering the words, with every warm wish and dance and toast, she'd floated in the clouds.

Married.

She was married to Jasper Degrailly. *She.*

"It doesn't seem real yet. I keep waiting for the dream to fade."

Jasper arched a brow. "What did I say about that?"

Amélie smiled with chagrin. "A habit not easily broken."

"Then diversion is the order of the day." He smiled sweetly. "That's a beautiful dress."

She smoothed her hand down the bodice. But for the woven brocade fabric and gigot sleeves, it was a modest, clean-lined, almost-simple dress. That was Jasper's design. While the marriage would be a scandal and the reception a decadent feast, the bride and her dress would be deceptively innocent.

"Take it off."

"Oh, Jasper, I'm so tired I can scarcely think."

"That's good. Thinking is excessively overrated in these matters."

Amélie chortled, then turned away from him and reached for the stays.

"Turn around and look at me while you do. Keep your eyes on me."

A blush warmed her whole body as she turned back. Why should she suddenly color like this? But whether he did it to arouse her or him, his intense perusal always made her skin come alive and her blood trickle to her sex.

She pulled clumsily, eagerly, at the laces.

"Relax." He stood and prowled closer. "Slow down. Seduce me."

Amélie relaxed her shoulders with a sigh. Then took a long, slow, deep breath. Slowly she peeled the outer bodice and skirt away, all the while exchanging a heated gaze with Jasper. Until finally leaving the pieces of her gown in a starched form at her ankles.

His eyes flew wide, then a slow, satisfied smile crept across his face.

"You've been very naughty today under your precious white dress, haven't you?"

He tipped a glass of Bénédictine to her mouth, and she swallowed.

"Now"—he set the glass down, took her nape, and brushed her lips with his—"you've forgotten some underthings." His lips and breath skated all over her face, coming so close without kissing.

Amélie shook her head.

"No?"

Jasper played with the gold satin ribbon at the top of her boned royal-blue corset. Then he drew a claiming hand down and *tsk*ed.

"You've forgotten your chemise and your knickers."

"Have I?" She peered down at herself.

"Take off your shoes and stockings. And enchant me while you do it."

She did, flirting with her eyes and her mouth and caressing her hands down her legs.

Then Jasper threaded his fingers through her coiffed hair and began pulling pins.

"I need this beautiful hair down."

When scores of pins lay like pine needles at her feet, he drew his hands over her scalp in a deep caress. All the while, his breath and lips skirted over her face until, finally, he pressed a chaste kiss to her forehead.

"Kneel on the bed facing the fire with your bottom on your ankles."

Amélie scrambled to obey, feeling heady once again, only this time with the grateful ease of submission.

"Now rest your hands on your thighs and fix your gaze down."

Eagerly she did. There was something so raw and restless in this now. She felt so naked and needy she panted and could feel her breasts straining against the tight corset.

At length, she waited, her ears leaning into the silence and the occasional crackle of the fire. But she heard nothing. Not the shuffle of shoes on the rug or the shush of clothes falling into a heap.

Long moments stretched. The more she waited, the more she wanted. She smiled to herself, knowing his game. She straightened her spine, took a bracing breath, and waited.

Patience, she implored herself. *You're fine. Warm, comfortable, relaxed.*

Yet the more she told herself this, the less she believed it. She itched to look up. To say something. But she knew she mustn't. This was a test, a simple test, really, of her submission. And she was failing. Because instead of waiting serenely on the bed, she wanted to climb right out of her skin and peel the elegant clothes from his body. She wanted to take him into her mouth. Wanted to make him wait. Make him beg.

Suddenly Jasper's hand wrapped around her throat, and his chin rested on the crown of her head. "Relax."

The warmth of his purring word, his firm hand on her, the citrus-chamomile-and-earthy-tobacco scent of him, this was what she wanted.

Leisurely he pulled the gold ribbon of her corset until it lay limply open. Then he moved to the hooks. One-by-one he deliberately, with such agonizing slowness, plucked them apart until the corset fell away, finally leaving her naked.

Once again, he left her to anticipate any word or touch.

After another agonizing wait, he said, "Do you want me to touch you?"

"Yes."

"Do you want me to lick and kiss you?"

"Yes."

"Do you want me to slide so deep inside you that you don't know where I begin and you end?"

Amélie's mouth fell open, and she couldn't help but look up at him. There he stood in his regal suit and commanding air and she naked and kneeling, waiting and begging. Desperate. She blushed, and her breath hitched.

"Yes."

"Yes, what?"

"Yes, Master. Please."

Jasper drew the pearl choker around her neck and clasped it. He dragged his wet lips around her ear and whispered, "Good girl." Then he lifted her chin, urging her to look at him.

"Now let's begin."

AUTHOR'S NOTE

The Laundry: Throughout the nineteenth century, there was an effort in Paris to render laundry and laundresses invisible. First women were forbidden from using the riverbanks of the Seine. Then bateaux-lavoirs, boats moored to riverbanks that acted as laundries, were abolished.

When the discovery of microbes focused attention on laundries and their ability to transmit disease, and after a cholera epidemic swept through Paris in 1884, they were regularly the target of public scorn as disease carriers. Laundresses lived and worked under the constant fear of tuberculosis (consumption) and diphtheria epidemics, and, even more, the powerful Conseil d' Hygiène raiding private homes and businesses to stamp out these diseases.

With working conditions so harsh, it was considered one of the meanest options for working-class women. Wine and brandy were cheap and plentiful. It was common for owners to provide it to stave off complaints. Alcoholism in laundries was rampant.

From Laundress to Queen of Paris: There was one time a year Paris treated its laundresses like queens. During the feast of Mid-Lent, Paris streets were consumed by the frenzy of carnival. With great fanfare, the women of each laundry elected a queen who, along with her retinue, paraded down the boulevards in masks and on floats.

The custom survived into the twentieth century when WWII interrupted it. It was never fully revived.

Performers and Sex:
"...The professional actress... these most lecherous women... can ignite an unchaste flame even in the snow."

—Fr. Michael Zampelli, S.J.,
on the Counter-Reformation view

The idea that a performer was a transactional being with few, if any, rights goes back to ancient Rome, where they were often slaves and if free, considered no better than slaves. For centuries afterward, performers, whether cross-dressing men or women performing in the public sphere, have been considered provocative, seen as using their bodies to arouse emotion in the same way prostitutes enflame the body, and deemed a threat to society and chaste marriage, even a threat to Christianity itself.

So conflated in society, a nineteenth-century French woman with few options became a courtesan through performing. A courtesan reigned at the top of the demimonde and made her means with her body, charm, and style. She was the bed mate of kings and generals, painters and princes, moving men as she moved society.

By the nineteenth century in France, courtesans were esteemed. So, when we meet Amélie Audet, the idea that she would want to be a performer simply for performing's sake was virtually unheard of still in the Paris of that era.

"Protest against the Tower of Monsieur Eiffel": The Eiffel Tower was conceived to commemorate the hundredth anniversary of the storming of the Bastille—a symbol of royal authority whose capture sparked the French Revolution—at the Paris Exposition Universelle in 1889.

To many, the proposed tower was akin to a war memorial, and the controversy surrounding it was considerable. In 1887, the newspaper *Le Temps* published the "Protest against the Tower of Monsieur Eiffel," signed by influential members of the literary and artistic community:

"We come, we writers, painters, sculptors, architects, lovers of the beauty of Paris which was until now intact, to protest with all our strength and all our indignation, in the name of the underestimated taste of the French, in the name of French art and history under threat, against the erection in the very heart of our capital, of the useless and monstrous Eiffel Tower, which popular ill-feeling, so often an arbiter of good sense and justice, has already christened the Tower of Babel."

The weight of public objection was so considerable Gustave Eiffel knew he had to develop clear functional capabilities for the tower to survive. He proposed it be used to further scientific study in areas such as meteorology and telecommunications. And in 1899, the first wireless transmitter was installed on the tower.

It established its permanent place in 1914, when its radiotelegraphic station jammed German radio communications, which contributed to the Allied success during the Battle of the Marne.

La Semaine Sanglante (The Bloody Week): Radicalized workers—resentful over the famine conditions during the Siege of Paris during the Franco-Prussian War, then the eventual defeat of France by Prussia—organized into a group called the Commune. For two months in the spring of 1871, they were the radical socialist and revolutionary government of France.

In May, the French regular army, revitalized after their ranks returned from German prisons, marched back into Paris. Outnumbering Commune forces five-to-one, they retook the city in only a week. One of the more decisive battles was the Battle for Montmartre, where the Commune uprising began.

Masculinity in Crisis in Fin-de-Siècle Paris:
"Every man has, in effect, some weak point in his mind or body, and there is no such thing as an *absolutely* normal condition for the one or the other."

—Eugène Gley,
"Les Aberrations de l'Instinct Sexuel"

Nineteenth-century medical and psychological understandings suggested that masculinity was a finite resource defined by the existence of semen. Medical authorities viewed the transfer of semen during sex as a loss for men and a gain for women. They argued it made women stronger and more masculine and men weaker, more impotent, and more feminized. These views were fueled by growing fears of women's empowerment and the anxieties of France having the lowest birth rate of any industrialized nation.

Later in the century, alienists began cataloguing aberrant sexual behaviors. The existence of which, they claimed, reinforced this notion that man and masculinity were in a serious state of decline.

Under these growing bourgeois and societal pressures emerged the luxury brothels. Men of means sought refuge in famous houses such as the Chabanais and the Monthyon, as well as Chez Christiane, which catered to the exploration of power exchange dynamics and BDSM.

The Russian Influenza Epidemic – Newspapers, Germs, and Travel: The largest nineteenth-century influenza epidemic, called "the Russian epidemic," arrived in Europe from the east in November and December of 1889. It was one of the first epidemics to occur during the period of bacteriology development initiated by the discoveries of Louis Pasteur and Robert Koch, one of the first to occur under the rapid expansion of railway lines, and the first epidemic to be so widely commented on and followed in the burgeoning daily press.

Because germ theory was so new and so often misunderstood, because the disease spread more rapidly than the world had heretofore seen, and because most major cities received early and detailed reports of the disease before it gripped them, it sparked a panic.

"The Great Dread," as newspaper articles dubbed it, grew uniquely from these three factors. In the end, while morbidity rates were high, mortality rates were low. This is sometimes credited as the first global instance of the distortion of a "media reality." Still, what lent to the discrepancy in perceptions was the near-obsessive media coverage of high-profile sufferers.

The Death of the Duke of Clarence: On January 14th, 1892—not in 1890 as I depicted here—Great Britain and the world were stunned by the news that HRH Prince Albert Victor, the Duke of Clarence and Avondale, Queen Victoria's grandson and the heir presumptive to the throne, succumbed to influenza. The loss was made more severe by the constant media coverage of his bedside vigil, the fact he'd just celebrated his 28th birthday, and that he was soon to marry Princess Victoria Mary of Teck.

To make a modern-day comparison, this would be the equivalent of Prince William dying only weeks before his wedding to Kate Middleton.

The much beloved "Prince Eddie" was widely mourned in Great Britain and beyond.

Paris – The City of Lights: Paris is considered by many to have been the capital of the world in the nineteenth century. At the epicenter of Enlightenment thought, emerging technologies, engineering marvels, a thriving avant-garde art scene, and a hedonist lifestyle, all things converged in Belle Époque Paris.

Many attribute the moniker "City of Lights" to either the brilliantly lit Eiffel Tower or Enlightenment thought. But the name actually stems from the mid-seventeenth-century, when Louis XIV was on the throne.

After a prolonged period of war and domestic strife, he sought to return confidence to his people with law and order. To make Paris safer, he employed Gabriel Nicolas de la Reynie as Lieutenant General of the Gendarme. The Lieutenant General quadrupled the number of officers, put lanterns on every main street, and residents were asked to fill their windows with candles and oil lamps.

The first European city to adopt street lighting, thereafter it became known as La Ville-Lumière.

SOME SUGGESTED READINGS

FROM MY BIBLIOGRAPHY

Chiesa, Sara. *French Cabaret Music: Songs of Aristide Bruant, Erik Satie, and Margeurite Monnot*, Florida State University (2013).

du Maurier, George. *Trilby* (1894).

Grüring, Jaimee. *Dirty Laundry: Public Hygiene and Public Space in Nineteenth-Century Paris*, Arizona State University (2011).

Hewitt, Catherine. *The Mistress of Paris: The 19th-Century Courtesan Who Built an Empire on a Secret* (2017).

Honigsbaum, Mark. "The Great Dread: Cultural and Psychological Impacts and Responses to the 'Russian' Influenza in the United Kingdom, 1889-1893." Social History of Medicine. Vol. 23, Issue 2, (August, 2010): pp. 299-319.

Johnson, Julie Ann. *Conflicted Selves: Women, Art, & Paris, 1880–1914*, Queen's University (2008).

Jullian, Phillipe. *La Belle Époque* (1982).

Loeb, Lori. "Beating the Flu: Orthodox and Commercial Responses to Influenza in Britain, 1888-1919." Social History of Medicine. Vol. 18, Issue 2, (August, 2005): pp. 203-224.

Merrill, Jane. *The Showgirl Costume: An Illustrated History* (2019).

Mogador, Céleste. *Memoirs of a Courtesan in Nineteenth-Century Paris* (1854).

Proust, Marcel. *In Search of Lost Time* (1913).

Scott, Virginia. *Women on the Stage in Early Modern France: 1540-1750* (2010).

Zola, Émile. *L'Assommoir* (1871)

Zola, Émile. *Nana* (1880).

https://victorianparis.wordpress.com

http://moorewomenartists.org/imagery-laundresses-19th-century-french-culture/

https://legacyseriesbooks.wordpress.com/the-price-of-innocence/laundress-in-19th-century-france/

http://catsmeatshop.blogspot.com/2010/11/what-opium-smoking-feels-like.html

https://frenchmoments.eu/moulin-rouge-paris/

https://www.messynessychic.com/2015/09/18/the-forgotten-elephant-of-the-moulin-rouge-garden-party/

http://digitool.library.mcgill.ca/webclient/StreamGate?folder_id=0&dvs=1511512321419~141

http://www.19thc-artworldwide.org/spring08/39-spring08/spring08article/108-reflections-of-desire-masculinity-and-fantasy-in-the-fin-de-siecle-luxury-brothel

TO EXPERIENCE MORE

OF MAY LEAVE STARS

Please visit:

www.pinterest.com/katestcroix/may-leave-stars

Spotify playlist:

spoti.fi/2ZBlTtR

ACKNOWLEDGEMENTS

My thanks first to contemporary romance author CD Reiss, without whose generosity this story simply would not exist. For your inspiration and encouragement there truly are no words.

To my dear friend contemporary romance author Amber Hadley, who has been there with me for this writing journey, the best critique partner, sounding board, and friend I could hope for. You renew my faith, friend.

To my first editor Cheri Johnson, who took a speechwriter back to school and turned me into a novelist. Your guidance and patience helped me climb a mountain I didn't know if I could climb.

To my beta readers Laura Bruinooge and Nikki Sansone. You raised your hands, read fast, and read thorough, asked every question and never spared the truth. Your suggestions always make my stories better.

To the amazing team of women who subcontracted on this project—Najla Qamber, Nada Qamber, Timea Gazdag, Jenny Loew, and Devon Burke. From editing and photography to graphic design, illustrations, and formatting, your tremendous talents helped me bring this story to life.

To my mom Karen Chalmers, who saved every story I ever wrote. "You were always a storyteller," she said. Thank you for believing in me! You inspire me more than you know.

To my husband Jeff Heywood, who I picked up at a bar in downtown Minneapolis. That was the best thing I've ever done! You never gave up on me. You never gave up on us. "You are incredible." ;)

To my sons Teddy and Abe Heywood. Being your mom is the great privilege of my life. For always saying, "Don't worry, Mommy, someone will buy your books," thank you, my little loves.

Finally to you, the reader. Thank you for taking a chance on this story and this new writer. I hope you enjoyed reading it as much as I enjoyed writing it.

ABOUT THE AUTHOR

Catherine C. Heywood is an Amazon bestselling author of romantic historical fiction, and a former political communications consultant and speechwriter.

Raised in Red Wing, Minnesota, she studied international politics at the University of Edinburgh and has degrees in politics, writing, and communications from the University of St. Thomas and Boston College.

She explored the law and improv before settling on storytelling. Her worst job was scraping year-old tobacco spit off a shoe factory wall. Her best is doing this.

She lives in western Wisconsin with her husband and sons, and her interests include architecture and design, fashion and food.

Find out more:
www.catherinecheywood.com

Stay connected:
www.catherinecheywood.com/newsletter